I0891338

Praise for
August Greenleaf's Last 7,000 Days

"*August Greenleaf's Last 7,000 Days* is lively, funny, nostalgic, and loaded with snappy dialogue."

—**Randall Beach,** columnist and reporter for the *New Haven Register,* coauthor of *The Legendary Toad's Place: Stories from New Haven's Famed Music Venue,* and author of *Connecticut Characters: Profiles of Rascals and Renegades*

"Quite often, we as humans sideline the three fundamental questions that quietly linger within us all: How did we get here? Why are we here? And where do we go when we die? *August Greenleaf's Last 7,000 Days* tells the story of one such human, an ordinary person whose life journey reveals he is anything but ordinary.

In these pages, you'll meet a character so genuine, so relatable, that his joys and sorrows will feel like your own. As a child, he navigates a world filled with both the quiet discovery of unique gifts and the shadow of fears that shaped his early days. From these beginnings to the reflective final moments of his life, you will laugh, cry, and confront the profound questions often buried beneath the noise of daily living. Above all, this story will leave you with a sense of hope—hope that is richer, deeper, and more enduring than you ever thought possible."

—**Charles F. Glassman,** MD, FACP, CoachMD™, author of the critically acclaimed *Brain Drain*

"Some books stay with you long after you turn the last page, and *August Greenleaf's Last 7,000 Days* is one of them. A poignant, deeply reflective memoir, this book unravels the extraordinary life of August Greenleaf, a man burdened with loss, addiction, and an unusual gift—one that allowed him to see what others could not.

"I relate to August completely as being 'special,' with all the good and despair that comes with that knowing.

"What stood out most was the intricate detail given to every character. Each person in August's life had a story that unfolded with care, making them feel real and significant. Their experiences, struggles, and connections reminded me of my own journey—how every person I meet seems to fit into the larger picture of my life in ways I may not fully understand yet.

"What follows is an intricate, immersive journey through August's life, chronicling his experiences, the souls he encountered, and the lessons hidden in the mundane and mystical alike. The writing is deeply emotional, painting vivid portraits of the people August loved, lost, and learned from. Every character is given depth and meaning, turning their stories into reflections of our own connections and losses.

"Though lengthy, the book never drags. The authors' meticulous attention to detail makes each character's arc feel like a standalone story, yet seamlessly woven into August's greater narrative. Reading it, I found myself contemplating my own life, the people who have come and gone, and the visible threads that tie us to our fates.

"By the time I reached the final pages, I felt as though I had lived a lifetime alongside August. His struggles, his sorrow, his fleeting moments of joy—they all resonated deeply. This is not just a memoir; it is an exploration of the human experience, a meditation on destiny, grief, and the possibility of something beyond.

"*August Greenleaf's Last 7,000 Days* is thought-provoking and utterly captivating. It made me reflect on my own past, my own losses, and the mysterious ways in which people and events shape who we become. It is a book that lingers, a book that makes you reconsider your own journey. And in the end, like August, I wasn't disappointed."

—**Vincent Genna,** MSW, psychic therapist, medium, master spiritual teacher, and bestselling author

To Ella

In second grade we read Jack London's *The Call of the Wild* together.
From then on I was hooked. Thank you, Mom!

To Joy

'Twas late you came, and too soon you left . . .
Ah, but the in-between!

MASCOT BOOKS
an imprint of Amplify Publishing Group

www.mascotbooks.com

August Greenleaf's Last 7,000 Days: A Memoir of Love, Loss, and the Miraculous

©2026 Stuart H. Greenblatt with David Connell. All Rights Reserved. No part of this publication may be reproduced, stored in a retrieval system or transmitted in any form by any means electronic, mechanical, or photocopying, recording or otherwise without the permission of the author.

Cover art by Marco Primo

For more information, please contact:
Mascot Books, an imprint of Amplify Publishing Group
620 Herndon Parkway, Suite 220
Herndon, VA 20170
info@mascotbooks.com

Library of Congress Control Number: 2024918344
CPSIA Code: PRV0525A
ISBN-13: 979-8-89138-377-7

Printed in the United States

August Greenleaf's Last 7,000 Days

A Memoir *of* Love, Loss, *and the* Miraculous

Stuart H. Greenblatt *with* David Connell

Contents

Prologue

8:30 a.m., Tuesday, January 25, 2033:

The following pages tell a true story; I know because it's my story. As I sit comfortably at my desk, here in my den, I share with you, my reader, the knowledge that I will die this afternoon. I am as sure of this elemental fact as the eagle is that he can fly or the fish that he can swim. Flanders Cremation Service has already been notified, and by Saturday at this time—if my wishes are carried out properly—I will be ashes. From then on, in this world, August Nathaniel Greenleaf will be just a memory. I can only hope that those whom I've loved will remember me with fondness, and perhaps a little forgiveness. Lord knows I have not always been easy to live with.

I am comforted now by a pervasive sense of peace—a peace that was promised to me seven thousand days ago. Unlike so many promises I've either made or been given, this one has never been broken, and for twenty years, through triumph and tribulation, I've come to rely on it. It enables me to sit here with equanimity, just hours before my death, knowing that in my end will be a new beginning. I am writing this—the prologue to my story—so near its end because it's only in the living of it that I've learned that there is nothing in life to fear—nothing, and if there should be anything at all that you take from this narrative, reader, let it be that.

A manila envelope addressed to my dear friend Dr. William can be found on my desk; inside is a copy of the entire manuscript—edited, proofread, and ready for the publisher. I've also left him a photocopy of an article I ran across about European monasteries. Did you know that many of these monasteries were much more than places of contemplation and prayer? Within their cloistered walls, the monks also fed and sheltered the poor and orphaned, educated the children, and nursed the sick—I like that. We have shared so much throughout the years, William and I, that I believe he'll enjoy this article too—this one last, modest gift to him from me.

Within the pages of my story, you will find characters who have suffered, healed, rejoiced, and loved; you may also find some interesting, if not useful, information. The episodes recounted in this book were taken from notes written at various times of my life, but primarily after my visit to the white house by the bay in November of 2013, when many of the questions that had been troubling me since childhood were answered. Over the past two years, I have been editing them—fleshing them out and rearranging them, hoping to make of them a more cogent and enjoyable narrative. Occasionally, in order to keep the story moving, I have taken certain liberties with the stylistic rules pertaining to "point of view" by unceremoniously switching from first person to third person omniscient. I believe the reader will find these breaches easy to ignore and will read on without hesitation or loss of comprehension. But however you find my story, reader—breaches or no breaches—please know it is offered in love.

This is an exceptionally cold January morning—the windchill is minus ten degrees. It's one of those mornings where parents worry over whether or not to send their kids to school. Already this winter, here in Connecticut, we've had three old-fashioned snowstorms, which together have resulted in four school-closing days. I imagine this fact has influenced the school superintendent's decision to open the schools today. I mention this because had my grandson, Sammy (who's at school now), had another unscheduled day off, it would certainly have presented me with a problem in light of my own plans for this afternoon.

But since Sammy's in school today, I've arranged for him to be picked up afterward by his friend Jimmy Walker's mother. She'll take Sammy to their house, where the boys will do their homework, play outside for an hour or so, and (I am told) have a fried-clam-strip dinner, a favorite of both boys. My daughter, Melissa (Sammy's mom), is at work at the hospital and will swing by the Walkers' to retrieve Sammy when she gets off at six o'clock this evening. Melissa and Sam have been living here with me for the last year and a half; she sold their house after the death of her husband, John. Since then, Sammy and I have grown very close.

I believe the boy is well prepared to cope with my death. The loss of both a father and a grandfather, less than three years apart, might well be devastating to many boys, but not Sam; he is not an average nine-year-old. Understanding him as I do, I have no doubt at all that he'll be fine—he knows the things I know. In any case, what has been fated for me cannot be changed.

11:15 a.m. on the same day:

I place a note in an envelope marked with Melissa's name and tape it to the front door. I go out for a short walk—it's cold, very cold—but it's a brilliantly clear winter's day, and the sky is a magnificent azure blue, which, seen through my watery eyes, scintillates in the winter sun. A blanket of frost covers the grass; the wintry wind freezes my mustache hair, and with each exhale a small mist rises, adding to the hoar under my nose.

Back inside, I take off my heavy coat, wool hat, and gloves and put them neatly in the hall closet. I head up to my den; the photographs on the wall leading up the stairs comfort me, for I'll be seeing my lost loved ones again soon. My beloved dog, Bowie, sits at my feet now; she seems to sense that something is amiss. Something is indeed different today.

"Good girl," I say, reaching down to scratch her ear. God, how many times have I spoken these words to her over the past thirteen years? I open a photo album that's been lying on my desk and flip through the pages; they are all there—all the people I have loved on earth, some of whom I will be leaving behind. Waves of sadness wash over me; I am going to miss them. Sadness gives way to gratitude when I reflect that mine has been a full and interesting, sometimes beautiful life. Finally, I am lifted by a flood of anticipation—anticipation free from fear, almost a longing—for what is to come.

Part One

A Special Boy

"Fear only has the power we give it. Hope works the same way."

—Bob Goff, *New York Times* bestselling author

"My tendency was self-disparagement so, for example, with the thought: 'I am Sumedho,' I'd think of myself in negative terms: 'I'm no good.' But listen, from where does that arise and where does it cease?"

—Ajahn Sumedho, The Four Noble Truths, "Realisation"

"Let everything happen to you: beauty and terror. Just keep going. No feeling is final . . ."

—Rainer Maria Rilke, "Go to the Limits of Your Longing"

Chapter 1

I Wore Brown

Before I retired in January of 2014, if you were to venture into my bedroom closet, you'd have discovered many uniforms, many brown uniforms—and all of these many brown uniforms would be fully laundered and pressed. Here, from the distant past, is an inventory of the damn things:

- Four pairs lightweight trousers—brown
- Two pairs heavyweight trousers—brown
- Four pairs shorts, knee-length—brown
- Four shirts, short-sleeve, button-down—brown
- Three shirts, short-sleeve, polo—brown
- Five shirts, long-sleeve, button-down—brown
- Two pairs shoes—brown, with brown laces
- One pair winter work boots—brown, with brown laces
- One sweater, crew neck—brown
- One sweatshirt—brown
- Two turtlenecks—brown
- Five T-shirts, crew neck—brown
- One vest—brown
- One rain jacket, nylon—brown
- One lightweight windbreaker—brown
- One mid-weight, mid-length jacket—brown

- One winter parka—brown
- One pullover hat, wool—brown
- One baseball cap with logo—brown
- Five pairs regular socks—brown
- Five pairs knee socks—brown

When I retired, I turned in all of these brown uniforms—except for one pair of lightweight trousers and one long-sleeve, button-down shirt, which I kept (believe it or not) for sentimental reasons. They have hung in my closet, untouched, for twenty years.

I never wore any of the uniforms listed above except for when I was required to wear them during working hours—nor have I ever purchased any piece of clothing for my private use that bore the slightest hint of the color brown. That said, I do own a pair of brown oxford dress shoes, which my late wife once coerced me into buying, thinking they made me look "sporty." I wore them only occasionally—and grudgingly—before she died, and never since.

Why all this brown, you may ask—and my aversion to it? Well, I was a UPS driver, and by the time my career came to an end, I had worked there for thirty-five years. All things considered, as you will see, it's a wonder I lasted that long. Although driving for UPS was a physically and emotionally demanding job, I stuck it out because of the security it provided; the benefits were excellent, especially the health coverage (which, over the years, I made liberal use of). It had a strong pension plan through the Teamsters Union, and it paid very well. I believe that, at the time, it was one of the top-paying jobs of its kind in the industry. With overtime, many drivers made over $100K a year driving those ugly brown trucks.

Much happened during my years of working for Brown, including a suicide (not mine), two marriages, one divorce, finding the love of my life, the birth of a beautiful baby girl, drug abuse (legal and illegal), rehab, therapy, a broken back, a broken heart, widowhood, a nervous breakdown, deep depression, an attempted suicide (mine), more rehab, more therapy, and my visit with a dead man. Through it all I waited—not without trepidation—for my inevitable return to Rockaway, New York, my boyhood home—and to a mysterious house that no one could see but me.

We have a lot of ground to cover, reader, so please, make yourself comfortable while I lead you into my story. Leave your troubled thoughts behind you and consider that, for the most part, they are not worth the investment of your valuable time and energy. Your thoughts are only thoughts; they may emanate from your mind, but they are not you! You are infinitely greater than these shadowy mental ruminations! You are the genuine article, perfectly you—as they say, "warts and all!" I can promise you that, and as you read on, I expect you'll come to understand this concept more clearly.

My story begins with a young boy, an emotional and very fragile boy. From an early age, this boy has known that he is different from other boys. He has always known that, at some point in his life, something miraculous will happen to him; he knew it even before he knew the meaning of the word *miraculous*. He knew it because he could feel it—he sensed it in his soul. Yet despite this knowledge, he's a sad boy; fear and anguish are his childhood companions. But please, do not feel sorry for him, because he will prevail. And as you'll see, we will all win in the end if we just allow ourselves to accept the victory! Now, reader, please allow me to introduce you to that boy, August Nathaniel Greenleaf.

Chapter 2

It's a Boy, Mrs. Greenleaf! It's a Boy!

Sunday, January 6, 1957:

Ella Greenleaf woke up at 1:15 a.m. on that bitterly cold winter evening, knowing that it was time. This was her second baby, and she knew that the feeling of peeing in her pants was not necessarily that—not even likely, since she was nine months and two days pregnant. No, this was her water breaking; it was time to get to the hospital and begin those dreaded contractions until August—or Agatha—came out of her into the world to extend their little family.

"Howie," she rasped, tugging at her husband's shoulder, "it's time."

"Howie," louder now, "please, my water just broke; we need to get to Maimonides—quickly!"

Another shoulder tug—no response. Then, louder still, this time accompanied by a punch to that same shoulder, *"Howard Greenleaf, I'm about to have my baby!"*

Howard awoke in a fog; his regular wake-up time was 3:30 a.m., ninety minutes before his shift was to begin at the Wall Street Post Office in downtown Manhattan.

After she'd confirmed that Howard was awake to stay, Ella went into the bathroom, cleaned herself up, put on a housedress, and got herself ready to go. She quietly lifted her six-year-old son, Michael, out of his bed, still sleeping, and carried him across the second-floor hallway to her friend Yetta's apartment, as they had arranged. When she got back to her own apartment, she found her husband sitting on the toilet with the bathroom door open. Five minutes later, Howard—incongruously, considering the situation and Ella's obvious expression of urgency—began shaving.

Howard and Ella arrived at Maimonides Hospital at exactly 2:15 a.m. After what Mom later described as "by far the worst pain in my life," I was born the same day at 8:57 p.m. The doctor who delivered me had an unusual name, which I'll never forget: Dr. Gregory Goodlife. As the good Doctor Goodlife guided me out of the birth canal and into this world, his first words to my exhausted mother were "It's a boy, Mrs. Greenleaf, it's a boy!"

I weighed eight pounds, three ounces; Mom would tell me that I came out crying and left the hospital the next day still crying. "Oh, but August," she'd say, "you were the most beautiful thing I had ever seen."

For as long as I knew him, Dad never offered his version of the story—nor, I believe, did I ever ask him for it.

Years later, out of curiosity, I'd sometimes ask my friends, "What's your very earliest memory?" Most often, they'd recount an event that had occurred sometime between the ages of four and six. When, in return, I'd describe my first memory, I was almost never believed, but it was true. I remembered Dr. Goodlife (although I never saw him), the wet warmth of my mother's womb, the pain and fear of being pushed out through the birth canal, my mother's grunts and screams, Dr. Goodlife's hands under me—the light, the cold air, the warmth and softness of the blanket they wrapped around me. Even now, I can remember the smell of the delivery room. I remember it all—believe me, reader, I remember it all—for I have the gift.

We moved out of our Brooklyn apartment, on the corner of East Thirty-First Street and Flatbush Avenue, in August of 1960. I was two and a half years old. I have many recollections of that apartment, the neighborhood, and our Brooklyn neighbors. Mom and Dad never took any photographs of our little second-floor walk-up, and there was only one photograph (that I've been able to find) taken during our family's tenancy there. This photo was taken by my mother's friend Rita. It shows Mom pushing me in a stroller alongside her friend Ruth Goldberg, who is pushing her son, Sheldon, in his bigger, fancier stroller. Sheldon is seen in the picture, cool as a cucumber, looking like the Little Prince of Flatbush Avenue. I, on the other hand, am shown bawling over some unspecified outrage. Perhaps I had a wet diaper, or I was hungry—or maybe I was jealous of Sheldon. Or did the unlucky photographer expose my fear of the camera being pointed at me—or of just being looked at?

[**Scopophobia: Fear of being stared at.**]

Behind me and my look of sheer terror, Mom flashed a "hurry-up-and-take-the-damn-picture" smile.

She was a slim five feet, seven inches tall, wearing a streamlined, red plaid coat. Although the photograph was in black and white, I remember clearly that red plaid coat with the big red buttons and tie belt. With her mid-length auburn hair neatly trimmed and her spare makeup expertly applied, she was as pretty as any picture could be.

I have other recollections that date from my earliest years. I can recall being awakened by loud voices coming from our small kitchen, which was adjacent to the bedroom that my older brother, Michael, and I shared. I stood up in my crib and listened. The room was dark except for a sliver of light filtering in through the bedroom door, which was ajar. Mom and Dad were yelling at each other, and I recall the ferocity of their argument. I was very frightened but too afraid to cry for fear that Dad might turn his anger toward me. Sadly, this was only the beginning; many more arguments were to follow until some years later, when Mom took matters into her own hands.

Another of my early memories concerns the Yang family, who lived on the first floor. The parents ran a laundromat down the street; they had a son named Tommy, who was a friend of Michael's. I recall watching as Tommy held a magnifying glass to an ant on the sidewalk. The sun's rays converged through the lens, focusing on this tiny creature, and *poof*—just like that, the ant disintegrated in a tiny puff of smoke. I cried and ran away—but I'll never forget the horror of that miniature immolation!

Michael, Tommy, and other neighborhood boys frequently played punchball on East Thirty-First Street; there were no other places to play in our Brooklyn neighborhood. My brother was the best player of the group, and I was proud of him. He could punch the ball the farthest and run the bases the fastest. Michael was already on his way to becoming a star athlete.

I remember my mom's uncle, Paul, who owned a shoe store. He was always very kind to our family, and at the beginning of every school year, he'd have Mom come into his store to pick out a new pair of shoes for Michael. Mom told me that my first several pairs of shoes were also gifts from Uncle Paul. Sadly, only a few years later, Uncle Paul died in an automobile accident; he was fifty-one years old. Mom told me that, although he was a successful businessman, Paul was always in a rush to get somewhere. Unfortunately, one day Uncle Paul rushed through a red light at the corner of Flatbush and Bedford Avenues and ran into a dump truck. Paul was ejected from his brand-new, white 1964 Ford Falcon and died on the street. The driver of the dump truck survived but suffered a broken collarbone, wrist, and pelvis. I was told much later (when I was able to understand such things) that he did very well in court. Let that be a lesson to us all: The seconds saved by moving too fast are seldom worth the risk. As my grieving grandfather, Josef, said with a sigh, "Act in haste; repent at leisure."

The most traumatic recollection from my early life, however, had to be the intentional dismemberment of my beloved stuffed monkey, Mr. Bim Zippy, by a party or parties unknown. I recall sitting on the front stoop of our apartment building, holding what was left of him. His arms and legs were scattered about the steps and sidewalk; an ear had been cut off, and his stuffing protruded from a slit in his side. Bim had been mutilated, murdered—and I cried inconsolably. I really loved that monkey, and it took me a long time to get over his loss. Mom brought a new monkey home just days later, but I wouldn't take to him; he just wasn't my Bim.

[Separation anxiety: Excessive anxiety of a child due to the absence of a parent or loved one.]

Mom then made it her mission (as she told me, only after the culprits were identified) to find out who would do such a cruel and wanton thing. Her prime suspects were Michael and Tommy Yang, but neither of them would confess to having done the deed. It was years later that my brother wrote me from Vietnam, and in his letter, he admitted that he and Tommy—with another friend, Mark Aberman—had dismembered Bim with Tommy's pocketknife. He apologized and asked me to forgive him.

I wrote back immediately: "I love and miss you, Michael, and of course I forgive you. Please, come home safe."

In August of 1960, Mom and Dad packed up the family, and we moved to an apartment on the top floor of a seven-story building in the Arverne neighborhood of Far Rockaway, Queens. Rockaway is a peninsula set between Jamaica Bay and the Atlantic Ocean. From our apartment's living room window, we had a clear view across the street to grass fields (where we would play for the next ten years), a real baseball diamond with dugouts and bleachers, a big white house by the bay, and Idlewild International Airport in the distance across the bay. It was a million-dollar view, seen from a moderate-income apartment building.

The most impressive thing to me, however, was the very first airplane I saw fly by our building, which was evidently in line with one of Idlewild's most frequently used runway approaches. Almost every plane flew past or directly over our building. The planes came in so low that you could read each airline's logo on its fuselage. Mom and Mike made a game of guessing which airline the next aircraft would represent: TWA, United, American Airlines, Pan American, Eastern, etc.

But it was the noise from these massive beasts that grabbed your attention. At certain times of the day, they might fly over our building every ten minutes or so, and good heavens, they were loud! It's the first one that you never forget: You're relaxing at home, maybe watching TV, innocent, unsuspecting, then—*boom!*—you've been initiated. You never really get used to it, but the effects diminish over time as your nerves learn to cope.

Mom and Dad grew to love our new apartment, though, and so did Michael. But I just found more things to fear—heights, elevators, the threat of an immense aircraft crashing into our building—and shortly, very shortly, it would be hurricanes too. And there'd be more.

Chapter 3

Life and Fear in Far Rockaway

We lived just five blocks north of the Atlantic Ocean and beautiful Rockaway Beach, with its five-and-a-half-mile-long boardwalk. West of us, visible from our living room window, was Somerville Basin, an arm of Jamaica Bay, less than one thousand feet from our apartment building. On the night of September 12, 1960, a month after moving into our new neighborhood, we watched whitecaps roiling on the bay. A hurricane was bearing down on us—her name was Donna.

Hurricane Donna was the strongest hurricane of the 1960 Atlantic hurricane season, causing severe damage in the Caribbean, in Florida, and along much of the East Coast of the United States. On September 6, Donna intensified to a Category 4 hurricane before making landfall in the Bahamas, where she generated gusts of 173 miles per hour. She went on to strike Florida's Gulf Coast before heading northeast across the state. Donna then danced northward along the Atlantic Seaboard, leaving destruction in her wake from North Carolina to New Jersey until, on the night of Monday, September 12, she arrived in Far Rockaway.

I recall all of this—not necessarily the factual accounts I've just cited, nor the damage statistics, but the experience of it—the windless, oppressive heat of the day before, the weather reports of the approaching storm, the growing realization that it was heading straight for us, unsettling stories of the monstrous 1938 hurricane, the silent preparation, the whitecaps, and the waiting. I'll never forget the events of that night and the following day. My tension grew as the storm approached, and by the end of the evening, I was nearly catatonic.

[**Catatonia: A state of immobility or stupor.**]

Mom and Dad watched Douglas Edwards on *CBS Television News* almost every night, but on the evening of September 12, they were paying particular attention to what he had to say. Two years later, in 1962, Walter Cronkite became the CBS news anchor, and the name of the program was changed to the *CBS Evening News*—but on that night, we were listening to Edwards. I took my cues from the words he used, many of which I did not understand, but his tone, and my family's reactions, told me all I needed to know: "Perhaps hundreds already dead . . . massive damage . . . killer storm heading to New York's Long Island."

"Mom," my brother shouted, "that's us!"

"Yes, it is, Michael, Long Island is just a few miles away."

Upon hearing that, whatever it was that was holding me together up to that point deserted me; I ran into the bedroom, buried my head under the covers, and cried. With the wind howling, the rain pounding on my bedroom window, and me screaming, Mom came into the room and sat down beside me.

"Augie," she said, "Mommy's going to get under the covers with you, dear. Move over and make some room."

She hugged me, and with her soft, delicate hand, she wiped away my tears and whispered in my ear, "There's nothing to be afraid of, Augie. We're very safe here. You, Michael, Daddy, and I are all going to be just fine."

"I'm afraid, Mommy."

"I understand that, Augie, and it's okay to be a little afraid, but it'll be over soon, and we are all going to be fine. I'll tell you what, little guy—we can all stay up late and watch TV, and I'll even make us some popcorn."

"I love you, Mommy."

"I love you, too, Augie—very, very much—and I'll never let anything happen to you."

With that, I got a big kiss, and Mom giggled as she wiped away the lipstick from my left cheek.

They all stayed up late that night—how could they not? The storm was a powerful one, with wind gusts up to 110 miles per hour. Our apartment building became part of Jamaica Bay; four feet of water surrounded us and the other buildings in our complex. All told, the storm killed an estimated fifty people in the US, and the total damage on the Eastern Seaboard was estimated to be $3.35 billion in 1960 dollars. I can only imagine how much that would be today.

At 10:00 that evening, I was sitting in my mother's lap, watching the *Armstrong Circle Theatre* on CBS. Dad and Michael had tried talking Mom into putting on the *Channel 5 News* so they could get storm updates, but Mom wouldn't hear of it, knowing it would upset me even more. I fell asleep shortly after that and woke up several times during the night—a combination of fear and exhaustion sending me back to sleep each time. I awoke the next morning at 9:00 a.m. By that time, the storm had already made its way northward, through southern New England. It was a sunny morning, and I couldn't help but notice the diluvium outside my window—it was as though our apartment building were Noah's Ark, afloat on Jamaica Bay. I went to the living room window and looked out at the big white house by the bay. It was flooded, too, and I wondered if the people who lived there were safe.

Life in Rockaway was far different from the life my family had grown accustomed to in Brooklyn. There were grass fields, and we didn't have to play on the streets and sidewalks. My mother was a stay-at-home mom until I started the first grade, when she took a job at Peninsula General Hospital, working the 9:00 a.m. to 2:30 p.m. shift as a file clerk. That year, Michael entered the fourth grade at PS 105, where he excelled in his schoolwork and demonstrated to his gym teacher that he was a budding athlete.

Having seen that our family survived Hurricane Donna was not enough to assuage my mounting fears. My next source of angst would be that very name, "Donna." I could no longer bear to watch *The Donna Reed Show*—as pretty as she was, just her name brought on nightmares of that stress-filled September night. Every holiday season, while my family watched *It's a Wonderful Life*, starring Jimmy Stewart and the aforementioned Ms. Reed, I went to my room and played by myself.

[**Alexinomia: A fear of names.**]

The fear of elevators—which I developed soon after moving into our new high-rise building—is aptly, though unofficially, called elevatophobia, and it may also involve one or more of the following:

[**Claustrophobia: The fear of enclosed spaces.**]

[**Agoraphobia: The fear of being trapped.**]

And especially with open or glass-enclosed elevators:

[**Acrophobia: The fear of heights.**]

As for the fear of heights, I had seen myself as brave for having the courage just to look out our seventh-floor apartment windows—but I'd never touch or lean against those windows, never! Michael, on the other hand, was fearless. He'd occasionally open the living room window and screen and stick his head way out beyond the outside wall. He'd say, "C'mon, Augie, try it. Oh, the humanity!"

One time, Mike dared me to do the same; when I refused, he shouted to my mother, "Mom, Augie's a chicken!"

Always sensitive to my fears, Mom scolded him: "Unlike you, Michael, maybe August doesn't have a death wish. Now get your head back in here, close the screen, and please, stop taunting your little brother!"

During my preschool years, a normal day began about 7:30 a.m., when I'd get up and have breakfast with Michael. Mom would say, "Augie, you don't have to get up so early—you can sleep in, you know. It won't be long before you're in the first grade and you'll have to be getting up." But I missed my big brother while he was at school, so I was determined to spend some time with him in the morning. Michael's school was only three blocks away, and he'd usually walk there with his friends. He just loved living in Rockaway. After Michael left for school, I'd go back to bed, sleeping until 9:30 or so, when my mom would wake me up and see that I got dressed.

Every morning, at about ten o'clock, Mom and I would go out to the playground in front of our apartment building. That involved going down to the first floor in the elevator, which for me was no easy task. Each morning, Mom's strategy was to hold my hand and try, somehow, to take my mind off the elevator. She might sing me a song or talk about what we were going to have for dinner—anything to divert my attention. It never worked—she'd literally have to carry or drag me into the damn thing. The big elevator doors would close, and I'd begin to howl. Other tenants soon learned to wait for the next elevator and leave that one to us.

"Augie," Mom would say, "we'll be living here in this building for a long time, and you'll be riding the elevator several times a day. It's very safe, son; you need to know that and get used to it."

With tear-filled eyes, I'd say, "Mommy, what about the stairs?"

"Augie, no—we will not be walking up and down seven flights of stairs every day. Mommy doesn't have the strength for that. Now, please calm down."

"But I like the stairs, Momma—please."

With that, she'd pick me up and carry me into the elevator.

Outside, at the playground, Mom would sit on a park bench with the other mothers and chat while the little ones played. I became friends with Hal Rosenthal, Federico Gutierrez, Jodie Sunderland, Kevin Feldman, and my very first little girlfriend, the stunning Susan Polowitz, who was four months older than me. My first love, Susan, was a cougar; in later years, there'd be other cougars for me to prowl with—but then, most often at night. After the park, Mom would wrangle me back to the apartment for lunch and a nap—and then Michael would be home.

My love for Michael was immense. But for his teasing me on occasion, he was the perfect big brother: he looked out for me; he taught me things, and he played with me—sometimes even though his friends were waiting for him to play with them. Every day, after he got home from school, weather permitting, he'd go out to the grass fields across the street to play sports with his friends. They'd play baseball in the spring, summer, and fall and football in the late fall and winter. Mike would often take me with him to watch. Crossing Almeda Avenue, he did just what Mom had taught him to do: He held my hand firmly, looked both ways (twice), and then—when no cars were coming—he walked swiftly across the street with me in tow.

Mike had grown up with most of the boys in our building, and by the fifth grade, he'd become friends with several other boys from his school. They'd bring their baseball gloves, bats, and balls, choose sides, and start a game. Sometimes, when the baseball diamond was free, they would start their game there, and I was able to watch from the bleachers—always on the bottom tier, of course. There was a group of teenage boys who'd normally arrive at the field first and, naturally, would take the diamond. But even if they arrived after Michael's group, the older boys would chase them off. Often, Michael and his friends had already started a game but were forced to cede the turf anyway.

At that point, Michael's group would set up their game in the large grass field near our apartment building. When I tagged along with Mike, I always hoped the big boys were already at the diamond. That way, there would be no confrontation. Another fear:

[**Conflict Phobia: Fear of conflict or disagreement.**]

One day, while Mike and his friends were playing on the baseball diamond, I saw the big boys coming, and my anxiety level went through the roof. Normally, Mike and his friends would have cleared off the diamond and moved their game to make room for the big kids. Not that day, though—that day, the younger boys decided they weren't going anywhere. Instead, they formed a huddle on the pitcher's mound, around Michael. Jimmy Williams, who seemed to be the unofficial leader of the older group, was a PAL (Police Athletic League) pitcher for our local team. At thirteen, he was tall and looked more like a sixteen-year-old . . . and boy, could he throw hard. As Dad would say, Jimmy threw darts.

Jimmy said, "Come on, guys, time to let the big boys play." Jimmy's friends tittered and jostled each other by way of emulating his derisive tone.

Watching this from the first row of the bleachers, I felt as if I were going to pee in my dungarees. Then, to my absolute horror, Michael, standing in front of his friends, said, "We were here first, so no matter how big you are, this field is ours to play on!"

"Really," said Jimmy's friend Keith McNulty.

"Yes, really," Michael said. At this point, I got up and went around behind the bleachers to hide.

"Okay, then," Jimmy said, playing the diplomat, "we'll make you a deal. We give you a half inning to bat against us. If you score a run, it's your field today. If you don't score, then we take over. Otherwise, we're playing on this field, and you guys are taking your game somewhere else."

My knees were shaking as I peered through the bleachers. I could see the younger boys huddling up again; Michael was doing the talking. When the huddle broke, Michael said, "Let's play that half an inning."

Now, Michael and his friends were ten or eleven years old; the big boys were all in their early teens and about a foot taller, on average, than the younger kids. Nevertheless, the stage was set: the teenagers were at their positions, and Jimmy Williams was on the mound. Our guys were in the dugout, ready to come to bat. Feeling calmer, I came out from behind the bleachers and sat down in the front row to watch.

Brian Gold came up to bat first. Brian exuded confidence, but after three pitches, three swings, and three misses, he walked back to the dugout with his chin on his chest.

Next up was Sean Connolly. When he came to the plate, Sean was looking as if he'd just seen a ghost. It didn't go any better for Sean than it had for Brian. Good morning, good afternoon, good night!

Then it was Michael's turn at bat. I was hoping that he'd bat Georgie White third and himself fourth so he wouldn't have to face the big Williams kid. I was afraid for Michael, but he approached the plate with a determined look on his face, a look that said he was ready for business. Jimmy Williams's first pitch was high, and Michael didn't swing. His next pitch was right down the middle; Mike took a big cut and didn't come close.

With the boys in the field chattering, "No batter, no batter" and "C'mon, Jimmy, he can't hit you, Jimmy," Williams's third pitch came in harder than the first two. This time Michael swung and foul tipped it to the backstop; Jimmy looked surprised. I saw Michael talking to himself, mouthing the words, "Okay, now; eyes on the ball."

All the boys were getting louder—not just the big kids but our guys in the dugout also. There was a glimmer of hope; maybe Michael could hit this Williams kid after all. Michael held his bat high, waving the tip in a tight circle, as he always did. Jimmy just smiled and went into his windup; his fourth pitch came in harder still. *Crack!* The ball left Michael's bat like a rocket and landed deep in left field, well beyond the left fielder's reach. I had never seen him hit a ball that far.

Michael tore around the bases, running with his head down. He circled first and second base like a young Jackie Robinson. As he approached third base, he looked up and saw the ball coming in to the third baseman from the cutoff man. When Michael started his slide, the ball was already there in the third baseman's glove, waiting for him. He was out by five feet.

That evening, over dinner, Michael told us that he'd thought for sure he had a home run—but he'd forgotten what Dad had once taught him: "Know your opponent." It wasn't a ten-year-old kid chasing down the baseball and throwing it back in. It was an athletic teenage player who'd made a perfect throw to the cutoff man. His name was Billy Alvarez, as Mike found out after the inning was over, when Billy approached him, patted him on the back, and said, "Good hit, Mike."

After that day, whenever the big kids were down a man, they'd ask Mike to play with them. But he'd accept their invitation only if his friends weren't around. Mike told me, "Augie, you never turn your back on your friends—never!" And he never did.

Chapter 4

Didaskaleinophobia

Tuesday, September 4, 1962, was a very troublesome day for Mrs. Ella Greenleaf. In the two or three years leading up to this day—the first day of kindergarten for her beloved second son, August—she had been a little uneasy concerning my mental state. "The boy is afraid of almost everything!" she confided to her neighbor and best friend, May Gold. "Honestly, May, I'm at my wits' end, and I pray that school will be a big help for him."

"Maybe the school guidance counselor, Mr. Phelps, can help. Why don't you call and make an appointment to speak with him?"

"Maybe—maybe that's a good idea. I'll call him. He's a wonderful little boy, May, you know that."

"He most certainly is, honey. All the mothers love him."

"He's so damn smart, he remembers everything—I'm a little embarrassed to tell you this . . . " She paused. "He even tells me all the details about his birth."

"Really! Maybe he's just repeating what he's overheard you say."

"No, May, he tells me things I would never know—hearing people talking while he was in the womb, his experience coming through the birth canal, the feel of the doctor's hands. Jesus, May, he even knows the name of the doctor!"

"What was the doctor's name?"

"Goodlife, Dr. Gregory Goodlife."

"Wow, what a cool name! Who could ever forget that?"

"But I never told him. I have never once mentioned it to him."

"Maybe Howard told him, Ella."

"Howard barely talks to Augie, and he would never bring that up. I don't think he even knows the doctor's name himself."

Ella became quiet for a moment and, speaking softly, confided in her new best friend. "You know, May, Howard doesn't care much about Augie. He's not Howard's kind of kid. It's all about Michael. Mike is certainly worthy of Howard's attention—he's such a great boy with many talents, and he's extremely confident. In many ways, he is the polar opposite of Augie." Ella began to tear up, and May handed her a tissue.

"I feel guilty, May—I feel guilty that I don't give enough attention to Michael; I feel as though I'm compensating for Howard's lack of attention to Augie. And Howard is so very hard to live with."

My mother then began to cry openly, and May, dear friend that she was, held her lovingly and said, "Well, I don't know about Howard, honey, but you are every bit the loving mother to Michael that you are to August. I've seen it; you're always hugging him and giving him the biggest, warmest smiles—the same as you do for Augie. You listen attentively when he speaks to you, and you make a point of going to all his games. Come on, Ella, you're the best of mothers. We all think that about you!"

"I love you, May."

"And I love you, Ella."

Mom did everything she could that summer to prepare me for school. She took me on a special trip to downtown Far Rockaway, where we had cheeseburgers and fries at Wetson's. From there, we went to the Army Navy Store, where she bought me three new pairs of pants and six new shirts.

"These are not your playclothes, Augie," she said. "You are to take them off as soon as you get home from school and fold them neatly or hang them up. I know you are positively, absolutely going to love school. It's going to be so much fun—and your teacher, Mrs. Fields, just can't wait to meet you!"

"Momma, how many boys and girls will there be in my class?"

"Twenty-four, Augie, and do you remember what Daddy said?"

"No, Momma."

"Well, he said that twenty-four is the number that Willie Mays wears on the back of his jersey. And whose favorite player is Willie Mays?"

"He's Michael's, Momma."

"That's right, Augie, and you are just going to love school, young man—just love it."

Mom could not have been more wrong.

Labor Day came after a long, hot summer, and Dad's brother, my uncle Robby, drove out from Brooklyn with my grandparents Saul and Anna. I loved all three of them, but I had a special place in my heart for Uncle Robby. He was a gentle and loving soul and always treated me with kindness. Secretly, I wished that he was my father instead of Dad. Mom showed off my new duds, and there was so much oohing, aahing, and excitement over them that I actually blushed. But I knew better—I saw through their little charade, and I thought to myself, *I am not going to school tomorrow, and that's that!*

The next day, at my new school, PS 105, twenty-three children lined up and walked obediently into the building, just like lambs to the slaughter. Not little Augie, though—the sixth lamb from the front, I balked. There was no way I was going to face the axe. The brief disturbance caused by my bleating refusal drew the attention of Mr. Phelps, the school guidance counselor, who watched over his flock like a border collie, just itching to nip at the heels of balky lambs. I could tell by the nimble way he moved that there was no way out of this; I'd have to concoct an alternative plan. Mom, who was looking especially pretty that day, was getting upset, and I knew it—I just couldn't do anything about it. I wanted to please her—to make her happy, but I was just too afraid to go into that school. Add another fear to the list:

[**Didaskaleinophobia: Fear of going to school.**]

So, I bargained with them: "If Momma holds my hand and walks me to the classroom, I'll go in."

And that's what we did: Mom and I walked into the school hand in hand, and Mr. Phelps led us all the way down the long, long corridor to my classroom. My plan was working. When we got to the classroom, room K2, I took my hand from Mom's and asked Mr. Phelps, "Can I kiss my Momma goodbye?" Before he could answer, I was halfway down the hall, running like the wind—making a break for it! But the nimble Mr. Phelps was a lot quicker than I'd figured, and he caught me just as I was about to open the exit door and flee the school. Phelps perp-walked me back to the classroom (although I don't remember my feet actually touching the floor), and as he pulled me into the classroom, I glanced over at my mother and saw the tears in her eyes.

That very same day, Michael was starting the seventh grade at JH 198. Daily dismissal at his school was 3:00 p.m., but for us kindergarteners, it was 1:30, which left Mom and me some time alone together. At dismissal, Mom was waiting by the school entrance door with the other mothers; I ran over to her and gave her a hug and a sobbing sigh of relief.

"How was school, Augie?" she asked.

"I don't like school, Momma, and I don't think Mrs. Fields likes me. She gave me a dirty look when Mr. Phelps dragged me into her classroom."

"He didn't drag you in, August, he walked you in—and I'm sure Mrs. Fields didn't give you a dirty look. She wouldn't do that."

"But she did, Momma, she gave me a dirty look just when Mr. Phelps was dragging me into the room."

"Okay, Augie, let's go get an ice cream at the truck to celebrate your first day of school—and then we can ride our bikes on the path near the ball field."

Despite all my other fears, riding a bicycle was never a problem for me. My training wheels came off quickly, and I loved the sense of freedom that riding my bike gave me. Dad had commented once, "Funny thing, when the boy really wants to do something, he puts his mind to it and does just fine. Otherwise, he's as stubborn as a brick!" My father often made barbed comments like that about me, and even more often about my mother, especially when he became moody. There were times when Mom would whisper to me, "He's in a dark mood, August. Just leave him be, and don't talk to him unless he speaks directly to you." Under those circumstances, I had no problem following her advice.

That beautiful September afternoon, Mom and I took a nice long ride. My first day of school was behind me now, and I was free, at least until tomorrow. Mom and I were together on our bikes, and our little world was in order—that is, until I asked her the question.

We had completed a loop back to the section of the path that lay across the street from the baseball diamond. We put our kickstands down and sat on a nearby park bench that looked out over the ball field and beyond. We sat quietly, enjoying the day and each other's company, when I asked, "Mom, who lives in the big white house over there by the bay?"

My question caught my mother by surprise. "I'm sorry, Augie, can you repeat that?"

I pointed at the house and said, "Mom, that big white house over there with all those rocking chairs on the porch—I never see people around. Who lives there?"

My mother was staring at me; she had a puzzled look on her face. "Where do you see a big white house, Augie?"

"Over there, Mom, don't you see it?"

"No, Augie, I'm afraid I don't."

"But it's right in front of us."

"Is today the first time that you've seen the house, Augie? I know that it's been kind of a full day for you, being your first day of school and all."

"No, Mom, I saw that house the very first day we moved in."

"And now you're seeing it again for the second time?"

"No, I see that house every day. Why, don't you see it?"

"Have you ever told anybody else about the house?"

"Yes, Mom."

"Who?"

"Michael—twice, but he just laughs at me."

Mom said that it was time for us to go home. She said Michael was probably there already, and she wanted to make sure that he was doing his homework.

Chapter 5

Ella Greenleaf

My mother, Ella Freedman, was born on Monday, October 26, 1931, the second of two children, three years after her brother, Mark. Ella's parents, Josef and Rachel Freedman, were both first-generation Jewish Americans from Poland. Josef arrived in the US in 1913 with his mother, Sarah, and his older brother, Benjamin; he was eleven years old. They lived with Josef's uncle, Isaac, for the better part of a year until their father, Abraham, arrived, and they took a place of their own. In 1914, at the age of ten, Rachel came over (also from Poland) with her parents, Heiman and Rose Berman, and her two brothers, Leonard and Sidney.

Both the Freedmans and the Bermans settled in the Lower East Side of Manhattan and assimilated into American life. There really wasn't much choice in those days; you got a job—jobs were plentiful at that time—the kids went to school, and everybody learned English and began their new lives in America, hoping someday to become citizens. Both families were Ashkenazic (Eastern European) Jews. Due to economic hardships and persecution in their home countries (especially Russia), 2.9 million Jews from Eastern Europe fled to America between 1880 and 1924.

By that time, New York City was producing 70 percent of women's clothing and 40 percent of men's clothing manufactured in the US, and this industry provided jobs for many newly arrived Jewish settlers. Roughly 10 percent of the Jewish immigrant labor force had been trained as tailors and seamsters—which were among the few occupations open to Jews in nineteenth-century Europe—and they brought their considerable skills with them.

So, it was only natural that both Abraham Freedman and Heiman Berman found work in New York's flourishing garment trade. Both men worked for Jakob Asch Co., on the corner of Seventh Avenue and West Thirty-Ninth Street. In the early spring of 1915, Abraham, Josef's father, and Heiman, Rachel's father, were assigned to work at adjacent sewing machines. Side by side they worked at their industrial Singers, stitching women's dresses. As Polish immigrants, the two men immediately took a liking to each other, and that summer, they planned a family outing at Coney Island in Brooklyn.

On a hot Sunday afternoon in August, with the sun moving slowly across a cloudless sky, the Freedman and Berman clans met for the first time, and lifelong friendships were begun. At the time, no one could have guessed that the two families would eventually become related. But when thirteen-year-old Josef Freedman first laid eyes on eleven-year-old Rachel Berman, it was love at first sight. It was a feeling that, years later, Josef would tell his daughter, Ella, he had never had before and would never have again. "We were only children, but I knew that, someday, I would marry your mother; she was the most beautiful and lively girl I had ever met." And marry her he did—on Sunday, October 14, 1923.

I never knew any of my great-grandparents on either side of my family, but my mom told me she absolutely adored her grandfather Abraham, who, she said, was quite a character. Mom liked to tell me stories from Abraham's early life, which she had gotten "directly from the horse's mouth."

One such story involved the Freedman family before they emigrated from Poland to the United States. The family was living in the city of Lodz, south of Warsaw, which at the time was an industrial town. Abraham, one of five children, learned at an early age to be resourceful. On this occasion, though, he used his resourcefulness with ill intent:

> One afternoon, when he was eleven years old, Abraham and two of his friends, Jacob and Dov, stole a chicken from a local butcher.

> Making this heist even trickier than it might otherwise have been was the fact that this chicken was still very much alive. How they pulled it off was all Abraham's idea. He waited until the butcher was busy with a customer, cutting meat and chatting all the while. He quietly entered the store through the front door, which was already open to let in the fresh air. He snuck behind the counter and into the back room, where there was a cage containing four live chickens. He removed one of the chickens—very carefully, so as not to cause a ruckus—then absconded through the back door. His friends were duly impressed by his chutzpah in pulling off this stunt, but now they had to figure out what to do with a live chicken.

"Truth be told, Abraham hadn't really thought this scheme through himself. None of the boys had the stomach for butchering a live chicken, and it didn't take a genius to know that taking the bird home alive wasn't a very good idea. After all, their parents may have been old-fashioned, but they were not stupid. Then another problem occurred to one of the boys: How were they going to split a live chicken three ways? To make matters even worse, the chicken in question was beginning to protest its confinement in young Abraham's arms. At this point, Jacob and Dov told Abraham that he could have the damn chicken; they were going home.

"Now, Abraham, besides being resourceful, was also stubborn, and he was not about to let this bird go to waste. So, he headed back to the butcher's shop, walked right in the front door, and asked the butcher to please slaughter and quarter the bird for his mother. The butcher, not recognizing it as his own chicken, did as Abraham asked. Abraham paid the man with money he had earned earlier in the week doing odd jobs, went home, and presented his smiling mother with a freshly butchered chicken.

"A year later, while studying Torah, Abraham came to regret his deception and felt the need to set things right with God. He purchased a chicken from a local farm and brought it to the butcher's shop where, a year earlier, he had stolen the chicken, which had been about the same size. He confessed his crime to the butcher, who said, 'It takes a mensch to admit his wrongdoing and even better to make restitution for it.'

"The butcher smiled, took the chicken from Abraham, and patted him on the back. 'You are a good young man,' he said. 'You know, I always wondered what became of that chicken. I thought I was going crazy.' Abraham left the butcher's shop smiling and feeling as if a heavy load had been lifted from his back."

Abraham was the last of my mother's grandparents to die. He passed away in his Brooklyn home in the month of May, 1956. He was eighty-eight years old. Ella and her father, Josef, were at his bedside. She was holding her beloved grandfather's hand.

Several years after Abraham's death, when she was sure I was old enough to understand (I was thirteen), Mom told me another story about her grandfather—this time as an old man in his seventies and living in America. "It seemed he'd had a fall on his front steps; nothing was broken, but he'd sprained his hip, and for the next several weeks, he needed a cane to get around. That didn't stop Grandpa from making his rounds, though. Several of the wives and widows of his friends were excellent bakers, and they loved having Abraham over for lunch or tea—so much so that they'd often bake something especially for him. There was such a gentleness about my grandpa that everyone felt comfortable in his presence; you couldn't help but love him. He certainly loved telling his stories, and he told them well—but more importantly, he knew how to listen, and he always remained discreet with the information they imparted. For that, he was greatly respected by all who knew him.

> "So, on one late April evening, my grandfather was walking home after tea and rugelach at a friend's house when he heard shouts coming from a nearby alleyway. When he got there, he saw three men kicking and punching a fourth man, who was doing all he could to fend off the others' blows. As the assailants pummeled

the unlucky man, they were screaming at him—heaping upon him the very worst of racial epithets.

"Without really thinking, Grandpa Abraham rushed into the alleyway to help the man—*'Stop it, get off him!'* he cried; he gripped his cane like a baseball bat and struck one of the assailants across his back. The man turned, wrested the cane away from Grandpa, broke it in two over his knee, and tossed it aside. Then the bully seized Grandpa by the shoulders and threw him to the alleyway dirt. Abraham was undaunted; he got up, grabbed another of the assailants around the waist, and tried to pull him away from the man he was kicking. Again, Grandpa was thrown to the ground; he landed headfirst and began to bleed from a two-inch cut on his forehead.

"As the beating continued, the defenseless victim managed to roll himself into a ball, desperately trying to protect himself from the onslaught. At that point, my grandfather, Yakov Abraham Freedman, did what he knew best to do—he prayed! Struggling to his knees, he balanced himself and placed his palms together in prayer. He'd completely lost track of his fedora, but his kippah remained in place, clipped to his thick gray hair. He began shuckling energetically, and with all the might he could muster—in a voice so authoritative that it caused the three assailants to pause and turn—he intoned a Jewish prayer of protection:

> My help comes from the Lord, the maker of heaven and earth. Indeed, he who watches over Israel will neither slumber nor sleep. The sun will not harm you by day, nor the moon by night. The Lord will watch over your coming and going both now and forevermore. Amen.

"From the ground behind the bemused brutes, Abraham thought he heard a meek and muted 'Amen.'

"The perpetrators were all facing Grandpa by then; what they'd seen and heard must have touched the little humanity that still resided within their souls. There, kneeling before them, was an old man—more courageous than all of them put together (and that much older too), his face covered with blood, so swollen that he could barely open his eyes; this for helping a man he didn't even know. Without turning back, the three men walked past Abraham and out of the alleyway.

"Then, in an act of love and determination, Grandpa got off his knees and gently helped the man to his feet. Though very badly injured, the man had his pride and was determined to walk out of that alleyway. Arm in arm, each leaning on the other for support, the two wounded men staggered out of the alley into the street.

"They spent that night—and two more days and nights—in Borough Park Hospital. The man told my grandfather that he was from Kentucky, that he was a truck driver. Earlier in the evening, before the assault on him, he had delivered a load of produce to a nearby distribution center. He'd planned to sleep that night in his truck, in the center's parking lot, and head home the next morning. But prior to turning in, he decided to go for a walk—after all, he'd never been in New York City before. While on his walk, he encountered the three thugs, and as they passed him by, he smiled. That was his offense—he'd smiled at them while Black—and for that, they knocked him down, dragged him into the alley, and fell to beating him mercilessly.

"After his release from the hospital, Abraham never saw the man again. Yet he'd seen enough to know that of all the marvelous qualities his new friend may have possessed, the one that eclipsed all the rest was his capacity for forgiveness. Here was a man of faith, who both forgave his assailants and prayed for them. Such a man, Grandpa thought, would make a fine angel."

My grandparents, Josef and Rachel, were a remarkable couple. Josef, Abraham's son, was a quiet, self-assured man who good-naturedly allowed his strong-willed wife, Rachel, to take the reins in most of the family's social and business affairs. She would have it no other way, and that was fine with him. She was an attentive and effective steward, and she rarely steered the family wrong.

Josef and Rachel owned a three-story, six-family apartment building in the Borough Park section of Brooklyn. Theirs was the large first-floor apartment, with tenants occupying the other five units—three on the second floor and two on the third. They had a modest backyard with a small garden that they made available to the tenants for planting vegetables and flowers. One morning, on his day off, a former tenant and good friend of Grandpa's came for a visit. Officer Bill Cunningham and Grandpa Josef were sitting in the backyard having their morning coffee and talking about old times. While Officer Cunningham was telling Josef some of the stories he'd picked up from the precinct, he suddenly stood up and walked over to the garden. He crouched down and broke off a leaf of a plant growing there. He brought the leaf to his nose and thought a moment. Then he came back to where Grandpa was sitting and asked, "Josef, who besides you and Rachel uses this garden?"

Grandpa said, "Why, the Hoffmans and Mr. Rodriguez."

"Who gardens where I just pulled the leaf from that plant?"

"That would be Mr. Rodriguez. Why, is there something wrong?"

"Yes, there is, Josef. It seems your tenant, Mr. Rodriguez, is growing marijuana. Pull it out before he gets you and Rachel into trouble."

As soon as Officer Cunningham left, Josef went into the house to confer with Rachel. After explaining the situation to her, he asked, "How do you think we should handle this, Rachel?"

"How should we handle it?" Rachel steamed. "Let me show you how we should handle it!"

Sternly, Rachel marched out to the garden with a paper bag; she got down on her knees and, one by one, tore out every plant that Mr. Rodriguez had planted. She shoved them into the paper bag, and when she finished, she stood up and looked directly up at Mr. Rodriguez's third-floor kitchen window, from where Mr. Victor Rodriguez was looking back down at her. Grandma pointed at Rodriguez, wagged her finger back and forth, and shouted, "No good, Victor! Never again!"

Rodriguez answered, "Sorry, Rachel, never again."

That's how it went with Rachel and Josef; they had their roles, and they acted them out without stepping on each other's lines. Oh, there might have been an occasional "Shut up, Josef!" from my grandmother's mouth when Grandpa voiced an opinion that failed to meet with her approval, but they were very much in love. Grandpa would just laugh and say, "Fine, Rachel—just fine."

There was no malice from him, only acceptance for Grandma's idiosyncrasies. I just loved him; he was the sweetest man I ever knew. Grandma, on the other hand, scared the shit out of me. One day, when we were visiting them at their Borough Park home, Grandma called me aside. I approached her nervously and soon found out I had good reason to be nervous. Grandma squatted down to my level, looked me in the eye, seized me by the collar with both hands, and said, "You're going to start behaving and be a good boy for your mother, aren't you?"

I was so scared, I could barely nod my head.

"Because if you're not, it's not going to go smoothly for you and me, August. Understand?" I was barely able to squeak out a "yes."

[**Giagiaphobia: Fear of one's grandmother.**]

My mother was a Depression baby and WWII child. In 1935, at the age of four, she was hospitalized with pneumonia. Her fever spiked to 107 degrees, and her doctors did not think she was going to make it. Rachel and Josef were worried sick about her but never gave up their faith that she would get better. Their faith was soon rewarded—little Ella pulled through.

At the age of thirteen, Ella was an above-average student who aspired to be a teacher. She took an after-school job with the Loft Candy Company, and there she made a new friend, Rose Levine. Several years later, Rose introduced Ella to her cousin, Howard Greenleaf—my father. Mom said he was one of the handsomest men she had ever met. Mom was seventeen, and Howard was twenty-two. He was a veteran who had seen action in the European Theater during WWII. They fell in love, much to the dismay of Josef and Rachel, both of whom felt that Howard was too subdued, even morose, and that their daughter deserved better.

Ella would have none of it—she believed Howard was a hurting man, damaged from the war, and in need of her love and affection. She thought she could fix him, but as it turned out, he was beyond repair, and it wasn't the war that had broken him. In retrospect, I believe that—war or no war—he was basically an angry, paranoid person, and that Mom, in love as she was, just refused to recognize that simple fact.

I wish I'd been around before they were married; I would have seized her by the shoulders, shaken her, and said, "You could have any number of men, good men; please, Momma, just not this one. Momma, you're making a huge mistake!" But then, I'd have been advocating against my own existence—and Michael's.

Seventeen-year-old Ella Freedman graduated from Erasmus Hall High School in June of 1949, and early in September, she eagerly began her first semester at Brooklyn College. Meanwhile, Howard was working for the US Postal Service in Manhattan. On a rainy September morning—her fourth day at Brooklyn College—an event occurred that would forever change young Ella's life. She woke up with extreme nausea; she ran to the bathroom and was sick. It was the same for the next several mornings. Actually, I suppose, the event that changed Ella's life had occurred on the evening of August 20, in the back seat of Howard's 1941 Ford Deluxe Coupe. The car was black with a cherry-red interior—as black as Josef's mood and as red as Rachel's face when Ella finally told them of her condition. Of that, reader, you will learn more later.

My mother's first week of college went smoothly; she couldn't have been happier. Her classmates were friendly and inquisitive, and her professors, with one exception, were enthusiastic, informed, and helpful. The exception was Dr. Joseph Confrey, her English literature professor. Dr. Confrey, it seemed, had a habit of repeating every word that came out of his mouth—sometimes twice, which drove Ella completely nuts. She might have been able to overlook it if it hadn't been for his other habit. Whenever Confrey came out with something that he deemed especially brilliant, he'd not only repeat it twice, he'd also stop and pose. Each time Confrey went into statue mode, Ella timed his poses. His record for that first week was a full seven seconds. *Absurd,* she thought, *this guy is absolutely absurd.*

Otherwise, everything would have been perfect for Ella if it hadn't been for the nausea. On Sunday, after three consecutive mornings of feeling lousy, Ella was becoming concerned, so she called a friend—whose sister had recently given birth to her third child—hoping to learn more about her own condition. She'd had sex with Howard two weeks before, but Howard had used a condom. Besides, what she knew about morning sickness during the pregnancy cycle was that it normally doesn't begin until about the sixth week. So, that Sunday afternoon, she and her trusted girlfriend, Suzanne Petrocelli, walked fourteen blocks to the home of Suzanne's older sister and mother of three boys, Gail Lastra.

When they arrived at Gail's Fifty-Ninth Street apartment, Mom felt completely welcome. Gail knew the girls were coming over, and like a good Italian hostess, she had laid out a spread of cold cuts, cheeses, and fresh rolls. Gail's husband, Donatello, was out with his brother, so the girls had plenty of privacy. Gail's three boys—Giovanni, seven; Vincenzo, five; and little Giorgio, two—were adorable and could not have been better behaved, and my mother took notice. *How nice to be a mother,* she thought. *Just not now, please. My mother is going to kill me, and my father will be so disappointed. And what about school—if I'm pregnant, I might never get to be a teacher!*

Her mind was racing when Gail said, "How was your first week of college, honey?"

Distracted by her own thoughts, she hadn't heard Gail's question and said, "I'm sorry?"

"College, Ella, how was your first week, dear?"

"I love it, it's even better than I could have imagined, it's just . . . " She paused; tears filled her eyes. Gail handed her a tissue, then reached over and took her hand.

"You're safe here, honey. Whatever we talk about stays here, okay?"

"Okay, thank you," Mom said.

My mother told her story to Gail while Suzanne sat quietly across from her and listened. She told Gail that she had been a virgin until three months before, when she and Howard went to a party at a friend's house. They had sex upstairs in her friend's bedroom while everyone else was downstairs. She said that she had had no intention of ever "doing it" with any boy until she got married, but it just happened. Then she explained that, a few weeks earlier, Howard had taken her out in his new car. They crossed over the Marine Parkway Bridge and stopped at a quiet spot along Rockaway Beach. They started necking, and "Howard coaxed me into the back seat—I really didn't want to do it . . . oh, I'm so ashamed."

Suzanne came around the table and hugged her. Ella told Gail about the morning sickness after her first missed period. "When are you due for your period, honey?" Gail asked.

"In a couple of days."

"Gail," Suzanne said, "about when did your morning sickness start with the babies?"

"Well, with Giovanni and Vincenzo, it was about six weeks after I got pregnant, but you know, I never had it with little Giorgio. Ella, did Howard use, you know—a condom?"

"Yes, both times."

"Ella, listen to me," Gail said, still holding her hand. "This could very well be just a stomach virus, and I want you to know this: The first time Don and I 'did it,' I was only sixteen."

Suzanne's eyes opened wide.

"I know, I never told you that, Suzie—but you were just a little kid. Listen, Ella, it's fine, we are human; in some cultures, girls start as young as twelve or thirteen. Ella, do you love Howard?"

"Yes, I do."

When it was time to leave the Lastra house, Gail gave each girl a big hug. She gave my mother her phone number and told her to call anytime, day or night.

By Friday morning of the same week, Mom was still having morning sickness, which made it difficult for her to get to her morning classes on time. Fortunately, most of her classes were later in the day. But by then, she was three days late for her period, and genuine panic was setting in. Also, by this point, her mother, Rachel, who had held her tongue for over a week, couldn't hold back any longer.

"Ella, what's wrong?"

"Nothing, Ma."

"Don't 'nothing, Ma' me, Ella Freedman. You have been running to the bathroom every morning for two weeks, and I know you are trying to be quiet, but I hear you."

"Really, Ma, I'm fine, I just have a queasy stomach is all. I think it's just nerves from school."

"Why are you nervous about school? You told me that you loved it and that you were doing well. Now come on—cut it out, Ella, I know you like a book. What's wrong, honey?"

"Mother, nothing is wrong. Leave me alone—I have to get ready for school!"

Rachel whispered, "Ella, have you been having sex with Howard?"

"For Christ's sake, Mother—no! Now please, leave me alone!"

My mother's bus ride to school that morning was tear filled. The summer had held so much promise, and now she felt as if her world were crumbling around her. I can only imagine the torment she felt over the consequences of a few unguarded moments.

By late November, after telling my dad, who seemed receptive to the idea of becoming a father, it was time for them to tell Josef and Rachel. Initially, Mom told Dad that she'd do this on her own, but surprisingly, he said, "No, we're in this together, Ella, and together we'll meet with your parents." And so they did.

Years later, Mom told me how Grandma Rachel mortified my father. No sooner had they sat down when she said, "Why buy the cow when the milk's for free, huh, Howard?" But after they'd talked for forty-five minutes, Grandma looked over at Grandpa and said, "It looks like we're going to be grandparents, Josef." Looking back at Ella—but now with a smile—she said, "I guess it's time to plan a wedding, and quickly!"

With that, Ella and Rachel hugged and cried, and Ella felt as if a colossal weight had been lifted from her shoulders. But deep in their hearts, Rachel and Josef feared this union. They had expected that Ella's infatuation with Howard would run its course and eventually come to an end. But now, there was no turning back, and all that was left for them to do was to pray for this young family and to love and support their daughter, come what may.

On February 26, 1950—a mild but gray Sunday afternoon—six-months-pregnant Ella Freedman was married to Howard Greenleaf, postponing her plans for college and placing her childhood ambition of being a grade-school teacher all but out of reach. People would talk, of course, as they always do, but if ever my Grandma Rachel heard of it, she'd tell them, "Shut up and mind your own business!"

Chapter 6

Howard Allen Greenleaf

I regret to say my dad and I never had much of a relationship; he was just not the kind of man who allowed many people to get close to him. I believe he might have, for a time, allowed my mother into his very private, guarded space, but that time was short-lived. Howard was a quiet man, prone to mood swings and extended periods of depression. You never knew when he might suddenly erupt. My mother usually bore the brunt of his anger, and less often, I did—but rarely were his tirades directed at Michael.

Mom avoided adding fuel to his outbursts, opting instead to use one of a variety of strategies, depending on the situation, to defuse his rage. She'd agree with him, or comfort him, or remain silent; on rare occasions she might leave the room—a tactic that required impeccable judgment on her part, since it might just as easily exacerbate his foul mood—but she'd never confront him directly. After each episode, she'd tell us that Dad's behavior was due mostly to the war, that he'd fought bravely for our freedom, and that we were always to respect him. Despite his temper, and however intensely I disliked him at times, I still loved my father and—God forgive my condescension—felt sorry for him.

Dad's grandfather, my great-grandfather, Ephraim Grünblatt, was one of 505,152 German nationals who immigrated to the United States during the period from 1891 to 1900. Ephraim arrived at Ellis Island in the month of July,

1900. He was twenty-three years of age. He had embarked in Hamburg, brokenhearted, aboard the SS *Deutschland*. Just three months earlier, he had lost his wife, Louise, in childbirth; their child, a boy, was stillborn. The Atlantic crossing took the *Deutschland* almost six weeks, which gave young Ephraim time to grieve and to regain his equilibrium.

Upon his arrival in New York, Ephraim needed no passport or visa; in fact, no paperwork of any kind was required. The arriving passengers formed two lines, one for women and children, the other for men. First, a medical examination was performed by a military doctor. Next came a brief interview with a customs inspector, who checked passengers' names against the ship's manifest and asked some routine questions. When Ephraim's turn came, the inspector asked, "'Blatt,' is that a leaf?"

Ephraim replied, "*Ja*, Grünblatt—it means Greenleaf, yes."

"Do you like that, Ephraim? It's easier, isn't it?"

"Yes, Greenleaf," Ephraim answered, not fully understanding the question.

Thus, after twenty-three years, two months, and nine days of being Ephraim Grünblatt, and with several strokes of a pen, Ephraim officially became Ephraim Greenleaf—new country, new life, new name.

While establishing himself in his new country, my great-grandfather met and married one Rose Fliegelman. Ephraim and Rose had five children: Simon, Elie, Andrea, Minna, and Saul, my grandfather. Saul went on to marry my grandmother Anna Moskowitz. They had four children: premature twin boys, who died shortly after birth, followed by Howard and then Robert. Try as you might, you'd not find two men more different than my father and his brother. Uncle Robbie (as we called him) was in every way his mother's son—kind, caring, and compassionate. As kids, Michael and I looked forward to his visiting us with Grandma Ruth and Grandpa Saul.

On the other hand, as we've seen, my father was aloof and moody—even sullen. But Dad was a hard worker, made a decent living, and supported his family. He put in his hours and never turned down an overtime assignment when it was offered. As a result, we never wanted for anything—except his love.

In September of 1944, at the age of eighteen, my father was drafted into the US Army. He was sent to Fort Benning, Georgia, for his fourteen-week basic training, after which, in December of that year, he was assigned to the Second Armored Division, "Hell on Wheels," in Europe. The Second, which was organized as a heavy armored division, was among the first to see ground combat in the European and Mediterranean theaters. They landed at Omaha Beach on the ninth of June, 1944—three days after the initial landing on D-Day. My father's first action was in mid-December of that year, at the Ardennes Forest. There, for six weeks in deep snow, his unit fought in the famous Battle of the Bulge to prevent the Wehrmacht from breaking through the American defensive lines as they moved eastward.

My father's division crossed the Rhine in March of 1945, and in July of that year, it was the first American unit to enter Berlin.

I've had to piece together this history of the Second Armored Division from independent sources, since (to the best of my knowledge) my father never spoke to any of us about the war or his wartime experiences. ANG

Chapter 7

Breaks, Bruises, Cuts, and a Dead Man

"So, August, tell me, do you like it here at PS 105?" Mr. Phelps asked.

"Not really," I said.

"Why is that?"

I glanced at my mother. "Because I like being home with my mom better."

"I see, August, and I understand that, because I like being home also."

"Home with your mom?"

"No, August," Mr. Phelps said, "I'm an adult; I don't live with my mother anymore. But I love being at home with my family. You know, August, you are a big boy now, and big boys go to school. A smart boy like you should have no problem doing well here."

Mr. Phelps was pitching the positive psychology crap, but I wasn't buying it. It was Friday, and I had completed my first week of kindergarten; Mom met me in Mr. Phelps's office to discuss my objection to sitting in class every day with twenty-three other brats and a flaky lady teacher who resembled an unshaven Humphrey Bogart.

"August," Mom said, "I've promised you that I will walk you to school every morning, and I'll be right outside the front door of the school waiting for you when you get out in the afternoon."

"You've told us, August, that there are things you don't like about school," Mr. Phelps said, "but besides not being home, is there anything in particular that's bothering you here?"

"No."

"Good then," Mr. Phelps said. "Monday starts a new week, and I expect you're going to do just fine! August, I would like to speak with you about one more thing. Mrs. Fields showed me this beautiful picture that you drew of a white house by the ocean. She thought it was wonderful and wanted to share it with me."

"It's not the ocean, it's the bay."

"Well, either way, it's very beautiful. Mrs. Fields had a wonderful idea, August. Because you're so good at drawing, she'd like you to help some of the other children with their artwork—if that's all right with you."

"How?"

"Well, you can sit down next to them and maybe help them draw something—like a smiling face, or a boat. I'm sure Mrs. Fields would appreciate that. At the same time, you can make friends with some of your classmates. So, what do you think?"

I nodded. "Okay." Mr. Phelps nodded at my mother, and together, she and I left the school for home.

As Mom and I left Mr. Phelps's office, I wasn't aware that the two of them had already had their own meeting. Mr. Phelps had confirmed that I was a very bright boy; they talked about my many fears and discussed strategies for motivating me to come to school more willingly. Then he asked her, "Is there anything else you'd like to discuss, Mrs. Greenleaf?"

"Well, yes, there is."

"What's that?"

"Augie thinks he sees a house in front of the bay, beyond the baseball field, across from our apartment building."

The guidance counselor tilted his head to one side.

"Mr. Phelps, there is no house there."

"When did he tell you this?"

"He told me on Monday afternoon and later that evening, when I asked him about it again. I didn't make a big deal over it, although he described the house to me in detail. It seems it's a large white house with a wide front porch and many windows—it's the same house August drew in the picture Mrs. Fields gave you."

"A child's imagination can conjure up many things," Mr. Phelps said. "Imaginary friends, animals, even large white houses with wide front porches. I wouldn't be too concerned, Mrs. Greenleaf. It's best just to nod your head if he mentions it again, and before long it'll be a thing of the past. The school bell's going to ring in a minute or two; I'll fetch August at his classroom and bring him in here."

Mr. Phelps and my mother certainly knew what they were doing. The rest of that school year went just fine, and I eventually became an "all-star" in Mrs. Fields's 1962–63 K2 class—with one exception: I was not at all confident in the schoolyard when it came to playing outdoor games with my classmates.

This problem continued to plague me throughout my childhood. My fear of participating in outdoor games and sports became so great that I'd actually hide during recess, and my attendance record suffered as a result.

[**Ludophobia: Fear of participating in sports or games.**]

My first grade year started on the Tuesday after Labor Day, in September of 1963, and it started with a bang—literally! Soon after Michael arrived home from his first day in the eighth grade, Dad came home from work. We all got into the family's 1959 Chevrolet Impala and went out to pick up a few things that Michael needed for class. After shopping, we went to Wetson's for burgers and fries and then headed back home.

My readers should be aware that these were the days before seat belts came into general use. I was in the back seat of the Impala, directly behind Mom; Mike was sitting on my left, behind Dad. We were coming down Beach Channel Drive, not far from the elevated tracks, heading south. I was still working on my Wetson's chocolate shake when the bang occurred. I never saw it coming—it was a complete surprise. A westbound '63 Chevrolet Corvair convertible, driven by one Gerard M. Charpentier, had run a red light at the intersection of Mott Avenue and Beach Channel Drive. The Corvair T-boned our car on the driver's side and spun us around. The impact broke Michael's left wrist and cracked one of Dad's ribs. Mom suffered two severely bruised knees; I was thrown into the back of Mom's seat, resulting in a spilt milkshake and a split lower lip, which would require eight stitches to close. Mr. Charpentier got the worst of it, though—he was ejected from the Corvair on impact and sent airborne over the hood of our Impala, landing fifteen feet further up Mott Avenue. He was later pronounced dead on arrival at Peninsula General Hospital.

With my lip bleeding profusely, and each of the others injured in some way, we all got out of the car on the passenger's side and moved to a safe place, just as my dad had instructed us. I made it to the corner of Mott and Beach Channel, near where Mr. Charpentier was lying in the street, face up, his eyes still open. I just stared at him, waiting for him to get up, but he never did. One of his feet looked like it was on backward, and his head was resting in a puddle of blood the size of a trash can lid. I realized then that he was dead—and I freaked out.

Seeing my distress, Dad immediately came over and directed me away from the gore. He took out his handkerchief and held it to my bleeding lip. Then he noticed that Mom was having trouble walking. He put my right hand up to my lip and said, "Hold the hanky tight against your lip, August. Put pressure on it, son."

He hurried over to Mom, picked her up, and carried her to a patch of grass on the side of the road. He gently put her down before going over to Michael, who was in obvious pain. Dad put his arm around Michael's shoulder and walked him over to the grass where Mom was sitting, got him settled, and then came back to me. It was my father, then, who rose to the occasion. Even with what later turned out to be a broken rib, he gave no indication of being in pain. I had never witnessed this side of him before, and I am touched whenever I think about his kind and tender actions on that Tuesday evening in September.

That eventful evening turned into a long night. Police cars, ambulances, and fire trucks soon arrived at the scene; I ended up riding to the hospital in an ambulance with my mom, while Michael went with Dad in a police car. We left the hospital around ten o'clock that evening—Mom in a wheelchair, Michael with his left hand and lower arm in a cast, Dad with a taped-up torso, and me with a very sore, stitched-up, fat lip. A taxi brought us home, and Grandma Rachel spent the next ten days with us—nursing, feeding, and loving all four of the Greenleaf wounded. As I had with Dad, I observed a tenderness in my grandmother that surprised me. These experiences—first with Dad and then with Grandma—made a strong impression on me. For the first time in my young life, I learned that there are hidden qualities in people, which need only the right opportunity to make themselves known. As a result of the accident, however, the lengthy list of my phobias increased by three, to wit:

[**Xafniasmaphobia: Fear of surprises.**]

[**Amaxophobia: Fear of driving or riding in a motorized vehicle.**]

[**Abiphobia: Fear of one's father.**]

The Impala was a total loss, and it took Dad three weeks to find a suitable replacement—a 1962 Chevy Bel Air four-door sedan. When he brought it home to take us for a spin, I refused to get in, and over the next several months, I'd do almost anything to avoid riding in that car. My poor mother—to what lengths hadn't she already gone to accommodate my many childhood fears? Yet, to her chagrin, they only seemed to accumulate. My father, on the other hand, had no patience for my erratic behavior and made his feelings known so forcefully that he'd literally frighten the fear out of me.

For the first few days after Dad got the Bel Air, each time I was expected to get into the car, I'd stand frozen at the rear passenger-side door—terrified. Mom would get into the back seat, and with the door open, she'd patiently coax me into the car. But this was a slow process, which had only occasional success.

My father used a different approach. He'd say gruffly, "August, get into the goddamn car!" If that didn't work, he'd growl, "August, if you don't get into the fucking car right now, I'm going to throw you in!" This threat was carried out only once, but once was enough. He snatched me up and roughly set me down on the rear seat; with the tip of his index finger wagging within an inch of my nose, he scolded me loudly for acting like a baby and slammed the door after me. I much preferred my mother's technique, but there was no denying that my father's method was more effective. By causing me to fear him more than I feared riding in his car, my dad got the results he wanted. But they came at a hefty price—and I was making the payments well into my adult life.

In any case, sooner or later I'd get into the car—I didn't have much choice. As my father drove our new "death trap on wheels" through the streets of Brooklyn or Queens, I'd close my eyes tightly and imitate a prayer I'd learned on the first Sunday after our accident. That morning, I was watching television—channel surfing, actually—and I came across a Catholic Mass. I had never seen anything like it before, and I was fascinated. What impressed me most was the priest's repetition of the words "in the name of the Father, the Son, and the Holy Spirit" while making the sign of the cross. So, from the start of any drive until we got to where we were going, that's what I'd do—over and over again! My brother would say something like "Augie, what are you doing? We're not Catholic, we're Jewish," or "Augie, that's enough—Mom, I can't take it anymore, he's driving me crazy! Please make him stop."

My exasperated mother, though—again, sensitive to my fears and anxieties—would simply say, "Michael, if it calms him down, let him do it—believe me, the alternative is even worse."

My father couldn't care less, just so long as I'd gotten into the car. One afternoon, Grandma Rachel was with us, sitting in the passenger's seat next to Dad. I was in the back, sitting between Mom and Michael. As soon as we pulled out of the parking lot, I began to pray—intoning my version of a Christian prayer and awkwardly crossing myself with each iteration:

In the name of the Father, the Son, and the Holy Spirit.

In the name of the Father, the Son, and the Holy Spirit.

In the name of the Father, the Son, and the Holy Spirit . . . Amen.

Grandma turned toward the back seat to confirm the unimaginable words emanating from my lips and gave me a look that would melt lead. She looked over at my mother and said in a stern voice, "Ella, dammit, what the hell is going on here! Why is your son reciting a Catholic prayer? Will we be seeing a crucifix dangling from his neck anytime soon?" She had an expression on her face that Mom later described as abject horror. If she were ever going to have a heart attack, Mom said, that would have been the time.

As was true of so many of my childhood hobgoblins, I eventually overcame my fear of riding on the open road in a motorized vehicle—a prerequisite for my thirty-five-year career as a UPS package car driver. Looking back on my amaxophobic years (as I've just done here), it occurs to me that I may owe that success—which has given my roller-coaster life much of its structure and purpose—to my late father, Howard Allen Greenleaf. But I never outgrew my deep loathing for surprises. ANG

Michael, though, was despondent. After an excellent season of PAL baseball, in which he led his team to a championship, he'd been looking forward to the football season. He had already tried out, and he was going to be the starting halfback and backup quarterback for the Arverne Knights. But after the car accident, the hospital physician, Dr. Klein, told my mom he'd require six weeks in a cast. Michael knew then that he'd miss most (if not all) of the season.

Dad moved very slowly through the house during his convalescence and returned to work a week later. I don't know how he did it.

Mom was in the wheelchair for about ten days when she decided to go back to the doctor. Her left knee was fine, but the pain and swelling in her right knee were not subsiding. A second X-ray of that knee revealed that she had a cracked patella, which would require her to be in a cast also. We Greenleafs were quite a sight whenever we went out—Mom in her wheelchair, Michael with his cast, et cetera—all of us limping, groaning, or grimacing in some way.

The second Monday after the accident was a day I was absolutely dreading. That was the day I was scheduled to have my stitches removed. I had a two o'clock appointment with our family doctor, and Grandma Rachel was to pick me up early from school and walk me the four interminable blocks to the doctor's office. I so did not want Grandma to take me that I begged my mother to do it—wheelchair, cast, and all. I told her I'd push her all the way to the doctor's office if she needed me to—I'd do anything to keep Grandma Rachel out of it. I needed TLC, not a lecture on being brave in the face of adversity. Although I'd recently seen the tender side of Grandma, I didn't want to push my luck. Now, as we marched those dreaded steps to Dr. Ryan's office, Grandma said, "August, you look like you're on your way to your own funeral!" I couldn't utter a peep.

"Listen to me, August," she said as she lowered herself to my level, which scared me even more, since I remembered very well the last time she'd done that. "You're going to be just fine, really, you'll see. It's one, two, three and over with—it'll hardly hurt at all. Time to grow up, young man." Grandma was right about the stitches (except there were eight of them, not three)—it didn't hurt a bit, but I cried just the same. That's what fear does; it creates an expectation of a negative outcome—it alters our perception of reality. It certainly plagued me for the first fifty-seven years of my life (fifty-six years, ten months, three weeks, and one day, to be exact—20,780 days) until that distant day came that would change everything.

Chapter 8

November 22, 1963

"God dammit, Ella, if I see you flirting with that guy one more time, I'll kill you both!"

"Howard, please—Augie."

"I don't give a shit about Augie; I don't give a shit about anyone, you fucking whore, you!"

"Howard!" my mother pleaded. "Please, I'm begging you—stop!"

The apartment door opened and then slammed shut. I was on my bed, lying face down, with a pillow pressed tightly over my head, trying to drown out my father's shouts; I just lay there whimpering. Mom immediately came to my room and sat down beside me. She gently removed the pillow, placing one hand on my back and stroking my head with the other.

"It's all right, Augie, your father's had a very hard week. Don't worry, I'm here."

And it was all right as long as *she* was there. Even though I was only six years old, I felt great empathy for her. We were both victims of my father's tirades—they frightened me, but she put up with them. I rarely heard her get caught up in the heat of his most hateful moments; she did everything she could to defuse each situation. She took all of his shit and gave none of it back. At least, that was the way she handled it when Michael and I were around. I don't know to this day if that was a good thing or a bad thing. That's just the way she was: she felt sorry for him—extremely sorry for him—so she took it all. Some might have said my mother was just a punching bag. I'd say she was a saint.

The absolute craziness of that morning was not really about Donald, our neighbor down the hall—the purported paramour. Mom was just being herself, friendly and courteous, but where other men were concerned, jealousy was my father's default setting. Men looked at my mother all the time—she was beautiful. I remember one time she was walking me to school, and as we walked past a group of construction workers, some of the men began whistling at her. She simply smiled and walked on. But being a kid, I had no idea what was going on, so I asked, "Why were those men whistling, Mom?"

"That's a birdcall, Augie," she said. "They're calling out the birdies to sing for them while they work."

"Will they sing, Momma?" I asked.

Mom stopped. "Quiet, let's listen." And sure enough, we heard birds singing.

"See, Augie," she said, "it worked." Then she gave me a smile so big it bordered on a laugh.

After lunch in the school cafeteria, I knew something terrible had happened. As we walked, single file, back to our classroom, we heard the sobbing; our first-grade teacher, Miss Rubins, looked distraught and was dabbing tears from her eyes with a Kleenex. She handed out art supplies and told us that we would not be doing our reading assignment for that day.

"Please draw and color whatever you wish, children. I just have to check on something very important. Please behave, and I will be back shortly." When she returned to the classroom, she brought Mr. Phelps.

"Class, I have some very sad news to share with you today," Mr. Phelps said. "Our president, President Kennedy, has died today. We are all very saddened by this news, and for the remainder of school today, we will not be doing our normal studies. Does anyone have any questions?"

I raised my hand, and Mr. Phelps called on me. "Yes, August."

"I saw a dead man in the street, at our car accident. Mom told me he was just hurt, but Dad said he was dead. Is the president dead like the man in the street was?"

"Well, August, that's a good question. I suppose dead is dead, so yes—the answer is yes."

"Is the president lying in the street like that man?" I asked.

"No, he is not. Does anyone else have any questions?"

Karen Plotnick raised her hand. "Will my mommy still be here to pick me up today?"

"Yes, she will, Karen. After school, today will not be different from any other day."

Nicholas Savastano raised his hand and said, "My father thinks that Nixon would have been a much better president. Will he be president now?"

"No, he will not."

"Why not?" Nicholas asked. "My dad says he would be a much better president."

"I see, Nicholas. Well, everyone is entitled to his or her own opinion, son, but our next president will be Vice President Lyndon Johnson." Mr. Phelps continued, "We might all gather for a special assembly at two o'clock; Principal Ryan will let us know shortly. Thank you, Miss Rubins. Thank you, class."

As the class sat at their desks, drawing, coloring, and processing what they'd just been told, I was suddenly gripped by fear and sadness. Would my father be there when Mom brought Michael and me home? Was there going to be more screaming? And what about President Kennedy—did he die in a car accident also? Was he thrown from his car? I knew my mom would be very sad; she loved President Kennedy and Jackie. I couldn't help myself; I put my head down on my desk and began to cry. It was as if I'd started a chain reaction in the classroom; before I knew it, most of the other kids were crying too—and so was Miss Rubins.

Chapter 9

Michael Adam Greenleaf

Michael was born on May 21, 1950, almost five years after the end of World War II and just three months after the wedding of Howard Greenleaf and Ella Freedman. He was a large baby, weighing in at eight pounds, six ounces. By the time of his high school graduation, he stood six feet, two inches tall and weighed 175 pounds. A star athlete, he was the starting quarterback on the high school football team, a starting forward in basketball, and in baseball—his best and favorite sport—he pitched and played center field. College and professional scouts often came to watch him, and my father made a point of attending every game he could, as did my mother, who, naturally, brought me along.

Michael was no slouch with the books either, posting a 3.7 grade point average over his four years at Far Rockaway High. But more important than all of his athletic and scholarly achievements was that Michael was growing up to be an outstanding person.

The favoritism my father showed toward Michael over me was very obvious, and it truly troubled Mike. Over the years, there were several occasions when I overheard Michael calling him out on it. Other times, I'd glimpse Mike nodding at Dad, prodding him just to look in my direction.

One day we were out on the field having a three-way catch—Dad throwing a baseball to Michael, Mike tossing it over to me, and me throwing it back to my father. We were at it for about ten minutes when Dad said, "Let's reverse it." On his first toss to me, he threw the ball much too hard; it was coming right at my face, and as I reached to catch it, the ball deflected off the heel of my glove and into my Adam's apple. I hit the ground in tears, but it was Michael, not Dad, who came running over to check on me. Dad just stood where he was and said, "Leave him alone, Michael, he needs to toughen up, he's fine. Come on, August, get up!"

Michael was enraged; he helped me to my feet, looked at Dad, and screamed, "Augie is eight years old—you had no business throwing the ball to him that hard!"

My father cut him off. "If I knew that he couldn't handle a ball thrown that hard, I would never have asked him to play catch with us."

"You didn't ask him," shouted Michael, "I did! You never ask Augie to play!"

Dad didn't have an answer. Michael put his arm around my shoulder and said, "Come on, Augie, let's go up and get a cold drink. Mom made lemonade, there's some in the fridge."

Later that night, both of us were lying quietly in bed, unable to sleep. I broke the silence: "Michael, do you think Dad hates me?"

"Of course not, Augie, he loves you. Mom says the war was very difficult for Dad, and he still hasn't gotten over it."

"I know he loves you, but I really don't believe he loves me, and that's okay. I'm happy—at least he has someone to love."

"Well, he loves us both, and that's the truth. Augie . . . "

"Yes, Michael."

"Do you still see a white house across the street, by the bay?"

"I see it every day. I know that no one believes me, Michael, but it's there."

"Do you see people, Augie?"

"No, I don't think anybody lives there. One day, after school, I watched that house all afternoon to see if I could see someone coming out or going in. I didn't see anyone. Michael . . . "

"Yes, Augie."

"Do you believe me?"

Michael paused for a few seconds. "If you believe it's really there, then yes, I believe you."

"But it is there. I see it just like I see you, like I see Mom and Dad—and my school. I don't know why no one else can see it, but I sure do."

"Well, I guess that makes you special—I mean, being able to see the house and all."

"Special? How, Michael?"

"Like, maybe you have a power that nobody else has. Sort of like Superman or someone like that."

"You think so, Michael?"

"Yeah, I do."

"Thank you."

"You're welcome. Good night."

"Good night, Michael. Michael . . . "

"Yes, "

"I love you."

"I love you, too, Augie."

The year was 1964; Michael was in his freshman year at Far Rockaway High, and I was in second grade at PS 105. Nicholas Savastano's dad had not gotten his way—Richard Nixon did not become president. It was as Mr. Phelps had told us on that terrible day in November: LBJ was our president now. I liked the sound of that—EL BEE JAY—better than his full name, Lyndon Baines Johnson. The Civil Rights Act had been signed into law, and men had gone into space and orbited the earth. The Beatles had come to America—we watched them on *The Ed Sullivan Show*, and Mike took me to the Far Rockaway movie theater to see *A Hard Day's Night*. In April, the New York Mets opened their third season at their new home, Shea Stadium, in Flushing Meadows, Queens.

The US had entered into a new war in support of South Vietnam, against the North Vietnamese and the Communist regime of Ho Chi Minh. Before the year ended, there were twenty-three thousand American troops in Vietnam.

Bishops of the Catholic Church were meeting in Rome at the Second Vatican Council (also called Vatican II, or the Ecumenical Council), which had been convened by Pope John XXIII to discuss significant changes in Church liturgy, interfaith cooperation, and general modernization of the Church itself.

Idlewild Airport, across Jamaica Bay from us, was renamed John Fitzgerald Kennedy International Airport (JFK) in honor of our fallen president. And (not least) Michael had a new girlfriend, Cynthia Brophy, whom he'd met in social studies class. Cynthia was a very attractive, red-headed Irish girl who lived on Beach Forty-Third Street.

Even in those ecumenical times, a Jewish boy with an Irish Catholic girlfriend might present a problem for both sides of that ethno-religious divide. But that depended on who you asked: Older people tended to prefer the safety and comfort of their traditional verities, while younger people were more open to testing the limits of the newly liberated mood of the country—making new friends and exposing themselves to new experiences.

Mom, for instance, was fine with it. She said Cynthia was "adorable" and "sweet," and Dad seemed to like her too. But Grandma Rachel? *That* was a different kettle of gefilte fish! When she got wind of the news that Mike was making time with an Irish girl, she had plenty to say. "She is a shiksa, Ella! Do you mean to tell me that you have allowed your son to get this friendly with a gentile? He's a Jewish boy, Ella—he had his bar mitzvah barely a year ago. Do you know what the Catholic Church teaches about Jews?"

"Momma, please."

"They teach that we killed their messiah. What they teach, Ella, is hatred for the Jews!"

"How do you know what they teach, Mother? When was the last time you set foot in a Catholic church, anyway?"

"I don't need to go into a church to know what is taught there. Your grandmother and grandfather fled Poland and came to this country because of persecution of the Jews by the Catholics."

"Momma, they are fourteen! At fourteen, it means nothing. She's a very sweet girl and their friendship is very innocent."

"Ella, this so-called friendship can, and will, only cause problems. Discourage it, and discourage it now, before he gets serious with this girl."

"Are you finished now, Mother?"

"I'm never finished, Ella."

Grandma Rachel was right on that last point. However, she was not the immediate concern for Mike and Cynthia's relationship. A more pressing problem came in the form of a group of pubescent boys from Cynthia's neighborhood who were not too keen that one of their own girls was making nice with a Jewish kid from the projects.

After breakfast, I followed my big brother down the stairs, avoiding the elevators entirely. Unlike Mom, Michael, knowing of my aversion to elevators, made a game of getting to the ground floor. The two of us raced down the stairs to the first floor and out the rear door of the apartment building. Sometimes, Mike would even let me win.

That morning, a Sunday, Michael was meeting the boys for a pickup football game at the field across the street. When we arrived, most of Michael's friends were already there, throwing the football around—Sean Connelly, Mark and Billy Harris, Brian Gold, the Meriano twins (Anthony and Salvatore), Kevin Frieman, Gerald White, and nine or ten other guys. I sat with Brian's brother, Andrew, who was a year younger than me, and we watched the game together. After the boys finished a really spirited game, everyone except Michael and me went home. The two of us stayed at the field and tossed the football while Mike worked on his passing technique.

I saw them first, because they came at Michael from behind. I shouted, "Look out, Mike!" He turned around just in time to see three boys bearing down on him. Until that day, I had never seen my brother fight—we had wrestled some, but that was just for fun—nothing like this. The way Michael moved, the way he ducked their punches and counterpunched, was a surprise to me. He threw one boy to the ground hard, and the kid hit the dirt face first. I thought Michael had killed him because he didn't get up—at least, not right away. One of the boys pulled off his belt and swung it at Michael, using belt and buckle like a mace and chain. Michael caught it in the air and swung it back at his assailant; the buckle caught the kid on the left side of his face, cutting his cheek wide open.

Blood was everywhere, and I could only stand there, frozen in place, shocked by what was happening before my eyes. The third kid, who hadn't been hurt (although I'd seen Mike punch him once in the stomach), started yelling, "Leave Cynthia alone, kike, because we'll be back, and next time we'll really kick your ass!"

Mike laughed and said, "Go back home to your mommies, micks."

Michael and I returned to our apartment; he was fairly composed, but I was in tears. Fortunately, Mom and Dad were not at home; they'd gone grocery shopping. I was really scared by what had just taken place, and even more afraid that those boys would come back again—maybe next time with more and bigger boys. I was confused as to why they wanted Michael to leave Cynthia alone, why they called him a kike, and why he called them micks. I was an emotional mess.

Michael said, "I'm sorry you had to see that, Augie."

"Why did those boys want to hurt you, Michael?"

"Those boys are just jerks."

"Do you know them?"

"Yes, two of them are from my school."

"Why did they tell you to leave Cynthia alone?"

"Because she's Irish and we are Jewish. It's ridiculous, Augie."

"Why did they call you a kike?"

"It's like a curse word for Jewish people."

"And you called them micks."

"That's a curse word for Irish people—I shouldn't have said that, Augie, I'm sorry."

That night, I couldn't sleep. I thought about Michael and about the Irish boys coming back to beat him up—or worse. I thought about the dead man lying in the street, not moving, never again to see his family and friends. I thought about President Kennedy, and how much Jackie and the children must be missing him. I thought about how I would feel if I ever lost Michael or my mother. I thought about some of the kids at school this past week, who made fun of me because I was afraid to play outside with them. I thought about my many fears, and why I was so afraid so much of the time.

I thought about the white house by the bay—why was I the only one who could see it? There had to be a reason, because it was there; it was real, and I knew it. I thought about what Michael had said about me. Maybe I was like Superman; maybe I *did* have special powers. I thought of the times (and there were many) when it had occurred to me that I was indeed different, that there was something in store for me—something very special—someday.

Then I fell asleep, and I dreamed. I was in the schoolyard, playing long jump. When my turn came, I took a long run, and then I jumped—only I did not come down. Instead, I started to fly. At first, I was just a few feet off the ground; all the children in the schoolyard stared in amazement. Then I rose higher and higher. Pretty soon, I was flying above the children's heads, soaring like an eagle. Above the school I flew, and then over and down Beach Channel Drive. I flew high above the projects and over our apartment building. I soared above the fields and the big, beautiful white house by the bay. I could see that there were people in the house, and I heard laughter coming from the open windows. I wanted to land and go into the house, but a quiet voice said, "Not now."

So, I continued my flight across the bay, high above Kennedy Airport and over the arriving and departing aircraft. I was climbing so fast that I was soon at an altitude where I could barely see the ground through the feathery cirrus clouds. Then, no longer an eagle, I was a rocket ship, thrusting deep into space, leaving all my earthly worries and fears behind. I was free.

Chapter 10

Mixed Feelings Concerning Principal Babjack

Early the following morning, Mom called her supervisor, Mr. Swoboda, at the hospital and notified him that she'd be taking a personal day off. After dropping me off at school, she drove the two miles to Far Rockaway High School in our family's Bel Air. She arrived with a purpose.

She went directly to the main office, introduced herself as the mother of Michael Greenleaf, and informed the receptionist, Betty, that she had an urgent matter to discuss with the school's principal, Mr. Babjack. Betty informed her that Principal Babjack was in a meeting but would be free soon, and asked that she take a seat.

In addition to being the school's receptionist, Betty Babjack happened to be the principal's daughter and was very much disliked by most of the school's faculty and staff. Anything Betty heard around school found its way back to her father, earning her the secret nickname "Big Ears Betty."

Twenty minutes later, Betty came for Ella. "Please follow me. Principal Babjack will see you now."

Upon entering the principal's office, Ella was struck by the resemblance between the principal and his receptionist and asked, "Are you two related?"

"Oh yes," said the principal, "Betty is my daughter and one of the school's finest assets; she knows everything about everyone. They all love her here at Far Rockaway High."

"I'm sure they do."

They exchanged pleasantries, and then Principal Babjack commented on her beauty, which caught my mother off guard. Hesitating only a moment to collect herself, she got right down to business. She told the principal about Michael and his girlfriend, Cynthia Brophy, explained that three boys had assaulted Michael, and that two of the boys were from Far Rockaway High. She repeated Michael's assertion that, before leaving the field, the boys had threatened him and warned him to stay away from Cynthia.

"My concern is that this issue is not finished, and that sometime, somewhere, these boys are going to come after my son again. Maybe there'll be more of them, and maybe it will be more than just a belt next time. I'm very much afraid for my son, Mr. Babjack, and I'm hoping you can help us."

While my mom and the principal were speaking privately in his office, Big Ears Betty was on the phone having a conversation of her own. After showing my mother into her father's office, Betty immediately called her friend Katherine Doyle, the mother of young William Doyle, who sported a gash on his cheek, which, the day before, had required four stitches to close. William, it seems, had told his mother that two Jewish boys had jumped him, that one of the boys had taken off his belt and swung it at him, and that the buckle had hit him on the cheek. He said the other kid, a smaller Jew, then called him a "dirty mick."

"Katherine, I think the mother of that Jewish kid who beat up Billy is in the office right now with my father. Her name is Greenleaf. The kid's name is Michael."

Meanwhile, in the principal's office, Mr. Babjack was asking Ella if she knew the names of the boys who got into the altercation with her son, Michael.

"Yes," my mother said, "the boy that Michael hit with the boy's own belt—his name is Billy Doyle. The other boy—Mike only knows his first name; it's Connor. As for the third boy, Michael says he never saw him before."

"Very good," said the principal. "I'm going to call young Mr. Doyle into my office; I'll find out who this Connor boy is, and we'll go from there. Leave your phone number with Betty, and I'll arrange a meeting with all the boys involved and their parents. I agree with you, Mrs. Greenleaf; we certainly do not want this to go any further. Although this incident did not take place on school grounds, I have a feeling this issue might very well wind up here if we don't nip it in the bud."

Later that morning a nervous, stitched-up, fifteen-year-old Billy Doyle found himself in the office of his high school principal, Mr. Ronald Babjack.

"So, William, that's quite a cut you've got there. Did that happen here at school?"

"No, sir, it happened yesterday afternoon," Doyle responded.

"I understand that a boy from this school gave you that gash?"

"No, I don't think so. At least—I don't know, I never saw them before."

"'Them,' William? How many of 'them' were there?"

"Two boys, one big kid and one smaller."

"And how old would you say these boys were?"

"About my age, I guess. The big one took off his belt and swung it at my face, and it hit me—right here."

"Hmm, nasty gash! How about the smaller boy, did he hit you also?"

"He swung at me and missed a couple of times, then he called me a 'dirty mick.' I think these kids are Jews, up from the projects. You know, they got some Jews living there."

"I see, William. Who is Connor?"

"Connor?"

"Yes, William, Connor."

"Well, I have a cousin named Connor."

"And what is his last name?"

An increasingly nervous William Doyle answered, "Doyle, like mine."

"And William, who is Cynthia Brophy?"

"M-my cousin," William stammered.

As William sank deeper into the leather Shaw-Walker office chair, Principal Babjack got on the intercom with his daughter/receptionist, Big Ears Betty.

"Please drop what you're doing now, Betty. Look up which class one of our students, Connor Doyle, is presently in. Go to that classroom, pull him out, and bring him directly to my office."

As soon as Betty delivered the second Doyle to her father's office, she hurriedly got back on the phone.

It didn't take long for Principal Babjack to elicit confessions from the Doyle cousins, or to learn that the third boy was an eighth grader named Sean Lynch. Sean was the boy whom Michael had thrown face down into the dirt. "Listen, you two," Babjack said, "leave Michael Greenleaf alone. If there are any more shenanigans, the both of you will be facing suspension. Have I made myself clear?"

Later in the day, he called the parents of both boys and filled them in on the events as they had actually transpired. Then he called Ella.

After reviewing with my mother what action he'd taken, Mr. Babjack found her exceedingly grateful for his help. He then ventured to say, "You know, Ella—is it all right if I call you Ella? My name is Ronald, but you can call me Ron."

"That's fine," my mother said, a little discomfited.

"I understand that Michael is an exceptional athlete. Sports are very important here at Far Rockaway High, and we are very excited to have your son competing for us in whatever sports he may decide to play. Please feel free at any time to reach out to me in the future. Perhaps we could have coffee together some morning."

"I'll bear that in mind. Thank you very much for going out of your way to help us, Mr. Babjack."

"Please, Ella, call me Ron. I'm just doing what they pay me to do, dear."

"Thanks again, Mr. Babjack, goodbye."

"Goodbye, Ella."

Chapter 11

38–48 Almeda Avenue

Thirty-Eight to Forty-Eight Almeda Avenue was the address we all shared in our seven-story, fifty-six-unit apartment building in Far Rockaway, Queens, New York. The building had eight apartments per floor; each floor was like a residential neighborhood, its hallway akin to a street. We lived on the seventh floor, in apartment 7D.

Apartment 7A was occupied by a widow, Mrs. Rose Eidelman, who represented our floor on the building's tenant committee. In her seventies, Rose was a very spry and energetic woman. The two things I remember most about Rose were her chicken soup—which she made for us almost every week (it was delicious)—and her wandering eye, which, as often as possible, was fixed on my father; she adored him. Whenever she bumped into me in the hallway, the elevator, or outside the building, she'd ask, "How's your father doing? What a lucky boy you are to have a father like Howard—such a handsome man!" Michael used to say that if Mom weren't around, Mrs. Eidelman would be delivering her chicken soup to Dad in a negligee.

Miriam Silverstein and her son, Steven, lived in apartment 7B. Steven was about Mike's age; he was mentally challenged. Kids being kids, some of the local boys called him "Stupid Steven." When Mike and I told Mom about it, she got very upset; she told us that we were never to behave that way ourselves and that we were to discourage that kind of behavior among our friends. Furthermore, we were always to defend Steven whenever anyone was making fun of him. From then on, Michael kept an eye on Steven; he'd often knock on the door and ask Mrs. Silverstein if Steven would like to go out and have a catch or take a walk with him. Mike stood up for Steven a couple of times when the neighborhood kids started to make fun of him. After that, there was no more teasing—at least, not while Mike was around.

One late winter's night in 1964, when I was seven, Mom woke Michael and me from a sound sleep. She put my slippers on and placed my winter coat over my shoulders. She told us that there was a fire in the Silversteins' apartment and that she was going to bring us to the first-floor lobby. When she opened our apartment door, the hallway was filled with smoke; the burning smell was acrid and very strong. My father and a couple of other men who lived on the floor were trying to break the Silversteins' door down, and I could hear the panicked voice of Mrs. Silverstein screaming for help—*"Help us! Oh, please help us! Help, help, help!"*

Mom said we were to take the stairs; we wouldn't want to tie up the elevators, because the fire department was on its way. When we reached the ground-floor lobby, the firemen were rushing into the building. Some of them headed for the elevators; others were moving toward the same stairwell we had just come down. It was two o'clock in the morning, and it looked as if all the residents of the building were in that lobby. Jodie Sunderland's mother, Joyce, came over to us and asked if we'd like to come into their apartment, which was on the first floor.

My mother thanked her and sent me with Mrs. Sunderland. Michael, who was very concerned about Dad, stayed with Mom and waited.

When it was over, Mike told me that the firemen had brought Mrs. Silverstein and Steven down in the elevator. Both of them were coughing, and Mike said they were covered with soot. "They were totally black, Augie—their faces, their hair, their arms, their pajamas—all black. It was really weird, Augie. Mom told me not to say anything to you, so don't tell her you heard it from me."

Evidently, Mrs. Silverstein had been smoking on the couch and had fallen asleep. She got up and went to bed, not noticing that her couch was smoldering. The couch eventually burst into flames, and in their panic, Steven and his mother shut themselves in Steven's bedroom. Fortunately for the two of them, the fire department arrived just in time, saving their lives and preventing further damage. The Silversteins were taken to the hospital, where they spent two days being treated for smoke inhalation. After their release from the hospital, they stayed with a relative for several weeks, until the necessary repairs had been made. Then they returned to their apartment.

It was a very long time before I got over the incident, though. Many years later, my wandering mind was still able to conjure up that terrible, acrid, burning odor; I just couldn't bear to think what it must have been like for Steven and his mother. Add another phobia to my list:

[**Pyrophobia: Fear of fire.**]

The Golds lived in apartment 7C. The kids were Brian and Sharon. Brian was Mike's age, and the two of them became very good friends. They played sports together, walked to and from school together, and shared many other interests. Sharon, three years older than I, was a total flirt. As I grew up, I could not keep my eyes off that girl—she was hot, and she knew it. As I watched, she'd pull back her hair and tie it in a ponytail—all the while sticking her chest out to enhance the tease. The first time I ever masturbated, I had the shining image of Sharon Gold in my mind—in full color and 3-D. Many years later I saw her at a party, and after a couple of drinks, I told her about my pubescent fantasy. With a wink and the hint of a smile, she said, "August, you weren't the only one, sweetie; a lot of boys did." Still a flirt in her adult years, Sharon went through two husbands before settling down with number three—an extremely successful interventional cardiologist—proving that there's more than one way into a woman's heart.

Brian and Sharon's father, Max, was a taxi driver who worked very long hours, so we never saw much of him. Their mother's name was May, and it was easy to see where Sharon got her good looks. My mother and May were to become lifelong friends and—in the end—were inseparable.

Apartment 7E was the home of the Berger family—Marvin and Bernice and their two toddlers, Jeffrey and Eva. Marvin was a printer by trade and did event photography on the side. He had the sensibilities of an artist; he was friendly and kind and got along well with everyone. Bernice, a housewife, was a very sweet lady; in the summer months she'd frequently offer Michael and me fresh lemonade. After high school, Jeffrey went to college and then to Fordham Medical School, eventually becoming a successful orthopedic surgeon. Eva, a flower child, moved to the West Coast, where she married the owner of a bakery. I've been told that they had six children and that the bakery made the best bagels and scones in Northern California.

Donald and Mya Jones lived in apartment 7F. They had no children, so I didn't know them very well. Donald was a postman and Mya a teacher. Over time, Mom and Mya became friends, and it was not unusual to find Mya in our apartment, having coffee with Mom and her anagrammatic friend May.

Apartment 7G was the home of the Brunos—Paul and Rita and their twin boys, Anthony and Salvatore. The boys were a year younger than Michael, and they all became friends. Paul and Rita owned a couple of laundromats in Far Rockaway, and they always had change on them, in case you ever needed to break a dollar. Paul's pockets literally jingled when he walked, and he had developed the habit of thrusting his hands in his pockets to jingle the coins manually whenever he was standing still. Marvin Berger often asked him what he jingled in bed.

Mr. and Mrs. Ramon Gutierrez lived in apartment 7H, at the far end of the hallway, with their large brood. Grandma Rachel used to call Ramon's wife, Mira, "a baby-making machine." She'd given birth nine times, for a total of ten children, all of them within a twelve-year span. The firstborn was Manny, followed by Christina. Then came Alonso, and right after him, Anita. Next was my good friend Federico; number six was Tia, followed by the twins, Raul and Reyna. Rafaela was number nine, and finally the baby, Marivel. Theirs was the largest apartment on the seventh floor; it had four bedrooms and two bathrooms. Mr. Gutierrez was a sergeant in the NYPD, and a nicer family you couldn't find anywhere. Mom called them the "Gutierrez Dozen."

It was Mr. Gutierrez who took me to my first-ever baseball game at Shea Stadium; he was kind enough to invite me along with him and his four boys.

I'd never been in a station wagon before, so that was a second first, so to speak. That day the Mets played the Chicago Cubs and won by a score of 6–2. I had a wonderful time, and not surprisingly, I'll never forget it.

It's interesting, though—in all the years our family lived in Far Rockaway, Queens, just twelve miles or so from Shea Stadium, Dad (a Mets fan himself) never took any of us to the ballpark. As I think about it now, it's more than interesting—it's sad, truly sad.

Chapter 12

The Man in the Window

All too many of my days at PS 105 were difficult for me. My manifold phobias were preventing me from discovering who I was—or could be. I was preoccupied with my fears and underperforming at school. I worried about recess in the schoolyard; I worried about my teacher calling on me; I worried that my homework and test results would be poor (which, increasingly, they were)—I worried so much I was worn out with worrying. In class, I was so distracted that I didn't hear half of what the teacher was saying. Yet even then, I knew all my worrying was useless—crazy; I just couldn't seem to do a darn thing about it. Worse still, I began to hide my fears and the problems they were causing me. I refused to discuss them—even with Michael or my mother.

[**Social anxiety disorder: Fear of humiliation.**]

I was morbidly afraid of one of the boys in my class, George Kendell, the class bully. He'd often shake me down for my lunch money, and I'd give it to him, which, of course, only emboldened George. Consequently, I became even more terrified of George—and ashamed of myself.

Also, ever since the fight between Michael and those three Irish kids, my fear of being beaten up became an obsession. Although not a hair on my head had been touched, and there had been no follow-up altercation, I found myself constantly looking over my shoulder.

[**Traumatophobia: Fear of pain or injury.**]

That particular fear, however, was eventually realized on a warm, late-September day in my fifth grade year.

It was a Friday afternoon, about two o'clock. My friend Jodie Sunderland and I had decided the day before to skip school. It was only a half day, and we thought we'd start our weekend a little early. We were across the street at the park, near the baseball field, playing on the large tire swing. Both Jodie and I looked up at the same time, and we saw half a dozen boys out by the baseball diamond heading our way. They weren't walking casually—they were striding with a purpose. Although at their distance from us I did not recognize any of the boys, both Jodie and I sensed trouble and began walking quickly toward our apartment building. Looking back over our shoulders, we saw the boys were then running straight toward us. I crossed Almeda Avenue in sheer terror, running as fast as my legs would carry me, without even checking for traffic! About halfway up the walkway to the building, I was knocked down from behind. I landed hard on the concrete pavement with a boy on top of me. Seconds later, other boys joined the first, taking turns jumping on me—kicking and punching me. As they proceeded with their assault, one boy growled about my being Michael Greenleaf's brother: "Tell him that we'll be kicking his ass too." Another boy called me a faggot—I didn't even know what that meant.

At that point, the nearby sound of a barking dog interrupted the fracas. A small woman walking a large, shaggy mutt saw what was happening and came to my defense. By then, I had completely lost track of Jodie.

"Leave that boy alone!" she said loudly and with surprising authority. "There are six of you and one of him! And look at you—the bunch of you—you're all older than he is!"

Then her voice became even louder, verging on a shriek. "Shame on you boys! Go on, get out of here—*now*!"

Fortunately for me the boys did as they were told. I was shaking as this kind and brave woman helped me to my feet. I could see that she was about seventy years old—all the more remarkable. She walked me to a nearby bench, and we sat down. She then asked, "Are you hurt, son? You have a cut on your forehead."

Trying to hold myself together and keep from crying, I shook my head and said, "No, ma'am. Do you know what happened to my friend?"

"He made it into the building; he's safe. Do you know those boys?" she asked.

I shook my head again. "Not really. I think they live up Beach Channel Drive."

"Are you sure you're okay? Those boys were stomping on you pretty hard."

I nodded, thanked her, and said, "I'm gonna go home now."

I ran into the building and up the seven flights of stairs, stopping occasionally to listen, in case the boys were there plotting to ambush me. When I reached our apartment, I had the key ready in my hand, but I was shaking so badly that I had trouble unlocking the door. After what seemed to be an eternity of fumbling, the door finally opened. I quickly stepped into the apartment and locked the door behind me, and leaning against it, I took a few minutes to calm down. Then I had to pee.

Michael was at football practice, and Mom was now working until 3:00 p.m., so I had a little time to wash up and think. My first thought was to tell everyone what had just happened. But then I realized if Mike knew, he'd want to go after those boys, and I didn't want him to get hurt. So, when the two of them got home, I lied. I told them that I had fallen off my bike. They believed me; Mike tousled my hair, and Mom cleaned out the cut and bandaged it, suggesting that I "be a little more careful next time."

By then, I was beginning to keep too much inside me, but I was acutely aware that nobody likes a "chickenshit," and I was determined not to let people think that of me. Michael had once told me that there were times when he got scared: "But sometimes you've just got to tough things out and not let them get to you, Augie; after you do that a few times, you kind of naturally get tougher. Like in football," he said, "the first few times you get tackled, it hurts, but if you don't let it bother you, after a while, it's no big deal."

The following Monday at school, we were all outside at recess when George Kendell approached me and said, "I heard that you got your ass kicked really bad on Friday, Greenleaf," and started to laugh.

I snapped; I tore into him like I'd never done to anyone before. I was throwing punches from every angle, and they kept coming until Mrs. Humphrey, the recess monitor, grabbed me from behind. George was so stunned that he wasn't able to return any of my punches. I was amazed at myself; I didn't think I had it in me.

Mrs. Humphrey brought me to the principal's office, where Principal Donavan asked me, "What happened, August?"

I told him exactly what Michael had told me: "Sometimes you just gotta tough things out." The principal frowned his official frown, but it seemed to me that in his eyes was the twinkle of a smile.

Physics is a science involving the study of energy and objects in motion. Baseball is a sport that puts physics on display. So, in the scientific sport of baseball (all other variables being equal), the faster the pitcher throws the ball, and the harder the batter swings the bat, the faster the ball will leave the bat, and the farther it will travel. This principle was in evidence just two weeks after my encounter with George Kendell.

Darren Raab was back in town. Darren was a hard-throwing Far Rockaway High School graduate who was currently pitching for the Syracuse Kings, a Triple-A affiliate of the New York Yankees. On this particular day, Darren was visiting our local field and pitching batting practice for the kids in our neighborhood. Everyone was there, including the local newspaper, *The Wave*, which had sent a reporter and photographer down to the field for a story. I was in the bleachers, sitting with Michael's girlfriend, Cynthia, and Mike brought Darren over to say hello to us. A local guy, Darren knew Michael well; all through Mike's high school sports career, Darren came to games whenever he could. He was very helpful to Michael as a tutor and in calling the attention of the pro scouts to Mike's skills on the ball field. Darren could not have been any nicer, and the four of us even posed for a picture in front of the bleachers. That photo was featured in the weekend edition of *The Wave*. I clipped it out and saved it; I still have it, and I'll hold onto it for the remaining days of my life.

It was a picture-perfect October day—sixty degrees, clear blue sky. Guys were playing in the field and taking turns at bat; Darren was pitching. Stanley Abramowitz had just popped to third when Darren looked over at Michael and said, "Come on, big guy, your turn."

Michael laughed and said, "Sure."

Darren delivered a medium-speed pitch that Michael slashed into left center field. "Not bad," Darren said. "Are you ready for the real heat?" Michael nodded, dug in, and assumed his stance; he waved the tip of his bat as he waited for Darren's next pitch.

With a full windup, Darren's next pitch was faster than I had ever seen a pitch thrown before. Michael's swing, always technically correct, this time was a thing of beauty—level, lightning quick, top hand rolling over his bottom hand at precisely the right moment—squarely meeting the spinning spheroid, and *crack*! Aided by an onshore breeze, the ball traced its majestic arc through the clear October air, landing far into the weeds, just twenty yards in front of the white house by the bay, and coming to rest more than 420 feet from home plate. Spectators' mouths hung open until the ball stopped bouncing in the weeds, and then they broke into broad smiles, accompanied by a chorus of "oohs" and "aahs." Darren, who was smiling from ear to ear, said, "Go on, Mike, take your home-run trot."

Cynthia seized my arm and said, "C'mon, Augie, we've got to get that ball for Michael." So off we went, running toward the weeds beyond left field.

I had not uttered a word about the white house by the bay to anyone—including Mom and Michael—for a very long time. Did I see it almost every day? Yes, I did. Could anyone else see it? Apparently not, so I judged it best not to talk about the big white house or anything else that might cause me to be taken away in a straitjacket. Until that October day, the closest I had ever come to the white house was the edge of the mown grass in deep left field, which was about a hundred and fifty feet from the house. I had been tempted, many times, to trudge through the weeds to the front of the house, climb the wooden steps, cross the wide porch, and knock on the large front door. But I just couldn't do it; fear held me back, although the temptation was certainly strong on that day, when Cynthia took my arm and said, "C'mon, Augie . . . "

As we ran after the ball, I was drawn by the excitement of retrieving the ball that Michael had hit a country mile off the famous Darren Raab, and curious to get closer to the house that had been such an enigma to me for so many years. But as Cynthia and I stepped from the short grass into the weeds, fear took over—fear of what we might see (or of what might see us)—fear of the unknown.

[**Xenophobia: Fear of anything out of one's comfort zone.**]

As hand in hand we picked our way through the sumac and Queen Anne's lace, my heart was thumping wildly; it felt as though it just might jump out of my chest and hop around in the weeds. From where I stood, I could see the big white house as I had never seen it before. It had a wide front porch, terminated at one end by a round tower. The windows were large, and some of them were open to the soft onshore breeze, ruffling the curtains and drapes within. The house was beautiful; just looking at it gave me goose bumps.

"Come on, Augie," Cynthia said. "It went deeper into the weeds than this. I think it's closer to the bay. I'll look here, you look over there."

"Over there" took me even closer to the house—approximately thirty feet from the front steps—and that's when I saw him. He stood, motionless, at a second-story window, staring directly out at me; linen curtains gently billowed around him like a lacy shroud. He wore a gray sport jacket and an open-collared blue shirt. Although he was quite old, he was possessed of a full head of gray hair; his wrinkled face was partially concealed by a well-trimmed gray beard. I was frozen in place; our eyes were locked in a reciprocal gaze, and I slowly became aware that I was shivering.

"Yes! I found it; I've got the ball. C'mon, let's go! Augie? Augie, what's wrong?" Cynthia was right behind me, but I just couldn't respond. She put her arm around me and said, "Augie, what are you looking at? Augie, you're shaking!"

She turned me around, walked me back through the weeds, and had me sit on the grass in left field foul territory. She told me to stay right where I was; then she ran off to find Michael.

Chapter 13

Augie's Secret

"Augie, answer me, Augie—I said answer me! Jesus, Augie, just say something, please!" Michael was worried and a little frustrated—but I couldn't utter a word.

"It's the house, isn't it?"

I nodded and began, finally, to stop shaking and to feel a sense of calm returning to me. Michael sat down on the grass next to me and said softly, "What did you see, Augie?"

"I saw an old man; he was in the house. He was looking at me from a second-floor window. But I don't know if he was real or not."

"So, you're not sure if you saw him?"

"No, I saw him for sure, but he wasn't moving—like he was one of those mannequins we saw at Macy's that time we went with Mom. But he sure looked real to me."

"I think we should go home and talk to Mom about this—okay? Do you mind if Cynthia comes, too, since she was here with you?"

I nodded hesitantly—the straitjacket might not be too far off.

When we got home, Dad was watching TV—a show about the Vietnam War. He felt that it wouldn't be much longer before we won the war and chased the communists out of South Vietnam. Mom was in the kitchen, on the phone with Grandma Rachel, who had taken a liking to Cynthia after all.

I went to the bathroom—I could hear Mom and Michael whispering, and I knew I was the whisperee. When I got back to the kitchen, Mom said, "August, it's been a long time since you've said anything about the big white house—come to think of it, I can't remember when you mentioned it last. But you saw it today?"

"I've never stopped seeing it, Mom; I see it almost every day. I just haven't mentioned it." Then I went on to tell the whole story. Cynthia answered a few questions from my mother, and we were done. Meanwhile, Dad never came out of the living room—he just kept watching TV.

I cannot begin to explain what it's like to see something that no one else is able to see. When you speak about it—even to those who love you, they think there's something wrong with you. Oh, they might not come out and say it, but you know what they're thinking, and it's very upsetting. On the other hand, I felt that I really was different from other people, and maybe that was a good thing. Maybe the old man in the window was not a mannequin—after all, do mannequins have gray hair and wrinkles? Maybe he was real—alive! What was I to make of that? Not surprisingly, Mom had her own thoughts on the subject and acted accordingly.

The plaque on the wall above his head read Barry A. Seltzer, PsyD, and Mom had just blown thirty-five of her hard-earned dollars on this quack. I don't know what the "A" stood for, but based on the hour I'd just spent with him, I'd have said it meant "Asshole."

"Let's play a game, Augie," he'd said. "If you wanted to say something to the old man in the window, what would it be?"

"Hello—I'd say hello."

"And then what? What might you have wished to ask him?"

"I'd have asked, why am I the only one who can see your house? Why won't you let anybody else see what I can see?"

"And what might the old man have said in return?"

"That I'm special—like Superman?"

"Are you Superman, Augie? What would you say to that?"

Seltzer was beginning to annoy me. "Maybe—yes, maybe I am. I see stuff that no one else sees."

"But why can no one else see this 'stuff' but you, Augie? Is it perhaps only make-believe?"

I could see through Seltzer's little game, and it was going nowhere. I hadn't spoken about the white house for over two years, and then came the incident that led to my being there. It seemed to me then that my best way out was to play along with this asshole—to pretend that the house wasn't really there.

"Yes, I suppose so; maybe it is make-believe."

"I see. So why get upset over something that probably isn't real? Is there something else bothering you, Augie? Something at school perhaps, or something at home? You can share it with me. What we say here is just between us."

How could this jerk possibly be of help if he was unable to accept that what I'd seen was real? Had he been able to assume my perspective—that perhaps those who do not see the white house have limitations that prevent them from seeing it—then maybe we might have gotten somewhere. Instead, he wasted our time and Mom's money by beginning with the assumption that I was deluded and then trying to elicit a confession from me—a confession that would make them all comfortable and leave me as fucked up as ever.

But little August was not in need of shock therapy, heavy medication, or even a straitjacket. Seltzer wanted a confession, so August confessed. He was pretending to be helpful, so August pretended to be helped.

Ironically, in one way, the session with Seltzer did help me: I decided that, from that day forward, I'd revert to my original strategy. For the benefit of my family, my friends, and the world at large, I'd affect to ignore the white house, the old man, and everything relating to them. Anything further I might learn about them, I'd learn on my own, and in secret—but learn I would!

Two weeks had passed; it was Saturday, and the Far Rockaway High football team had a big game against Flushing High. Dad wanted to leave home early so we could get good seats in the bleachers. I was up early and told Mom that I was going outside for a bike ride. I rode aimlessly along the path for ten or fifteen minutes, and then I headed straight for the weeds beyond left field. I hid my bike in the weeds and started walking toward the big white house to search for answers to questions I hadn't yet formulated. No longer afraid, I was confident—even emboldened. After all, it was only a few weeks ago that I'd taken on and beaten George Kendell; why should I be afraid of an old man who looked out at me from the second-story window of a house that no one else could even see?

The windows were closed this time, and there was no one staring out at me. I ran up the front steps, crossed the wide porch to the front door, and knocked—no answer. So, I knocked harder—still nothing. Nervous, but in control, I called out: "Hello." Only silence. The porch was welcoming; overhead, a seagull slid past, and I listened to the wind blowing through the reeds between the house and the bay; it was a beautiful sound. Strangely, I felt as though I belonged there. I tried peering through the first-floor windows, but all the shades were drawn. I reached into my pocket for the note that I had written the night before and left it under the doormat by the front door. It read as follows:

> *Hello,*
> *I have many questions. You know*
> *what they are. Can you please answer*
> *them for me? I will be back in one week.*
> *August Nathaniel Greenleaf*

The game did not go well for Far Rockaway. Michael threw two interceptions and fumbled once; we lost 20–7. On the drive home, he was inconsolable, blaming himself for the loss.

"I should just stick to baseball," he said. "After I get out of the Marine

Corps, that's what I'll do."

"Excuse me, Michael?" Mom said. "When did you decide this? There's a war going on, and you're not going to Vietnam to fight in it. It's not our war!"

"That's what I want to do, Mom. And you're wrong; it is our war. It's up to us to stop the communists in Vietnam now."

"Howard, please, tell him how foolish this idea is."

"The boy is going to be eighteen next year. It'll be his decision, Ella—whether or not to serve his country."

"Howard, you fought in a war—you, of all people, know what it's like. Are you encouraging this?"

"I'm not encouraging anything!"

"Michael, at least get your degree; if you still want to join after that, then you can join as an officer," Mom said.

Uncharacteristically, Michael, who rarely raised his voice, shouted, "Please, you two, just shut up! It's my life, and I'll decide what I want to do with it!"

The subject didn't come up again—not for a few months, anyway.

The next week, I went back to the big white house, hoping to make some progress in solving my enigma. Meanwhile, Michael was watching *Wide World of Sports* with Dad. They were in celebration mode; earlier in the day, the football team had beaten Astoria by a score of 44–7. Mike had passed for two touchdowns and rushed for another. He was wearing his bright blue Far Rockaway T-shirt with white lettering.

Mom was visiting with May Gold, and I told Dad and Mike that I was going out to ride my bike with my friends. I raced down the stairs (I was still a little uncomfortable in the elevator) and rode out to left field as fast as my legs could pedal me. I dropped the bike in the weeds and headed straight for the big white house. As I stood in front of those seven wooden steps, my heart was pounding. I was so afraid of what I might find. The house was quiet; the windows were closed, as they had been the week before, and the drapes were drawn. When I reached the top step, I saw a note poking out from under the doormat. I picked it up and saw that it was my own note from the week before.

Disappointed, I turned and slowly walked back down the front steps. When I reached the bottom, I turned to look at the house one more time. Only then did I think to turn my note over and look on the back. Written there, in a beautiful hand, was a date—nothing more:

November 26, 2013

A chill ran through my bones; I hadn't expected any of this (although, in truth, I hadn't known what to expect). The note was real, tangible, and tears filled my eyes. At the time, I couldn't say where these tears came from, but now—looking back—I realize they were tears of joy and relief. I knew then that I was not crazy, that I was truly different—different in a powerful and profound way. I had no idea what the inscribed date signified except that, for me, it was a validation. It was as real as the house was, as the old man in the window was (whoever he might be). I stuck the note in my right front pocket, looked up at the house again, and called out, "Thank you."

I bounded back through the weeds, feeling weightless—I wanted to tell the world about my epiphany, but I knew I couldn't do that. If only I could share my secret with just one person, it would be enough! As I straddled my bike and began to ride off, I glanced up at our building across the field, and there, looking out from our seventh-floor living room window, in his bright blue Far Rockaway T-shirt with the white lettering, was Michael Adam Greenleaf. From that distance, it seemed he was looking straight back at me.

Chapter 14

Gettysburg, Pennsylvania

He didn't say a word over dinner, nor at any other time during the evening. It wasn't until we were both in bed that Michael asked, "Is everything all right, Augie?"

"I know you saw me, Michael. I saw you in the window, looking at me."

"I did—it's the white house again, isn't it?"

I got up and went over to his bed; I turned on his reading light and handed him my note. Then I sat down at the foot of the bed and told him what had happened. Mike sat up and, after reading my note, gave me a look of surprise and compassion.

"Turn it over, Mike."

He looked down at my note and slowly turned it over. "That's not your handwriting, Augie." It was both a statement and a question.

"No, I don't write like that."

"It's old-fashioned penmanship. Did you have someone write this for you?"

I shook my head, and for several seconds, we just stared at one another.

Thanksgiving came and went—then Hanukkah, Christmas, and New Year's Day. Cynthia was spending more time with Michael than I'd have wished, since it cut into my time with him. But Mike was happy, and that's what mattered most. As a boy, I had the best big brother around, and Michael's happiness was mine also. The football season had ended on a sour note for Michael; Far Rockaway High lost the borough championship game to Flushing High. Nevertheless, many colleges sent scouts to watch Mike play, and there'd be many more when baseball season came.

Michael's high school athletic career was winding down, and he had several decisions to make. Two of his friends, Sean Connelly and Gerald White, had told him that they planned to join the military. Mike had always had a fascination for the Marine Corps and was contemplating joining up, but Mom strongly disapproved. If he should decide against the marines, Mike would have several baseball and football scholarship offers to choose from. Almost all of these options involved leaving home, though, and the very thought of his going away made me sad.

At the end of the year, Mom quit her job at the hospital and took a job at a school for special education as a teacher's aide. She loved it and vowed that after I grew up, she would go back to college and get her degree in teaching. Dad was Dad—perhaps even more so. What can I say; my father never changed and never would. He had been especially quiet lately, and that was good news for everybody. I believe the only one of us he truly loved was Michael. He took pride in Mike's athletic achievements and in his fascination with the Marine Corps.

Around this time, I found myself constantly looking over my shoulder. I had never spoken to Michael about my second run-in with the Irish boys, for fear he might go after them—who knows what would have happened then! My many fears still dogged me, but despite that, I was able to develop a modicum of self-confidence. The fifth grade was not so bad. The classwork wasn't too difficult for me, and I had friends and other diversions to keep me busy. Yet there was still plenty of time to think about a certain cryptic note.

November 26, 2013: I would be fifty-six years old on that date. Would I be married—a father, perhaps even a grandfather? And why that date? It was forty-six years away. The more I thought about it, the more my curiosity grew. For the next several months, I was obsessed with it. Was this the date when all my questions would be answered? Did it need to take that long? Who was the old man? Was he the one who wrote the date on the back of my note? How could that be? He would no longer be alive in 2013. It was all so perplexing; my mind was in constant overdrive.

In the spring of 1968, Mike's senior year, Far Rockaway's baseball season began in a big way. They won their first four games by a combined score of forty-six runs to nine. Michael had five home runs during that stretch, with thirteen RBIs and a .440 batting average. Professional and college scouts were in the stands at every game to watch Mike play. Mike's talent was primarily as a hitter—and he was probably the best pitcher on the staff. But his greatest value to the team was as an everyday player, playing center field and hitting cleanup. Although he was flattered by the professional scouts' interest in him, Mike was most impressed by Bennie Squatrito, from Bucknell University. The school offered an excellent civil engineering curriculum, which was Michael's primary academic interest; it also had a very competitive Division 1 baseball program. To Michael, it was a perfect combination.

It appeared the school was poised to offer Michael a full scholarship and was already making plans for Mike to come to central Pennsylvania to visit the campus and its baseball facilities. Since Michael was very interested in the Bucknell program, Mom and Dad decided to help sell it by planning a five-day family trip to the school and its environs. Mom was willing to do anything to dissuade Michael from joining the marines, and if that involved pulling both of us out of school for a few days to take a trip to Lewisburg, Pennsylvania, well, for her it was a small price to pay. Mike would miss one game, but he thought a visit to Bucknell would be worth it. Personally, I was thrilled with the prospect of a family trip that included three days off from school.

Whenever we prepared for a family vacation, my father would be transformed: his mood became lighter, and he appeared to be far less stressed; he actually laughed and even sang a song or two. We all liked this side of my father; we just never saw enough of it. It manifested itself only during vacations, some holidays, and otherwise on extremely rare occasions, none of which I am now able to call to mind. Why couldn't this have been Dad's default setting? He loved the itinerary that Mom had prepared and was ready to roll, as were we all.

Wednesday, 4/17:	9 a.m.	Leave home.
	Wednesday p.m., and	Tour Amish Country,
Thursday:	All day.	Lancaster County, PA.
Friday:	All day.	Tour Gettysburg National
	Military Park, Gettysburg, PA.	
Saturday and Sunday:	All day	Visit Bucknell University,
	Lewisburg, PA.	
Sunday, 4/21:	5 p.m.	Leave for home.

We were charmed by Amish country, with its rolling hills, neatly kept farms, colorful farm stands, horse-and-buggy rigs, craft and quilt shops, smorgasbords, and the quaint old ways of Amish life. Towns with names like Bird-In-Hand, Blue Ball, Ephrata, and Intercourse reflect the earthiness and directness of their plainspoken people and take the visitor back, however briefly, to simpler times. They did just that for my dad; he loved it, and it was he who suggested, "Next summer, let's spend a week here." Mom, Michael, and I agreed that it was a great idea.

We had just finished dinner at Miller's Smorgasbord and were walking out to the car. Dad, with his arm around Mom, led the way; he was singing a Sinatra song. Michael and I were trailing behind; we glanced at each other and smiled. When Dad got to the car, he did something that I had rarely seen him do: He opened Mom's door first, waited until she got in, then closed the door behind her. As he came around to his side of the car, Michael surprised him.

"Why, Dad?" he asked.

"Excuse me, son, what was that?"

"You've been so nice to us all day—especially to Mom. Why can't you be this way more often? Don't you realize how much happier we'd all be if you could? Do you even think about that—how we feel?"

I was stunned, and so was Dad—stunned and hurt. He didn't get into the car, and he never made eye contact with Michael. He just kept walking—he walked past the car, out of the parking lot, and down the road. Mom was seated in the car with the windows rolled up and heard none of this. By the time she opened the passenger-side door and got out of the car, Dad was already out of sight.

"Where's your father?" Mom asked, bewildered.

"He walked off down the road, Mom," Michael said.

"Why? What's going on?"

After Michael explained, she told him to stay with me at the car; she was going to take a walk down the road to see if she could find Dad.

Mike and I leaned quietly against the car for twenty minutes or so until they returned. Neither of them said anything as we all got into the car. Dad drove us back to the motel cottages; there was a silence in the car that you could cut with a knife.

When we got to the cottages, Dad parked, turned off the lights and the ignition, and then turned toward us in the back and said, "Michael is right; your mother has been right all these years. I just can't help myself, and I want to do better. When we get home, I will seek help." But he never did.

That night, I asked Mike, "Do you think Dad could ever change?"

"Sure he can, why not?"

I appreciated Michael's reassurance, but I was eleven years old, and the father I had known my whole life just didn't seem to be capable of changing. Then I asked, "Have you ever talked to Dad before like the way you talked to him at the restaurant tonight?"

"Yes, a few times."

"Well, if he didn't change then, what makes you think he'll change now?"

Mike got quiet and then said, "Confidence, Augie. You have to believe that something good will come of this."

"Mom deserves better; she really does, Michael."

Again, Mike was silent for a few moments. Then he said softly, "You know, some people in this world are givers, and some are takers. Mom is a giver; she gives of herself tirelessly, and she's really good at it. You and me, well, we have learned from her. You're a giver, and I hope I am too. But Dad—he doesn't really know how to give. He's a taker, and that's how Mom and Dad's relationship works. But I pray all the time that one day, he might learn from Mom and start giving. We had a glimpse of it tonight."

"I hope you're right, because he's our dad and all, but I still say Mom deserves better."

Then I asked, "Even though you're visiting Bucknell this weekend, Michael, are you still thinking about joining the marines?"

"I'm still not sure, Augie, but I am going to decide soon. I don't talk about it with Mom, because I know it upsets her. We really need to stop the Communists in Vietnam, and the military could use guys like me. On the other hand, playing minor league baseball, or going to a school like Bucknell, does sound pretty darn good."

On Friday, the family arrived at the Gettysburg National Military Park in Gettysburg, PA. We got there in a state of what I can only describe as collective heightened emotion. We had been silent the whole trip, and in the silence, the emotional energy was palpable.

Mom had signed us up for a four-hour bus tour around the Gettysburg Civil War site, and as a way of taking our minds off the family's problems, it appeared to be just what the doctor ordered. We saw the Devil's Den, Rose Woods, and Little Round Top. We saw the Rebel positions where Pickett's Charge originated; we walked the Union positions along Cemetery Ridge. We stopped at countless monuments dedicated to military units from the various states, both Union and Confederate, and to the individual heroes who had contributed to the Union victory. We visited the David Wells House, where President Lincoln stayed the night before he delivered his immortal Gettysburg Address on November 19, 1863.

But for some, the ghosts can never be fully laid to rest; they arise whenever the opportunity presents itself. This visit to Gettysburg had apparently awakened my father's ghosts. I don't believe Dad had thought it through; perhaps he'd underestimated the power and longevity of the ghosts of battles past. His demeanor changed completely; his initial enthusiasm abandoned him and was replaced immediately by a serious and somber mood that took over his entire persona.

As I said earlier, my father never discussed his experience in WWII; perhaps he'd seen some truly horrible things. As a frontline soldier, he'd likely seen death and destruction on a daily basis, and as a tank driver, it's possible he'd even caused a good deal of it himself. At the time, Dad was just Michael's age—an eighteen-year-old kid from Brooklyn. He was shipped across the ocean to a strange land and thrown into the midst of one of the bloodiest battles of a bloody war. How was he to prepare for that? I can't imagine now what he'd gone through then. But being with him here, in Gettysburg, and seeing the pain in his eyes, I felt close to him—perhaps closer than I'd ever felt before—or ever would again.

What Michael saw in Gettysburg, on the other hand, was the bravery and heroism of men like Colonel Harrison Jeffords of the Fourth Michigan Volunteer Infantry, whose regiment found themselves in the Wheatfield, engaged in hand-to-hand combat with the men of Kershaw's South Carolina Brigade. In the chaos, Jeffords spotted his regimental flag—which he had sworn to defend with his life—seized by the enemy. As he rushed toward the flag, he was shot through the thigh and then took a bayonet thrust to his abdomen. His men rescued their colonel and wrested their flag from the enemy's grip. Jeffords, however, died of his wounds.

Then there was the story of Union First Lieutenant Alonzo Cushing, commander of Battery A, Fourth US Artillery. As the battle entered its third and final day on July 3, 1863, Cushing stood at a pivot point of history. The Confederates had been successfully held at bay during the first two days of the battle, but on the third day, Confederate General Robert E. Lee unleashed a massive infantry attack, which has since become known as Pickett's Charge. Cushing, who had graduated from the US Military Academy just two years before, had seen action at Bull Run, Antietam, Fredericksburg, and Chancellorsville. Nothing, however, had prepared him for the carnage of what followed.

Chaos engulfed the 110 men of Battery A. Although the Confederates had been inflicting considerable casualties, the Union forces were causing even greater damage and opening gaps in the enemy lines that would ultimately allow them to repel the attack and win the battle. Lieutenant Cushing was standing tall in the face of the Rebel charge, peering through his field glasses to direct the fire of his battery, when a shell fragment ripped through his shoulder. A second shot tore through his abdomen and groin. Bleeding profusely and holding in his exposed intestines with his hands, Cushing continued to direct the movement of his lone remaining field piece. With ebbing strength, he ordered his men to keep firing at the advancing Confederate troops. Then, Cushing was struck in the mouth by a bullet and fell dead beside his gun. He was twenty-two years old.

More than 150 years later, on November 6, 2014, First Lieutenant Alonzo H. Cushing was awarded the Congressional Medal of Honor, his country's highest award, for "conspicuous gallantry . . . at the risk of life, above and beyond the call of duty." ANG

Mom had hoped that our visit to Gettysburg would convince Michael of the horrors of war, of the devastation and death it leaves behind. She believed that, once exposed to the tragic realities of battle, Michael would be dissuaded from his inchoate thoughts of enlisting. Combined with the trip to Bucknell—its promise of a college education and the attraction of college-level athletics—she expected that Mike would abandon his idea of joining the marines. But Mom had miscalculated. Before they'd left Gettysburg, Michael—perhaps without even realizing it himself—had decided to join the Marine Corps, and Mom sensed it. She drew closer to Dad; I saw her taking his hand that Friday afternoon and gently rubbing his back. She was hurting, and she knew that, all too soon, Dad would be too.

For me, Gettysburg turned out to be more than just the most famous battlefield of the American Civil War. It was further confirmation that I was, indeed, different, that I had an ability to see what others could not see—and even more important, that I was not alone.

Our tour guide was a knowledgeable and genial local man by the name of Guy William Ginter. Although the badge clipped to his shirt pocket bore only his first name, he told us his full name and proudly shared a bit of his family's military history. Guy had served two separate tours in the navy, seeing action as a gunner on the USS *Massachusetts* in WWII. His father, John Bernard Ginter, was a naval officer during the Spanish-American War of 1898. He was aboard the USS *Maine* when it was sunk in Havana Harbor by a massive explosion, killing 250 of the 355 men aboard. John Bernard survived unscathed.

Guy saved the story of his grandfather Zachary Isaac Ginter for last. Zachary had fought with the Fifty-Third Pennsylvania Infantry Regiment, right here at Gettysburg. At the battle site known as Devil's Den, he suffered bayonet wounds, which resulted in the amputation of his right arm just below the shoulder. Zachary recovered and lived on to start a family, which, eventually, included Guy.

Guy himself looked like a character from the Civil War, tall and slim, with silver hair and a full beard to match. He took his job seriously; he had been a guide for twenty-one years. Our group numbered about twenty people. At the beginning of the tour, Guy asked us our first names, and we were amazed when he referred to everyone by name throughout the tour. Since I was clearly the youngest of the group, he'd affect to ask my opinion on various points of his commentary. "What do you think of that, August?" he might ask, or "Pretty cool, August, isn't it?"

The last stop on the tour was Little Round Top. This is the smaller of two rocky promontories at the southern end of Cemetery Ridge. It was the site of an unsuccessful assault by Confederate troops against the Union's left flank on July 2. Little Round Top was successfully defended by a brigade under Colonel Strong Vincent, who was wounded in the fighting and died five days later. This hill was the vantage point for our tour as we looked out over the fields below us, to the west and northwest. These were the same fields that were covered with the blood of the combatants 105 years before.

It was from Little Round Top that I saw my second house—that is, the second house that, I believed, only I could see. It was a large, cream-colored, three-story house. Like the Far Rockaway house, it had large windows and a broad, inviting porch with rocking chairs spaced around on it, facing out. It stood out on the landscape with nothing around it but open fields and scrub.

I waited for someone in our group other than me to ask Guy about the house. After all, we were all looking directly at it as Guy lectured us on one or another aspect of the fierce battle that had taken place here. But I waited in vain; no questions or explanations were forthcoming. They all behaved as though they didn't see it—didn't see the man sitting motionless in one of the rocking chairs.

Guy then led the group over to a monument that stood directly behind us. But all of my attention was focused on the cream-colored house, just a hundred yards or so from where I stood. I was staring at it when, suddenly, I felt a hand on my shoulder—it startled me. Guy drew up beside me and asked in a serious tone, "What is it, August, what are you looking at?"

"A house, Guy."

Guy followed my gaze and was silent for a moment. Then, without turning his head, he rolled his eyes toward me and said, "A house—what color is it?"

"It's cream colored. You know, like light tan," I said. "Do you see it?"

"No, I don't, but can you tell me anything more about it?"

"It's got a large front porch with some rocking chairs. There's a man sitting in one of them; he's looking right up here at us."

"A man, August? What's he wearing, son?"

"A blue uniform, like the Union soldiers wore. He looks young—like Michael's age."

Guy swallowed hard and became very still. By then, some people in the tour group, including my family, were drifting back toward us. Guy asked me to point directly at the house, which I did. "How many floors does it have?" Guy asked.

"Three," I said, holding up three fingers.

The returning tour group gathered around Guy and me. There was a look of concern on some of their faces; they were reading our body language and facial expressions and were looking as though they had some questions of their own.

Mom definitely noticed; she reached out and gently took my hand in hers and asked, "What were you pointing at, Augie?"

"Just the field," I said.

"And what were there three of? I saw you hold up three fingers."

Guy interrupted, "Folks, this is the last stop of the tour. I will be taking you back to the visitors center now. If you have any questions at all, please feel free to ask on the bus ride back."

As we were walking back to the bus, Guy came over to Mom and Dad and said in a low voice, "When we get back to the visitors center, we'll need to talk."

Chapter 15

A Special Boy

The five of us sat in a small conference room at the visitors center. Guy was choosing his words carefully.

"I have been working here at Battlefields Tours for twenty-one years. The first tour I ever gave was back in June 1947, two years after the war ended. About fifteen years ago—1953, I'd say—I had a funny little man on one of my tours. I'll never forget him; he was about fifty years old and wore a toupee—not a very flattering one, though—like it belonged to someone else. Now, this was before I started asking tourists for their first names, so I never got his.

"Anyway, the group was up on Little Round Top, looking down at the field, just as you folks were a little while ago, and he says, 'What about that old house down there—was that there during the battle?'

"Now, clearly there was no house there, so I said, 'What house?'

"He let out a nervous little laugh and said, 'There, right down the hill—that cream-colored house with the big front porch and all those rocking chairs.' With that, he looked around at the other folks, hoping for confirmation of what he alone was seeing. It became really awkward for all of us—many of the tourists just stared at him; some started to walk away, shaking their heads. I didn't know what to do, so I said to the group, 'It's time we went back to the visitors center.' On the drive back, the little man was silent, and when we got there, he left immediately, without saying another word to anyone—not even goodbye.

"It had occurred to me that this strange little man was—how shall I say it?—disorientated. But I'm not one to criticize or prejudge people, so I just let it ride—until three weeks later, when I was having a few beers at a local tavern with some of the other tour guides. We got to talking about some of our recent experiences on the job, and I told my story about the little gentleman up on Little Round Top. Two of the guys, Blaine Taylor and Stevie Richmond, chuckled, made a few wisecracks, and asked some perfunctory questions. But out of the corner of my eye, I could see that Ryan Kelly was waiting for the other two to finish talking. Ryan had been working at the park for about thirty years by that time and was nearing retirement. When his turn came, he told the three of us about a woman he'd had on one of his tours two years before." The following is Ryan's story, as told to us by Guy Ginter—seventeen years after it happened:

"'She was fifty-five or sixty years old,' Ryan said. 'It's hard to tell sometimes, and of course, you never ask. Her name was Eleanor, and up there on Little Round Top, she took me aside and said, very matter-of-factly, 'You know, there's a house down at the bottom of that hill, don't you?'

"'Oh, really,' I said, 'is there?'

"'Yes, it's there,' she said, 'except you can't see it.'

"'And why is that?' I asked.

"'Because not many have the gift. You have to be born with it; you have to be able to remember everything in your life—everything you've experienced, everything you've seen or heard. I know that you probably don't believe me, most people don't—but that doesn't mean a thing to me—not at all. I've seen quite a few houses that others don't see, but nothing like this one—it's being in a National Military Park and all. See those rocking chairs, there on the porch? Well, of course you don't. There are six of them; no one's sitting in them now, but they're rocking anyway. It's a grand old house, three stories high, you know—tan with white trim, well maintained . . . '

"Ninety-nine times out of one hundred, I'd have assumed this lady was crazy—but she was so darn convincing that I asked her, 'Do you ever see any people?'

"'Not here I don't,' she said, 'but I have—at the house that's on my family's property in Maryland.'

"By then, the tour group was beginning to gather around us, and I didn't want things to get out of hand, so I herded the group onto the bus, and we drove back to the visitors center. When we got there, I went over to Eleanor and told her that I wished we had more time to talk, but I had another group waiting. So we smiled and said goodbye."

As soon as Guy finished Ryan's story, he turned to me and said, "Something quite remarkable is going on here, August, something beyond our comprehension." Then he said to my parents, "Mr. and Mrs. Greenleaf, your son is a very special boy." I got up from my chair and went over to him; I put my arms around him and began to cry. Moments later, Mom did the same with me. We were both crying, and even Guy had a tear in his eye.

Then Dad asked, "Does Mr. Kelly live near here?"

"Oh, no," said Guy. "Ryan died about five years ago—cancer."

"How about Eleanor," said Mom. "Would you by any chance know her last name?"

"No, unfortunately not," Guy said.

That evening, during an early dinner at Howard Johnson's, I filled my parents in about what had taken place at the house by the bay. After dinner, we drove the two hours to Lewisburg, home of Bucknell University, and settled into the campus accommodations that the school had arranged for us. That night, Mom and I had a really great talk. With watery eyes, she said, "August, I always knew you were a special boy, from the very night you were born. I felt it, right here, in my heart," and she placed her right hand on her sternum. "I'm so sorry that I ever doubted what you've been telling me. It was just—all so hard to digest . . . "

I interrupted her. "It's okay, Momma—who would have believed it anyway? Someday, though, I'd like to meet someone else who sees what I see. You know, so we could talk about it and all."

"I don't doubt for a minute that one day you will, August."

"What do you think it all means, Mom?"

"I really don't know, but that date in 2013 obviously means something. I suppose that you are going to have to go back to the house on that day, and then maybe you'll find out."

"It sure is a long way off." I said.

"It sure is, Augie boy," she said. "You'll be fifty-six, and if I'm still around, well, I'll be a wrinkled old lady."

"You're never going to have wrinkles, Mom."

"Augie—believe me, I hope to be around to get them someday."

Our weekend at Bucknell was an exciting one—the four of us were treated like royalty. That's what they do, I suppose, for the family of a star athlete they covet, like Michael Greenleaf. Our guide for the weekend was an upperclassman named Charles Cheswick. Charles declared, "Please call me Chuck, everybody does."

Chuck was amiable enough and gave us a spirited tour of the school's campus. From there we met with the university's president, Dr. Charles Henry Watts, who could not have been nicer; I could see that Mom and Dad were impressed, although I couldn't read Mike's reaction. He had his game face on, the same one I'd seen him wear when he came up to the plate for a clutch at-bat.

Chuck then brought us over to the athletic facilities, where we met with the varsity baseball coach, Tommy Thompson. It was obvious that Mr. Thompson was very interested in selling Bucknell's baseball program to my brother; he spent a considerable amount of time with him. He showed him the ball field where he would be playing and introduced him to some of the team's assistant coaches and several of the players who were loosening up on the field. Later that night we were treated to a lovely dinner with the athletic director, Noel Preston.

Lying in bed that night, I asked my brother, "So what do you think,

Michael?" He didn't answer, so I repeated the question—again, no answer. I was not surprised. Mike often fell asleep as soon as his head hit the pillow. He was not one to ruminate; he was a straightforward, self-assured young man. I was Michael's opposite; in bed my mind was always racing—that was my normal state of consciousness until I'd finally fall asleep from exhaustion.

When sleep finally overtook me, I dreamed I was running as fast as I could. Behind me, the Amish were in hot pursuit in two horse-and-buggy rigs. I was in a field—it was the field leading up to Little Round Top. The house was there in front of me, and I ran toward it. As I bounded up the steps, I turned back to look. The Amish were gone. I was alone on the broad porch of the cream-colored house. Six rocking chairs were aligned on the porch, and one of them began to rock. Another started rocking, and then another, until all six were rocking with nobody in them—randomly at first, and soon in unison.

I knocked on the front door and heard a man's voice say, "Go away, you don't belong here; this isn't your house." Then from behind me a hand touched my shoulder; I turned, and there was Guy Ginter wearing the uniform of a Confederate soldier. "This house belongs to the Yanks; it's not for us," he said. A shot rang out, and Guy's blood spattered on me; he spun around and fell, dead, into one of the rocking chairs—and there he sat, rocking . . . back and forth, back and forth, back and forth . . .

Chapter 16

1968/69

Nineteen sixty-eight was an eventful and turbulent year. It saw two tragic assassinations: On April 4, Dr. Martin Luther King Jr. was killed at the Lorraine Motel in Memphis, Tennessee, by a single shot from a Remington hunting rifle fired by James Earl Ray. Just two months later, on June 8, in the kitchen of the Ambassador Hotel in Los Angeles, Robert F. Kennedy, a candidate for president of the United States that year, was struck by three shots from a handgun fired by Sirhan Sirhan, a Palestinian Christian who was angered by Kennedy's support for Israel.

In Vietnam, on January 30, the North Vietnamese and Viet Cong launched their vaunted Tet Offensive, a coordinated series of surprise attacks on scores of cities and military posts in South Vietnam. The objective of the operation, which continued through the month of September, was to demoralize the South—to undermine the South Vietnamese Army's commitment to prosecuting the war and drive a wedge between the South Vietnamese and their US allies. US troop numbers in Vietnam peaked at 555,000 in 1968, and that year was also to become the deadliest of the war for American forces, with 16,592 killed and 87,338 wounded.

At home, American society was in a state of upheaval. Young men were burning their draft cards, the feminist movement was gathering momentum, and the Black Panther Party was advancing its creed of Black Power.

Together, these movements were having a profound effect—especially in US cities and universities—through antiwar protests and civil rights demonstrations, which led to rioting in many parts of the country. This internal strife turned increasing numbers of Americans against any further involvement in overseas hostilities.

My brother had turned eighteen on May 21, 1968, and graduated from Far Rockaway High School in mid-June. The baseball team won the borough championship, due in part to my brother's record-breaking season. Mike's batting average was just shy of .400 that year, and he had the most home runs and RBIs of any high school player in the city of New York. He was positioned either to sign with one of three professional baseball clubs or to attend any of several colleges on a full scholarship. On June 25, five days after graduating, Michael took a bus to downtown Far Rockaway, walked into a building at 525 Rockaway Avenue—the US Marine Corps recruitment center—and enlisted.

That evening—over a dinner of fried chicken, mashed potatoes, corn on the cob, and green bean casserole—Michael announced to the family that he had enlisted in the Marine Corps. Mom said nothing; I believe she knew his enlistment was imminent. Michael would turn down every other career offer that had come his way—and there were many—opting instead to do what he saw as his duty. Mom had had one long talk after another with him concerning the questionable validity of the war in Vietnam, frantically working against the increasing likelihood of his enlisting.

Some of these talks became heated. Mom would argue, "This is not our war, Michael; it's not our fight! It's between the Vietnamese themselves." She cited a report by Walter Cronkite from February, in which Cronkite had stated that the US war effort was "mired in stalemate" and that there was broad-based public skepticism regarding the effectiveness of the war.

Michael's usual response went something like this: "A large segment of the US population was against our getting involved in World War II. Luckily, tens of thousands of men like Dad joined up, and thank God, we eventually won the war—because the ramifications of losing it were unthinkable." Mom's reasonable observation that "what was true of WWII is not necessarily, nor even likely, true of Vietnam" fell on deaf ears. At this point, Michael would add, "This is very much our fight, Mom. If we let the communists win in Vietnam, what's next?"—and my mother's heart would break.

Discussions like this were being held in families throughout our bleeding nation. Mom had often pleaded with Dad to speak to Michael about the horrors of war, to deny any glory in his own experience—to do or say anything to dissuade him from this course of action. On this particular evening, though, after Michael's announcement, Mom and Dad had nothing to say. There was no offer of support, no stiff upper lip, no meek dissent—only a silent meal. But the silence screamed of frustration, exhaustion, and despair; it wept for the irreconcilability of a shining ideal on one side and a loss of hope on the other. It trembled in fear for the life of this beautiful young man—their firstborn son, my only brother. They sat in their silence as though it were the very air they breathed, looking down absently at their half-eaten dinner and, with their forks, aimlessly pushing the remnants of their meal around on their plates—seeking deliverance from their unspeakable pain, groping for the shelter of their boundless love.

A few days later, I overheard my father talking to Michael. Dad said, "Please don't tell your mother this, but I'm proud of you, son; it takes a real man to reach a difficult decision like this, and you are a man." I was proud of Michael too. Dad was right—this was obviously not an easy decision for Mike to make, and when he made it, he was following his conscience, postponing his plans for a career. Mom was still very emotional about what had taken place that evening at dinner. She hugged him almost every time he was within arm's reach of her; her eyes teared up as she whispered in his ear that she loved him—would always love him.

Later that summer, we spent three weeks vacationing in the White Mountains of New Hampshire, at one of the family's favorite spots, the Baggish

Cottages, in the town of Bethlehem. Cynthia came with us for the first ten days, and we all had a great time. For me, looming on the horizon when we got back home was the sixth grade—my last year at PS 105. For Mike there would be a mid-August train ride down to Port Royal, South Carolina, and then to Parris Island, for boot camp, USMC style. There, Mike would undergo eight weeks of rigorous training (marine boot camp had been shortened from eleven to eight weeks due to the war in Vietnam) and would come out the other side a marine.

The summer was flying by, and on the night of August 17—two days before Mike's departure—Mom threw a surprise party for him at Amaro's Italian Restaurant in Far Rockaway center. Everyone was there—all our relatives and friends. It was wonderful to see them all together, and Mike seemed to be enjoying himself immensely. Cynthia was there, of course, as were her parents, Adrian and MaryAnn Brophy. They were very nice and appeared to be totally accepting of Michael—they were every bit as worried about him as we were. Cynthia had visited us on a couple of occasions during the prior few weeks, when Michael was not in, to spend time with Mom. I listened in on one of their conversations from my room. Cynthia had broken down crying, and my mother was bravely trying to console her.

It was a rough time for all of us. Those who loved my brother knew what was at stake. After boot camp, Michael was going to fly halfway around the world to engage in a jungle war against the natives of that jungle, the North Vietnamese and Viet Cong. Grandma Rachel and Grandpa Josef were very emotional; I overheard Grandma telling Michael, "Don't you try to be a hero, Michael, just do your job, and come back to us safe and sound." The party ended with many long hugs and tearful goodbyes—and with the departure of each guest, the mood became a little more somber.

That night Michael came in very late; I had fallen asleep sometime around midnight, and when I looked at the time, it was four o'clock in the morning. He tried to be quiet, but, erratic sleeper that I am, I woke up anyway.

"Good party," I said.

"Yes, it was, Augie. I'm sorry I woke you up."

"It's okay," I said. " . . . Michael?"

"Yes, Augie."

"Are you scared?"

"I'm nervous," he said, "but not scared. Scared and nervous are different. It's okay to be nervous sometimes; it can keep you alert. But like I've told you before, Augie, being scared incapacitates you; it ties you up in knots, and you become ineffective—useless." Then he said, "Just now, when I came into the room—well, I did make some noise on purpose, hoping you'd wake up."

"I'm glad you did."

"I won't be seeing you, or Mom and Dad, for the next eight weeks while I'm at boot camp. It's going to seem strange."

"Or Cynthia," I said. "Were you with her tonight, Michael?"

"Yes, I was."

"Are you going to marry Cynthia?"

"When I finish my tour of duty with the marines, I plan on it . . . Augie, I want to talk to you about something very important to me."

"What's that?"

"You, Augie—you are very important to me. I want you to know that I love you."

"Thank you, Michael, and I love you."

"You're finishing grade school this year, and junior high is only a year away for you. You're a thinker, Augie, and deeply empathetic; maybe that's why you've been given the gift you have. I have no idea why you've been given this gift, and unless you know something you're not telling me, you don't either. Just remember and accept how truly special you are. Whenever you get lost in your worries, remember that you have this gift for a reason—that there is a plan for you, and that there's absolutely nothing to worry about. Do you understand?"

"Yes, Michael, I understand."

"Good night, Augie."

"Good night, Michael."

Two days later, Michael left for boot camp. Three weeks after that, I started sixth grade and immediately hated it. Our teacher, Miss Broccoli, was an absolute witch—and for whatever reason, she did not take kindly to me. Honestly, it wasn't my didaskaleinophobia (which by that time was under control), yet her disdain for me was obvious to everyone. I didn't know what I'd done to earn her opprobrium, and I tried my best to win her over, but it was a losing battle. It's true that at times in class, I would lose focus and daydream—and Miss Broccoli made a point of calling on me at those times. And when, inevitably, I failed to provide her with the correct answer, she'd say, "There goes August Greenleaf—daydreaming again. You are in school, young man, pay attention!"

Broccoli didn't aim her wrath at me alone; there were several other boys with bull's-eyes on their backs. Oh, she had her favorites, all right—she adored Lisa Waldman, Patty Ann McNulty, and Kathy Sear, who just happened to be the three prettiest girls in the class. My friend Jodie Sunderland and I came to the conclusion that Broccoli was a lesbian who hated boys and lusted after pretty young girls.

One day in early October, during a math lesson, Miss Broccoli was discussing the associative properties of addition and multiplication. She turned abruptly from the blackboard and directed a question to the class. I hadn't been listening—I'd been thinking about Michael, who would be coming home soon from boot camp for his ten-day pre-deployment leave. I had no idea what Broccoli's question was, so naturally, she called on me!

"Would you please repeat the question, Miss Broccoli?" I asked as meekly as I could manage.

Broccoli fumed, "Not only will I not repeat the question, August, I will have you come to the blackboard and write out for the class, 'Enough is enough of my silly daydreaming in school!' Now get up here!"

Something snapped in my brain. As I strode from my desk to the blackboard at the front of the class, I shot back, "You're right—enough is enough!"

I seized the biggest piece of chalk I could find and wrote, large enough to be read from the back row:

Broccoli = Bully + Boy hater + Lesbian!

When I got home from school, my mother called me into the kitchen; she had already been notified of my chalkboard caper and was not very happy. "August Nathaniel Greenleaf—please tell me you didn't write on the blackboard that your teacher is a bully, a boy-hater, and a lesbian!"

"I can't, Mom."

"You can't what, August?"

"I can't tell you I didn't write what you just said."

"August, jeez, what am I to do with you? Listen to me, you have no idea what Miss Broccoli's sexual orientation is, but whatever it may be, it's none of your damn business. And now you've been given a week's suspension—shame on you!"

She grounded me, of course, but even so, I thoroughly enjoyed my Broccoli-free week off. In any case, it all turned out for the best; the school administration decided that sending me back to Miss Broccoli's class was not in the best interest of public education, so instead, I was placed in Miss Yamamoto's sixth grade class.

On my arrival back at school, accompanied by my mother, we were ushered into Principal Donavan's office. Already there were Mr. Phelps, the guidance counselor, and Miss Broccoli—the school's Wicked Witch of the West and leading lesbian. The first order of business was to elicit an apology from me to Miss Broccoli, which I thought went reasonably well.

"Miss Broccoli," I said, "I am sorry that I called you a bully, a boy-hater, and a lesb—"

"August!" Principal Donavan broke in. "There is no need to use those offensive words again. Now, start over, please!"

"Miss Broccoli, I am extremely sorry for the insult that I wrote on the blackboard. You are an excellent teacher and were only trying to teach me a lesson about paying attention in class. Please accept my sincere apology."

"I accept your apology, August," Miss Broccoli said. "However, it is my hope that you will not turn on Miss Yamamoto and disrupt her class as you did mine last week."

"Miss Broccoli," Mom said, "I wish to apologize also; I can assure you that August was not raised to behave as he did in your class."

Broccoli aimed low. "Regardless of how you've been raising August, Mrs. Greenleaf, he remains a very immature boy."

With a knitted brow, Mom shot back, "It seems to me, madam, that the words 'immature' and 'boy' are linked by definition. As a teacher, you'd do well to remember that from time to time—it might make your life a little easier."

"Mrs. Greenleaf, Miss Broccoli," Mr. Phelps interrupted. "That will do—please!"

After the meeting (which ended without further damage), and after Miss Broccoli had left his office, Principal Donavan instructed me on the importance of respecting our school's teachers. As we were leaving, Mr. Phelps added, "August, I'd like to see you in a week to discuss how you and Miss Yamamoto are getting along."

Michael arrived home for his ten-day leave shortly after my triumphant return to PS 105. His stay with us went by much too fast. Good times have a way of doing that.

He took a lot of ribbing about his marine buzz cut, but both Mom and Cynthia loved running their hands over it. He had a lot of stories about boot camp to tell us, and he said it was "crazy hard," but in an odd sort of way, he loved it. His drill instructor, Sergeant Wilson, sounded like a real tyrant, yet that was not at all how Mike saw him. To Mike, his DI was more a mentor—a "father figure." Surprisingly, Mike actually seemed to miss him.

Mike balanced those ten days among us very well, just as he did most things in his life. I got to spend some quality time with him—it was wonderful to share meals with him again, especially breakfast—and we had some serious nighttime chats, as we'd done so many times before. And then, again, he was gone.

NASA's *Apollo 8* space mission was launched from the Kennedy Space Center in Florida on December 21, 1968. During its twenty hours in lunar orbit, the crew of three became the first humans to view, directly, the back side of the moon—and to witness an "earthrise." On Christmas Eve, the three astronauts took turns reading the first ten verses of the Book of Genesis. After making ten orbits of the moon, the command module and its crew returned safely to Earth.

I had a recurring dream throughout my early childhood: My mother is crying uncontrollably, and I can do nothing to console her. By the dream's end, we are hanging on to each other, both of us crying bitter tears, but I don't know why. That dream became reality on Friday, January 10, 1969—four days after my twelfth birthday—when two men in blue uniforms showed up at our apartment door. One of the men had red stripes down the sides of his pants; they both carried white hats tucked under their left arms. Speaking softly, the man with the red stripes reported to my mother that her son, PFC Michael Adam Greenleaf, USMC, had, just the day before, been killed in action.

Chapter 17

Bethlehem, New Hampshire, July 1968

The Baggish Cottages softball team of Bethlehem had a darn good squad in the summer of 1968. Arthur Klein was their catcher, and Steven Goldberg, a lefty, pitched. The infield, from third to first, was made up of Greg Steiner, Jack Orenstein, and the Silverman brothers, Marty and Harry. The outfielders were Charlie Baggish—the owner of the Cottages—in left field and Max Lipke in right. Left and right center field were patrolled by the father-son combo of Howard and Michael Greenleaf.

On a gorgeous Saturday afternoon in July of that year, the Baggish team was playing Twin Pines Resorts. Mom, Cynthia, and I were in the bleachers, cheering for the Baggish boys. It was the bottom half of the seventh (and last) inning; Baggish was down by a run. We had runners on second and third with two outs. Mike was up next, and it didn't take long for him to resolve the situation. He drove the first pitch far over the left center fielder's head; it bounced twice on the grass and rolled into the woods beyond, and dear old Baggish won the game. Mom, Cynthia, and I beamed with pride, and Dad, pumping both fists in the air, joined the team's welcoming committee at home plate. Everyone on our side of the bleachers went out to congratulate Michael, but before he greeted us, he turned, approached the opposing team, and shook each player's hand, saying, "Good game, good game . . . "

That was my brother: fiercely competitive, calm under pressure, and gracious in victory. He was very much the person I was not, the kind of person who, for much of my life, I couldn't even imagine myself to be.

Every weekday afternoon at the Cottages, there was a pickup softball game. Many of the fathers and sons played—as (occasionally) did moms and daughters. Mike tried his best to talk me into playing, but I was much too self-conscious (and just plain scared—ludophobic) to put myself forward in such a public way. Behind the Cottages was a half-mile-long wooded path leading to a small, secluded, and very beautiful pond, which teemed with wildlife. One afternoon, while a game was in progress, Cynthia asked if I'd like to take a walk with her down to the pond. I was more than happy to go; in many ways she had become like a sister to me—after all, she was almost one of the family. Cynthia was easygoing, kind, gentle, and considerate—and she was fun to be with. Mike had found the perfect girl.

"You know, Augie, I'm so glad that your mom asked me to join you guys up here," she said. "I would love to have stayed the entire three weeks, but my parents want me back for our family's trip to Delaware to visit my grandparents."

"I know," I said, "my mom told me about it."

"Augie, may I ask you a question?"

"Sure."

"When your brother is away with the marines, I would still love to come over and visit with you and your mom. Would that be okay with you?"

It touched my heart that Cynthia felt that way—that without Michael, she still cared enough for Mom and me to want to spend time with us. But I couldn't put my feelings into words; I couldn't tell her that her question touched me. Again, all I could say was, "Sure."

It took many more years before I was able to speak truthfully—that is, to speak plainly and from the heart. I had always felt as though I had something to hide from the people I encountered—something they'd figure out about me that they might find odious. Even at a young age, there were always secrets, always my little deceptions, and I was forever carrying this burden of my own making. In later years, I'd resort to sex and drugs to take me outside of myself—to overcome my insecurity and escape the fear living inside me.

When Cynthia and I reached the pond, we sat down on a bench and, for a little while, silently took in the beauty of nature. Cynthia loved birds—my brother had given her a copy of *All About Birds: Northeast* (from the Cornell Lab of Ornithology series) for her birthday a few months earlier, and she was getting pretty good at identifying the various regional species.

"Look, Augie, a black-capped chickadee! And over there—cardinals! They don't migrate, so they're pretty close to the northern limit of their range. They retain their plumage year-round, even in the snow. The greenish brown one is the female. Aren't they beautiful!"

Her enthusiasm was contagious; I couldn't help but be infected by it, and I thought, *I hope, one day, to be as lucky as Michael—to find a girl like Cynthia.*

"Hey! What are you two talking about over there?" It was Mom. She was coming down the trail toward us with Michael.

"Maybe we should leave you two lovebirds," Mike teased.

Cynthia surprised—and embarrassed—me a little when she wrapped her arms around me and said, "Augie's all mine; you two go away now!"

"Augie, have you gone and stolen my girlfriend while my back was turned?" Mike said, pretending to scold me.

"Well, Michael Adam Greenleaf, you seem to think that softball is more important than your girlfriend," Cynthia said, "and you gave your brother the chance to move in, and August did just that—he's all mine now."

"Just hold on there, Miss Brophy," Mom said, grabbing my arm in a mock attempt to pull me away. "This one belongs to me. You can have his big brother, but August is all mine."

I was with some of the people I loved most in the world. If I could have stopped time, I would have done it, right then and there—on that wooden bench near the pond, amid the laughter and the love—among the chickadees and cardinals, the jumping fish, the turtles and the frogs. But time can't be stopped at a whim, and every magical moment must end, lest real life catch us unawares. But if we are patient, the magic will return, and if we're alert, we'll catch it again.

Together, we made our way back up the path to the Cottages. Cynthia and Mom led the way, walking hand in hand; my brother and I followed at a little distance. Michael leaned toward me and said quietly, "See those two ladies in front of us, Augie? One day there'll be three; your girl will be walking with Mom and Cynthia. You have to choose wisely, though, and you have to treat your girl with respect, Augie. Then watch—your life will be transformed."

Throughout my childhood, Michael watched over me constantly, and he made a point of letting me know that my manifold fears were only my own thoughts gone bad. "Those thoughts are all in your head, Augie," he'd say. "They're not real. I've seen you gaining confidence every day, becoming the real August Greenleaf! If you'll just continue believing in yourself, you'll be just fine, Augie, I guarantee it."

In the years following Michael's death, I had little interest in the world around me; I was in a perpetual torpor. In middle school and high school, I paid little attention to my studies, and my grades suffered accordingly. I avoided extracurricular activities, and the few girls who showed any interest in me were quickly put off by my moodiness. After graduation, I went to community college for a year but was ill-prepared and even less stimulated than I'd been in high school.

But I needed money, so I spent a couple of years flipping burgers, mowing lawns, and shoveling snow, and was surprised to find that my many fears and phobias began to leave me. Michael was right: As my hobgoblins were forced out of my mind by more constructive thoughts, I became increasingly confident and sociable. Again I found that women were attracted to me, and that realization gave my confidence another bump. I was developing a sense of purpose and began to suspect I had something to offer the world after all . . . and vice versa.

Shortly after I turned twenty-two, I took on a truly demanding job at UPS as a package car driver. I was required to show up, work hard, drive carefully, and take responsibility—and I did well. Yet steady work is no panacea; it comes with its own problems, and eventually my anxieties began again to dog me. But by then I'd acquired the means to purchase the chemicals I needed to keep my demons at bay. ANG

As the four of us left the wooded path on that beautiful summer day and stepped onto the Cottages' property, I caught a glimpse of Dad sitting in a lawn chair, in the shade of a sugar maple, watching. He didn't say a word, and I wondered if he felt like an outsider (because, in fact, he was, and that made me sad).

Steven Goldberg, the pitcher for the Baggish Cottages team, was also staying with his family for a few weeks at the Cottages. Steve had two daughters—buxom, seventeen-year-old Mindy and her twelve-year-old sister, Bonnie, whose smile featured a set of braces that made it look like she had a cheese grater in her mouth. Mindy had her eyes on Michael the whole time we were there, and I knew that the only thing holding her back had been the presence of Cynthia, who had just left to visit her grandparents in Delaware. With the door wide open, the pretty, big-chested brunette jezebel was putting all her moves on Michael, and it appeared Mike might be falling for it. As for jezebel's younger sister, Bonnie Braces, something very strange was going on: she was flashing her pretty brown eyes and metallic smile—at me!

On day twelve of our vacation, during Wednesday bingo night, the Goldberg sisters got the chance they were waiting for. With a large segment of the Cottages community glued to their gridded number cards and a prize of fifty cents a game tantalizing the adults, the girls suggested the four of us take a nighttime walk down to the pond. Mike seemed to like the idea and grabbed from our cottage a couple of flashlights that Dad had packed for the trip. Mike handed me one of the flashlights, and the four of us set off for the pond.

Picking our way down the wooded path that led to the pond, I stayed as close to Michael as I could, walking beside him with flashlight in hand—scared shitless of the dark.

[**Nyctophobia: Extreme fear of night or darkness.**]

This wasn't Far Rockaway, with streetlights and neon signs illuminating the night. This was the country, raw nature; it was pitch-black, and we were walking in the woods with the giggling Goldberg girls, who tittered and squealed at every bullfrog, peeper, and owl—but seemed, nevertheless, to be having a jolly good time. ANG

Somewhere along the path, Mindy bumped me out of the way and was now walking with Michael. Meanwhile, sister Bonnie, who had been slowly edging toward me, was now at my side, holding my hand. If I'd had any clue at all about what was going on, I'd have had to admit that these girls were good. When we reached the pond, Bonnie maneuvered the two of us onto the wooden bench. Then she leaned over and kissed me smack on the lips and said, "You're so cute, Augie." I liked it, and in the darkness, I smiled.

The night ended with a second kiss; Bonnie planted this one noisily on my right cheek, directly in front of Michael and Mindy. Michael got a big kick out of it, but Mindy seemed distracted, a little out of sorts. Evidently, Mike had not fallen into the trap she'd set—always the gentleman, he'd been true to his girlfriend, Cynthia, after all. I must have been visibly relieved, because for the remainder of our trip, Mike teased me about my own loose morals. He'd say, for instance, that he'd had no idea I was so attracted to shiny objects; or, if I liked kissing chrome, he knew a '58 Oldsmobile he could fix me up with. My brother could be merciless once he got going.

By summer's end, despite my many fears, I was beginning to develop some confidence in myself. The house by Jamaica Bay and the house at Little Round Top were not apparitions after all—they were real, the former confirmed by a tangible (albeit somewhat cryptic) note, the latter by two separate and independent accounts of other Gettysburg tourists who evidently shared my gift. In the sixth grade, I had taken on two bullies, George Kendell and Miss Broccoli, and prevailed—and most recently, I'd kissed a girl!

But despite my modest successes of the past year, I knew I still had a long way to go. And when January brought the news of Michael's death, everything in my life fell apart.

Part Two

My Last 7,000 Days

To know yourself as the
Being underneath the thinker,
the stillness underneath the
mental noise, the love and joy
underneath the pain,
is freedom, salvation,
enlightenment.

—Bob Goff

Red sky at night, sailors delight;
red sky in the morning, sailors take warning.

—Mariners' aphorism, based on Matthew 16: 2–3

En ma fin gÎt mon commencement.
In my end is my beginning.

—Mary, Queen of Scots (1542–1587), while imprisoned at Fotheringhay, awaiting execution by her cousin, Elizabeth I of England

Death is the mother of beauty; hence from her,
Alone, shall come fulfillment to our dreams . . .

—Wallace Stevens, "Sunday Morning"

Chapter 18

Ten Years Later

Saturday, January 6, 1979 (journal entry):

I am twenty-two years old today. Although I am well aware of the date and its significance (Christians, for instance, call this day the Epiphany—a feast day, a holy day), I no longer celebrate my birthdays. I have not done so for ten years—nor will I ever again. Others try to put me in a celebratory mood, but I do not oblige them; I just can't do it. Each birthday is a reminder of what took place three days after my twelfth birthday—half a fucking world away.

The pain has never left me. The guilt I feel enwraps me to this day; it immobilizes me like a straitjacket one I fear I shall wear until my dying breath brings release. During this cold, dark time of the year, like nature, I retreat into myself; I remain aloof, even from those closest to me, while I mourn him, the brother I allowed, perhaps encouraged, to go to war—a war that was largely a lie.

It was I who did not object—they both did. From the beginning, my mother objected vehemently—so much so that, eventually, even my father came around—attempting, on several occasions, to change my brother's mind. But I never once protested, nor did I voice any concern over his decision to go to Vietnam. "Michael, the family needs you . . . Michael, I need you, and if anything ever happened to you . . . Michael, I beg you—please don't go!" These never-spoken words still echo in my brain. I had invested my own pride in him; I basked in his glory, convinced that he would prevail, as he'd always done before.

On Tuesday, January 9, it will have been ten years since he died. There was no preparing us for it—only a knock on the door. It was 5:15 p.m.; my father was napping, and my mother was in the kitchen preparing dinner. She went to the door and opened it. Two men in dress blue uniforms filled the door frame. One was a marine captain; the other, with lieutenant commander's stripes on his sleeves, a navy chaplain.

Mom invited them in and told me to wake up my father. All four of them sat at the kitchen table; my mother had a queer look on her face, a look I'd never seen before. It scared me. Dad told me to go to my room, so I listened from there with the door ajar; I heard one of the men say "killed in action."

"Oh no," my mother said softly. She repeated those two words and kept repeating them until, in her anguish, they became the perfervid plea of the helpless—"Oh no, oh no, oh no, oh *no, oh no, OH NO!*"

I ran to the kitchen; Dad was holding her in his arms. Mom just kept repeating those two words as though, in their repetition, the truth they decried might be altered, and in my father's embrace, she clasped her arms tightly over her breast, as though to keep her heart from exploding.

I ran back to my bedroom and fell into my bed face down. I placed my hands over my ears to drown out my mother's screaming—to drown out the world—and I cried. I cried for my dear brother, Michael, and I know, somewhere deep inside, I shall forever shed my tears.

Chapter 19

Connecticut

Winter 1974:

We sat sideways, like bookends, on the long living room couch in apartment 7D, Far Rockaway, Queens, New York. "Augie," he said, "you've got to get it together, man—stop acting the part of the lost kid! What's going on?"

I just stared at him and shook my head, happy to see him again yet entirely lacking the words to explain the feeling of constant dejection I'd been suffering since he died.

"Let's grab our gloves and go out and have a catch," he said.

Out on the field across the street from our building, we were tossing the ball back and forth, except Michael wasn't tossing—he was firing the ball at me, and to my great surprise, I was catching it effortlessly. Before long, a wide smile crossed my face—I was with Michael; he was with me—all was well again.

"There you go, Augie—good job, little brother."

"I'm really glad you're here, Michael."

"Glad to be here."

"How have you been, Michael? I've missed you."

"Really great."

"Can I see you anytime I want to, Michael?"

"Only when you dream, Augie, only when you dream."

The alarm clock woke me, with its annoying beep-beep-beep; it read 6:45 a.m. If I decided to go to school that day, I'd need to get out to the bus stop within forty-five minutes. It was only March, and I had already skipped a handful of days in this, the second term of my sophomore year in high school. So what was one more day?

Before rolling out of bed, I thought a little while longer about the dream I'd just had. He had been coming back to me lately in my dreams—they seemed so real! The dreams were a recent development; it had been over five years since I'd last seen him alive, and in all that time I rarely, if ever, dreamed of him. But lately there'd been several nights when he, according to my mother, "was visiting us." Evidently, Mom was having dreams of Michael too. On one recent Saturday morning, I got up early and heard her sobbing in her bedroom across the hall. I rapped on her door and stepped into the dark room. "Are you okay, Mom?" I asked.

"It was your brother, August; I was just dreaming about him—he was a little boy, so handsome. I'm so sorry to wake you, please go back to bed, dear."

The house was chilly that morning. Mom usually turned the heat down at bedtime to save on the heating bill. This was our first winter in our new Connecticut home. Grandpa Josef and Grandma Rachel had made a generous down payment on it. Grandpa's older brother, Benjamin, who lived in Westville, a predominantly Jewish section of New Haven, had told him about this house in Branford, a shoreline town about ten miles east of New Haven.

"Branford is a very nice old Connecticut town, Josef," Benjamin said. "The school system is a good one for your grandson, and I should be able to get Ella a job at the hospital here in New Haven. You and Rachel can take the train out from New York whenever you wish—Branford is only fifteen minutes or so out of New Haven. I'm looking at a house now; it's modest, but it has three bedrooms, and it's within walking distance of Long Island Sound. I believe this will offer the two of them a fresh start, Josef. They certainly deserve one."

In May of the prior year, the four of us—Mom and I and my grandparents—took the train to New Haven. Benjamin picked us up at the station and drove us out to Branford to have a look at the house. The adults all loved it, but I was indifferent. I had no qualms about leaving the city, but living out here would take a lot of getting used to, and even though our current living situation was far from ideal, I had neither the energy nor the desire to move.

At day's end, Benjamin told Mom that he was going to give her his spare car; Mom broke into tears and gave him a big hug. "This is what families do in trying times, Ella," he said. "I only wish I could do more."

Two days later, my grandparents put down a deposit to hold the house and later, at the closing, followed up with the down payment, which was sufficient to make Mom's monthly mortgage payments affordable.

Mom and I moved into the house that summer—July of 1973; it had been a little over a year since the divorce. For the previous six months, we had been living with my grandparents in Brooklyn, and quite frankly, during that entire time, my grandmother never let up on me: "August, did you go to school today? . . . August, if you were in school as you say, then let me see your work assignments . . . August, it's hard, I know; you've been through a lot lately . . . August, if you continue to drive your mother crazy, then you're going to have to deal with me . . . " as though I hadn't been dealing with her already—day after day!

Michael's death was hard on my father too. He was, I'm sure, just as bereft as Mom and I were, but he suffered his pain alone, and his moods became even darker and stormier than they had been before. Mom saw the effect that Dad's behavior was having on me, and it was certainly taking at least as heavy a toll on her. She'd finally had enough of his arguing, his anger, his debilitating moods—in short, all of his bullshit. One Wednesday morning, after Dad had left for work, Mom woke me up early. "Get up, Augie," she said. "We're packing up and moving in with Grandma and Grandpa."

"What about Dad?"

"He's not coming with us, Augie. It's just the two of us now."

"I don't understand, Mom."

"I've decided to divorce your father—I should have done this years ago, Augie, years ago!"

We loaded up the trunk of her girlfriend May's family car, a 1968 Chrysler Newport—and with May behind the wheel, Mom seated next to her, and me in the back, we drove away. Looking out the rear window, I watched with sadness as it all shrank in the distance—our building, the ball fields, the bay, and the white house by the bay. In a minute's time they were gone. I closed my tear-filled eyes, and in my mind's eye, I saw Michael up at the plate—the bigger boys were talking it up, trying to unnerve him, but Mike would have none of that. He hit the ball way over the left fielder's head and was rounding the bases like a young Jackie Robinson.

In all the remaining years of my life, I would return to Far Rockaway just three times, and each time I came, it would be there, waiting—of that I'd had no doubt: my beautiful white house by the bay.

Chapter 20

Jessica

Summer 1981:

I parked my UPS truck and stepped up to the front door of her condominium unit with a package from J. C. Penney. I knew this was it—she had told me as much the day before. "Augie," she'd said, "I'm expecting a package tomorrow, and I really think you're going to like your tip. If the package doesn't come, you come anyway—you've a one-hour lunch break, right?"

Augie is going to get laid today, I thought, or maybe get a blow job. Or just maybe, if I can squeeze it into my lunch break, I'll get laid *and* get a blow job. But then I'll have to go down on her, of course—fair's fair. God, she's beautiful, I can't wait to go down on her. So much to do in one lunch break!

Twenty-five-year-old Jessica Ann Gilbert was a sublessee of Unit 6G at Dawson's Landing Condominiums in the town of Madison, Connecticut, a tony shoreline community on Long Island Sound, twenty miles east of New Haven. Just as I reached down to ring her bell, Jessica opened the door, wearing only a sheer bra and panties. Having a man look at her in such scanty attire didn't appear to faze her at all. Jessica danced for a living at the Glitter Girls and Gentlemen's Club in New Haven; she was accustomed to having men ogle her and search her lithe and lightly draped body for new and more creative places to sequester their tightly folded dollar bills.

"Like it, Augie?" she said as she struck a piquant pose, with her front door wide open.

"Nice," I said.

"Come on, you can do better than *that*."

I sidled in as she closed the door behind us; I set her Penney's package down and placed my clipboard on top of it. Then I gently lifted all 110 well-distributed pounds of her off the polished hardwood floor, and with her arms already around my neck, she wrapped her strong, shapely legs around my waist. We locked lips for a long moment, and then she whispered, "The bedroom's to the right, Augie."

About two weeks later, we got together again for a weeknight date. After dinner and a couple of drinks, I took her back to my place, where we smoked a bowl, made love, and stayed up talking until morning. In those nighttime hours, we exposed much of our hidden selves to each other. I felt comfortable with Jessica, free to tell her of my insecurities and phobias—the houses I saw, my brother's death, bullshit from my job at UPS, et cetera. In turn, she told me how her parents had died in a motorcycle accident on I-95 in Mystic, Connecticut. It was a Sunday afternoon in July; they were on their way back from a weekend at Cape Cod. Jess was staying with her grandmother and her seventeen-year-old uncle, Louis. She was nine years old at the time. A tractor trailer had swerved into the Harley her parents were riding as her father was attempting to pass; the police estimated that they were going seventy miles per hour. Both of them were pronounced dead at the scene.

Jessica's grandmother took the initial call from the state police. When she hung up, she went into the living room, where Jess was watching an Abbott and Costello movie on TV. Her grandmother said, "Jessica, I have some very bad news—your mother and father were both killed this afternoon on that goddamn motorcycle." She went on in front of her shocked granddaughter, "I knew this would happen one day, I knew it. I warned them. You heard me, Jess, didn't you?"

Now an orphan, Jessica went on living with her grandmother and uncle. The fondling started soon afterward, and the sexual abuse by her uncle continued until shortly after her thirteenth birthday, when, finally, she told her school guidance counselor about it. Jess's uncle denied everything, of course, and her grandmother chose to believe him. So, the next time it happened, Jessica ran away from home. She was picked up at a bus station by two Norwich, Connecticut, police officers and returned to her grandmother and abusive uncle. Soon after that, Connecticut Family Services stepped in, and Jess was moved to a foster home, where her foster parents, the Manuellis, took good care of Jess and eventually adopted her.

After some wild and turbulent years in her late teens and early twenties, she began to pull her life together. She was taking courses at a local community college and working four nights a week at the club to support herself and pay for her education. "I'm majoring in business administration," she told me. "Two down and two more years to go until I can start fresh. I am so ready to move on—I swear, I'd quit dancing right now if I could, but the money is too good; it's the only reason I stay. Some nights I look into their eyes and it sickens me, Augie. Some nights I see his eyes in theirs, and when I get offstage—I'm physically ill."

Our friendship grew in the months following our marathon date, but not so much in a romantic sense. It's rather odd—although I was very attracted to Jess physically, I'd begun to see her in a completely different light. Oh, we made love a few more times, but that was all. Our relationship was evolving into something much more important to us than sex. What developed—and it developed quite naturally—was a spiritual kinship: an unconditional bond between trusted, and trusting, friends. Each of us suffered from bouts of depression and anxiety, and we'd both known emotional pain—the kind of debilitating pain that takes hold of you and won't let go, that comes out of nowhere and leaves you feeling cold and alone—isolated, even from those closest to you. We were both all too familiar with it and often had to talk each other down from the ledge when the shit got serious.

Jess knew that I had gained a certain level of confidence in myself, largely because women were attracted to me. I was told that the attraction was a combination of my looks and the gentle way I came on to people, especially women. I understood the looks part, maybe—but the latter, not so much.

Women were evidently unaware that my gentle demeanor floated on an ocean of pure terror, and that my insides crawled with the fear of being found out.

Nevertheless, I became addicted to the attention the ladies lavished on me, and with the help of sex and weed, I managed to hide in plain sight from my worst nightmare. Jessica could read me like a book—she'd say, "Augie, for fuck's sakes, please stop trying to screw every attractive woman you meet. Your problem is that you're too damn sweet and good looking. I swear to you, Augie, I don't know how you juggle them all—no wonder you suffer from anxiety."

With the passage of time, our friendship has endured and become steadily stronger. Although circumstances eventually led us to make our lives on opposite coasts, Jess has remained available to me whenever I've needed her—by phone or email. On several occasions, she boarded a plane back east when I'd hit bottom—and I've done as much for her.

Luckily, Jess and I found that we had something much more valuable than sex to give each other—something we were both infinitely more in need of: genuine empathy, true understanding. Although we had loved being lovers, each of us came to the realization that it wasn't desire that drew us together—rather, it was the need for the refuge we afforded each other, especially when the wind howled and the storm clouds gathered, as they often did. In fact (and I think Jess would agree with this), it was the only thing that truly mattered in our relationship, and sex had become, if anything, less help than hindrance in fulfilling that other, more pressing need.

So, our feelings evolved away from the passion of lovers toward a constancy akin to the friendship between brother and sister—but there were times when, even more, they resembled the love between parent and child. At those times, we would deftly assume alternate roles as might be required, in each case, by the vicissitudes of our erratic, bipolar lives.

Yet, for me, there was another dimension to our friendship—one that I've never discussed with Jessica—that now, even as I write this, I'm admitting to myself for the first time. In a strangely unselfconscious way, Jess would occasionally tender me a transcendent kind of spiritual support, a certain grace, for which I had once relied solely on my dead brother, Michael—and my heart would be full to overflowing.

Chapter 21

A Sunday in June with the Greenleafs

Sunday, June 13, 1982:

- August Greenleaf, 7:30 a.m.:

My regular 8:00 a.m. Sunday wake-up call from my mother in Florida was preceded by another call at 7:30, which woke me from a deep sleep. I had not gone to bed until three o'clock that morning, and I answered in a fog, with a raspy voice—the result of too much weed the night before.

"Good morning, August," Grandma Rachel said. "Did I wake you? I thought you had said that your mother calls you at seven on Sunday mornings."

"That's okay, Grandma, I had to get up anyway. Big day today. I'm really looking forward to seeing you and Grandpa."

"August, I'm listening to WCBS radio; there is an accident on the Throgs Neck Bridge. Listen to me—take the Whitestone Bridge instead."

"Sounds good, Grandma."

"August, is William still coming?"

"Yes, he is, Grandma. I'm picking him up at nine."

"Good, Grandpa and I love William—and August, please drive the speed limit."

"Will do, Grandma."

"About what time will you be arriving, August?"

"Around eleven, Grandma."

"Bring a rain jacket, there's a chance of showers."

"Okay, Grandma."

"Love you, August."

"Love you more, Grandma."

The William my grandmother was referring to was Bill Salinger. Bill and I had met in history class at Branford High. We were two misfits mired at the bottom of a repressive social hierarchy—known in the '70s as high school—so we formed an ad hoc defensive alliance that, within a year, grew into the friendship that has now lasted almost a lifetime. In the summer of 1982, having completed his third year at the University of Connecticut School of Medicine, Bill was doing his surgical rotations at the UConn Medical Center in Farmington. He was just a year away from graduating and becoming known ever afterward as William Salinger, MD. So, after he graduated, I began to call him "Dr. William." I liked the sound of it, and I eventually dropped the "Bill" entirely in favor of "William"—it seemed more fitting.

- Ella Greenleaf Santoro, 8:00 a.m.:

"Good morning, Mom."

"Good morning, Augie—why, you answered on the first ring, that's not like you," she said with a chuckle.

"Grandma called me at 7:30 to tell me that there was an accident on the Throgs Neck and that I should take the Whitestone instead, so I was up already."

"That's your grandma," she said, again with a laugh. "Is Bill still going with you?"

"Yes, he is."

"Augie, I know I've said it before, but it pleases me so much that you drive into the city to see your grandma and grandpa every few months. You're a wonderful grandson, August Nathaniel!"

"And you're not such a bad mother, either, Ella Santoro."

"That's Ella Greenleaf Santoro to you, Augie boy."

"That's right, my Jewish Italian mother, who left me five years ago for warmer environs to teach in Clearwater, Florida. How's school going?"

"Just three more weeks to go this year—I can't believe it. I'm really going to miss them—I have such a great little group of fourth graders. There's that one boy I told you about, Jack Gibson. I could eat him alive; he so reminds me of you when you were small."

"A real head case, huh?"

"Not at all, Augie, he's a sweet, beautiful boy—just as you were, son."

- Howard Greenleaf, 8:45 a.m.:

My dad sat in the bleachers watching the boys play baseball. It had been sixteen years since he'd seen his own son Michael play ball. "Oh, Michael," he said to himself, "why, why didn't I stop you? What a fucking idiot I was!" He got up from the bleachers and walked along the path adjacent to the ball field. She had left ten years ago, and he hadn't seen her since the divorce. He heard that she was married again and living on the Gulf Coast of Florida. A teacher now, he thought; she had always wanted to be a teacher. He had been meaning to see his son, but the truth was, seeing him would bring back too many more memories—memories he'd rather be rid of.

He had never married again; marriage wasn't worth all the bullshit that came with it. He'd dated several women, but only with the thought of getting laid. If they got the least bit serious, he'd dump them. He worked as much overtime as he could these days—what else was there to do? He was eligible for retirement, but that was the last thing on his mind. Currently, what was foremost in his mind was the Smith & Wesson Model 10 .38 Special with a four-inch barrel—a revolver he'd recently purchased from a coworker at the post office. It had been resting atop his bedroom dresser for a week.

- August Greenleaf, 9:00 a.m.:

I picked Bill up at his house, and we got on I-95 South toward Brooklyn, New York. The drive would take about an hour and forty-five minutes, which would give us a decent chance to catch up on each other's lives.

"You go out with that new girl from Clinton last night?" Bill asked.

"I did—she's a real pothead."

"Oh, and you're not, August?" He smiled.

"Well—yes, but she's an even bigger one."

"How much did you two smoke?"

"About three or four joints."

"Jeez—so, which was it, three or four?"

"I don't know, I was so stoned I lost count."

"You really need to slow it down."

"I know."

"Any 'no strings attached' sex?"

"I think so."

"You think so, August?" Bill was laughing now.

"I don't know if we did it or if I dreamed it."

"You really are a piece of work—I hope you didn't drive her home last night. Tell me you didn't; tell me that you took her home this morning."

"I didn't."

"You didn't what?"

"Drive her home," I said.

"So she's still at your house?"

"No."

"Where is she, then?"

"I can't answer that question. I got up this morning, and she was gone."

"Gone, August?"

"Gone," I said.

"Did you check the closets? Maybe she stumbled into one of your closets and fell asleep."

"No, Inspector Clouseau, I did not."

"Really, Augie, this is serious. This girl could turn up dead somewhere."

"I'm just having some fun with you, Doctor. Somehow, last night she made it to the rug in the living room, and that's where I found her this morning—fast asleep on the rug, smack in the middle of my living room floor. Her girlfriend came by this morning to pick her up, just before I headed over to get you."

"You had me going there," Bill said. "You know, I'm serious, Augie, you really need to cut back on the weed, it's not good for you."

"It helps with my anxiety, it really does. When I smoke, it calms me down—I feel peaceful, and the nerves disappear. I mean, I function well when I smoke—but I do agree with you, man, I've been smoking way too much."

"Have you been doing anything else besides weed?"

"A little hash and some coke—but not much."

After Bill finished giving me the complete version of his antidrug lecture—and, I must admit, he could be very persuasive—he asked about my mom. Bill had confessed to me many times, as had some of my other friends, that he was in love with my mother.

"How's my girlfriend Ella doing?"

"She's fine. She's going to be staying with me for the first two weeks of July. I'll tell her you were asking about her. How are things going on your end? I've got to hear some of your surgical-rounds stories."

"Well, let's see—would you like to hear the pus story or the motorcycle accident story first?"

"Let's go with the pus story, and you can work your way up to the motorcycle accident."

"So, on Tuesday, I'm called to the emergency room to see a guy with a diabetic foot."

"What's that?"

"When your diabetes is uncontrolled, you can lose feeling in your feet. You might not feel a sore, a cut, or a blister. The lack of feeling is called sensory diabetic neuropathy. So, this older guy comes in with a nasty blister under his big toe. Poor guy, he can't even walk. When I come in, he's in a wheelchair, and his right leg is propped up on a folding chair, with a pillow under his foot. His blister is a rather large and nasty one, extending to the ball of his foot, so I put on a pair of gloves, and very gently I run my fingers around it, and as I'm doing that, the freaking thing pops. Smelly yellow pus shoots out of it and sprays all over my lab coat—and the pus that misses me shoots halfway across the room."

"That's enough, I get the idea." Since I was already sufficiently sickened by his pus story, I asked Bill to save the motorcycle saga for the ride home.

When we got to my grandparents' house in the Borough Park section of Brooklyn—the same home they'd lived in for the past forty-five years—we were welcomed with open arms. My grandparents, both in their early eighties, were looking well, and since I hadn't seen them for a few months, I was happy to be there with them again. After a full hour of interrogation by my relentlessly inquisitive grandmother and a few knowing smiles from Grandpa, we sat down to a delicious lunch. Grandma Rachel had prepared a spread consisting of matzo ball soup, bagels and lox, cream cheese, real Jewish rye bread, whitefish salad, tuna salad, chicken salad, and chopped liver—and for dessert, a fabulously rich, five-layer chocolate cake.

- Ella Greenleaf Santoro, 1:00 p.m.:

Ella was the best of wives, and Marco knew it. On this particular Sunday in June, after playing an early morning round of golf, he showered, and with his friend Dominick (the atypical terminal *k* was perhaps the contribution of an overzealous immigration agent) di Gioia headed over to the Sand Bar for lunch, where they'd planned to meet Mom and her friend May. She had thought it would be an ideal place for May and Dominick to meet.

Marco remembered his first date with Ella, five years earlier. It, too, was at the Sand Bar; she was beautiful, and he'd fallen in love with her before dessert. It was a sunny May afternoon; they had met the night before at a cocktail party hosted by a mutual friend. He had asked her to join him for lunch the following day, and she accepted. My mother wore a long, flowing white skirt and a teal blouse that set off her remarkable green eyes; the lucid blue of the Gulf of Mexico shimmered at her back.

They covered the routine subjects: her teaching job, his architectural work, family issues, et cetera, and before long, the conversation went much deeper. They spoke of the pain they'd each been through—she had lost her firstborn son to the war in Vietnam when he was eighteen years old. His wife had died five years earlier, after a long battle with cancer. Both of them had experienced the kind of pain that hurts so deeply you feel as though it will never go away. They spoke of the love in your heart that keeps you going, and although you are forever changed, you recover and move forward—baggage and all.

- Howard Greenleaf, 4:00 p.m.:

Driving back from his brother's house in Sheepshead Bay, my father was thinking how good it was to see them. His brother, Robert, was happily married, and his mother, Ruth, who now lived with them, seemed to be getting along just fine. His father, Saul, had passed away four years before—and as Howard thought about it, he realized his father's funeral was the last time he had seen his son August. Four years!

- August Greenleaf, 6:00 p.m.:

Early that evening, as Bill and I headed home from my grandparents' house, traffic was very heavy. "What a mess," Bill said.

"When is it not?" I grumbled.

"Three in the morning on Tuesdays."

"And how do we know this to be true, William?"

"Because last year, when I took the red-eye back from California, we landed at Kennedy, and the drive home at three a.m. was a breeze. That's how I know this to be a *fact*, sir."

"So, you're assuming that every Tuesday is like that one Tuesday when you drove home from Kennedy in the wee hours of the morning?"

"I believe it to be a safe assumption, yes. That is, barring an accident, of course—or road construction."

"Aha, you're hedging your bet already," I said. "Not so sure, are you, that every Tuesday morning at three a.m. is clear sailing?"

We had a good laugh at our meaningless verbal sparring, and then the conversation turned to my concern about my father.

"It's been a very long time since I've seen him, Bill. I never went back to Far Rockaway, I just couldn't—too many memories. So, whenever we did get together, it was at my grandparents'—his parents' home. Being with him was always uncomfortable for me; I only went because he's my dad, but very few words of any consequence were ever exchanged between us during my visits. He loved my brother, Michael, but he—well, he didn't have much use for me. It's all so fucking sad, it truly is, William. I believe I'm the head case that I am today largely because of him."

"Augie, you're no damn head case! We just spent the day with your mom's parents in Brooklyn—I don't know many guys who would do that."

"You sound like my mother. I wish that were true, Bill, but I tell you, man, I feel anxious so much of the time—often to the point of nausea."

"Yeah, anxious," he said, "like a modern-day Casanova, collecting girlfriends like postage stamps—as a hobby."

"You know, much of that's not even my doing."

"That's right, they just fall into your lap—from out of the sky."

"For some reason, they do . . . Hey, why don't I just throw a few of them your way, buddy, okay?"

"That won't be necessary, Augie."

Sensing a serious tone in Bill's response, I doubled down. "You're right, Doctor, you're going to be making the big bucks soon enough—then they'll be all over you."

Bill was silent and looked out his side window for a very long moment; then he turned to me and said, "That's beside the point, my friend."

Something had sucked the fun out of conversational byplay. "Are you okay, man?"

Bill paused for a moment, collecting his thoughts. "I have something to tell you, Augie." He was silent for a while longer; then he said, "I know what it feels like to be anxious all the time, too, Augie—because I'm gay."

"You're gay?" It was more than a reaction, it was a sincere question—born of surprise, yes, yet seeking confirmation of what he'd just said.

"Yes, I'm gay."

"When did you find this out, Bill?"

"I've known for many years, Augie, since I was a kid. It's not something you just 'find out,' it's something you *know*—it's part of who you are. So, I've been deceiving myself for most of my life. I've been lying to you—I've been fucking lying to everyone I know. I've dated women, pretending to be someone I'm not—but I can't live that way any longer, I just can't!"

"Why didn't you say something, Bill? You could have told me, you know that."

"It's not as easy as that, Augie. It's been difficult keeping it a secret for all these years—all the lying and pretending—it sucks! It's like building a cage and locking yourself in."

"Have you told your parents?"

"Yes, last weekend—and do you know what my mother said? She said, 'I could have told you that ten years ago.' Imagine that!"

"Who else knows?"

"I've told most of my family. Except for them, you're the only one."

"Look, man, I love you like a brother—you are a brother to me, and I'm just so proud of you now. There's nothing more to hide—shit, man, there never was anything to hide—I just want you to be happy."

"I am, Augie, I truly am—especially now that I'm out."

"Well, you can forget about you and me hooking up," I said. "That just ain't gonna happen."

"You're right about that, Augie. Frankly, you're just not my type."

- Ella Greenleaf Santoro, 8:00 p.m.:

It was a busy and productive Sunday, Ella thought, as she stepped out of the shower in their beautiful Dunedin, Florida, beach home. It had all of Marco's signature touches, the work that made him a very popular area architect. It was certainly the kind of home that she never dreamed she'd be living in—tasteful, spacious, efficient, and comfortable—and she never dreamed she'd be so lucky as to meet a man like Marco, either. He was a gentle, kind, and loving man—talented, humble, well principled, and supportive of her in every way. He was three years older than she, fifty-five, graying, and elegant—the kind of man that people noticed and respected.

"Well, I believe that went very well today," she said as she slipped into bed and cozied up to the man who had convinced her that true love between a man and a woman was possible, and then had made it happen . . . to her, of all people! That night they made love, and after their lovemaking, she'd had that wonderful feeling again—the feeling of being truly blessed—and then she cried. He asked if she was all right; she nodded, and he wiped away her tears, knowing that these were tears of joy. Then he kissed his beautiful wife good night—a long, tender, innocent kiss that brought their souls into alignment.

- Howard Greenleaf, 11:30 p.m.:

He sat, despondent, at the kitchen table, all alone in his seventh-floor apartment; the gun lay on the table in front of him. Staring at it then, he thought again of his son Michael; it had been over fifteen years. His boy, had he lived, would have been thirty-four years old. Howard should have intervened—should have stepped up and not allowed him to follow through with that dreadful decision. He was just a boy—a remarkable boy with a very bright future ahead of him—but a boy nonetheless. The guilt consumed him still, and he knew he would never be able to put it to rest. Had she stayed, maybe she could have helped him, but she was gone now—had been gone for many years, and would never be coming back.

He thought of the war—his war. He had come close, very close to death on a couple of occasions. Once, they rolled into a small, abandoned village that had been bombed out by the Allies. They secured the village, and some of the tank crews were assigned to assist the infantry in mopping up. My father and several other armored troopers were organized into a search party and ordered to go through the structures that remained standing to ensure that they were clear of the enemy. He'd climbed the steps of a two-story stone house, rifle at the ready. At the head of the stairs, he turned to his right and entered the first of the two rooms on that floor.

He heard him before he ever saw him—the German soldier who was hiding in the far corner of the dark room. The soldier had attempted to fire, but his rifle had jammed. My father fired into the shadows in the direction of the sound; the soldier gasped and gurgled, and fell silent. Keeping low, he moved quickly to the soldier's position and saw that he was just a boy like himself. Looking up at him, the dying boy murmured, "Hilf mir, bitte hilf mir." My dad turned away and cautiously moved on to the next room. He would find out later, when he asked a sergeant who spoke fluent German, that the words spoken by the dying soldier were "Help me, please help me." Seeing my father's eyes fill up, the sergeant patted him on the shoulder and said softly, "Best to forget about it, soldier."

That close; he had been that close to avoiding all of this—the pain, the guilt, the hopelessness, and the misery of a life without meaning. He folded the note he had written earlier in the day and put it in an envelope, which he then marked: "For My Mother and Brother." He looked for a long time at the revolver lying dormant on the table and wondered at its purposeful design, its precise, blue-black metal parts. Then he picked it up, loaded the cylinder with six .38-caliber rounds, and retracted the hammer. Using his left hand to steady the piece, he carefully placed the muzzle in his mouth. He tilted the short barrel upward, toward his brain, and with his right thumb—gently, almost lovingly—pressed the trigger.

Chapter 22

Fly Away, Little Bird

My father's suicide brought on the same anguish I had felt with the death of my brother, Michael, nearly fifteen years before—a noxious mixture of pain and guilt. Voices in my head were telling me that I hadn't done enough, that I'd let him down. How could I have allowed so many years to go by without ever visiting him? Those who loved me (especially those who had known my father) stood by me and helped me fend off the demons of self-doubt. They embraced and comforted me, and I welcomed their love—craved it. I accepted their support with gratitude and listened patiently to their arguments against the destructive narrative I'd concocted and had myself believing. But I knew then that I would never forget him and that only time would bury my sadness.

Mom flew in the next morning and attended my father's funeral, which was held that afternoon in Brooklyn. Jessica and William were there, of course, helping me to maintain focus and to manage the emotions that came over me in random waves. Michael's high school girlfriend, Cynthia Brophy, by then Cynthia Rogers, was also there with her husband, George. The Rogerses had two boys and were living in Morristown, New Jersey. Cynthia and I had stayed in touch with each other throughout the years since my brother's death—we had never allowed the friendship we'd built through Michael to die.

Later that afternoon, after the mourners had left the cemetery, I drove my mother to LaGuardia Airport for her flight back to Florida. Mom had some time to spare, so on the way to the airport, we stopped at a small restaurant in Forest Hills, where we sat down for a quiet dinner. Hardly a word had been spoken between us that day; neither of us had known what to say.

So, we sat in silence for a minute or two until my mother said, "Quite a day, Augie."

"Yeah, quite a day, Mom."

"You know," she said, "leaving your father was the right thing for the two of us to do, August. I've felt that way from the very first, but I never imagined that our leaving would have led to this. My God if only he'd sought help, or met someone else—someone who might have looked after him better than I was willing to do."

"There was nothing you could have done about that, Mom, and staying with him would have sunk us both."

Mom sighed. "I suppose you're right about that, Augie."

"As I think back on it now, I see he was more an adversary than a father to me. He was a father to Michael but never to me—except in the biological sense. In the years since we left, while I've felt sorry for him, I haven't missed him—I really haven't thought all that much about him."

With uncharacteristic candor, Mom said, "I'm sure he never thought much about you, either, Augie, that's just how he was."

"I agree, but you know something, Mom—whether I like it or not, part of him lives on in me."

"August, you're nothing like your father."

"How can I not be?"

"Believe me, August . . . nothing!"

For the next hour or so, the two of us sat eating, talking, and trying to make some sense of it all—as if any sense could be made. Mom insisted on paying the bill, and before getting up from the table, she said something even more uncharacteristic of her:

"What a fucking day, huh, August Nathaniel?"

"What a fucking life," I said.

We continued on to LaGuardia, where I saw my mother off—back to Florida and her new, happier life.

In those days, I smoked a lot of weed, but I wouldn't say that at the time it was a bad thing. It quelled my anxiety and helped to open spiritual doors for me (although some of those doors were subsequently slammed in my face). I was high when I first meditated and seriously contemplated the larger questions of life. Was there a God who acted in history, as my Jewish forebears believed? If so, did he make himself known to me by allowing me to see two houses—one in Far Rockaway, the other in Gettysburg—that no one else could see? What was the significance of November 26, 2013? Would I meet him then? Was it he looking out at me from the second-story window of the house by the bay?

I was searching for my religious identity then; I studied Torah and read extensively in Jewish mysticism; I read the Bible, both Old and New Testaments, and the exegetical works of Christian authors; I read Hindu texts and went on week-long yoga retreats. I was baptized in my midthirties but eventually came to an understanding of the world that might be considered more in line with Buddhist principles. Yet it was in my twenties, at the cool end of a roach, that my spiritual flame was kindled, and although it has waxed and waned over the years, it has never been extinguished.

Karen Binder and I met on a Saturday afternoon in October. Jessica and her fiancé, Kenneth, had recently broken up, and knowing she had been down in the dumps over the past few weeks, I called her to ask if she'd like to join me for some fresh air. So, we decided to go to a popular local orchard and farm market to have a snack, enjoy the crisp New England autumn day, and perhaps pick up some fresh produce and a few pumpkins for Halloween.

She and Kenneth had been together for two years, and Jess really loved the guy. Kenneth, a graduate of the Yale Law School, now an attorney in New York City, had recently proposed to her, but no sooner had the echo of his proposal faded than he decided to break it off. It seems his firm, Monroe, Aldrich & Schwarz, LLC, about that time had hired a new attorney—a divorce lawyer with long legs and other qualifications who had eyes for Kenneth, and (as it turned out) he had the same for her. Why anyone would want to break up with Jessica, though, was beyond me, and I told her so. "Augie," she said when I picked her up at her East Haven apartment, "I'm done with men—finished! I think I'll start dating women, they're far more reliable."

During our visit to the farm market, we got some mulled cider and a couple of apple cider donuts and took a seat at an empty picnic table—one of a half dozen or so set out for customers to enjoy their food al fresco. Jess was in the process of venting her anger when she suddenly stopped herself and said, "Don't look now, Augie, but there's a real hot chick sitting with another girl to your right; she's checking you out."

"Maybe she's checking you out," I said.

"No, she's got her eyes on you; every time I look away, she stares at you. She probably thinks I'm your girlfriend and doesn't want to be rude. Why don't you go over and say hello?"

"No, Jess, I'm with you."

"Augie, go on over—it's not like we're on a date or anything."

"Maybe the two of them are on a date," I said.

"I don't think so," Jess said. "Not from the way she's staring at you."

"I can't, Jess, it would be rude."

"Do her good looks intimidate you, August Greenleaf?"

"No, they do not," I said a little too emphatically. With that, Jess abruptly got up and made a beeline to the other table. She talked with the two women for a minute or so while I pretended not to notice. Then, as Jess took a small, spiral notepad and pen out of her purse, I looked over and locked eyes with the "hot chick," as Jess had described her. This was Karen Binder—soon to be my bride.

Jess had given Karen my phone number, and she called me that night.

We talked for nearly an hour and made a date for the following Saturday evening. I picked her up at her Old Saybrook apartment, and we drove to a local fish house. There, over my broiled scallops, baked potato, and house salad, I fell in love. She was gorgeous: blond and blue-eyed, with a slender but shapely figure. She told me she'd been married once before, but he had cheated on her, which brought her brief marriage to an unceremonious and unlamented end. She was twenty-six years old, she said, and told me she worked at a travel agency. Three weeks and four dates later, Karen told me she had fallen madly in love with me. It was, she said, a combination of my good looks and even better lovemaking.

In front of a gathering of twenty-five guests, we were married on January 15, 1984—less than three months after we'd met and a week after my thirtieth birthday. Marrying Karen would prove to be the stupidest thing I'd ever done in my adult life—and that's saying something! My friends had tried to stop me, calling my attention to some of the more obvious warning signs; even one of Karen's friends told me that she was not the right woman for me. I ignored them all. Love can be blind, but it's a temporary blindness. In my case, I was so dazzled by Karen's beauty that I was unable to see anything else—for almost three days.

It all started on our honeymoon in Acapulco, with a temper tantrum over my refusal to rent minibikes for the two of us—which had nothing to do with a fear of minibikes; I just lacked all confidence in the drivers of Acapulco. "No," I said, "I don't trust these Mexican drivers—let alone the drunken tourists—with our lives. I'd rather not return to Connecticut in a box, thank you very much . . . and why are you yelling at me?"

Karen had gone ballistic. "What the fuck is wrong with you? If only I'd known that I was marrying a fucking wimp . . . " et cetera, et cetera.

There are a couple of lines in a postmodern song recorded by the Talking Heads in 1992 entitled "Once in a Lifetime," where David Byrne sings (or rather recites), "This is not my beautiful house . . . This is not my beautiful wife." These words express exactly how I was feeling when we got back home to Branford. My normally peaceful house—the house I'd lived in since the age of sixteen, the house my mother had given me when she moved to Florida—was suddenly anything but peaceful. It was now inhabited by a madwoman. This was no longer "my beautiful house," it was a psychiatric ward, and Karen was no longer "my beautiful wife," she had become a shrill, maniacal harpy!

January was drawing to a close, and my mood had soured with the weather. I'd lie awake on the couch during those cold, lonely nights and say to myself something very much like what Byrne says (sings?) in that song: "My God! What [the fuck] have I done?" After toying with fantasies of homicide in its various forms, my musings would be mollified, and I'd eventually arrive at the realization that, one way or another, this mistake of a marriage would soon come to an end—legally; it might cost me, but it would be over and done with. Only then would my mind be sufficiently at peace that I'd be able to get some sleep.

On May 17, 1984, exactly five months into our ill-fated marriage, Karen was at work, and I was at home with the flu. I had a headache, and my search for Tylenol in the medicine cabinet turned up empty. Then I remembered that Karen had once gone into one of her night table drawers for Tylenol. I opened the top drawer and rummaged around; I didn't find the Tylenol, but I noticed an opened envelope marked "Karen." I removed the neatly folded note inside. It read:

> *Dear Karen,*
>
> *Come fly away with me today! Let's not waste another moment, my dearest, life is too short. From that first moment I laid eyes on you, the day I sat at your desk, I knew you had to be mine. The afternoons of lovemaking at the hotel were incredible, and I know they were for you also, my sweet lover.*
>
> *I know it's a bit complicated—you made a mistake several months ago, but mistakes can be rectified, and I have the means to resolve*

that problem for you. I promise you, my dear, that you will no longer be sitting behind a desk, booking trips for others—and I'll see to it that you'll never have to work another day for the rest of your life—you'll be traveling with me.

Sincerely, Bruce

P.S. I'm coming in next week to book a trip for two to Puerto Rico—please say that you'll join me and fly away for a week in the sun.

Karen arrived home at 7:30 that evening; I was at the kitchen table waiting for her. When she entered the room, I motioned her to an empty chair. "Please, have a seat—my dear," I said.

"How are you feeling today, August, any better?"

"Why, yes, I am doing wonderfully well. Thank you for asking."

"That's good."

"Karen, I have a question . . . "

"S-sure," she said tentatively.

"Have you planned any trips lately? Say, to Puerto Rico? Like, maybe, a trip for two?"

"What the fuck are you talking about?" she shouted.

"Fly away, little bird!" I roared. "Fly away—your lover awaits you in the sun!"

She looked at me without expression as I said, in a very quiet and controlled voice, "Now pack your things and get the fuck out of here—as fast as humanly possible."

"Fuck you, August!"

"No, Karen, fuck you—and why are you still here—do I have to say it again? Pack your things and get the fuck out of my house!"

The divorce was finalized in August—and apart from my own legal fees, it didn't cost me a dime!

Chapter 23

Anna Sokolova—January 28, 1986

It was 11:00 a.m., and I was already behind on my new Guilford route. Having delivered the last of my next-day air packages before the 10:30 time commitment, and after making several business stops, which counted as morning deliveries, I parked my package car near the front of a two-story duplex that matched the address on the largest package I had on the truck that day. The address label read:

Mrs. Anna Sokolova
17 Sharon Street
Guilford, CT 06437

The box sitting in the rear of the truck was marked WGT: 115 LBS. It was not only heavy, it was also quite bulky. As I approached the modest building on the front walk, I was hoping that Mrs. Sokolova lived on the first floor, not the second. I had mistakenly left the UPS hub without a hand truck that day, so there was absolutely no way I was going to lug this monster up a flight of stairs by myself. I climbed the five steps leading to the front porch, and to the right of the front door, I found two doorbells: the bottom button read Miller, the top, Sokolova. This was not a good sign.

I pressed the top button and waited. I rang again, and I waited some more. I was becoming increasingly frustrated—I had 125 stops on the truck, and this single stop was already taking much too long. I was just about to ring a third time when the front door opened. An older woman wearing a yellow apron greeted me cheerfully. "Good morning, you must be bringing my bedroom bureau."

I nodded. "Yes, I believe so; the box is pretty big—115 pounds."

"Could you please bring it up to my apartment? I'm on the second floor. It would be greatly appreciated."

I quickly surveyed the stairway leading up to her apartment and saw that the steps were high and steep and the staircase quite narrow. "Mrs. Sokolova," I said (hoping for a compromise), "this package is far too heavy for me to bring up to the second floor without assistance, and at this time there are no other drivers available to help me. May I please leave it here on your front porch?"

"My son, Alex, lives with me; he's upstairs—can he help you?"

"Yes, absolutely," I said. "It would be great if he could."

"Sasha, Sasha!" she called up the stairs.

From beyond the open door of the apartment, a high male voice answered, "One moment, Mother, I'll be right down."

By then, I was already a little anxious—what was I getting myself into? Two minutes later, a small, thin, balding man who appeared to be in his fifties came down the stairs. I neither needed nor wanted a formal introduction, but Mrs. Sokolova insisted on it. "This is my son, Alex Sokolova—and your name is . . . ?"

"August," I said, and I thought to myself, *Jesus Christ, lady, I'm not dating your son, I just need him to help me carry this goddamn box up to your apartment.*

Alex and I shook hands; then Mrs. Sokolova extended her hand to me and said, "My name is Anna." Regretfully, I recognized the worst side of my nature beginning to show itself—which often happened when I became anxious—and I thought, *What the fuck!*

Let me pause here for a moment to provide the reader with a brief description of what it means to be a UPS package car driver. When you take a job as a driver for UPS, you have to be prepared for the intense pressure that comes with it. Just the day before, I was summoned to the manager's office to answer for a delivery problem that had purportedly occurred that day—total bullshit. It took almost an hour to convince him that there was no problem after all. So, understandably, I was already feeling somewhat put-upon when I arrived at Mrs. Sokolova's door. ANG

Alex was gamely following me out to the truck when Mrs. Sokolova shouted to him from the house, "Sasha, you're still wearing your slippers. Please go upstairs and put on your shoes and socks."

"What the flying fuck! A middle-aged mama's boy—jeez," I muttered to myself, turning toward the truck to avoid being heard. After what seemed like forever, Alex came out again, wearing shoes and socks just as his mother had instructed him to do. "Good boy, Alex," I mumbled.

I slid the box to the edge of the open tailgate. With little faith that Alex was up to the task, I told him to grab the opposite corners at his end of the box and said that I would do the same at my end. I instructed him that, on the count of three, we were both to lift, and with the clearest, firmest voice I could muster (short of pique), I counted out, "One, two, three!" and a groan came out of Alex that (I swear) could be heard halfway down the block. More impressive, though, was that he was actually holding up his end of the damn box. Shuffling along, the two of us inched the box up the walk toward the porch. We were about halfway there when Alex pleaded to put it down. "Break, break—I need a break," he gasped.

"Okay, Alex," I said. By that time, I was feeling sorry for him, and as we set the box down on the front walk, Mrs. Sokolova, from her perch on the porch, turned to me and said, "Alex has a lung condition—asthma; please be patient with him."

A minute later, Alex said he was ready, and again I counted to three. As we lifted, there was another groan from Alex, this one even louder than the first. It was the equal in every way of the sound weight lifters make when they snatch prodigious weights from gym floors and lift them over their pointed heads—and it cast this timid little man from whom that Olympian sound had emanated in an entirely new light. This time we made it to the porch steps, and again, Alex petitioned for a break.

Before we lifted the package for a third time, I instructed Alex to back up the front porch steps while holding onto the box. "The brunt of the weight will be on my end, Alex—the bottom end." We made it up and onto the porch, and noticing that his mother was nowhere to be seen, I signaled Alex to set the box down again. I glanced at my watch. I had already spent nearly twenty minutes at this stop.

Mrs. Sokolova reappeared carrying two glasses of orange juice and gave each of us a glass. "Here," she said, "take a little break, boys—that box must be very heavy." Then she reached into the side pocket of her apron and took out an inhaler, which she placed in Alex's hand. "Go on, Sasha, take a couple of puffs—I heard you wheezing." After Alex had taken two pronounced puffs from his inhaler, and we had both finished our orange juice, we got back to the task at hand, which (it seemed to me) had begun to resemble a freaking comedy routine.

"One step at a time, Alex, nice and easy now," I said. The orange juice was having its effect on the dopamine level in my brain; my mood was becoming lighter, and it began to dawn on me that life was just too short not to appreciate the humor in this encounter with these very nice but very strange people.

We lifted again on the three count, and Alex followed my instructions attentively as we readied ourselves for the thirteen steep steps that led up to the Sokolovas' apartment. We got through the outside door into the foyer, and we'd made it up two or three steps when Alex blurted out, "Down, put it down!" I heard but (due to the size of the package) was not able to see Mrs. Sokolova, who was at the head of the stairs, micromanaging her son's ascent. "Easy, easy, Sasha, don't strain; watch out for your hands. Stop when you need to, honey."

We made it up a few more steps, and Alex was starting to wheeze again. Urgently, he declared, "August, I have to drop it!" Then, as if this whole situation were not already weird enough, I heard Mrs. Sokolova from up the stairs exclaim in a panicky voice, "My baby, my baby, Sasha! Daddy, please be careful with my baby!"

For a fleeting moment, I felt a twinge of sadness for this odd little family—but mostly I felt the weight of that large package as I strained to keep it from sliding down the stairs and killing me. While I struggled to hold the box steady, Alex got his second wind. This time we made it up another four or five steps; we were about three-quarters of the way to the top when, sweating profusely and aching from the weight I'd been supporting for the past several minutes, I gasped, "Come on, Alex! Just a few more steps to go!"

When we finally reached the second-floor landing, an intense feeling of joy and relief came over me. We made it; we'd climbed our Everest! I pushed the box into the apartment, and returning to the hallway, I said with unalloyed pleasure, "We did it, Alex; way to go, baby!" I reached out and gave him a big hug.

Surprised and a little confused by my show of emotion, Alex stood still and received my embrace stiffly. After an awkward moment, he said quietly, "Thank you very much, August."

Then it was Mrs. Sokolova's turn. As I hugged her, I had no idea that there would be many more hugs between us in the years to come; how could I possibly have known? I glanced at my watch again; it was 11:35 a.m.

Mrs. Sokolova said, "Please, August, come in and sit for a few minutes; I'll get you some more orange juice." As she showed me into the living room, I knew I was already way behind schedule—but what the hell! Anyway, her television was on, and it appeared that the space shuttle *Challenger* was about to blast off. This was to be the second orbiter of NASA's space shuttle program, and its crew would include the first civilian to leave Earth's atmo sphere and fly into space.

Her name was Sharon Christa McAuliffe. Christa, a social studies teacher at Concord High School in New Hampshire, had been selected from more than eleven thousand applicants who participated in NASA's Teacher in Space Project. She was expected to conduct a few experiments and teach two lessons from the space shuttle. The mission had captured the imagination of millions of Americans, including me, and I was glad for this unexpected opportunity to see the launch.

It was perfect timing; just as I sat down in an easy chair, the spokesman at

NASA launch control announced, "T-minus ninety seconds and counting." Together, the three of us watched the historic liftoff on their twenty-five-inch Zenith color TV. Then, only seventy-three seconds into the flight, came the heartbreaking explosion that turned our mood from confidence and pride into apprehension, horror—and grief. With tears in our eyes, we regarded each other in disbelief.

After several minutes of silence, I got up to leave, and Anna said, "They're going to their homes now, August. They're going to their homes."

Chapter 24

The Night Shift

Some things in life just happen—there is no plan for them; they evolve organically and then present themselves unexpectedly. Such was my short-lived side job as a male prostitute. Please, reader, try not to judge me; what seemed like a good idea at the time turned out to be (you should pardon the expression) a mixed blessing. What I gained in lucre and pleasure of the flesh was *almost* offset by the rolling cycle of anxiety and drug use that this episode engendered.

It all began in the merry month of May, 1987. I'd been on my Guilford route for several months and had made regular deliveries to the Shelter Brook Condominiums. Shelter Brook is an upscale retirement community, more than 250 luxury dwelling units within its gates. As their UPS deliveryman, I had become acquainted with many of the residents rather quickly—they all get a lot of packages.

One of the things you learn early in the delivery business is that retirees like to talk. For them, time is such a plentiful commodity that they'll seize on any opportunity to engage in small talk, or better still—gossip. The residents of Shelter Brook were no exception; they could not have been more gregarious. One resident in particular was perhaps a little too friendly.

Her name was Gabrielle Bonnet. I learned that her last name was to be pronounced Bon-*nay* when she corrected my pronunciation the first time we met. Monoglot that I was, I had pronounced it as you would a hat worn by ladies of the Victorian era. Anything but Victorian, Gabrielle was a superbly fit and attractive, modern woman in her midfifties. She was born in France and had come to the States in her late twenties to marry a wealthy American businessman, eighteen years her elder, named Wilson Carter. They lived in New York City for twenty-four years before Wilson sold his business. Having retired here in Connecticut, the sixty-nine-year-old Wilson didn't last long—within a year, he died on the tennis court of a massive heart attack.

A year after that, having settled her husband's estate, Gabrielle decided to reassume her maiden name and "to screw as many good-looking young men as possible before becoming a wrinkled-up and proper old lady." She spoke fluent English with an appealing French accent. Still, I was a bit surprised when, one afternoon during a delivery, she said matter-of-factly, "August, nothing would please me more than to rent you for a night. How much?"

Half-jokingly, and equally matter-of-factly, I said, "Two hundred dollars."

"It's a deal," she said, extending her right hand to shake on it. And just like that, I had a second job—"moonlighting," you might say. She explained that it had been a longtime fantasy of hers to pay a handsome young man for sex and to have him "devour" her. "August," she said, "I believe I could have seduced you and had you gratis, but I just had to fulfill this gigolo fantasy of mine, and you strike me as the perfect candidate for the role."

We exchanged phone numbers and settled on Friday, three days later, as the day of our rendezvous. All of this was done so smoothly that I was beginning to think I'd not been wise—when my phone rang.

"August," she said, even before I spoke, "take me from behind, gently at first, and slowly build it up to where you are fucking me hard—so hard that you make my eyes pop out of my skull." In the next call she said, "August, take me into the shower, soap me up, and fuck me there." And on another call—this one left on my message machine—"August, I'd like you to tie me up and . . . " I hung up and reflected on just how far I had come from the frightened boy I once was—but maybe this was a little too far. I was in over my head, and I knew it.

Whatever she was looking for, it wasn't me. I was good at lovemaking; I had learned by experience with many willing and patient partners. I listened to my lovers and responded; it pleased me to please them. But I was not the kind of lover to fuck a woman so hard as to make her "eyes pop out of her skull." That was not my style; I made love tenderly, attentively—I made love in a way that (as many of my partners would tell me afterward) felt like more than mere sex, that felt, well, like making love—and that pleased me.

When I arrived at the Shelter Brook Condominiums security gate in my 1984 Dodge Daytona, the security guard recognized me immediately, since I had been coming through that gate in my package van for the past three or four months. His name was Stan; he normally worked the day shift, so I didn't expect to see him on this particular evening. As it happened, Stan was covering for a coworker, and he loved to chatter. Not surprisingly, he was full of questions. "Nice car, Augie. Who're you here to see?"

"One fifty-two B," I said.

"Why, that's the Frenchie, Ms. Bonnet—ahem, excuse me—Madame Bon-*nay*," he said sarcastically. "You fucking her, Augie, you dirty dog, you?"

"No, Stan, I'm not having sex with Ms. Bonnet—Gabrielle and I are just friends."

"You can't bullshit a bullshitter, Augie. Come on, tell me—you're fucking her, aren't you? How is she, Augie? She's great in bed, I'll—"

"Stan!" I cut him off—I was running out of patience. "Please ring her and open the gate for me. Please! Thank you very much."

It had come to me during my fifteen-minute drive to Gabrielle's condo that I should stick to what I'm good at—that I should make tender love to this lovely older woman, and if she wasn't happy, then no problem, I'd give her her money back. It was just that simple.

So, I proceeded on that basis, and at no time did she ask for anything more. "August," she said with that pretty little French accent of hers, "that was incredible—you are incredible." The following morning, before I left, I offered to return her $200, but she wouldn't hear of it. Instead, she patted me on the ass and said, "It's yours, *mon cher*, you've earned it. Now, let me see if I can bring in more business for you."

On Tuesday of the following week, Gabrielle called and said, "August, I believe I have another client for you."

Another client, I thought—was this woman now my French pimp? "Gabrielle, please. Thank you—but no thanks!"

"August," she said, "don't be silly. Carolyn is divorced, and she's very beautiful. I've already told her all about you; she wants to know if you're free on Friday night."

"Actually no, I'm going out with some friends, and I'm not really interested, but thanks again."

But she persisted, and finally, reluctantly, I caved. "August," she said, "there will be a special surprise for you."

"Please, Gabrielle, no surprises; I can't do this if there are any surprises. I don't like surprises."

"August, trust me. You're going to like this surprise."

I found it nearly impossible to refuse this woman; she was as fluid as water and as determined as ice—but I must admit, I loved it, and why not? I was still in my twenties (although by then pushing thirty) and unattached; these women were attractive and experienced, and they were paying me $200 for a night's work—if you could call it that.

Friday evening, when I showed up at the door of Carolyn Larsen's condo, I was pleasantly surprised. She was an exquisite woman, tall and slim; she wore a low-cut, cerulean-blue silk blouse over a beige, knee-length pencil skirt and matching leather pumps. I had been told by Gabrielle that she was fifty-eight, but she could have easily passed for a woman in her forties. As I came through the door of her unit, she immediately handed me an envelope and said, "This is for you, August. We might as well get the business part of our evening out of the way now, don't you think?"

I nodded, and she motioned me to sit on the couch so we could become acquainted. We talked for ten minutes or so until my curiosity got the best of me. I was afraid to ask, but I did anyway. "Gabrielle said that there'd be a surprise this evening; I'm hoping she was mistaken. Please tell me there will be no surprises, Carolyn."

"Oh, but there will be a surprise, August, a big surprise."

Oh, God, I thought. I could feel my heart rate double; what kind of surprise did this woman have in store for me, and what had I gotten myself into?

She got up from the couch, took my hand, and led me down a wide hallway. We stopped at a closed door, which, as I was about to learn, was Carolyn's bedroom. I half closed my eyes, not sure what to expect; she turned the doorknob and, like a game show host, announced, "Now, let's find out what's behind Door Number One!" She opened the door wide, and standing there before me was the gloriously naked (save for a pair of open-toed slippers with four-inch heels) Gabrielle Bon-*nay*!

Chapter 25

The House on Sharon Street

With Karen Binder out of my home and out of my life, I was a free and happy man. I borrowed the epithet that Traveling Bruce had used for me in his note and, turning it around, dubbed Karen "the Mistake." I vowed then never to speak her name again . . . and until just now (when it hardly matters), I never have. I also vowed never to remarry; but as the reader will soon learn, I reneged on that one.

By that fall, I had been on the Guilford route for nearly two years, and for several months, I'd been keeping an eye on a rather curious house on Sharon Street, the same dead-end street where the Sokolovas lived. The house was situated at the very end of the street, nestled into the woods. There was no driveway leading to the house, no street number, nor any mailbox for that matter. As far as I could determine, the house never received mail or package deliveries, and I never saw anyone enter or leave the property. Yet it was in surprisingly good repair. Oddly, the house seemed to face away from Sharon Street; from the rear, it appeared to be a Victorian or Gothic-style home—at least a hundred years old—painted a dark blue-gray, with cream-colored trim. On the other side of the house, opposite Sharon Street, were only deep woods.

One of the many duties of a UPS driver is to make a delivery attempt for every package that is on your truck. If, for instance, you find a package on your truck that hadn't been loaded in the proper sequence, then even if you've already passed that address on your route, you must return on the same day and attempt to deliver it.

Toward the end of one mid-November day, I found an undelivered package for an address on Sharon Street. It was dusk and getting dark quickly, as autumn afternoons do. So, I returned to Sharon Street, and after making the delivery (to a very nice young couple at 32 Sharon), I drove to the dead end of the street, where normally I'd just turn around and head back to the main road. On this particular evening, though, the old Victorian, illuminated by my headlights, eerily beckoned to me. I was consumed by curiosity, so I decided to investigate.

I stepped down from my package car, and with my flashlight in hand, I groped my way through the woods, toward the front of the house. It was dark by then, and I was glad to have the flashlight, especially in the woods. Goose bumps covered my arms, even under my UPS jacket. When I reached the house, I called out, "Hello?" But there was no reply—nor was I anticipating any. Feeling my way, I stepped carefully along the side of the house, and as I neared the front corner, it was all becoming familiar to me. I turned the corner at the front of the house, and in the flashlight's beam, I saw the wide porch I'd been expecting—and arrayed on the porch, mute and motionless, were six rocking chairs.

The weather on Monday of Thanksgiving week was cold and rainy. With Christmas fast approaching, the package volume on our trucks was picking up. I had a package that morning for Anna Sokolova, and when she said, "August, you're soaked, come in for a few minutes—have a cup of coffee and a piece of pound cake," I readily accepted.

We sat at her kitchen table, sipping coffee and exchanging pleasantries, as we had done before—and then I asked her about the house. "Anna, that old blue Victorian at the end of your street—do you know anything about it, who might live there?"

"August," she said quietly and with a look of surprise, "did Alex tell you to ask me about that house?"

"No, not at all. He's said nothing to me about it, but I find it strange that I've never had a delivery there, and in the two years I've been driving this route, I have never seen anyone in or near it. It has no mailbox or driveway, and—"

Anna interrupted me, and I watched as her eyes welled up. She placed her hand on my arm and said softly, "And you see it, August? Do you really?"

"Yes, I see it." Her reaction struck me—an expression of relief followed by tears of joy—and I understood it perfectly; I'd had the same feeling twenty years before in a small conference room in the visitors center at Gettysburg. "Yes, Anna, I do see it," I repeated, and I knew then that this old blue Victorian house at the end of Sharon Street had no other reason for being there.

We looked into each other's eyes and smiled—beautiful broad smiles. Then she cried again, and I laughed—I don't know why I laughed, but it was the heartiest, most cathartic laugh of my young life.

In the short time we had before I continued on my route, I shared with Anna as much as I could of what I knew. Then I had to go, so I got up from the table and said goodbye. We hugged, and as I walked to the door, Anna said, "Please come back after you've finished work tonight, August—seven o'clock? I'll have dinner ready when you get here." So, I hurried through my day, skipped lunch, and was home by 5:30 p.m. I took a shower, dressed, and immediately called my mother to tell her about Anna. Mom, of course, shared in my joy and asked me to call her as soon as I got back home, "no matter what time it is." I quickly confirmed with her that yes, I would be going to Grandma Rachel's for Thanksgiving, and yes, I was really looking forward to my annual visit to Florida in December. Then I left for Anna's house.

When I arrived back at the Sokolovas', Alex, Anna, and I sat down to an old-fashioned pot roast dinner. For me, as a bachelor, having a home-cooked meal like this waiting for me was a rare treat. Alex was the first to point out the "elephant in the room," but Anna stopped him. "Sasha, we will eat and enjoy our dinner first, and then we'll move to the living room to talk." Turning to me, she added, "If that's all right with you, August." With my mouth full of pot roast, I nodded my assent.

Forty-five minutes later, with dinner over, the table cleared, and the dishes rinsed and stacked in the sink, the three of us sat in the living room and talked. I reviewed with Anna and Alex everything I knew and had seen—the Far Rockaway house, the old man in the window, the note with the 2013 date on it, the house in the field below Little Round Top at Gettysburg, the story told to me and my family by the tour guide, Guy Ginter, describing a tourist named Eleanor who (several decades earlier) had told another tour guide, among other things, "Not many have this gift. You have to be born with it. You have to remember everything."

When I finished telling Anna and Alex what I knew, I went on to share my thoughts (mostly guesses) concerning what it all might mean. By then, I'd been talking for over an hour. Now it was Anna's turn.

Chapter 26

The Gift

"Yes, you have to remember everything, August, and we—you and I—certainly do. We have the gift," Anna said.

"Yes, Anna, I do: my birth, my childhood, my whole life."

"Do you recall your mother singing to you when you were a little baby—do you remember that, August?"

"Yes, I do," I said softly.

"Me too, August. I was born on March 7, 1905, in the village of Kirillov, near the lakes of Siverskoye and Dolgoye, in Vologda Oblast, a subdivision of Imperial Russia. My mother sang to me old Russian lullabies; she was such a sweet woman. She died when I was a girl—eight years old. My little brother, Leonid, and I were raised by my *babushka* and *dedushka*—my grandparents. We saw my father only occasionally; he was always working. Leonid drowned in Lake Siverskoye—he was just six years old. He was roughhousing in the lake with friends and evidently hit his head on a rock at the bottom. The other children didn't realize he was still under until it was too late. He was such a lovely little boy.

"In our village of Kirillov was the Kirillo-Belozersky Monastyr—in English it means the White Lake Monastery. It was the grandest of monasteries in all of Russia. There Dedushka became friendly with a *monakh*, a monk, named Petya. Dedushka, a mason, did stone repair and restoration inside the monastery.

Petya became a regular visitor to our home, but I don't know if he was more attracted to Dedushka's companionship or Babushka's cooking. Either way, he was a welcome and honored visitor whenever he came into our house.

"Petya taught me all about Jesus, about his love for all mankind, and how he gave himself up on the cross to pay for our sins. Babushka told Petya about my gift of memory—she said, 'Anna, tell Petya what you remember.' After I'd told him some of my many recollections, Petya shared a story with us about a very old woman who also remembered everything. This woman lived in the town of Kasimov, about 320 kilometers (200 miles) south of the monastery, where Petya himself was born and raised. This is Petya's story, as he told it to Babushka and me." Anna then proceeded to recite the story, word for word:

Her name was Irina Ivanovna Novikova. Many in town called her Ved'ma (the witch). Some of the townspeople, especially the children, stood clear of Irina Ivanovna; they said she could see visions that others could not see. There was a great big field outside her home, and the villagers reported that often she could be seen alone in the middle of that field, all by herself, speaking to the spirits.

One day, when I was a twelve-year-old boy, my curiosity got the better of me, so I walked the four kilometers to the home of Irina Ivanovna. I was not afraid; I had faith that God would protect me, no matter who or what I might encounter. When I arrived, I was surprised to find that her home was not much different from most of the other villagers' homes, and not at all what I expected a witch's house would look like. When I reached her yard, I stepped off the road, and as I cautiously made my way toward her front door, I must admit I had become a little nervous.

Just steps away from the front door, and prepared to flee at any moment, I was startled when, suddenly, the door opened. There stood a woman of about seventy years—wrinkled face, wearing a tan dress and gray wool stockings, her gray hair pulled back in a bun—in short, her appearance was quite unremarkable.

"*Dobroye utro*—good morning," she said.

"*Dobroye utro*," I replied.

"Tell me, what can I do for you, young man?"

"They say that you are a witch. I wanted to see for myself if you are."

"Who are *they*?"

"People in the village."

"Well, do I look like a witch to you?"

"Not really."

"What's your name?" she asked.

"Pyotr, but everybody calls me Petya."

"Pyotr, the rock," she said.

"Yes, rock," I said.

"My name is Irina Ivanovna. Would you like to come in and have some tea, Petya?"

"Yes, please."

Irina had a very clean and well-arranged home. We sat at her kitchen table, and she put out a plate of ginger cookies to go with the tea. When I told her that I had walked four kilometers to see her, she said, "That's a long distance to walk—why, you must have some important questions to ask of me, Petya."

"Yes, I do," I said.

"Please . . . ask."

"Some of the people say that you talk to the spirits out in the field in front of your house. Is that true?"

"Yes, it is true. However, 'spirits' is not how I would describe them, Petya. They are deceased and thus no longer in our world, but they are quite alive in theirs."

"And what world is that?"

"The next world, Petya, the life beyond the death. You see, Petya, we continue onward after we leave our bodies—this world. We are called to a special place—a familiar place, with familiar faces, some of whom walked this earth many years before us, yet they are our family, and we recognize them, regardless of how long ago they left this world. It's a home, Petya—a house with loving family and dear friends. There we will stay until summoned onward again. My family's home stands just outside, in the field in front of this little house."

"And why can you see it, while others cannot?"

"Because I have the gift, Petya," said Irina, "and if you have the gift, you see things, and you have to remember everything."

When she finished Petya's story about his encounter with Irina Ivanovna, Anna told me of how she came to be in America.

"Five years after the death of my mother, my father married a woman named Vera; she was very kind to me, and I liked her very much. When I was fifteen, my father informed my grandparents that he and his new wife were planning to emigrate to America, and that he wished to take me with them. I did not want to go, I so loved my grandparents—they had raised me, and the thought of leaving them broke my heart. But Babushka and Dedushka thought it best that I go with my father and Vera, and so, on April 17, 1920, the three of us set sail for America.

"I met Nikolai Alexeyevich Sokolova in New York when I was eighteen. He was a good man; he worked as a machinist. We were married in 1925; I was twenty years old. I miscarried twice, and then, in 1933, Alex was born. Nikolai had an older brother who lived in New Haven; he was a foreman at Winchester Repeating Arms Company. He got Nikolai a job there, and we moved to Connecticut. It was just after World War II that we bought this two-family house here in Guilford. We were quite happy here—Nikolai loved it. He passed away in 1974, and it's been just Alex and me since. After Nikolai's death, Alex and I moved up to the second-floor apartment—which is not as large as the first-floor apartment—so we'd have a little more rental income.

"I never saw a 'special house' as a child, August, as you did—at least I don't believe I'd ever seen one in Russia—you'd think I'd remember if I had. Yet less than two months after we came to Guilford from New York, on a fine Sunday afternoon, Nikolai suggested we go for a walk. So, we walked to the end of the street here, and I saw it for the first time."

"'Kolya,' I said, 'I wonder who lives there, in that big house—it's so beautiful.'

"'What's so big and beautiful, Anya?'

"'That house, right there,' I said, pointing to it.

"'What house, Anya—are you seeing things? Anna Sokolova, did you get into the vodka?' he teased and started to laugh.

"So, I grabbed his arm, and I pointed directly at it and said, 'Right there in front of you, you blind bat.'

"Nikolai grew very serious and said, 'There's nothing there but woods, my darling—are you all right?'

"The following day, after Alex got home from school, he and I took a walk to the end of the street. I pointed in the direction of the big blue house and asked him, 'Do you see where I'm pointing, Sasha? What do you see in that direction?'

"'Woods,' he told me.

"'Anything else?' I asked.

"'No, only woods, Mama,' he said.

"So, August, when you asked me earlier today about the blue house in the woods . . . " Anna began to weep. "It's been forty years—forty years of keeping this to myself. I walked back there so many times through those years—with friends, with visiting family. I would goad them by saying things about the woods—how lovely they were, for instance, especially in autumn—but never once did any of them say anything about the big blue Victorian house standing there—in my eyes, as plain as the noses on their faces. I'd havc thought I was a crazy woman if it hadn't been for Petya's story from so many years ago."

As the years of my life have gone, 1987 turned out to be one of the more transformative: I learned that Anna Sokolova and I shared a special gift that connected the two of us—an Old World woman in her eighties from the western plains of Russia and a thirty-something UPS driver born in Brooklyn—in a profound way.

On a Friday evening in October of that year, after a late dinner in New Haven, William, Jessica, and I stopped at Toad's Place, a popular destination for live music and dancing. Years before, at my father's funeral, I had introduced William and Jessica, and the three of us had since become very close friends.

That night, a local rock group named Los Tres Amigos (lead guitar, bass, and drums) was pushing the limits of the speaker system while the three of us were drinking our beer and enjoying the music from a safe distance. Suddenly, I was seized by a panic attack; I became disoriented and short of breath—my heart rate went through the roof, and I began to sweat profusely. I needed to get out of the bar and into the fresh air immediately. Meanwhile, William was talking with a preppy young man whom I took to be an acquaintance from the hospital; Jess was on the dance floor, trying to keep up with an athletic young woman who had the grace of a dancer and the power of a gymnast. Neither of them was aware of what was going on with me.

On the sidewalk outside the club, I leaned against a tree and greedily breathed in the cool evening air; my heart settled down, and I gradually came back to myself. After twenty minutes or so, I reluctantly went back into the club, in case William and Jessica were wondering what had become of me. Pushing through the reveling children of Bacchus, I spotted Jess and wended my way over to her. With the music pulsing in our ears, I shouted, "Where's the doctor?"

"Follow me," she shouted back, and grasping my hand, she pulled me toward the dance floor and pointed out William amid the dancing throng, pumping and spinning with the young man I'd seen him talking to earlier. He was obviously into it, moving unselfconsciously—uninhibited and free, as the music insisted he do. I smiled, and without a hope of being heard, I shouted at the top of my lungs, "Way to go, William!" A moment later, I noticed that Jess was back on the dance floor—she and the gymnast were dancing, with reckless abandon, directly in front of the band. I watched the two of them, transfixed, until the set ended and the music stopped. Jess planted a wet and sensuous kiss on the lips of her receptive partner and walked off the dance floor. As she approached me, she smiled and said, "Whatever is this world coming to, huh, August?"

A short while later, the three of us left the club; I had kept my panic attack to myself—that was no longer important. What was important was that I was with my two best friends in the world—both of them had come a long way, and it was clear to me that I had some catching up to do.

But the year wasn't over yet; December lay ahead, and I was soon to begin a new chapter in my life.

Chapter 27

Christmas 1987

At UPS, the weeks between Thanksgiving and Christmas Day are known as "peak season"—when all hell breaks loose in the world of Brown. During this hectic time, the saving grace for package car drivers like me are the "helpers;" drivers really wouldn't be able to do their jobs without them. When a helper is assigned to a driver, most often the two will work together throughout the peak season. Many drivers will work with a relative during this time, and it's not at all unusual for a driver to have a son or daughter as a helper.

As I was punching in on Monday morning, November 30, I was given a helper's time card and told that I was to meet my helper en route at a local supermarket parking lot at 10:00 a.m. I glanced at the time card and did a quick double take; the helper's name, as typed on the card, was Ricky Ricardo. Was this for real, I thought, or was someone playing games with me? I smiled as I heard a voice in my head announcing, in a Cuban accent, "Lucy—I'm home!"

Well, the time card was genuine, but Ricky Ricardo turned out to be nothing short of *un gran decepción*—a big disappointment. Perhaps it was my fault; maybe I shouldn't have asked him to sing "Babalú" for me on his first day on the job (I was just kidding). And possibly we'd have gotten along better had he shown up for work on either Wednesday, December 2, or Friday, December 4, preferably both. Or maybe, on Monday, December 7 (Pearl Harbor

Day), had I been a little nicer when I chewed him out for his truancy of the prior week, things might have gone more smoothly between us. And, you know, if he hadn't responded by saying, "Go fuck yourself, Jew boy, you can sing 'Hava Nagila' or some other Jew song for *me!*"—then perhaps we might have been able to salvage our relationship. Alas, Ricky Ricardo had left me no choice but to end it all, right then and there.

"Ricky Ricardo," I said, "to borrow a line from Franklin Delano Roosevelt: Today is a date which will live in infamy—you're fired!"

"You can't fire me," Ricky Ricardo shouted. "You're not a supervisor."

"That's true, Ricky Ricardo," I said, "but what I can do is tell you to get the fuck off my truck—right here, right now!" That was the last I ever saw of Ricky Ricardo. I worked the rest of that day without a helper and finished at 11:00 that evening.

The following morning, I was handed a new helper's time card; this one bore the name Christina Esposito. I was told that Christina was a college student, that she had worked peak season the year before, and that she was a very good worker. I checked to see which driver she had been assigned to the prior year, and before he headed out on the road, I asked him why—if she was so good—he wasn't using her again this season. The driver, Kevin, told me that his son was working with him this year and said, "Chris was an excellent helper—I'm sure she'll do a great job for you, Augie, and she wears the brown pretty well, if you know what I mean." He gave me a smile and a wink and stepped up into his package car.

On that second Tuesday of December, I learned Kevin had not been lying. This young woman, Christina, knew how to work, and she was certainly attractive—but beyond that, she had a genuinely winning personality. During that peak season, we worked together for a total of twelve days, averaging ten hours per day—ample time to get to know a person.

Christina was twenty-four years old and a third-year law student at Western New England University in Springfield, Massachusetts, concentrating in criminal law. She had done her undergraduate studies at the University of Connecticut in Storrs. When not at school in Springfield, she lived at home in North Haven with her parents, John and Patty, and her live-in grandfather.

She had two older brothers: James, an electrician, and David, a New Haven cop. She loved her grandfather Alphonse and told me he was the sweetest person she ever knew. She enjoyed studying the law and was an avid reader of fiction, when time permitted. She raved about Margaret Atwood's *The Handmaid's Tale* and "craved" anything written by John Irving or William Styron. She "adored" rock music, especially Billy Joel and Bruce Springsteen, and she was a huge fan of the New York Yankees (as was I).

That peak season at UPS went by incredibly fast—good company is the best antidote for the torpor of routine. On Christmas Eve, I gave Christina a gift card to a local bookstore as thanks for her fine work in assisting me. I joked with her that she wasn't quite as good as Ricky Ricardo, though, whose major contribution had been in *not* singing "Babalú"! Then I asked her if she'd like to join me for dinner one evening after the holidays, when I got back from visiting my mother in Florida. To my delight, she accepted.

Chapter 28

Dunedin, Florida

The announcement came over the PA system in the Delta Airlines terminal at JFK International Airport: "Delta flight 246, with service to Atlanta and Tampa, Florida, has been delayed. Estimated departure time is now 7:20 p.m." A two-hour delay! I sank down in my black Naugahyde seat in the waiting area of Gate 16 and closed my eyes in frustration. When I opened them again, I saw a column of US Marines, six abreast, in camouflage gear and backpacks, marching through the concourse, past Gate 16—there must have been fifty of them. Strangely, they had no rifles, and the only sound they made was the muffled tramp, tramp of their polished combat boots on the terminal's terrazzo floor. Since I wasn't going anywhere anytime soon, I got up to follow them. As they passed me by, I saw him—on the far side of the formation, third from the rear—it was Michael. I stepped lively through the column of unresisting marines, who silently, fluidly closed ranks behind me as I moved past. But when I reached his position, I saw it wasn't Michael after all.

Stepping to the side, I looked toward the front of the column. I could see that Michael was now at the starboard end of the front rank; I had to jog to gain on him. Just as I reached him, he made a flanking movement to the right, and I followed. Suddenly we were outside the terminal on the darkened infield of an unused runway. Michael had come to a halt and was standing at "parade rest," facing south toward Jamaica Bay, which was directly in front of him. As I drew next to him, I noticed the chevron and crossed rifles on his sleeve, signifying the rank of lance corporal. The placid bay reflected beautifully the lights of the buildings of Far Rockaway in the distance.

Without turning his head, his eyes fixed on the bay and the lights beyond, he said, "See, straight ahead? That's our building, Augie, that's where we live with Mom and Dad; seventh floor. And look over there—just below and to the right, all lit up. That's the big white house by the bay! Do you see it, Augie, do you?"

"No, Michael, I don't see it," I said softly.

"But it's there, Augie. You might not see it, but it's always there—I can see it, you have to remember everything."

I woke up, dry mouthed and disoriented, and stared at the alarm clock until the display registered in my brain. It was 3:47 a.m. It took another moment for me to remember where I was—Marco and Mom's house in Dunedin, Florida. The night light in the guest room emitted a warm glow that I found restful, and through the open windows, I could hear the waves of the Gulf gently lapping the beach nearby. As they lulled me back to sleep, I thought again about my dear, dead brother. Oh, how I missed him and wished that he were here to reassure me, as he had done so often in our youth.

"Nine days, Augie, I have you for nine days," Mom said.

"You are all your mother has been talking about since Thanksgiving, August, I was beginning to get jealous," Marco said.

My mother laughed as she set a plateful of crisp bacon on the table. "Your favorite breakfast, Augie boy, pancakes and bacon," she said as she came over to my end of the table to deliver my breakfast and give me a hug. "More coffee, dear?" she asked.

"Yes please, Mom."

"So, tell me more about your helper, Christina," Mom said.

"She's a very nice person. She works hard; she's smart, attractive, kind, and funny. We were so busy that it didn't occur to me to ask her out until the last day before peak ended—but I'm glad I did."

"It's been a hard year for you, son, and you deserve some happiness."

"It sure has, Mom—I'm glad to be here with you two to say goodbye to this old year and welcome in the new one. Hey, Grandma Rachel says that you and the Italian Stallion have been working her over to get the two of them to move down here."

"Yeah—that's what she calls Marco now."

"I kinda like it, honey," Marco said. "Your mother is absolutely hilarious."

"And the thing is, she's *not* really trying to be funny," said Mom. "Try growing up with her—the woman was a holy terror. Just ask August."

"She used to scare the shit out of me. I'm still afraid of her," I said.

"Augie, tell Marco the story about the phone call from Grandma when you were in the fifth grade."

"Yeah, well, one week I played hooky from school for three days, so the school notifies Mom, who is at her wits' end with me, and she tells Grandma Rachel about what I did.

"So, the following Monday I get home from school, and Mom's not out of work yet. The telephone rings, and I answer it; it's Grandma. She says, 'August, is that you?' I say yes, and that's when all hell breaks loose.

"'August, listen to me, and listen good,' she says. 'When your mother's older brother—your uncle Mark—was a boy, he pulled some similar nonsense like you just pulled. Would you like to know what I did to him?'

"So, I say, 'Not really.'

"'Wrong answer, weisenheimer,' she barks. 'I'll tell you what I did to him. The very next morning, when he was all dressed and ready, I grabbed him by the ear and marched him all the way to the school. Three blocks we walked with me holding onto his ear. I walked him right into the classroom, and in front of his classmates, I made him apologize to his teacher and promise her that he would be a better boy and a more conscientious student. And do you know what, August?'

"I don't answer; I cannot get any words out of my mouth—I'm that scared. So, she repeats, a little louder, 'And do you know what, August?'

"'What, Grandma,' I mutter meekly.

"'From that day forward, he was a near perfect student. Would you like me to pay you a visit, August? How many blocks is it to *your* school? I'll have no problem doing the same thing for you, understand me?'

"'Yes,' I say, halfway between a gulp and a whisper.

"'Have a good rest of your day, August,' she says and hangs up. She doesn't even wait for me to say goodbye."

On Sunday, my first full day in Florida, the three of us—Mom, Marco, and I—were out on Marco's boat, *Serenity*, a 1985 Sea Ray 340 Sundancer. It was a balmy late December day, seventy-three degrees and sunny. Whenever I came down to Florida to visit my mother, I couldn't help but notice how truly happy she was. At the time of this visit, she was fifty-six years old and savoring every day of her new life. If anyone deserved to be happy, she certainly did—she had paid her dues and then some—and here she was on this beautiful boat with the two men she loved most in this world.

Marco's architectural firm was doing quite well; more and more people were moving to Florida to retire, bringing their money with them, and each year, his business grew. Mom really didn't need to work, but she loved teaching; it was the dream of a lifetime come true. These two were a contented couple and very much in love; it gave me a sense of well-being to see my mother settling so comfortably into her late middle-age years. As we sat cruising the placid Gulf, with the warm ocean breeze in our faces, my eyes filled with tears; I could barely hold them back. Mom put her arm around me as if I were a child again and said, "Are you all right, Augie?"

"Yeah, Mom," I said, "I'm just so happy for you." She put her other arm around me and gave me a big squeeze. Self-consciously, I glanced over at Marco; he was smiling from ear to ear.

Chapter 29

Christina

Christina and I dated for two full years, and in due course, we fell in love. But I was determined not to make the same mistake twice, so this time, I was taking it more slowly, trying to stay in better control of my emotions.

On a Saturday afternoon in mid-January of 1988, I drove seventy miles from Branford to Springfield, Massachusetts, for my first date with Christina. She was enrolled at the WNE School of Law and lived in an off-campus apartment she shared with two other women. I picked her up there, and we drove to the center of Springfield. I parked the car, and to use up the remaining daylight, we walked the city for an hour or so in the cold and bracing air. Just after dark, we ducked into a local pizza place, where we chatted for a couple of hours over a medium pepperoni pie and a pitcher of beer. I drove her back to her apartment, and before she got out of the car, she thanked me for the evening and told me that she'd had a wonderful time. I reached out and, gently taking her hand, assured her that I had too.

"Can I see you again next week?" I asked.

"Yes, I'd like that," she said.

"Okay, then, it's a date!" I said with a smile. Then, impulsively, and still holding her left hand, I kissed her on the lips.

A little surprised but not displeased, Chris smiled demurely and said, "Good night, Augie."

We saw each other on most Saturdays, holidays, and school breaks for the balance of the spring semester (her last at WNE). I didn't want to push our relationship too hard, knowing that every hour she spent with me instead of studying was a real sacrifice for her—and truth be told, I had other things to do myself. But I was pleased with the progress we were making, and I believed she was too.

Chris graduated from law school in May of that year and passed the Connecticut bar exam just two months later, in July. She went on living with her parents for a short time until she got her first job; by October, she and an old high school girlfriend were sharing the rent on a two-bedroom apartment on Olive Street, near the center of New Haven.

During the months when Chris and I were building our relationship, I was having long talks with Jessica and William about her. Jess had taken to Christina immediately and told me early on that Chris was the one for me—of that she had no doubt. She often joked that if Chris and I ever broke up, she would ask her out. "Don't lose her, Augie," she told me. "Keep taking it slow; give her space. She's going through a transition in her life—she needs time to think and a little room to breathe."

For his part, William wasn't so sure about the match: He had some concerns about the social disparities we might be faced with—the circles that, as an attorney, Chris would be moving in as compared with the facts of my "time-clock-punching, union-dues-paying, blue-collar work at Brown." He actually said that!

"It's a different world from yours, Augie; believe me, I don't say that to discourage you—but it just is." William could be like a mother hen, and I loved him for it. "It's a gay thing," he quipped.

So, I took both Jessica's *and* William's advice—as contradictory as it was. On one hand, I continued to move slowly, giving Christina lots of space—and on the other hand, I fretted constantly that she was much too good for me. Consequently, many months went by before Chris and I made love. It was on a beach on Nantucket Island, off the coast of Massachusetts; we both knew it was time and wanted it to happen. We talked about it for hours afterward and agreed that it was the slow cultivation of our friendship and love that made that night possible—and so very, very special. She'd fallen asleep in my arms, and I knew that she was the one I'd spend the rest of my life with. I thought of my dear brother, Michael, and remembered the words he'd spoken to me one beautiful summer afternoon on a wooded path in Bethlehem, New Hampshire: "You have to choose wisely—and you have to treat your girl with respect, Augie. Then watch—your life will be transformed."

Christina and I celebrated Christmas Eve of 1989 at her family's home in North Haven. After sharing a traditional Neapolitan meal—seven fishes, including gnocchi with clam sauce, baccalà, roasted sea bream, and so on—served with baked penne and *insalata di rinforzo* (a warm salad consisting of cauliflower, carrots, pepperoncini, et cetera, for this occasion spiced with anchovies). The fishes were followed by dried fruit and nuts—and we washed everything down with copious amounts of Lacryma Christi (a traditional white Christmas wine) and espresso. Then we settled down in the den to open gifts.

The whole Esposito family was there—Christina's parents, John and Patty; her grandfather Alphonse; her maternal grandparents, Dominic and Madeline de Luca; her older brother, James, with his wife, Andrea, and their three children, Martina, Angela, and Joseph; and her younger brother, David, his wife, Rita, and their son, Thomas.

After the last gift had been opened, and in accordance with a certain conversation I'd had with her parents earlier in the day, Christina's father announced, "Hold on, everyone, we have one last gift to open," and turning to me, he said, "The floor is yours, August."

Thus introduced, I got up from the couch where Chris and I were sitting, and turning to face her, I took a small box from the inside breast pocket of my jacket. I knelt and, with both hands, tendered the gift-wrapped box to Christina. She was caught completely by surprise, and with extreme care, she unwrapped and opened the box. As tears ran down her cheeks, I took her hand in mine and said, "Christina Esposito—will you please be my wife?"

We were married on October 6, 1990, in Christina's church, Saint Theresa, in North Haven. She was beautiful; I was proud and grateful, and we would always be true to the vows we swore that day. With open hearts, we promised to love and honor each other until death did us part. Our daughter, Melissa, was born on November 7, 1991, and (as it turned out) our little family was complete.

I loved most things about being a dad, but I did not like diapers—dirty diapers, and I cared even less for changing diapers. However, with a mixture of love and a grudging sense of duty, I changed my fair share.

Melissa's toddler years were the best years of our lives. We played with her dishes, her dolls, and her Sesame Street Farm set. We spent hours at various local children's parks, playing on the swings, seesaws, slides, carousels, and jungle gyms. Dunkin' Donuts was a favorite stop; I drank my coffee (dark, no sugar), and Melissa sipped chocolate milk through a straw while making crumbs of Dunkin's Munchkins—glazed were her favorite; they were the sweetest and made the stickiest messes. We went on hikes at a nearby state park, walking on dead leaves through wooded trails. When she got tired, she'd reach up for a piggyback ride—and I'd joyfully carry her all the way back to the car.

Christina left her job at a local New Haven law firm to be a stay-at-home mom. She raised Melissa through her first four years, until pre-K; it was then that Chris got her dream job. Always a strong advocate for equal rights, due process, and the presumption of innocence, Christina was hired by the Connecticut State public defender's office, New Haven division, as a public defender. During the four years that she was at home with Melissa, money was tight, but we made do. She was an attentive wife and mother, and although I could not have asked for anything more, I began to feel that old sense of unease growing inside me. Anxiety and depression had always had their insidious way with me, and they were never very far away, regardless of the external circumstances of my existence. My dear friend William—by then also my family doctor—was a practicing internist with an office in our hometown of Branford. He suggested I try fluoxetine and wrote me a prescription for Prozac. That helped somewhat, but when my anxiety amped up in earnest, I'd take a Valium. Over the years, William had suggested that I try psychotherapy—and I did, but it never helped all that much.

I continued to smoke a little weed, but in deference to Christina, I picked my spots, keeping it to a minimum at first. Pot was never her thing; a glass or two of Italian red wine was more to her liking. I missed it, though, and felt that I was suffering by not smoking as regularly as I'd been used to—so I smoked more. If there was any cloud hanging over my relationship with Chris, it was that I was not completely honest with her about how much marijuana I was actually using. I was afraid it would be a deal-breaker, and I couldn't bear to lose her. Both William and Jessica thought that, if it helped, it was probably all right, although they felt that my use of the drug was getting a little out of hand.

It worked for me, though; it calmed me down and mollified my anxieties. But eventually, my fears began to catch up with me, and I needed ever-increasing amounts of the drug to function—I was psychologically addicted. Naturally, I worked assiduously to keep my problem from Christina, but inevitably, one Saturday morning it all came out.

Chris and I were shopping in a local supermarket, with Melissa in the shopping cart, when an anxiety attack hit me. I suddenly felt light-headed and claustrophobic—as though I couldn't breathe. The ceiling seemed to be bearing down on me, and I raced out of the supermarket to find some sky. I was standing in the parking lot, my chest heaving, when Chris came out, with Melissa in her arms. She rushed over to me and hugged me, the baby sandwiched between us. With a furrowed brow, she asked, "Augie, what's happening?" I assured her that I was okay now that I was outside.

That afternoon, during Melissa's nap, Chris placed her hand on my cheek and said, "Augie, honey, don't think you have to hide anything from me. People have anxiety attacks—they get depressed. You're a wonderful husband and father, and you're my best friend. Please, from now on, share with me how you're feeling. I'm your wife." It occurred to me then that I'd married the Italian version of my mother. This woman loved me—how or why, I didn't know, but she did—and I loved her, more than my life.

That same evening, I confessed everything to her. I acknowledged the periodic bouts of anxiety and depression—hell, she knew about that already. I told her about my past abuse of marijuana—even my dependency on it. She looked me in the eye and said, "I just need you always to be honest, Augie." From that day forward, I was—and when I needed to smoke, I did, and she understood.

By the time the '90s rolled around, William and Jessica were well established, and in 1992, both were married. William exchanged vows with a nurse named Jeremy Sage, whom he'd met at Yale New Haven Hospital three years before. Ten years earlier, in June of 1982, on our way back from visiting my grandparents in Brooklyn, William had confided to me that he was gay. In the years that followed, he and I had many heart-to-heart conversations, some tearful, centering around his place—as a gay man and a physician—in a society that was only beginning to come to grips with the persistent fact of homosexuality. While the intervening decades have seen improvements in gay and lesbian rights—in the treatment of AIDS, for instance, and the acceptance of gay marriage—there is still room for continued understanding and goodwill. For me personally, however, when made aware that my best friend was gay, the issue was far simpler: William had become my best friend while gay, and he would remain my best friend—with all the attendant joys and sorrows, benefits and obligations—for as long as we both lived. Just as William had been the best man at my wedding, so would I be his—and in June of 1992, in a small Unitarian ceremony in Madison, Connecticut, I was honored to bear witness as he and Jeremy pledged their eternal love for each other.

I say above that William was married in 1992; in effect that's true but technically incorrect. Marriage of same-sex couples was not legal in Connecticut in 1992. At that time, the Unitarian Universalist Society was providing services for same-sex couples who wished to make public expression of their mutual love and loyalty. In October of 2005, the state instituted "civil unions" for gay and lesbian couples, which purported to afford benefits equivalent to those attendant to marriage between a man and a woman, but the law proved to be inadequate for that purpose. So, in November of 2008, Connecticut legalized same-sex marriage (only the third state to do so), and in April of 2009, William and Jeremy were "remarried"—after living together for seventeen years. ANG

Jessica, on the other hand, had moved out to the coast in 1989 and was amassing a small fortune selling real estate in Southern California. There she met a professional baseball player—a left-handed pitcher named Clint Andrews, who labored for an unaffiliated minor league franchise in Orange County. They were married in October, after the end of the 1992 baseball season. Unfortunately, the marriage didn't get much past the second inning. It seems old Clint had a problem finding home plate, and when Jessica confronted him with it, he balked—so she gave him his unconditional release. The couple separated, and just prior to opening day of the 1995 season, they were divorced. After that, as Jess liked to say, she was "a free agent."

In California, Jess had come a long way from that Connecticut waif who'd lost both her parents in a motorcycle accident and was then condemned by state authorities to continue living with her pedophilic uncle and her enabling grandmother—the very people who'd made her preteen years a living hell. But Jess was determined that nothing and nobody was going to stand in the way of her happiness. She'd willed herself through hard times to become a resilient, intelligent, and competent adult, a successful businesswoman, and a caring human being. For more than forty years, Jess was a volunteer and generous donor at her regional chapter of RAINN (Rape, Abuse & Incest National Network) in Orange County, California. Throughout her active years, working with countless teenage girls—many of whom were, like Jess herself, victims of sexual abuse in the family—she was a source of comfort, inspiration, and hope.

In the spring of 1994, I lost two of my favorite people in the world. On Friday, May 13, my mother called me with the news that Grandma Rachel had died in her sleep; she was eighty-nine years old. She was buried in a cemetery plot on Long Island that she and Josef had purchased several years before. At Rachel's funeral, Grandpa Josef said to me, "Augie, some people think that this is the saddest day of my life, but it's not; I got to spend seven decades with the only woman I ever loved—not many guys can say that. Will I miss her? Of course I will, but my memories of her will keep me going until the time comes for me to join her." (Five years later, Grandpa Josef was laid to rest there beside his beloved Rachel. I loved my grandparents dearly, and I miss them to this day.)

On a weekday evening in early June, three weeks after Grandma Rachel died, I received a call from Anna Sokolova. "August," she said, "can you come over to my house on Saturday morning at ten o'clock? I need you to accompany me to the blue Victorian house at the end of my street. I want to see the front of the house—and I want to see the porch that you once told me about."

"Are you all right, Anna?" I asked.

"Yes, August, I'm fine."

Just a week or two before, she'd confided to me that in all the times she'd seen the old house from the street, she'd never dared to approach it for a closer look, had never seen the front of the house or the porch that I'd described to her years before. She said that she was too afraid even to venture onto the grounds.

Anna's request was, for her, quite unusual; the words she used—"I need" and "I want"—almost never came out of her mouth. Although I'd detected no urgency in her tone, it seemed to me that Anna wasn't quite herself, so I thought it best that I accede, enthusiastically, to her request.

"Of course, I'd be happy to help, Anna. Saturday at ten? I'll see you then."

I arrived at Anna's house on Saturday morning as promised; the weather was fair, and I was in good spirits.

"Thank you for coming, August," she said. "I think we should set off immediately."

She explained that Alex—who was a member of a chess club that met at the local community center on Saturday mornings—had just been picked up by another member of his group and would be coming home around one o'clock in the afternoon.

The house at the end of Sharon Street was a slow fifteen-minute walk from the Sokolovas' apartment, and as we walked, Anna didn't say a word. After ten minutes or so, the house came into view, and as we approached it, she took my hand and held it tightly. When we reached the old house, we stood awhile in the street, looking at it through the trees. As we looked, Anna's grip grew tighter.

"Ready, Anna?"

"Yes, August, as ready as I'll ever be." We stepped off the street and carefully made our way through the woods to the front of the house. Before long, we were standing at the foot of seven wide wooden steps, which led up to the broad front porch. We paused for a minute or so to admire the elegance of this old Victorian building; then, slowly, we climbed the steps. As we stepped onto the porch, Anna gasped and squeezed my hand again. In a low, quavering voice, she whispered, "August! Do you see her?"

"Yes, Anna, I do."

The woman looked to be in her late thirties or early forties; she was wearing a calf-length print dress, gathered at the waist, with a form-fitting bodice, square neckline, and long sleeves. On her feet she wore long, black wool stockings and sturdy, woven bast shoes. Her only adornments were a pair of small, simple amber earrings and a plain gold wedding band that she wore on the fourth finger of her right hand. From the moment we saw her, she'd fixed her gaze on Anna. She held out her arms and spoke a few words in (what I recognized to be) Russian.

Anna let go of my hand and left my side; she took a few tentative steps toward the woman. Then, moving quickly, she fell into her arms, and they stood entwined in a long embrace. Face-to-face, and with tear-filled eyes, the two women carefully examined each other from head to toe, chattering in Russian all the while. Presently, Anna looked over at me, waved modestly, and smiled. Then she turned and walked with her mother, arm in arm, into the house, and the door slowly closed behind them.

I was so stunned by the suddenness and finality of Anna's departure from me that I lingered by the old house for another hour or so while I decided what I should do next. Initially, I had expected that Anna would soon be coming back out of the house, but as I waited, it occurred to me that the time of my visit had been arranged to coincide with Alex's chess club meeting, so that I might be there when he came home.

I hurried back to Anna's house; I mounted the front steps and ran up the stairs. When I entered the Sokolovas' apartment, I knew instinctively where to go, and what I'd find when I got there. I went directly to Anna's bedroom, and there she was, lying peacefully on her bed, her head on a pillow, her eyes closed as if she were taking her midday nap. On her night table I found two envelopes—one bearing Alex's name, in Anna's script, the other, mine. I opened the envelope addressed to me and read her note:

Thank you, August, you have been a great friend, and a second son to me. Please look after Alex, he is not as familiar as he should be with the ways of the world. I blame myself for that. He may need some practical advice from time to time, and I know I can rely on you for that. Alex is financially secure, and mostly self-sufficient—and I truly believe that, with time and your wise counsel, he will blossom, even at his age.

Goodbye, my dear friend—I am going home.

Fondly,

Anna S.

I put the note back in its envelope, folded the envelope, and slipped it in my shirt pocket. Then I pulled up a chair and sat with Anna, waiting for her only child to come home.

Chapter 30

The Love of a Grandfather

The passage of time is perceived differently by each of us and differently by each of us under different circumstances—it's entirely subjective. For most of us, time passes more slowly when we're young and accelerates as we age. Do you remember when you were a kid in school how the last two months of each school year seemed endless, but the summer days, lubricated by the fun you were having, raced by, and then it was September again? Then, as you grow older, the days, weeks, months, and years melt away faster and faster (even as they become more routine) so that by the age of seventy or so, you count your weeks as you once counted your days. For those of my readers who haven't yet reached that venerable stage of life, trust me—it's true.

At his ninetieth birthday celebration, my grandfather Josef said to me, "I blinked, and then I was ninety."

I was thirty-five at the time, and I asked him, "Grandpa Josef, if there were just one piece of advice on life that you'd give a guy like me, what would it be?"

Grandpa paused, smiled, and said, "That's easy, August: Don't be an asshole."

"Don't be an asshole," I mused.

"That's right," Grandpa said. "Don't be an asshole."

I wasn't sure how to respond. Was Grandpa telling me that I was an asshole and that I should not be an asshole, or was he just saying don't be an asshole like nobody should be an asshole?

So, knowing my grandfather not to be one to pull any punches, I asked him, "Grandpa, are you telling me that I am an asshole and that I should stop being an asshole, or are you simply saying, 'Don't be an asshole'?"

Grandpa looked at me very seriously and said, "Which do you think, August?"

I greatly respected my grandfather and valued his opinion, so I said nervously, "I'm not sure, Grandpa."

My grandfather drew closer to me, hugged me, and said softly in my ear, "August, you will never be an asshole. It's not in your nature to be an asshole."

With tears in my eyes and a smile on my face, I said, "Thank you, Grandpa."

"August, like I have told you before—you think too much. Most of the time, what we fear never even happens. We worry, lose sleep, and grow gray hair like me." He paused and smiled. "What little I have left, anyway."

Josef Freedman died on April 5, 1999; it was the day of his ninety-seventh birthday. At the time, he was living with his son, my uncle Mark. One evening, Grandpa told Mark that he wasn't feeling well, and seeing that something was not right with his father, Mark wisely called for an ambulance.

My grandfather was taken to New York-Presbyterian Hospital, where, after an initial checkup in the ER, he told the treating physician that he was feeling somewhat better and was taken to a temporary staging room. As they waited, Mark was growing nervous and a little irritable. Grandpa Josef, who was lying on a hospital gurney, looked his way and said, "There's nothing to be nervous about, Mark, I'm going to be fine."

With those words, my grandfather closed his eyes and quietly passed away.

Chapter 31

Oxy

The 1990s had brought two special girls into my life—Christina and Melissa. I could not have imagined, just a few years before, that I would be in the emotionally secure and loving place I was; but then, my life has been nothing if not full of surprises. Before Christina and I were married, I had renovated the house (it had really needed it), and I was thrilled that she loved it so much. What was not to like? We were living in a lovely shoreline community, just a short walk from the beach, a ten-minute drive from the center of town and several fine restaurants, and only a half-hour drive to Christina's parents—which was especially important to her.

Chris, Mel, and I were a tight-knit family. My weekdays at UPS were long and very busy, but we took full advantage of our weekends. The work at UPS was quite physical, and although that's what I did for a living, I wasn't really cut out for it. I'd never been a very physical person, but I hadn't gone to college, and UPS paid well, so that's just what I wound up doing. When I was a young man, it provided me with enough cash to support my eccentric lifestyle and keep me in weed; later on, it offered ample remuneration to support my family and to provide a comfortable home and roof over our heads.

Toward the end of the '90s, I suffered two debilitating injuries at UPS, each of which required surgery and a lengthy recovery. The first was a torn labrum in my right shoulder, and the second involved lower-back surgery to repair two herniated discs—plus, in each case, several months of rehabilitation. The positive side of these two surgeries was that I was able to spend a considerable amount of quality time with Melissa—Mel, as we had begun to call her. In both her first and third grade school years, I got to play the role of house dad, and I loved it. For a considerable time in each of those years, I brought Mel to school in the morning and picked her up in the afternoon. The joy of spending so much time with my daughter made the pain from my injuries more bearable. The oxycodone didn't hurt either—at least, that's what I thought then.

I've always been a quirky kind of guy; I'm fearful of things that most people are comfortable with and take in their stride—and yet I'll try other things that many will avoid like the plague. Included in the latter category were drugs—expensive, mind-altering, addictive, and often illegal drugs, toward which I'd been drawn throughout much of my adult life.

Elsewhere in these pages, I've written about my voracious appetite for marijuana and my dabbling with cocaine. In the late '90s, following my shoulder surgery, I was introduced to another species of drug, oxycodone—on the street, called "oxy" (and in its plural, pill form, "oxys")—which, besides being mind-altering and addictive, had the advantage of being legal (prescribed by my doctor) and free of charge (covered by my Teamsters health insurance). I liked oxys—I liked how they made me feel. They deadened the pain from my injuries, and they relaxed me, settled my mind. I felt a sense of peace and supreme well-being when I took them. Some nights, when Christina and Mel were asleep, I'd go outside and smoke a joint; when I was on oxys, the high was incredible—indescribable. On January 6, 1997, I turned forty, and by the end of that year, I was addicted to oxycodone.

Oxycodone is an opiate, derived from the seed capsules of the opium poppy (*Papaver somniferum*). A relative of morphine and heroine, it has a high potential for abuse, and I was one of its abusers. Taken in pill form or time-release tablets, the drug can be chewed or swallowed. Some users inhale its vapors by heating the tablets on aluminum foil over a small flame; others will crush and sniff the drug, as I sometimes did. Still others, seeking a more potent high, will dissolve it in water and inject it.

My doctor had written me a ninety-day script when I injured my shoulder. Then, ninety days later, I found myself asking for more, which he gave me (albeit reluctantly), advising me that this would be the last prescription for oxycodone he would write for me. Soon after that, I realized that my body had become physically dependent on the pills; I was beginning to experience withdrawal symptoms from being without the drug. These symptoms included hot flashes, muscular aches, cramps, headaches, upset stomach, restlessness, and weird cravings.

I had wanted oxys less for their analgesic effect than for the mental calm they brought me. So, I spoke with a fellow UPS employee who had been injured on the job a few years before. He had once mentioned to me that, after his doctor stopped prescribing pain medications for him, he sought them out from a friend "who knew someone who knew about such things." I'd never considered obtaining oxycodone through anyone but my doctor—but I was desperate. My contact told me he would be able to score me thirty-milligram oxycodone tablets for fifteen dollars a pill. He said I would only need a few to get me through the withdrawal. I bought the pills, I took them—and immediately wanted more. Even after the withdrawal symptoms had abated, I still wanted more.

Chris and Mel were unaware of what I was going through; I'd learned to be a damn good drug-addicted actor. One pill a day became three, then four, and sometimes five. I had been buying oxycodone continuously for almost two years, until my back injury in 1999. For me to say I was upset about needing another surgery would be a lie—I was thrilled. I'd be getting another script from the doctor, and I'd be able to stop my illegal purchasing of the drug, which would mollify my growing sense of guilt and save me at least sixty dollars a day. But of course, it didn't end there—even after the prescriptions from the back surgery ran out, I was soon looking for other ways to get my oxycodone.

This ordeal lasted for well over two years, and it was taking a toll on my marriage. Christina, of course, had noticed I was becoming less and less sociable, and although I tried to hide it, there were clues for her to pick up on—after all, she was an attorney. By late 1999, I was no longer able to afford my habit, and I was tired of concealing the missing income from Chris. I was again in physical and psychological hell; my withdrawal symptoms from not using for a week were a form of torture. It was time to confess. I no longer wanted to live the lie—I needed help.

Within a week, through the love of my family and the support of my friends, I was on my way to Silver Lakes, a psychiatric and substance abuse hospital in Fairfield, Connecticut. As we passed through the entrance gate, I had no way of knowing that this would not be my last visit.

Rehab is something like high school; you're grouped together with a random and eclectic population of misfits who are just as fucked up as you are. For me personally, it would be four weeks of soul-searching, disclosure, and general emptying out of a hopelessly tangled network of conflicting emotions and cleansing of the chemicals that both contributed to my disaffection and stood in the way of my ameliorating it. Detox was difficult and painful. Initially, I was as sick as a dog, but once I got beyond the physical sickness, my assigned shrink said it was time to work on my emotional well-being. For me, August Nathaniel Greenleaf, that would involve a hell of a lot of work.

Silver Lakes is an upper-class psychiatric hospital in lower Fairfield County, an extremely affluent area of Connecticut. Let's just say that treatment there was not cheap, and I found myself among some very wealthy people, many of whom had more—and more serious—issues than I could ever have imagined. It's certainly true what they say, that money cannot buy happiness, and nowhere I've ever been has the truth of that adage been more clearly illustrated than at Silver Lakes. During my stay, I met some fascinating people; among those I became friendly with were a popular rap artist and a well-known author. One evening, the rap artist and I got together and wrote a rap "song"—long on lyrics and rhythm, short on melody—about a deliveryman who fucks a lot of bitches, makes tubs of money, smokes blunts day and night, and generally doesn't give a shit about anything. The rapper entitled our song "Just Shut Up and Blow Me, Bitch" (which, although punchy, struck me as something of a non sequitur). The famous author, on the other hand, who found me "engaging and a bit droll," had no interest in collaborating with me on anything.

After twenty-eight days, it was time for my discharge. I'd gained a renewed sense of purpose that did not involve illegal substances in any way—but alas, it was also the end of my short-lived rap career.

Chapter 32

A New Millennium, A New August

The twenty-first century was underway, and our family was thriving. Melissa was doing extremely well in school and was an all-around good kid—kind, smart, and funny—in every respect she was the image of her mother. Christina was happy with her job and gaining a solid reputation. She was grateful and relieved that my recent crisis was behind us. I wanted desperately to justify her faith in me, and I was working hard at it; I was free of all substances and determined to stay that way. At Silver Lakes I'd had extensive therapy, and I continued with follow-up therapy after my release. In addition, I did an IOP (intensive outpatient program) for six weeks, and I was attending AA meetings at a local church.

I was also taking a renewed interest in my spiritual life. I read works by Eckhart Tolle, Thich Nhat Hanh, Stephen Batchelor, His Holiness the Dalai Lama, and others. I spent some time studying Judaism, the religion of my birth, but was naturally drawn to Eastern thought, and I was beginning to feel, for the first time in my life, a deeper sense of peace and understanding. Or, perhaps more accurately, Eastern philosophy helped reveal to me the many blessings that already lay spread out before me, directly in front of my scaly eyes.

I had been introduced to the art of meditation at Silver Lakes, and when I meditated regularly, I felt myself folded into something much greater than myself—something universal. At those times, I was able to look beyond *myself* and thus forget my conjured problems—or, insofar as they were real, to keep them in their proper perspective. But the old feeling of dread hung on me like a shroud; though the rays of the rising sun might fill the sky with golden light, I'd sense the dark wall of a storm gnawing at the edge of an oblique horizon.

Our February visits to Mom and Marco's home in Florida had become a family tradition for us, and after Melissa started school, we'd go during her winter holiday. Each April, during her spring break, Melissa and I would head down to Florida while Christina stayed home in Connecticut. This gave Mel and me some special father-daughter time and Chris a well-deserved respite from the rigors of being a working mom. During the summer, typically in July, Mom and Marco would spend two weeks up north with us. Then, in October, I'd take a four-day weekend and fly alone down to Florida for some mother-son time. All in all, although we lived over 1,200 miles apart, our family got to spend a significant amount of time together each year.

So, in the third week of the first February of the new millennium, we took our annual winter vacation to visit Mom and Marco in Florida. Melissa loved their pool (what kid wouldn't?), and we couldn't get her out of there unless Marco promised to take her for a ride in his boat. I loved watching my mother's interactions with Melissa. I knew when Mel was born that Mom would be a wonderful grandmother, and I was not disappointed. These were truly the times of our lives, and I couldn't have been any happier than I was when I saw the expressions of joy that passed among Marco and these three special ladies in my life.

One evening, after Melissa had passed out from an entire day spent in the pool, we four adults were sitting around on the patio; Marco had just uncorked a bottle of a fine Nebbiolo and poured a glass for each of us. (He had checked with me first to see if alcohol was taboo for me. I explained that it was okay, that my problem was never the booze, it was always the drugs.)

Mom, who was sitting to my right, stood up and, raising her glass, offered a toast: "To my dear son, August, who never gives up, who has always persevered, even in the darkest of times, and who does not realize how truly special he is—and"—she turned to me—"you are, son." Then, turning to Chris: "And to Christina—a mother could never have hoped for a better daughter-in-law, wife to her son, and mother to her granddaughter than you. You have stood by our Augie through a difficult time, and I am so very thankful for you, the daughter I never had."

Later that night, while Chris was asleep, I lay thinking about the words my mother had spoken in her toast. It's true that I have often thought of myself as special in that I have a gift that, evidently, not many have. Apart from that, I have generally suffered from low self-esteem. I've tended to think of myself as a person who's had to struggle through life, one who has, all too frequently, seen himself in a negative light. But whence does that idea arise, and where will it end?

On the wind, the answer comes: in the mind, of course! It starts in the mind, and if it is ever to end, it must end there, where it began. It's as Michael had once said, it's only a thought, and thoughts are evanescent things—insubstantial, not what we are made of—not what we are. As creatures of our minds, our thoughts ought not to control us but rather to be subject to control by us. I had spent most of my life in the thrall of my negative thoughts—immobilized or misdirected by the self-judgmental, self-defeating obstacles I had placed in my own way, like the sorry spectacle of a latter-day Don Quixote, tilting at the windmills of my imagination as though they were "the unbeatable foe."

As my mother said, I have persevered in this life; I have been through a lot of shit—granted, much of it self-shat, but shit nonetheless—and somehow I've made it this far, scarred but still standing. So, how hard can it be? That very night, I vowed that I would begin to see myself in a different—more positive, more hopeful—light. I vowed that I would no longer listen to, nor take instruction from, the Sisyphean story I'd been telling myself for so many years. I vowed that, with the new millennium, would come a new Augie.

Chapter 33

Italy

By the summer of the year 2000, Marco's business was doing extremely well, so he treated us all to a family vacation in Italy. On a pleasant, early August evening, we boarded an Alitalia flight at JFK, and after a long night in the air, we touched down at Naples International Airport.

We were met at the airport by Marco's younger brother, Carlo, who drove us straight to his home in Avellino, about thirty-five miles due east, where both he and Marco grew up and where Carlo still lived with his wife, Maria; his three married sons, Gianni, Umberto, and Franco; their wives; and (among them) a total of seven energetic children. Introductions were exchanged all around, and we all shared a light meal, enlivened by joyful conversation.

For the next two days, we were treated like royalty by Carlo and his family. The love between Marco and his younger brother was on full display, and our visit was all the richer and more convivial for that. On Saturday morning, we picked up the rental car that Marco had reserved—a red Alfa Romeo 156 Sportwagon—that we'd be using during our entire stay in Italy. We bid farewell to the extended Santoro family and drove back to Naples, where many of the Esposito family still lived. Chris had never been to Naples and was looking forward to meeting her relatives, but Melissa was inexplicably sad to leave Avellino. After some gentle interrogation by her mother, Mel admitted that she had developed a crush on Gianni's second son, ten-year-old

Giuseppe. Ella suggested that she and Giuseppe might become pen pals, and she cheered up.

Later that afternoon—when we arrived at their lovely Naples neighborhood—we were tearfully greeted by a small corps of Christina's aunts, uncles, and cousins. They fed us, toasted us, sang to us, fawned over us, and regaled us in their Neapolitan dialect—interspersed with surprisingly passable English phrases. In short, they did everything they could to make us all feel at home. Marco, who spoke the dialect fluently, translated for us, which made communication a breeze. It was all very beautiful, and Christina was profoundly touched. Besides meeting her relatives, she also got to see the old homes of her grandparents and great-grandparents (which had remained in the family), and on Sunday, we attended Mass at the little church where her grandmother had been baptized.

After making our Neapolitan goodbyes, our travels took us to Sorrento, Rome, and Tuscany—where we visited Siena and Florence—Bologna, Ferrara, and finally to the Adriatic coast and the romantic city of Venice. Through it all, Marco was our interpreter and guide—wise, kind, patient, generous, and an attentive husband to my mother. Marco had had one child, a son, whom he'd lost in a plane crash in 1972. Davide, twenty-five years old, was flying with a friend who had, not long before, gotten his private pilot's license. Their single-engine aircraft crashed, killing them both, as they attempted to land in a squall at a small airport in upstate New York. So, Marco—having earlier lost his first wife to cancer—had known suffering and loss and yet was able to pull his life together and find happiness. I thought of him as a friend, exemplar, and father figure—and I loved him.

Our first sightseeing destination was the resort town of Sorrento. That first evening we walked through the lovely town, taking in the sights. The women shopped, strolling from one shop to the next; at times they left Marco and me standing outside to chat, breathe the sea air, and admire the beautiful Italian women who happened by, appropriately dressed for the sultry Sorrento summer night. When the ladies had had their fill of shopping, the five of us went to a charming restaurant that Marco's brother had recommended, called Il Piatto Gustoso (The Tasty Plate). Carlo and the restaurant's owner, Ernesto Martinelli, had been close childhood friends, and Marco had also known Ernesto during his youth in their Avellino neighborhood.

We were shown to a table outdoors, seated, and served like royalty for the rest of the evening. Ernesto's staff brought out plate after plate of the most delicious Italian cuisine I'd ever tasted—and bottle after bottle of a wonderful local red wine. By dinner's end, we had gone through three bottles, and I (I admit it) had drunk more than my share. After our meal, while Ernesto was refusing Marco's euros, I got up from the table, and a wine buzz hit me. I suddenly became very dizzy, and as I sidled around the table on my way to the sidewalk, my right foot caught the leg of a chair at an adjacent table, where a rather elderly Italian woman was sitting. Tipsy as I was, I stumbled and began to fall. In an attempt to right myself, I instinctively grabbed for the back of the old woman's chair, which began its own downward trajectory. As the poor woman sensed herself being involuntarily separated from her linguini with clam sauce, she reached for the table and seized a fistful of tablecloth, pulling her juicy meal perilously close to the table's edge. Fortunately for everyone, Marco saved the day: with the reflexes of the goalie for SSC Napoli, he reached over and (thank God!) brought her chair upright while her linguini teetered on the brink, threatening to fall into her lap—until, just in time, an alert server rescued it.

So, I was the only one to kiss the pavement that evening—and as I struggled awkwardly to my feet, Ernesto was there to help me up and steady me while I gained my equilibrium. He then turned to the patrons, and with a smile, exclaimed in accented English, "Too much-a the vino!" This declaration was made to the good-natured applause of many and the abject embarrassment of only one—me. And it didn't enhance my self-esteem that the elderly woman whom I'd almost sent crashing to the patio pavement with a lapful of linguini looked me in the eye, shook her head, and muttered, "Americano intossicato—stupido!"

Over the following three days, using Sorrento as a base, we visited the nearby towns of Amalfi and Positano, the ancient Roman city of Pompeii, and the Isle of Capri. Amalfi is the ancestral home of many Italians who emigrated to America in the late nineteenth and early twentieth centuries to the city of New Haven, Connecticut. It is absolutely stunning, with its views of the Tyrrhenian Sea and its magnificent cathedral and campanile standing high above the Piazza del Duomo, where the citizens sit sipping espresso in the shade of colorful patio umbrellas while enjoying the soft sea breezes. I'd have been content to spend the remainder of our trip right there.

On our second day in Sorrento, we booked a tour to the ruins of the ancient Roman city of Pompeii. This once beautiful city was destroyed by an eruption of Mount Vesuvius in 79 CE and was buried under twenty to thirty feet of lava and hot volcanic ash. Its ruins were discovered in the late sixteenth century, but excavation of its treasures did not begin until 1740.

Pompeii is a haunting place; I was not sure how Melissa would take to it, but as it turned out, she was every bit as fascinated as we adults were. During our tour, she listened carefully and asked many pertinent questions of our guide, Lorena, including one we were all wondering about: "Why didn't the people try to run away when Vesuvius erupted?"

"Excellent question, Melissa," Lorena said. "The residents were simply not aware that Vesuvius was a volcano—the word didn't even exist in their language. They had thought it to be a mountain like any other, and they were unprepared when it started to spew out smoke and flames. Even when the lava began to flow, they had no idea that it would reach their city, or that it would engulf everything in its path. Not knowing what else to do, they remained in their homes, and perished."

Mel was growing up quickly; naturally curious, she was thinking for herself and developing an adult capacity for empathy. I was proud of her.

The next morning we left Sorrento and drove along the coast, past Naples, to Rome. Marco had reserved two rooms at a bed and breakfast in Trastevere, a neighborhood on the west side of the Tiber River, near the Vatican. We arrived late that afternoon, and after settling in at our B&B, we went out for dinner at a nearby restaurant that had been recommended by our host.

As we strolled along the tidy streets, drinking in the sights and sounds of this ancient corner of a world-class city that had taken 2,700 years to build (and rebuild), we came upon a UPS package car parked on our side of the street. At the rear of the truck, unloading boxes, was a handsome young man dressed in the familiar brown uniform I'd been wearing for the prior twenty-one years of my life.

"Hello," I said.

He stopped what he was doing, looked up, and said with a smile, "Buon giorno, signore."

"Do you speak English?"

"Mi dispiace, no," he said, shaking his head and frowning with polite regret.

I turned to Marco and asked him to tell my fellow UPS driver that I also worked for UPS back home in the US and that I'd like to know what he thought about his job and the management at UPS here in Italy.

Marco repeated my question to my counterpart in Italian: "Devo dire che, per me, il lavoro va bene, ma que'i nella gestione sono veramente dei rompipalle."

Marco translated the response for me. "He says the job is fine, but the management—how shall I say it—are real 'ball breakers.'"

I couldn't help smiling. "Agreed," I said, looking over at my Roman compadre and nodding with amusement.

Again, Marco translated for him: "Lui è d'accordo."

"Godetevi la vostra vacanza," the driver said cheerfully. "Arrivederci, signori."

Translation: "Enjoy your vacation. Goodbye, gentlemen."

And I, nearly depleting my entire inventory of the Italian language, said, "Grazie—buona sera!"

With so much to see in the Vatican, Marco arranged a private tour, which enabled us to see a lot more than we'd have been able to see on our own. We toured Saint Peter's Basilica (c. 1506–1626 CE) with its massive, 138-foot dome, designed by Michelangelo Buonarroti—a magnificent structure at the center of the Roman Catholic world.

Next, we visited the nearby Sistine Chapel (dating from the fifteenth century) to see its famed frescoes, which adorn the chapel's walls and ceiling. These frescoes were painted by various artists of the time, but by far the most admired are those painted by Michelangelo, including his depiction of the creation of Adam, at the center of the ceiling.

On our second full day in Rome, we toured several classical sites in the old city, including the Roman Forum, the Capitoline Hill, the Colosseum, the Pantheon, and two Baroque monuments—the Trevi Fountain and the Spanish Steps.

The following morning, we drove north to the Tuscan city of Siena. Immediately upon checking into our hotel, Marco began to ask around for details of the annual Palio dell'Assunta, a traditional horse race, which was scheduled to take place the next day.

Palio, a bareback race held twice annually, is Siena's most popular attraction. Ten of the city's seventeen present-day contrade (neighborhoods) compete in either one or both of the Palio races each year.

Each contrada is represented by its own standard, displaying the neighborhood's distinctive colors and its unique symbol or mascot. Included among the symbols, for example, are the caterpillar (Bruco), snail (Chiocciola), little owl (Civetta), dragon (Drago), unicorn (Leocorno), and goose (Oca).

The contestants arrive at the Piazza del Campo (il Campo), replete with entourage and paraphernalia, at their neighborhood's traditional entrance on the piazza to the shouts and cheers of their supporters and join the prerace procession around the square. There is much fanfare, with flags waving, trumpets blaring, and partisans singing, dancing, shouting, and marching behind their favored entries. Spectators crowd the infield of the racecourse or cheer from temporary bleachers.

When we arrived at Il Campo for the race, the infield was already crowded, and I looked over at Marco, who met my gaze with a wink. He then led the four of us to a section of temporary bleachers, where the late afternoon sun would be at our backs. It seemed he'd been able to procure five seats for our group on very short notice, and as I inched past him to my seat, I gave him a quizzical look, as though to ask, "How . . . ?" He only shrugged and said simply, "In Italia, c'è sempre un modo." ("In Italy, there's always a way.")

Earlier in the day, we had placed our bets in our own little family pool. As it happened, the winner that day was Leocorno (the unicorn), a *contrada* that had been selected by my nine-year-old daughter, Melissa, who pocketed the twenty-five-dollar prize. The light in her eyes and the smile on her face as I sat her on my shoulders and trotted her off to dinner were priceless—and it occurred to me that I was the winner after all.

Marco was behind the wheel as the five of us traveled north on a narrow country road between Siena and Florence. Every bend and turn revealed a new vista, each more stunning than the last. We had just stopped at a charming local winery for lunch and were still about an hour from Florence, the capital of Tuscany—"la Citta del Giglio" (the City of the Lily), as Marco called it—where we would spend the next three days.

As we drove, a familiar sensation suddenly came over me. I felt an adrenaline rush, like an aura, and goose bumps covered my arms. We rounded another curve, and I immediately saw the source of my premonition. "Marco," I said, "pull over!"

I opened the passenger door and got out of the car. I heard Melissa say from the back seat, "Mom, look at the little girl standing up there, all alone on that hill—so far from anywhere." I'd seen her, too, and a minute later, as I climbed the hill toward her, I could see that she was barefoot; her long brown arms hung loosely at her sides, and her light-brown hair was blowing gently in the summer breeze at the top of the hill. She was wearing a white, sleeveless cotton blouse and a knee-length lavender skirt.

She was standing at the crest of the hill, looking up at a lemon-colored stucco house in the Tuscan country style, with a broad, roofed veranda that overlooked the road and the rolling hills in the distance. I knew instinctively that only she and I were able to see the house, that my family—by then standing around the car, shaded by the mature cypress trees lining the road below, and looking up at the two of us—saw only us, the grassy hill, and the endless Tuscan sky above.

As I drew nearer to the girl, I saw that she was, at most, six or seven years old; she was calm and relaxed—apparently unfazed by my approach. Soon, I was standing beside her, breathing somewhat heavily from my exertion.

The girl remained silent for a minute or so while I caught my breath. Then she said, "It's beautiful, isn't it?"

"Yes it is," I said, "very beautiful . . . What's your name?"

"Mirabella—it means 'wondrous beauty.'"

"That's a pretty name. My name is August."

"What does that mean?" she asked.

"It means 'great' or 'exalted'—very grown up."

She turned her head, looked up at me, and laughed. "I like that." She paused for a moment, then said, "My mother says that I am wondrous, because I see what others cannot see—and I remember everything."

"Yes, I know—you are a special person," I said.

"I come here every day. Sometimes, I see an old woman in that window right up there." She pointed to a window on the second floor, about thirty feet from where we were standing. "But she's not there today—only sometimes do I see her."

"Do you know who she is—does she wave to you?"

"No, I don't recognize her. She's very old."

"Ah, too bad . . . Mirabella, never let anyone tell you that what you see does not exist, because they will be wrong. Speak of it only to those you trust, and always trust yourself—do you understand?"

"Yes, August, I do."

We talked for eight or ten more minutes about the yellow house and the gift we shared, and then I had to go.

"I'd like to stay longer, Mirabella, but I must leave now; my family is waiting."

"Arrivederci, August."

"Goodbye, Mirabella."

"Sono felice che tu possa vedere la mia casa, August, nessun altro lo fa."

As I turned to go, it struck me that the entire time we talked, Mirabella spoke only Italian, and I, only English—yet we'd understood each other perfectly well. I can't explain it, other than to say the two of us shared a special gift—one that afforded us a privileged glimpse into another, less familiar world where, as far as either of us knew, anything was possible. I slowly picked my way back down the hill to my waiting family, and as I descended, Mirabella's parting words echoed in my mind:

"I'm happy that you can see my house, August. No one else does."

We reached Florence that afternoon, but before we crossed the Arno into the city center, Marco drove us to the Piazzale Michelangelo, an outdoor terrace carved into a slope on the south side of the Arno, which offered stunning views of the old city, the birthplace of the Italian Renaissance. Marco gathered us around him so he could describe for us, in detail, the stunning cityscape that lay before us. For reference, he produced a guidebook from his backpack, brandished it for all to see, and then spoke to us for almost an hour without ever looking at the guidebook again.

Our hotel, the Grand Hotel Cavour, was ideally located near the Duomo, Alberti's reconstruction of the Basilica di Santa Maria Novella, the Ponte Vecchio, and the Uffizi Gallery. Nearby was a small restaurant, Osteria Lungarno (Inn on the Arno), that, thirty-five years earlier, Marco had visited with his first wife, Francesca, and their young son, Davide. A year or so before (in planning our own trip to Italy), Marco had casually mentioned it to my mother. Possessed of a memory second only to mine, Ella insisted we have dinner there. In doing so, she was hoping to remove all barriers that might still lie between them—all the secret places where his heart might hide from her. She had long ago emptied her heart and mind to Marco about Howard and Michael, but men are more taciturn, more reticent—so she wanted to make it easier for her husband to open his heart about his late wife and son. It evidently worked: The following morning, when the two of them came down for breakfast, they looked tired and happy, and behaved like newlyweds.

We made stops in Bologna, where we enjoyed an afternoon and early evening in and around the city's magnificent Piazza Maggiore, and Ferrara, where we spent the better part of two days investigating the history of Jewish life in Italy. Then, with full bellies and happy hearts, we were off to our final destination—Venice, "Queen of the Adriatic."

During our three-plus-day stay in Venice, we visited many of its best-known sites, including il Molo (the Wharf, which is the ceremonial entrance to the city by water), the Doge's (Duke's) Palace, Saint Mark's Basilica, the Piazza San Marco (the central square), the Campanile, the Jewish Ghetto, the Gallerie dell' Accademia, and several churches to view their celebrated works of art. Of course, we just had to take a gondola ride through some of the city's many small canals and neighborhoods, where we stopped occasionally to browse the shops and markets. Mom, Chris, and (especially) Melissa loved it; I thought it was kind of cool too.

Of special importance to me, though, were the three mornings when I awoke in the dawn's gray light and went out alone to walk the quiet streets of the still-sleeping city. I walked along the quays and across bridges over narrow neighborhood canals, each day a different route. With daybreak, the mist vanished, and the low sun threw sharp shadows at the glowing-gold buildings, one to the next—which, in their turn, cast muted reflections on the placid surfaces of the canals. The early morning silence, pierced only by the intermittent cries of hungry, low-flying gulls, suggested in me a sense of shared ownership in a pristine world of wonder. I walked on, past bakeries, where the yeasty smell of fresh-baked bread filled my nostrils, reminding me that I, too, was hungry.

On the last day, toward the end of my walk, I poked along the Grand Canal, stopping occasionally to watch a vaporetto dock and unload its consignment of city workers, whose sleepy, downcast eyes and purposeful gait betrayed little awareness of the beauty through which they moved. As I started back to the hotel, I turned for one more look at the Piazza San Marco and the lagoon beyond, and smiled.

That evening, our last in Venice, we decided to try a restaurant that specialized in traditional Venetian cuisine. Marco suggested La Caravella, near the Piazza San Marco, which was known for some of the most authentic food of the Veneto region, especially its seafood. The maître d' seated us outside in a small courtyard adjacent to the restaurant. As he distributed our menus, I asked him to recommend a seafood dish traditionally prepared for the Venetian palate. Without hesitation, he said, "Today, signore, we have fresh branzino. This is a European sea bass, which here is roasted to perfection." And then, kissing his clustered fingertips, he exclaimed enthusiastically, "Squisito!"

So, I went with it. About the time we were finishing off a round of drinks, our dinners arrived. In front of Marco, the waiter placed a plate of capesante alla veneziana, a traditional scallop dish, served with sauteed spinach; Mom, who loved creamed dishes, was having gamberetti alla crema, prawns in a garlicky cream sauce, over linguine; and Chris and Mel, both meat eaters (despite our waiter's polite but barely concealed disapproval), were having vitello alla Milanese—Milanese, for heaven's sake!—breaded veal fillet fried in butter (which the house kept on the menu for emergencies such as this), served with risotto and white asparagus.

My dish was the last to be served, and when the waiter proudly placed it before me, it came—to say the least—as something of a surprise. I had expected a nicely filleted piece of fish, neatly trimmed, glistening under whatever transformative sauce the chef deemed appropriate, and nestled demurely between my zucchini and roasted tomatoes. Instead, staring up at me from a pure white china plate, supine among slices of lemon and a sprig of something green, was the whole damn thing: head, tail, fins, scales, gills, eyes, and all! (The veggies were served on the side.) Even as the others started to eat, I was still staring down at my plate, not knowing where the hell to begin. I looked over at Marco, and rolling my palms upward, I shrugged, with a slight forward projection of the chin.

Marco chuckled and said, "Incomincia cogl'occhi, August!"

And I: "Which means . . . ?"

Still smiling, he said, "Start with the eyes, Augie, start with the eyes!"

Too soon it was time to leave Italy; our trip had come to an end. Christina, Melissa, and I thanked Marco and my mother profusely for sharing this remarkable country with us—this rich and bountiful peninsula.

We checked out of our hotel, took a water taxi to the airport, and boarded an evening flight from Marco Polo to JFK, which was due to arrive in New York in the morning of the following day. By 8:00 p.m., we were flying into the sun just as it was setting, in a burst of red and gold, over the blue-gray Alps. In my mind it was Italy, consummate host, wishing us *addio*—and slowly pulling down the shades.

By the midpoint of our flight, at an altitude of thirty-six thousand feet, somewhere over the Atlantic, my family slept while I—never able to sleep in an airplane—reflected on Mirabella, that supremely habituated little girl of the Tuscan countryside, who, so self-assured despite her age, openly shared with me the magic of her own "special" house.

I had been reading an article in *Time* magazine; it was a review of a newly published memoir by veteran NASA flight director Gene Kranz entitled *Failure Is Not an Option*. According to the review, "Mr. Kranz's memoir tells us riveting stories from the early days of the Mercury program, to *Apollo 13* and beyond." By the time I finished the article, I'd decided that this book was certainly one I'd like to read; it had planted a dream in my restful mind. Mr. Kranz doubtless had many fascinating stories to tell . . . well, so did I (although perhaps not quite so "riveting"), and as the years wore on, there'd be more—of that I was sure.

So, it was aboard that Alitalia flight 1217, three decades ago, that the journey of writing my own memoir began. Although at the time I had only scattered notes—scribbled in notebooks and on miscellaneous scraps of paper—I knew that, by journey's end, I could have enough to fill volumes. I turned off the overhead light, closed my eyes, and thought on it.

Chapter 34

Far Rockaway Redux

July 20, 2003:

It had been almost thirty years since my mother and I left Far Rockaway—since we left Dad, left the apartment we had lived in for twelve and a half years, left the house by the bay, and left the ghost of my brother, Michael. We'd talked about returning on several occasions, but each time, it was I, not Mom, who wasn't ready to go back. I'd held onto the pain and sadness for far too long; I wouldn't let go of it—couldn't let go of it. But at last, thirty years later, I was ready—thirty years! Michael would have been forty-eight years old; my dad would have been seventy seven. In ten years, on November 26, 2013, I'd be returning to Far Rockaway again. Was it to be "a date with destiny"?

On this muggy July morning—during Mom and Marco's summer visit to Connecticut—Christina (who had just turned forty), Mom, Marco, and I got into my silver 2001 Volkswagen Passat and headed south on I-95, toward the borough of Queens, New York—a seventy-mile drive. But first, we'd planned to drive to Long Island via the Throgs Neck Bridge to the town of West Babylon for a visit to the grave sites of Mom's parents, Josef and Rachel Freedman, and my father, Howard Greenleaf—all of whom were buried in the New Montefiore Jewish Cemetery.

After an hour of walking between the two grave sites at Montefiore and sharing our carefully selected memories, we got back in the car and drove six miles north to Farmingdale, where the Long Island National Cemetery is located—the military cemetery where Michael was buried. Mom placed a bouquet of white roses at his headstone, and we all stood somberly around Michael's grave, weeping and thinking our own thoughts about this magnificent young man who had been taken so early—and so needlessly—from us.

When Mom was sufficiently composed and ready to move on, we drove east to Far Rockaway, via the Southern State Parkway and the Marine Parkway Bridge. We had left Melissa back in Connecticut with Christina's parents; we'd thought it best not to bring her, knowing that, between our visits to the grave sites of her uncle, grandfather, and great-grandparents—and our long delay in returning to Far Rockaway—emotions might be running high among the adults.

Crossing the Marine Parkway Bridge (which is just minutes from our old neighborhood) for the first time in three decades was a sentimental experience for Mom and me. We had crossed this bridge many, many times during my childhood on our visits to my grandparents—both the Freedmans (whose grave we'd just visited) and the Greenleafs. But this time, I wasn't a child riding in the back seat, with my father at the wheel; this time it was I, a middle-aged man, driving over this familiar span. I chuckled with wry amusement at how long it had taken me to come this far.

Some things just seem never to change—seem suspended in time—and so it was with 38–48 Almeda Avenue and the old Arverne neighborhood. But was it there? Of course it was; of that I'd had no doubt! It was every bit as beautiful as it was the first time I laid eyes on it, so many years before. We found a parking spot on Almeda Avenue, almost directly in front of our old building. The four of us sat quietly in the car. No one moved to get out; no one uttered a word. At last, Christina asked quietly, "Do you see it, Augie?"

Just as quietly, I said, "Yes, I do." My mother reached out from the back seat and gently placed her hand on my shoulder. We all got out of the car, and Mom came around to my side and took my hand. They all seemed to be waiting for me to decide where we were going first—across the street to the playing fields and Jamaica Bay or to the apartment building that had been our family's home more than three decades past. I chose the latter. Marco and Christina followed as Mom and I, hand in hand, walked slowly toward the front entrance of the building. The front walk seemed shorter and narrower than I remembered—everything seems bigger when you're a kid. I led our little group into the building and straight to the elevators. Without fear, I pressed the call button, and we all watched as the floor indicator went through its itinerary: 5-4-3-2-ding. When the door opened, we silently stepped in; instinctively, I pressed 7, and the door closed in front of us.

There was no plan—it all just happened; I guess you can say I followed my heart. When we reached the seventh floor, Mom, Marco, and Christina followed me down the hallway to apartment 7D. I took a deep breath, and not knowing what to expect, I rang the doorbell. A woman answered the bell, and after I explained on the intercom why we were there, she opened the door.

She appeared to be in her early thirties, neatly dressed, hair in a ponytail, and attractive. I introduced myself and the others in my group and explained as best I could how we happened to be standing at her front door.

To my surprise—and before I could even ask—she invited us all in. Her name was Bianca, and she couldn't have been any kinder; she understood. Her apartment was immaculate and tastefully furnished, yet strangely, it was just as I remembered it. Bianca walked us into her kitchen—where my father had ended his own life. I wondered if Bianca knew or how she would react if she were ever to find out.

Then she showed us into the living room—our living room—and without hearing another word, I went directly to the large picture window that looked out over the ball field toward Jamaica Bay and the stately white house. I stood there for a few silent moments, taking in that familiar scene, then sighed, turned away, and rejoined the group. Bianca took us into each of the bedrooms, and in my old bedroom I swear (a trick of the mind?) I saw Michael sitting on the edge of his bed, looking straight at me. He was eighteen years old, as he'd been on the day I last saw him alive.

When it was time to leave, we thanked Bianca, and Mom gave her a hug.

Mom's eyes were brimming with the emotion of it; they'd been moist all day since, at Michael's grave site, she'd broken down completely and wept bitter tears. We left the building and crossed Almeda Avenue, toward the playground where we had romped as children—the benches where we sat with our moms; the swings where we swung as high as we dared to go; the paved path where we walked and rode our bikes; the baseball field, the site of many of Michael's finest moments; the beautiful Jamaica Bay; and for me alone, the enigmatic white house, just as I remembered it. I was thrilled to be in its presence again, as I would any reunion with a dear friend after a long separation.

It was (I had since learned), a Victorian style home; it had an asymmetrical facade, with broad, overhanging eaves, gabled dormers, bay windows, and—at the northeast corner nearest Jamaica Bay—a round pergola with a conical roof. Seven wide wooden steps, with railings on either side, led up to the large, airy porch, which stretched across the entire front of the house and along the north side, overlooking the bay.

At the front of the house, above the porch, was a small, covered balcony off the second floor. The exterior walls were sided with painted cedar shingles. With the use of specially shaped shingles, some surfaces formed diamond patterns, while others resembled fish scales. The large windows, flanked by their dark-green shutters, were closed, and all the drapes were drawn. The house was beautifully proportioned and immaculately maintained—and on the porch, six rocking chairs sat in perfect alignment.

Although the day was warm and fine, I sensed a chill wave running down my naked arms.

Chapter 35

He Knows Me

He comes to me often in my dreams, as he has ever since I was a boy—since I first saw him staring at me from the second-story window of the house by the bay. Often, at night, when I am in the midst of one of my very worst nightmares, he will interrupt. I have come to know his voice; it has become familiar to me, and it soothes me. He assures me that everything will be all right, that there is order and purpose to the events of my life, and that there is nothing to fear. He says that, one day, we will all be together again. When he speaks to me, he speaks softly; he knows me, he knows my name. I cannot explain how—yet he does.

Chapter 36

A Morning on the Job

June 9, 2004:

On most mornings during the school year, before work, it was my job to drop our daughter off at school. As had Christina, Melissa attended local Catholic schools. From pre-K through eighth grade, she went to Saint Bernadette's School in the Morris Cove section of New Haven; her high school years were spent at Sacred Heart Academy in the town of Hamden, directly north of New Haven. Driving Mel to school was an unalloyed pleasure for me; the twenty or thirty minutes it took to drive her from home to school gave us a chance to stay current with each other's lives, especially hers, which was ever-changing.

Often, we'd leave home a half hour early so we could stop on the way for an egg sandwich or breakfast pastry at a local Italian market. Those days were extra special, and I cherished them, knowing that one day they'd come to an end, as all good things must. Yet, occasionally, there were days when Melissa stretched my patience to the limit. Enough said—those of my readers who have raised a daughter through her early teens know exactly what I'm talking about.

On this unusually hot and humid early June morning, after dropping my seventh grader off at school, I arrived at my UPS hub at 8:30 and was immediately summoned to my center manager's office. There, I was greeted by a middle-aged man wearing a blue jacket with white lettering on the back that read "FBI." My first thought was, *Oh, shit, Augie, what the hell have you done now?*, but I was relieved to learn that Hector, as the agent had been introduced to me, was not after me. His reason for being at UPS that morning was to inquire about a customer on my Clinton route. Evidently, this particular customer was suspected of being associated with a credit-card and identity-theft ring operating out of southern Florida.

The customer's name was Grace Goodwill (no, really), and I immediately thought of the obstetrician who delivered me, Dr. Gregory Goodlife. I thought, too, how could someone with a name like that possibly go bad? Perhaps, having been hung with such a sugarcoated moniker, Grace found it just too much to live up to and took the alternate route. Or maybe she'd taken the name as an alias to throw the feds off her trail. Either way, the FBI was coming after her, and that's never a good thing.

The package, addressed to Ms. Goodwill, was a two pound box, sent via next-day air, from Miami, Florida. On the box, just above Grace's name—placed there by my center manager, at the FBI agent's request—was a "Signature Required" sticker. My curiosity got the better of me, and I inquired as to what, exactly, was in the box. I was told, politely, that the contents of the box were classified and could not be divulged, as I had "no need to know."

Instead, Hector outlined a plan according to which I was to meet him at the commuter parking lot off exit 64, on the northbound side of I-95, in Clinton. From there, he would ride with me in my UPS truck to Ms. Goodwill's house. Before we turned into her long, wooded driveway, Hector was to sequester himself in the package compartment of my truck. My assignment was simple: I was to make the delivery, have Ms. Goodwill sign for it (on a special handheld computer given to me for the purpose), get back into the truck, and drive back down the driveway. Just before reaching the main road, I was to give the handheld computer (with the signed digital receipt) to Hector, let him out of the truck, and continue on my route as though none of this had ever happened. Hector asked if I was okay with the plan; if not, they would have someone else do it. I told him that I was fine with it.

Three-quarters of an hour later, I got off the highway at the Clinton exit and was greeted at the commuter lot by three black Ford Tauruses and six FBI agents, two in each vehicle. Clearly, Grace Goodwill was in deep shit. Hector got out from the passenger side of one of the cars and took a seat in my truck. During the ten-minute drive to the suspect's house, Hector asked if I had ever met "this Goodwill character." I said no, that I did not recall ever having delivered to that address before. When we reached the Goodwill driveway, Hector stepped into the package compartment, and I closed the door behind him. As I drove up the driveway, the three Tauruses pulled over and parked along the main road, near the bottom of the driveway, concealed from the house by dense woods.

The driveway ended at a two-car garage attached to the house; a raised ranch—big but otherwise unremarkable—extended to the left. I parked the truck and stepped out, carrying the two-pound package, and walked up the path leading to the front door. I mounted the three steps onto the stoop, and before I could ring the doorbell, the door opened. There in front of me stood a very attractive blond woman—I'd guess in her midtwenties—and in her arms, she was bouncing a chubby little baby (a boy, I assumed, because of the blue PJs). "Good morning," I said. "I have a next-day air package for Grace Goodwill."

"That's me," she said.

"Great," I said and turned the handheld computer toward her. "I'll just need your signature right . . . here."

"Do I have to sign?" she asked.

"Yes, ma'am, you do," I told her, pointing to the "Signature Required" sticker. After she signed, I solemnly handed her the package and said half-heartedly, "Have a nice day," knowing full well that this was the beginning of what might well turn out to be one of the worst days of her life.

I stepped back into the truck, and as I drove back down the long driveway, I heard Hector ask from behind the package compartment door, "Did everything go okay—did she sign? Did you see or hear anyone else in the house?" I told him about the baby in her arms, and by then, we'd reached the bottom of the driveway, near the road. I opened the interior door of the truck and gave Hector the handheld computer that Grace had signed. He shook my hand and thanked me; then he stepped down off the truck and got into one of the Fords. As I turned onto the main road, I glanced at my rearview mirror and saw the three cars speeding up the driveway toward the house.

That was the last I ever saw or heard of either Agent Hector or Grace Goodwill, but through the years I've often thought about her and the baby. I pray that the child had a good home to go to, one where he was cared for and raised properly. As for Grace Goodwill, maybe she did some hard time, or maybe there were mitigating and extenuating circumstances that got her off the hook—who knows? I just hate to think of that lovely young woman—with the bouncing baby boy and the beautiful name—gone bad.

Memorable events and bizarre people are plentiful for those of us whose job it is to drive those brown trucks, and on that uncomfortably hot June day, when the temperature would ultimately reach a record ninety-five degrees, more was soon to come. Just a couple of hours after watching the FBI on their way to keeping our country safe from the crimes perpetrated by its domestic miscreants, I was about to make a delivery to one of my all-time favorite customers, a genuine character by the name of Mitchell Goldberg.

Mitchell was an eccentric, free-spirited, and successful artist whose house was also on my Clinton route. His paintings fetched remarkably high prices for the Connecticut market, and you could clearly see why: The man was extremely good at his craft. He'd have had even greater financial success in New York, but he didn't like the city; he considered it pretentious—too "uptight" and (believe it or not) too "parochial." For the most part, his canvases were moderately sized, intended for hanging in residential spaces or private offices; they consisted primarily of landscapes and village scenes but included some still lifes and a few portraits. I ran across this review of his work online; it's from an article in the *New Haven Register*:

> Stylistically, Goldberg's work doesn't fit easily into any category; if anything, you'd have to say it most closely aligns with the Impressionists, but with more strongly geometrical arrangements, and more saturated colors—drifting toward Cubism. Everything on his canvases seems to be in the right place, and comfortable with where it is. Although the eye tends to chase his seductive linework around the surface of each painting, the overall composition is always focused—the center of an expanding universe.

Many of Mitchell's paintings, especially his smaller "color sketches," depicted different aspects of his property. It was not unusual for me to come up his driveway to find him sitting pensively with brush and palette in hand, his easel and canvas standing before him, awaiting his loving touch.

In the two years that I had been doing the Clinton route, I had driven up and down that driveway countless times; packages were always coming in and out of Mitchell's house and studio. He shipped his paintings to dealers all across the country and around the world, primarily Europe and Japan. Nevertheless, as I've said, Mitchell was a true eccentric; you never knew what to expect from him. Stories about him abound, but a few of my own, recounted below, may help to better acquaint the reader with this unique and remarkable man.

On the very first day I met him, two years before, I introduced myself and told him that I was going to be his new UPS deliveryman. "Mr. Goldberg," I'd said, "my name is August—"

"Listen," Mitchell interrupted, "I may be a hot-shit artist, but a memory for names I don't have. So, what I do is this—I call all my delivery people 'Ace.' The mailman, FedEx, UPS—everyone is Ace; it's much easier for me, and I don't have to tax the old brain. After all, you guys are a bunch of aces, the best in the business, as far as I'm concerned. So can the 'Mr. Goldberg' crap. It's Mitch."

Another time, on a cold, late-December day in 2002 (my first year on the Clinton route), I drove up Mitchell's driveway to find him swimming nude in his pond. When I reached the house, Mitchell, who was essentially treading ice water, called over to me, "Happy winter solstice, Ace! Why don't you throw off that uniform of yours and jump in the pond with me. Come on, Ace, let's celebrate together!" With that he shouted at the top of his voice, "God, I love it!"

Then there was the afternoon I happened to be making a delivery while a gentleman from a posh New York gallery was visiting with Mitchell. He was there to view a series of eight of Mitch's paintings and to discuss a purchase price for the entire series. My delivery that afternoon required Mitchell's signature, and as I approached the two men, I apologized for the interruption. Mitchell bellowed, "Augie [Mitch had given up calling me Ace since he'd gotten to know me better], say hello to Winthrop. Winthrop is here representing his New York gallery, Chartier's, and he's about to make an offer for eight of my paintings, which I did after my visit to Montana last summer and the Palouse in eastern Washington."

Winthrop and I shook hands, and Mitchell said, "Augie, you and I have discussed my work before, and I've shared with you some of the prices that my paintings have sold for. So, why don't you set a price for Winthrop here for all eight paintings." Winthrop looked to be as astounded as I was by Mitchell's suggestion, but picking up on his scheme to have some fun at Winthrop's expense, I played along. Winthrop's mouth hung open through my entire performance.

"Well, Winthrop," I said, "I imagine you can get anywhere between four and five thousand for each of the paintings in this series. So, we'd like $2,750 per painting. That's a total of—let's see—$22,000 for all eight."

Winthrop looked at me, then at Mitchell, then back at me. Finally, his eyes settled on Mitchell. Without blinking an eye, Mitchell surprised both of us when he said, "Augie here is about right, Winthrop—twenty-two K for the lot of them sounds to me like the right number. That's my final price."

Winthrop paused for a few moments and said, "I was thinking more in the line of twenty K, but I guess twenty-two will have to do."

After shaking Winthrop's hand, Mitchell saw me out the door. In the foyer he reached out, gave me a hug, and whispered in my ear, "Great job, Augie. I was going to ask for $2,500 each. I'll see you tomorrow."

The next morning, when I showed up at Mitchell's place to deliver a package, he came running out of the house with a cup of coffee in one hand and an envelope in the other. He crowed to me that I'd netted him an extra two grand over what he thought Winthrop would pay for the paintings. "Here, this is for you," he said, and he handed me the envelope. "Your agent's fee, Augie—great job, my boy, great job!" I tried to tell him that a fee was unnecessary, but he wouldn't hear of it. I thanked him and put the envelope in the pocket of my brown jacket. Then I asked, "What would you have done if I'd quoted Winthrop a lowball price?"

Mitch answered with a smile, "Why, I would have told him, 'Clearly, Winthrop, August here has been out in the sun a little too long.'" After I left Mitchell, I continued with my route, and when I stopped for my lunch break, I took out the envelope and opened it. Inside were fifteen crisp one-hundred-dollar bills.

As an eclectic—a person of varied interests and tastes—Mitchell was a very wise, kind, generous, and patient man. In the spring and summer, I'd often find him in his backyard, on his knees, tending his garden. He enjoyed feeding the wildlife on his property—oats for the deer (they were plentiful, but venison was never on the menu) and seed for the various species of birds, including wild pheasant and turkey. But the messy, noisy, and aggressive Canada geese had to fend for themselves. Over time, I developed a real affection for Mitchell, and (I think) he for me. A week almost never went by that he didn't invite me to join him for lunch, and I quickly learned that the man was as much an artist in the kitchen as he was in his studio.

So, on that hot June morning in 2004, about two hours after leaving Grace Goodwill and the six FBI agents to sort out the rest of their lives, I was coming up Mitchell's driveway to make a delivery, and there he was, sitting on his porch—his bandy legs resting on a hassock, slightly spread—smoking a joint. He was totally naked, his nuts being fanned by the warm summer breeze. After parking my truck, I paused a moment before getting out, thinking, WTF?

Then I heard Mitchell shout, "What's the matter, Augie—never seen a naked man smoking a joint before?"

With somewhat less enthusiasm, I shouted back, "Actually, no, Mitchell, but it's your property to do with as you wish, sir."

"Exactly, and actually, y'know what I'm doing, Augie?"

"Yes, I do, Mitchell. It looks to me like you're sitting naked on the porch, smoking a joint."

Laughing, Mitchell said, "I'm airing the boys out—on a hot day like this, it's always important to air them out. And do you know why, Augie?"

I got out of the truck with Mitchell's package. "Please tell me," I said.

"Because if you don't air them out, they get chafed—and Augie, we don't want that. You ever have chafed balls, Augie?"

"Yes, I have, Mitchell, yes, I have."

"That's because you don't air them out, Augie."

I quickly placed Mitchell's package on the porch and retreated to the safety of my package car. I put the truck in gear and waved "so long" to Mitchell. As I drove off his property, I checked the time—it was 11:59 a.m., and I thought, *What a strange morning, indeed.*

Chapter 37

The Surprise Party

In the autumn of 2006, we celebrated my mother's seventy-fifth birthday in Florida. The timing was perfect, since it coincided with my regular October visit with her and Marco. She was older but as lively and gracious as ever. We had a wonderful evening with Mom's old friend May and her husband, Dominick, who had been introduced to each other by Mom and Marco twenty years before. Two Jewish girls from Queens, both with off-the-boat Italian husbands—go figure.

A few weeks later, on November 7, Melissa turned fifteen. Mel was in her freshman year at Sacred Heart Academy and was as pretty as a peach, but her fifteen-year-old attitude—well, that was another matter. She had gained enough confidence that she'd begun to assert herself, and my Lord, I thought our home might never be the same again. Overnight, it seemed, I had devolved from the ideal father, font of all wisdom, into a totally clueless and definitely uncool old fart.

In January of 2007, I turned fifty, but despite knowing my negative feelings about celebrating my own birthdays—and about surprises—Christina went ahead and organized a surprise birthday party for me. Surprise parties—depending on how large they are and who gets invited—can be very hard to keep secret. Evidently, this surprise was going to be a big one, and although I've never been the most observant of people (even for a man), I began to put two and two together.

First, let me say that in no way would I ever eavesdrop or intrude on private conversations between my wife and my daughter, nor would I monkey with their personal effects—their cell phones, for instance. I'm not that kind of guy. But I just couldn't help myself, really; Christina's cell phone happened to be sitting right there on the kitchen counter in front of me while she was outside chatting with our next-door neighbor.

It was the Saturday before New Year's Day, and by then I had a pretty good idea that Chris was up to something. So, I picked up her phone (after peeking out the kitchen window to confirm that she was still engaged in conversation, of course), scrolled through her recent calls, and—bingo! There had been five calls between Chris and my mother, just in the past week. Add to that the three calls Chris made to Jessica, plus the conversation I "happened" to overhear between my daughter and her latest best friend, Sydney. Yes, her bedroom door was closed, and it's true, I was standing in the hall with my ear pressed against it, when I heard Melissa say, "My dad's going to be really surprised—and freaked out. He absolutely hates surprises."

By now, reader, you are surely aware of my feelings about surprises—as Melissa had confided to Sydney, I absolutely hate them. So, at the time, that was my excuse, and the rationale for my sneaky, underhanded, and otherwise totally inexcusable behavior in sniffing out the facts. I just had to save them from their own good intentions. See, then, for me the party would no longer be a surprise—it would be just another social event; I'd have known all about it, but they wouldn't know I knew.

That was the beauty of the whole thing. They thought they were surprising me, but although I would act surprised, I would not be surprised. Thus, the party would not be a problem for me, and I would not ruin everyone's evening by behaving badly. Instead, everyone would be happy and have a good time. The fact that my dear loved ones had worked so assiduously in plotting the event, and had then contrived so furtively to keep it a secret from me, still touches my heart—deeply. I was, indeed (as I remain to this day), a *very* lucky man.

"*Surprise!*" My family and eighty invited guests shouted as Christina and I entered Il Suono dell'Aqua (The Sound of Water), an Italian restaurant in New Haven's Long Wharf section. I put on my best surprised face, assured them all that I'd had "no idea," and everyone was indeed happy. The only one I'd confided in about my little charade was my dear friend Dr. William, who I knew could keep a secret. It really was a beautiful party, and for the first time in my adult life, I was able to let the ghost of my brother go and to truly enjoy my own birthday. Mom and Marco were up from Florida, Jessica had flown in from California, and my father's brother, Robert (Uncle Robbie), came up from New York. There were many from Christina's family in attendance, friends from UPS, and neighborhood friends—even friends I didn't recognize. It was really quite special.

I had not seen Uncle Robbie in six years; it was at his seventieth birthday party, in New York, that I'd seen him last. He really was a good man and one of my favorite people—but after my mother left my father, Uncle Robbie and I had drifted apart; I wished we hadn't. We talked about my father—Robbie knew how my dad was; he'd known his older brother well. He didn't blame Mom for leaving him, and he told her as much that very evening. At seventy-six, Robbie was looking good, very healthy. I'd always been struck by how different he and Dad were—polar opposites, really. Was this due to the difference in their genes, the order of their birth (Dad was five years older), life experience (the war, for instance)—what? I never knew, and now, I suppose, I never will.

Jessica had flown in the day before and was staying with friends for a few days. She was doing well in California, and after her failed marriage to the baseball player, she had remained single, as she'd vowed to do. She had turned fifty the year before, and she looked great. She told me she dated quite a bit, but if a guy got too serious, she'd move on. Jess said that she wasn't looking for "serious," that she liked having fun, but life was full enough without that kind of commitment. Later that weekend, we got together for lunch, and I realized then how much I'd missed my old friend and confidante.

Mom and Marco were spending a few days with us, and after coming home late on the night of the party, the four of us stayed up until the wee hours, reminiscing. Mom shared with us a touching story about Michael—a story I remembered well, although at the time, my six-year-old brain was not able to fully comprehend its poignancy. In May of 1963, Mom gave a party for Michael on his thirteenth birthday. All of his friends were there, including Steven Silverstein, the mentally challenged boy who lived down the hall with his mother. Michael had always looked after Steven, protected him, and, of course, insisted that he be at the party. When it came time to light the candles on the birthday cake, Mike noticed that Steven was not there, so he asked several of the other kids if they had seen him. One of the boys told him that Steven had gone back to his apartment.

Mike asked Mom to hold off lighting the cake; he was going to go over to the Silversteins' apartment and bring Steven back to the party. About ten minutes went by, and Mom decided to go over to the Silversteins' to see what was going on. When she got there, she found Michael and Steven sitting on the floor. Mike had his arm around Steven's shoulder; he was speaking softly, telling Steven that everything was all right, that the boy who said that bad word to him was a jerk, and that if he didn't want to come back to the party, that was okay—he would be back in a few minutes with a big piece of cake for him, a lit candle and all.

When she finished telling her story, my mother's eyes were moist. Marco put his arm around her, and for a long moment, none of us said a word. It was I who broke the silence. With eyes closed, I said, "Michael, I miss you, big brother. I wish you were here with us tonight—with all our family and friends—here, with your great big smile and your even bigger heart. I love you, Michael."

The room was quiet again for another few moments, and then Mom spoke. "Michael, you were—and in our memory, always will be—an exceptional human being. You graced us for eighteen years with your presence, and you are forever in our hearts."

Again, a brief silence followed; then Marco said, "Michael, your mother speaks of you so often, I feel as if I know you—and with the same longing that she expresses her love for you, I do mine."

Then, finally, Christina said, "Michael, in so many ways, the reason your brother—my husband, August—is the man he is today is due to you—to your guidance and your love—and I wish to thank you with all my heart."

And so it was.

Chapter 38

2011

In the fall of 2008, Melissa entered her senior year at Sacred Heart Academy; in the spring of the following year, our "little girl" (who was by then five feet, nine inches tall) was a high school graduate, ready to begin her college studies at Quinnipiac University in Hamden, Connecticut, with aspirations of becoming a physician's assistant. I cried at her graduation ceremony, and when we dropped her off at Quinnipiac on move-in day, I cried again. Christina was the rock of the family; she organized and planned and, in general, did what had to be done. I was mostly sentimental mush—but useful mush, not idle mush. I ran errands, carried stuff—lots of stuff—for the move into Mel's college dorm, picked up (and paid for) tons of takeout, and took pictures—hundreds of pictures.

It was strange not having Melissa at home; the place was eerily quiet. Chris and I sorely missed her, but there were perks. Food didn't disappear from the fridge and cupboards as fast as it had before, and there was no one to yell at me for playing my Pink Floyd CDs too loud. It seemed the time required to clean the house, wash the dishes, and do the laundry was cut in half. Sex between Christina and me got a little wilder, and we didn't have to close the bedroom door (didn't even have to use the bedroom), and I could sleep half an hour later in the morning. But I'd have swapped it all—except maybe the sex part—to be needed for driving Melissa to school again.

At about 8:00 a.m. on Tuesday, January 4, the phone rang. Christina had already left for her office, and I was about to head off to work myself but hadn't yet gotten out the door, so I answered it. It was my mother; she was at Mease Dunedin Hospital and sounded very distraught. She told me that Marco had woken up at 2:00 a.m. with a terrible headache. He was in excruciating pain, so she called for an ambulance. According to the hospital doctors, Marco had suffered an intracranial hemorrhage (bleeding in the brain), and he was in critical condition. I caught a 1:00 p.m. connecting flight to Atlanta, out of Bradley International Airport in Windsor Locks, and got into Tampa at 6:30 that evening. I rented a car and drove directly to the hospital in Dunedin.

Marco's prognosis was not good, and Mom held his hand as he lay unconscious in the intensive care unit. By 10:00 p.m., he was gone. After spending some time alone with him, Mom came out of his room. I held her close, and we stood together, shedding silent tears.

Marco was eighty-two years old; he and Mom had been together for thirty-one years. Christina and Melissa flew down the next day, and a well-attended funeral Mass was held two days later at Marco's church. Mom kept herself together, but we know that she was still in shock. "It all happened so fast," she said, "so very fast."

Marco's wish was to be cremated and to have his ashes deposited in the Gulf of Mexico, but Mom just wasn't ready for that. Mom, Christina, Melissa, and I decided that, on our next trip to Florida, we would fulfill Marco's wish. Christina and Melissa returned to Connecticut two days after the funeral; I stayed on for a few more days to help Mom with the hundred things she had to do in the aftermath of Marco's death.

We were, obviously, very concerned about my mother; Marco's death had come so suddenly that she'd had no time to prepare for it. Later in January, I took a couple of days off and flew down to spend a long weekend with her. I noticed that she wasn't looking well and that she'd lost several pounds. "Mom, have you been skipping meals?" I asked.

"I'm just not that hungry lately, Augie. Don't worry, I'll get over it," she said.

"Of course I worry. I've only got one of you," I told her.

"And I have only one of you," she said, smiling back at me.

She was right, of course; one mother—one son. We had come a long way together, and I was determined to see her through this sad and stressful chapter of her life, to help her in any way I possibly could.

Mom came up north in February; we'd decided that she should spend a few weeks with us, perhaps even a month or two. But there was clearly something wrong with her. She was not eating well, had a recurrent cough, and admitted to having pain at the upper right side of her back. Christina took her to see our dear friend and family physician, Dr. William. He examined her and sent her to a radiologist for a chest X-ray. Two days later, Mom, Christina, and I were back in William's office; he explained that a shadow had been found on Mom's right lung and that he was going to send her back to the radiologist for a CT scan so they could get a closer look from different angles.

We were hoping that this would turn out to be nothing—a false alarm. With the sudden loss of Marco just weeks behind us, it just didn't seem fair that we'd be heading down this road again so soon. A day later, Mom and Christina were back at the radiologist's office for Mom's CT scan. The following day, a Friday, we all gathered in William's office, where he gave us the news that we'd been praying not to hear.

"Ella," he said, "you have a five-centimeter lesion on your right lung—that's approximately two inches." William took off his glasses, drew a breath, and looked directly at Mom. "The CT scan confirms that this is an irregular mass, which is a likely indication of cancer. The most qualified doctor I know of to decide how to proceed beyond this point is Dr. Thomas Warner at the Smilow Cancer Center at Yale New Haven. Tom is a personal friend and an excellent thoracic oncologist. I'm going to schedule an appointment for you immediately."

We saw Dr. Warner on Tuesday of the following week, and from there it was back to radiology on Wednesday for an abdominal and pelvic CT scan.

Warner's staff scheduled an appointment for ten o'clock on Friday morning to review the results of the scans and to go over her case with the doctor.

I lay awake all Thursday night—it hurt so badly. My fear of hearing the news that I'd do anything to avoid hearing was palpable. Here was that old feeling of dread, that "mother of all fears," spawning litters of the lesser fears that had had such an insidious effect on my childhood. It occurred to me then that these childish fears had never really left me but had merely transmuted into the roster of my adult fears: fear of losing my job; fear of what people might be thinking of me; fear for my mental health; fear of surprises—of the unknown; and now, fear of losing my mother, the last remaining link to the family of my childhood. Except for her, they were all gone—Michael, my father, my grandparents, and tomorrow . . .

I just couldn't bear to hear the news. "Death, please don't take my mother—not now!" It appeared that my adult self was little better equipped to cope with my grown-up pain than my juvenile self had been with his petty hobgoblins. Still, there was my daughter, Melissa; if the worst were to come, she would need her mother and me—especially me—to help her cope with the loss of her grandmother.

Christina loved my mother, and it touched me to see how emotional she was about Mom's suffering. Lying together in bed that night, we wept and prayed. I wasn't sure who or what I was praying to, but Chris knew. "Faith, Augie, have faith—everything is in God's hands now."

In the morning, Chris made a lovely breakfast for us: omelets with cheddar cheese, tomato, and onion, fresh bagels with cream cheese and lox, and coffee. Mom ate a decent breakfast, and I said to her, "There you go, girl, good job!"

Mom smiled indulgently and said, "Listen, you two, I love you and Melissa more than anything in this world, but please, I'm okay. I know that I've been quiet lately; it's because I was letting fear get the better of me. But you know what? Last night, a feeling of peace came over me, and a voice in my head was saying, 'It's going to be all right, Ella, everything is going to be all right.' I know, regardless of what Dr. Warner tells me today, that I am blessed. I've been blessed with the three of you; blessed with Marco; blessed with Michael, for the short time I had him; blessed with wonderful parents, family, and friends—blessed for all seventy-nine years of my life." Then she said softly, "I'm not expecting favorable news today, but I'm ready for it—whatever it is, it's going to be all right."

"Ella, your CT scan shows multiple metastases in your liver and in your adrenal glands," Dr. Warner said. "At this point we could try chemotherapy, which could very well make you sick but might also extend your life by several more months. The other option is to do nothing medically except to keep you comfortable and, when the time comes, to arrange hospice care for you."

"What would you do if you were sitting in my chair, Doctor?" my mother asked pointedly.

Warner sighed and said, "Probably the latter, Ella, probably the latter."

"How much time would you say I have left, Doctor?"

"I'm thinking less than a year. It could be as much as six months or as little as several weeks."

"I see," my mother said.

"I'm sorry to have to give you this news, Ella."

"I was expecting it, Doctor . . . Google," she said with a slight smile and, I swear, the merest hint of a wink.

"Yes, pretty soon, with modern technology advancing the way it is, I won't be needed at all," Dr. Warner said, smiling softly at my mother. "You're a brave woman, Ella; please know that I'm here for you in case you have questions—or if there's anything else you might need."

The following Monday, I applied for FMLA (Family and Medical Leave Act) benefits at work, which provided me with additional (albeit unpaid) days off to spend more time with my mother. Mom went on to live for another eight months, exceeding Dr. Warner's more optimistic estimate by two months. She returned with me to Florida for a week to tie up loose ends. After that, until she went into hospice, she stayed with us here at home. She and I spent our days playing cards, watching movies, and talking for hours on end. I had not spent this much time with her since I was a very young boy, before I started school. We both smiled ruefully at the irony of it—that she had to be given a death sentence in order to enjoy the uninterrupted company of her only surviving son.

Mom's dear friend May came up from Florida three times during those eight months, for a week each time. We put her up in Melissa's room. The two of them, as close as ever, became even closer with each visit. I suspected that May's visits helped extend Mom's life—they certainly improved the quality of her waning days. Their friendship, which had begun in Far Rockaway when I was a toddler, had lasted fifty years—one of the many blessings Mom had listed that morning at breakfast on the day we learned the worst.

My mother looked death straight in the eye and never flinched—her strength strengthened the rest of us. On October 21, Mom was admitted to Connecticut Hospice in Branford; five days later we celebrated her eightieth birthday.

On the thirtieth of October, 2011, at 10:25 in the morning, Ella Greenleaf Santoro passed away. I was there, holding her hand as she took her last breath—and a long, deep breath it was.

Chapter 39

Goodbye

"There's so much to do, Chris—I have no freaking clue where to begin!"

"Augie, calm down, it's only been two weeks. Let's just do as we've planned—after the New Year, we'll fly down to Tampa, meet with the attorney, and take it from there." Chris was right, of course. I had learned by then that it's never a good idea to quibble with a lawyer, especially one as organized and clearheaded as my wife.

On Monday, January 2, 2012, Chris, Melissa, and I flew to Tampa and took a cab to Marco and Mom's home in Dunedin. It was sad to be in that lovely house with both of them gone; as beautiful as it was, it seemed hollow—bereft of the love and laughter that we had grown so accustomed to over the years. Only the faintest echo of those happier times remained, but we had our memories—enough to last us a lifetime.

On the following day, we had an appointment with Marco's attorney, Anthony Russo, for the reading of Marco's and Mom's wills and to discuss the legal and financial details of their estates. After the reading, Attorney Russo explained some of the legal jargon and answered our questions. All this took two hours. Mom and Marco had left a sizable sum of money to Marco's brother, Carlo, and his family in Italy, a generous amount to Melissa, and to Christina and me, they'd left the remainder of their estates. Chris and I decided that there was no rush in disposing of the Florida house; for the time being, we'd hold onto it. Perhaps, with retirement not too far off, we might use it as a winter home and—who knew?—we might even start a collection of new memories.

On Saturday morning, we had a small, informal memorial service, led by Fr. John Garvey, the pastor at Our Lady of Lourdes Catholic Church, where Mom and Marco often attended Mass. The service was held on the spacious patio of their home. May and Dominick were there, as were several of Mom and Marco's other closest friends in Florida. I don't believe there was a dry eye among us as Fr. John held the urn containing my mother's ashes, poured them into the urn with Marco's ashes, and said, "Beloved husband and wife, Marco and Ella Santoro together now, and for eternity. Amen."

That afternoon, May, Dominick, Christina, Melissa, and I boarded Marco's boat, and with Dominick at the helm, we headed out to the Gulf of Mexico to deposit Mom's and Marco's ashes in accordance with their wishes. When we were about two miles offshore, due west of Dunedin, and in an area where the depth of the sandy bottom was between forty and fifty feet below the surface of the Gulf, Dominick maneuvered the boat into the proper position with respect to sun and current, cut the engine, and set anchors fore and aft.

May—who some years before had been to an ocean burial off Seal Beach in California—suggested how I might deposit the ashes and helped me with the preparations. Before leaving for the marina, May and I had placed the ashes in a weighted, tightly woven wicker basket with a woven-in handle. We covered the ashes with rose petals, then covered the petals with a fine white linen cloth for the drive to the marina. On the boat, Dominick tied a length of sisal rope to the basket's handle.

The five of us stood along the landward gunwale, opposite the sun, where we would be able to see below the surface of the Gulf. After removing the linen cloth, I held the basket over the gunwale and, slowly paying out the rope, lowered it into the water. As the basket passed beneath a placid swell, the rose petals floated free and began to disperse with the gentle breeze.

Between the spreading petals we were able to see clouds of ashes billowing out of the descending basket, which by then was four or five feet below the surface. I held the basket at that depth for a moment and said, just loud enough for all to hear, "You were the best of us; you brought smiles to all our faces and made us happy; and the two of you, Ella Greenleaf Santoro and Marco Vincenzo Santoro, shall forever be as one—in our hearts and in the sight of God."

Using the sound system's remote, Dominick played their favorite song, "My Funny Valentine," sung by Frank Sinatra, and as the CD softly played, I continued to lower the basket deeper and deeper into the sea while we thought our thoughts and prayed our prayers—until the basket and its precious contents disappeared in our tears, and the music faded on the breeze.

Chapter 40

Northbound

On Monday, we put Melissa on a plane back to Connecticut. The rest of our week in Dunedin was full of emotion. The outpouring of love and support we received from the community meant a great deal to us and ameliorated our sadness. It seemed that everywhere we went, people knew who we were and greeted us with a smile and a hello. Marco and Mom had been greatly respected in Dunedin, and many in town wanted us to know it.

Chris and I continued to sleep in the guest bedroom we'd been using; the master bedroom would remain Mom and Marco's until some unspecified future time when we came to regard the house as truly ours. We made love several times that week, and we held each other close until sleep came. We reminisced about Mom and Marco, how fortunate we were to have had them in our lives, and how suddenly they had left us. Melissa was a college sophomore by that time, and Chris had been a public defender for over fifteen years. I was just two years from retirement, and I couldn't wait—suddenly the Brown seemed awfully old.

We left Dunedin on Sunday, January 15, in my mother's silver Volvo XC90—she'd wanted Melissa to have it—and we took several keepsakes from the Florida house (mostly photographs) that we wanted to have with us in

Connecticut. Chris and I were returning home as inheritors of the major portion of Mom and Marco's estate, but there was no joy for either of us in that. Although we had gained considerably in financial security, in our hearts, that was absolutely no compensation for the loss we'd suffered. In planning for my retirement, I'd had visions of making longer and more frequent visits to Florida—of spending a lot more time in the company of these two people I loved so much—than I'd been able to do while I was driving for UPS. But alas, it was not to be, so I resolved to put these thoughts aside during our trip back north and instead be the very best traveling companion I could be for my wife, whom I also loved dearly.

The trip home would be over twelve hundred miles, and we were on the road by 5:30 that morning. Our plan was to drive until sunset, find a room, have something to eat, get a good night's rest, and finish our journey the following day. I did the bulk of the driving, although Chris took the wheel for a couple of hours, between ten and noon. The drive that day was a fairly easy one; Sunday traffic on the highway was very light, and despite stopping for lunch, we made very good time. At one point, Chris even suggested that we drive straight through the night and make it home by sometime Monday morning. But I didn't feel up to it; my night vision wasn't what it once was, and I thought it better, and safer, to stick to our plan.

By late afternoon, we were in Rocky Mount, North Carolina. The sky was beginning to darken, and Christina searched the car's GPS for area hotels. She found a Hilton Double Tree on North Winstead Avenue, in Rocky Mount, and called ahead for a reservation. Within ten minutes, we got off the highway and checked in. We were both in the mood for a burger, so Chris asked the desk clerk for the location of a fast-food restaurant nearby. He suggested a Hardee's about a mile south, just off North Winstead Avenue. We thanked him and went up to our room. Chris unlocked the door and held it for me as I squeezed past her with the luggage. Inside, I dropped the bags and immediately stretched out on the bed.

"In for the night, Augie, or just checking to see how comfy it is?" Chris chided.

"You know," I said, "I'm exhausted—it's been a stressful week and a long drive. I could use the rest. I think I'm in for the night."

"I'll tell you what, good lookin', you flip me the keys and grab yourself a little beauty snooze; I'll go get us a couple of greasy cheeseburgers and some fries."

"You sure, honey?" I said.

"Absolutely," she said as she bent down and gave me a long, soft kiss on the forehead.

Chapter 41

Two Men of Carolina

He was a loner; at thirty-five he had never slept with a woman, never even had a girlfriend. He never really knew his father, who had left home when he was a small boy. His mother had raised him, but she was in the process of becoming an alcoholic, and what little of herself she had to give him wasn't nearly enough. His was just another sad story—another boy who was fucked from the beginning—and where he came from, there was far too much of that.

He'd had five jobs in the past three years. Alcohol had become a real problem for him. He didn't try to hide it; he was beyond that. When he was drinking, everyone knew it; he was a sloppy drunk, and when he drank, he got awfully loud. When he drank, he felt really good, like everyone was his friend. When he drank, he felt uninhibited—free.

So, he drank to kill his pain, to drown the self he could no longer bear to face in the mirror—the self who once had hope, once tried, once cared. On this Sunday, he stayed home in his dingy, second-floor apartment. He had picked up a case of Budweiser the day before; his mission was to stay home all day, watch the NFL playoffs, and polish off most if not all of that case—and so, he got to work.

By the second quarter of the Giants-Packers game, he was already well into his case of Bud—two cans short of three sixes. As he watched the game and drank his beer, he'd been chain-smoking Camels, and when he finished off what remained of the pack in his shirt pocket, he got up, took a leak, and went to the bureau in his bedroom, where he kept his stash. But there were none there, and this really pissed him off.

It was almost 5:30; he checked his wallet, which was sitting on the bureau, next to his car keys, and found that he had a twenty. He tucked the wallet into the back pocket of his saggy jeans and grabbed his keys. The minimart at the Mobile station on North Winstead, just past US-64, was only a couple of miles up the road, and he decided that he'd take a quick ride over there at halftime and pick up some cigarettes and a bag of chips. If he hurried, he could be back in time for the second-half kickoff. As soon as the first half ended, he headed out; he didn't care jack shit about the halftime show. He gingerly made his way down the rickety old staircase to the ground floor, climbed into his red 2003 Ford F-150 pickup, and took off up the road.

Officer Darren Robinson had been a member of the Rocky Mount Police Department for over thirty years. At fifty-two, and a third-generation law enforcement officer, he had seen it all. Father of four and grandfather of two, he should have been home today. Over the years, he had done his share of weekend shifts, but that day, with the NFL playoffs underway and a half dozen of Rocky Mount's finest booking off (most, he guessed, to watch football), he answered the call. Anyway, the overtime pay always came in handy, and he was going to be a retired man in two years—so why not? Sundays during the football season were generally quiet (until the bars closed), so he figured this would be an easy shift.

Over his thirty-year career, Robinson had seen things change in town. When he was a young cop, back in the '80s, people had more respect for law enforcement. These days, especially among the younger crowd, there was little or no regard for the badge. This just wasn't the way he'd been raised. At times, he had half a mind to rap some of these youngsters right across their filthy mouths, but he was too smart for that. He knew very well that one moment's loss of temper could cost him his job—possibly even his pension—and that wasn't going to happen to him. He was a fine officer and a compassionate man, perfectly suited for this line of work. He was the kind of cop who, if he stopped you for a traffic violation, would accept almost any old sob story (and he'd heard them all) as an excuse to let you go with a warning—that kind of cop.

He'd had to fire his gun only once in his career (although he had pulled it out of his holster on a few other occasions), when he responded to a domestic on Heights Avenue. It was half past ten in the evening. A woman had called 911, and speaking quickly, in an agitated whisper, she told the operator that her husband was drunk, that he had punched her on the side of her head, and that he was just then threatening to blow her brains out with his shotgun. She had locked herself in the bathroom and was afraid to come out. She was lying in the bathtub, pleading for help.

A young officer, only twenty-five at the time, Robinson drove to the scene. He was ordered to wait for backup, so he pulled his patrol car over to the curb opposite the house, got out, and, as he had been trained to do, crouched behind his patrol car, using the car as a shield between him and the house. Moments later, a second patrol car arrived on the scene; as Robinson glanced over to acknowledge its arrival, the woman's husband barged out of the house, armed with a pump-action shotgun, and headed straight for him—pumping and firing. The driver's side window of the squad car exploded in broken glass, and tiny shards rained down on Robinson.

With his gun drawn and ready, Officer Robinson had no alternative but to return fire. Three of the four shots he fired stopped his assailant, who never got off another shot. As the man lay dying, Robinson did all he could to help him. Meanwhile, the other officer moved quickly into the house to check on the man's wife. She was unharmed, except for a bruise on the left side of her face, where she had been struck by her husband—who, lying on the lawn, had just breathed his last.

On this Sunday in January, though, his shift had been a quiet one, as he'd expected it to be. Parked at the curb on the northbound side of North Winstead Avenue, with only a half hour to go on his shift, Robinson watched as a red Ford pickup went speeding past him, heading north. The speed limit on that section of road was thirty-five; as he switched on his siren and pulled out in pursuit, he judged the pickup to be doing at least twice that. Robinson followed at speed until, suddenly, the pickup swerved across the double yellow line and headed straight for a southbound silver SUV.

Chapter 42

If Only It Were a Dream

"... **forty-eight, forty-nine, fifty!** Ready or not, here I come." I was It, and we were children, playing our childhood game of hide-and-seek. I searched high and low, but I couldn't find him. It was getting late, and I was getting scared. I called out at the top of my lungs, "Michael, where are you? Michael!"

"I'm here, Augie," I heard him say.

"I hear you, Michael, but I can't see you," I said. "Where are you?"

"Here, Augie, right in front of you—but you can't see me because I'm dead."

"Michael, I'm scared."

"Augie, don't be scared; it's just like Mom said, it's going to be all right, and it will be—all you have to do is knock on the door—that's all, Augie, and he'll answer it. Go ahead, Augie, knock . . . knock real loud."

Suddenly, I was standing in front of a big door. It wasn't just any old door; it was the front door of the big white house by the bay. The afternoon sun was pouring itself into a bank of clouds on the western horizon, and I did just as Michael had urged me to do—I began to knock.

The knocking at the door woke me from a sound sleep, and it took me a few seconds to get my bearings. I rolled out of the bed and tottered over to the hotel room door. "Coming, honey," I said, expecting it to be Chris with our cheeseburgers and fries.

Chapter 43

Deliverance

The "gift" of total recall I've been endowed with has not been an unmixed blessing. Although it has been of immeasurable help in my life (in school, at work, remembering names, faces, birthdays, impressing the ladies, etc.), it has, almost as often, been a curse. There have been times when I've wanted, *needed*, to forget, but my dogged memory prevented it.

I remember everything about my beloved Christina—clearly, vividly, as though a motion picture were being projected on my mind. In most of these images I find consolation—indeed, they sustain me—but some are chaotic, jagged, and confusing; these tear at my viscera like shards of broken glass.

I remember that Tuesday morning in early December of 1987—the first time I saw her at the UPS hub in Wallingford—like it was yesterday. She was wearing her brown company-issue uniform so well that all the drivers' eyes were on her, mine among them. She had a gentle but confident air about her and a soft, unassuming smile that instantly (and always thereafter) put me at ease. As the teamwork between us grew into friendship, and friendship into love, I was always reassured by her presence, her competence, and how she moved—the natural beauty of her being. She was loving and kind, supportive in every way—and then she was dead.

Still, she fills my mind—our first date, our first kiss, the first time we made love. It was on our first vacation together, Sconset Beach on Nantucket

Island. We were lying on our blanket, holding each other close in the early morning chill, and suddenly I knew—I just had to spend the rest of my life with her. "August," she said, our eyes caught in an out-of-focus, lovers' gaze, "I haven't given myself to many." Nothing more was said. We lay there on that little patch of beach as the sun breached the Atlantic horizon and slowly floated upward until it popped free and fully round in the reddening sky. We drove back to the small cottage I had rented and took our first shower together.

At times like this, it comes to me in flashes: that I don't remember anything at all but rather that I'm living my life all at once.

"Daddy, I love you, but you need to be *here*—please, Daddy," my daughter pleaded.

"Melissa, I know, I'm so sorry, forgive me."

"It's just until the doctors regulate your medication, Daddy. Dr. Flynn said you could be out of here in as little as two weeks." Melissa and I held each other tightly; we were all that was left of our little family, and here she was, at twenty-one, just six months after the death of her mother, looking after her fifty-five-year-old wreck of a father. It should have been the other way around; I knew it, and the guilt associated with that knowledge only deepened the depression that came with the loss of Christina. Moreover, I'd become aware of an inexorable sense of dread. The feeling that I just couldn't live another day lay before me at every turn.

Earlier that afternoon, I had arrived back at Silver Lakes for another course of treatment. I was greeted by Amanda, a social worker on Main One, which was to be my unit for this stint. Amanda gave me a tour of the unit and showed me my bedroom. She told me that my roommate's name was Henry but that he liked to be called Hank, and that he was currently in a meeting—otherwise she would have introduced him to me. Dinner, she said, was at 5:15, which left me about an hour to relax. This being my second time in rehab, I knew how precious an hour of downtime really was, so I decided to rest.

My bedroom was similar to the one I'd had the last time I was at Silver Lakes, but I sensed something was different. Now, I knew I was not completely right in the head, but neither was I hallucinating, so what I saw on my bed threw me for a loop. Resting there, with his head on the pillow, was my old friend Mr. Bim Zippy, the stuffed monkey who had always been there for me when, as a boy, I needed him most . . . that is, before he was mutilated by my brother, Tommy Yang, and Mark Aberman. I had no idea how he got there, but there he was. Seeing him again after so many years brought all my emotions to the surface and dredged up thoughts of my checkered life since I'd seen him last. So, I curled up on the bed with him and cried leftover tears from my childhood. How did I come to be here . . . and for the second time? Where the hell had I gone wrong?

As I lay beside Bim, my emotions slowly subsided. Sometime after we'd settled in for a nice rest, I heard the bedroom door open, followed by a pathetic groan. I opened my eyes, and there, looming over us, was a morbidly obese, middle-aged man with a random stack of graying hair covering his head like a sleeping cat—and a look of terror on his face.

"What in the hell are you doing with Bim?" he shouted. "And what in God's name are you doing on my bed?"

"Oh, hi—you must be Hank. I'm August, your new roommate; I just got here an hour ago."

"That doesn't answer my question! Why are you in my bed—and napping with my monkey?" he demanded.

It was only then that it dawned on me—Bim wasn't here for me after all; he belonged to Hank, and Hank was justifiably upset. But the comfort Bim had given me for that restful hour was, in retrospect, something that I would always be grateful for.

After a four-hour period of observation and a few consultations, Dr. Erica

Rubenstein, my treating psychiatrist, diagnosed me with "cannabis-induced psychosis," coupled with anhedonia (the inability to feel pleasure). She suggested a combination of antidepressants she believed might very well "bump" me out of my deep depression. Dr. Rubenstein was an "eclectic physician" and clairvoyant. She had spent years of her life studying parapsychology, as well as traditional medicine. Her personality was somewhere between Dr. Joyce Brothers and Joan Rivers, yet for some reason, I was expected to trust her judgment. Dr. Rubenstein had prescribed a combination of drugs she called "California rocket fuel." She must have repeated the phrase a dozen times before I agreed to go on the regimen. When you're in the worn-out shoes I was wearing—hopelessly lost, with no particular desire to go on living—there really isn't much choice, and what the hell difference would it make anyway?

She showed me a few published case studies in which this grouping of medications was found helpful in relieving depressive symptoms in a "statistically significant" number of patients. She started with Effexor, a well-known serotonin and norepinephrine reuptake inhibitor (SNRI), part of a class of antidepressants that work by increasing amounts of serotonin in the brain—something I was clearly in critical need of. Next, she prescribed Remeron, another antidepressant, that I was to take in the evenings to help with my insomnia. Finally, she prescribed BuSpar, an antianxiety medication to control my generalized anxiety, which had become an increasingly debilitating problem for me.

I had come a long way in the six months between Christina's death and my second stay at Silver Lakes. This dark journey had begun with a knock on the door of a hotel room in Rocky Mount, North Carolina. When I opened the door, instead of looking into my wife's beautiful brown eyes, I was staring at the badge of a Rocky Mount policeman, who introduced himself as Officer Darren Robinson and asked if he might step into my room.

"Mr. Greenleaf," he said, "there's been an accident and—I'm so sorry to have to tell you this—your wife has been killed."

I saw his mouth moving, but I couldn't hear him—my brain wouldn't process the words. I felt dizzy.

"Mr. Greenleaf, why don't you sit down." Still, the words came faster than I was hearing them.

I sat on the edge of the bed and silently stared at the door through which, an hour before, Christina had left my life. "Are you sure it's Christina? She just went to pick up some burgers down the street."

"Yes, sir, we believe it to be your wife. She was driving a silver Volvo SUV, Florida plates, ST1274."

As though still in a dream, I put on my jacket and meekly followed Officer Robinson to his car. He drove me to the local hospital to identify Christina's body. No words were spoken between us on the way, but I sensed the empathy emanating from Robinson. His calm nature and professional demeanor helped me to remain as focused and lucid as I could possibly be, given the circumstances, to comprehend the enormity that he'd presented me with just fifteen minutes before.

How do you handle such a thing? How do you tell your twenty-one-year-old daughter that her mother is no longer alive, that she was killed by a drunk driver in a head-on collision, and that she will never see her again? That as she died (due to "blunt force trauma"), while trapped in the driver's seat of her mother-in-law's car, her mother's last words were, "Tell them that I love them—please, tell them that I love them . . ."

We brought Christina back to Connecticut; the wake was held at a North Haven funeral home. Her parents, John and Patty, gazed about with vacant eyes; they were obviously in shock, as was the rest of the family. I know that wakes (or calling hours) are a long-standing Christian tradition, especially for Catholics, and that they provide an opportunity for extended family, friends, and neighbors to pay their respects to the departed and her immediate family. But my God! Standing only a few feet from my beloved Christina's casket while a seemingly endless procession of mourners paid its respects was one of the hardest things I've ever had to do. Yet I was moved and comforted by the outpouring of support we received that evening, and that offered me a new perspective on the purpose and process of a wake—and, in general, of the efficacy of social ritual.

Earlier, I said that my road back to Silver Lakes began on the night of Christina's death, and that's true—but it really started going downhill about a month after that. By then, Melissa was back at Quinnipiac, with a heavy heart, to finish her last semester of undergraduate studies. We'd had lengthy discussions about this; she was leaning toward sitting out a semester, but with my help, she came to the realization that her mother would never have wanted that. There's no doubt that Christina's wish would have been that Melissa stay the course, finish out the semester, and, in the spring, walk at graduation with her classmates.

So, I was alone in our home for the first time since my bachelor years, following my divorce from my first wife. After two decades of marriage to Christina, the house bore all her personal touches. At times, I found it almost unbearable to be living there, among the memories. One evening, I so needed to get away from it all that I actually checked into a local hotel and had a relatively restful night in that anodyne, memory-free milieu. During those weeks, Melissa and I were in contact every day, either in person or by phone, to assure each other that we were well and functioning. I did my best to ease her mind, and she mine, but we both knew that we were struggling—there was no hiding it. Still, Melissa had the optimism and resilience of youth; I just felt . . . bereft.

I visited John and Patty Esposito to learn how they were coping with Chris's loss. But they had the refuge of a large family to spread the weight of their pain. I attended Mass every Sunday at Christina's church in North Haven and met three times with the pastor. He encouraged me to pray, but I was no good at it. I asked God, "Why?" But God was silent!

Angry and at my wits' end, I decided to drive the two-plus hours to Far Rockaway, back to my old friend, the white house by the bay. I desperately needed answers—an explanation of why this horrible thing had happened to my beloved Christina and how I was expected to deal with it.

I slept fitfully that night, and early the next morning it was pouring—a cold and persistent late winter's rain. But that didn't stop me; I put on an insulated rain jacket, got in my car, and headed for I-95 South. After a treacherous drive though wet and occasionally icy conditions, I pulled into a parking space in front of our old apartment building. I glanced through my side window, but I couldn't see the white house through the fog that covered the southern shore of Jamaica Bay. I stepped out of the car and walked, head down, across the grass fields and into the wet weeds beyond. I stopped and looked up, fully expecting that it would be there as it always was—but this time it wasn't. "Where the fuck did you go?" I shouted. "I need you; I need some fucking answers!"

I could barely see anything now; the rain was beating down on me, and my eyes were inundated by the downpour. Bone-tired and dejected, I kicked at the weeds under my muddy boots and headed back to my car. I sat there—for how long I couldn't say; an hour? Two? I don't know. Then he spoke to me in a voice I recognized from my dreams.

"August," he said. "Sometimes there are no answers, only questions. This is true for you and for everyone who has ever walked this earth. It's something we have to live with; there are no exceptions. Be patient—all of your questions will be answered in due time. Go home now." Just at that moment the rain stopped, the fog lifted, and the afternoon sun peeked through the clouds. I looked back through my side window, and there she was—my beautiful white house by the bay.

I wish I could have hung onto that moment and let the wondrous nature of it carry me forward—like a leaf caught in the wind—twisting and turning, and eventually coming down for a soft landing. But I was weak; I couldn't do it. My grief overwhelmed me.

I was back to work and going through the motions. I coped as best I could, but I missed Christina badly. The pain I was experiencing was intense, and my reflections on her death became a constant accusation. I shouldn't have been so dismissive of her suggestion that we drive straight home instead of stopping in Rocky Mount; I should have been the one who went out for the burgers, but instead, I'd preemptively plopped myself on the hotel bed like a lazy slob, leaving Chris to run the risk of driving after dark in a strange town. I could still hear Christina's last words to me; I could still feel her kiss on my forehead; I could still see her lifeless body on the hospital gurney. These recollections cycled through my brain endlessly; they just wouldn't stop. I thought I'd go mad. William insisted that I call a therapist friend of his, but I never did—I had other ideas.

I held out as long as I could before I called my old drug connection, looking for some weed. I figured, what the fuck—I needed something to cut the edge, and weed had always done that for me before. He told me about these marijuana brownies that he was able to get on a regular basis. They contained fifty milligrams of THC per brownie—extremely potent. He recommended that, for starters, I do a quarter brownie at a time, so I ordered a dozen. Initially, the brownies separated me from the heavy depression, but before long, it came back even stronger. By then, I was doing a full brownie after work, and in the months that followed, as I did more and more brownies, my depression became steadily worse.

In May of 2012, a short time after Mel's graduation, I stopped going to work. William and Melissa contacted my center manager at UPS; they informed him of my condition, and he arranged another leave of absence for me. By then, I was hardly eating—I had lost twenty-five pounds. Each morning, I would get up dreading the thought of going through another day. Life for me held no interest; I was suffering from anhedonia and an all-consuming guilt over what I was doing to Melissa—my sweet, loving, and trusting daughter. I began to think it best that I make myself disappear—that Melissa would be better off without me in her life.

Moreover, I was harboring a growing suspicion that those who professed to love me were, in reality, just feeling sorry for me, that I was an object of pity, a burden—that, behind my back, they were complaining about my weakness, my lack of courage.

So, on the night of Sunday, June 3, 2012, I drove to a rest stop on I-95, parked my car, and went inside with a pen and some notepaper. I got a cup of coffee at Dunkin' Donuts, sat down at a table, and wrote a suicide note. When it was finished, I set it on the dashboard of my car, closed the car door, and walked directly from the parking lot out onto the highway.

The lights of the oncoming tractor trailer were blinding, and the asphalt trembled beneath my feet. The driver blasted his horn again and again; I squeezed my eyes shut and whispered, "God forgive me." Suddenly I was seized in a bear hug and lifted off the pavement; I was hauled off the highway with little or no time to spare. His powerful arms held me so tight that by the time I was set down safely on a nearby patch of grass, I could hardly breathe—but I was alive.

I looked up at him. He was a tall man, dark-skinned, with a handsome face creased with care. His brown eyes were soft and, in the beams of a hundred headlights rushing by, seemed to shine with a light of their own. He wore jeans and a blue T-shirt. Quietly he said, "Please, sit here awhile on the grass." I did as I was told. The man knelt beside me, leaned over, and, with his lips mere inches from my ear, said in a low voice, "You ought not do that again, August." Without even thinking how this man knew my name, I began to cry.

The Connecticut state police arrived shortly afterward. They asked the man some questions about the incident, and he told them what he knew. He told them his name was Otis Mills, that he was from Louisville, Kentucky, and used to be a truck driver. That was all they got out of him. Then they turned to me.

I would see Otis Mills but one more time—on a cold winter's night, twenty years later.

Whoever he was, Otis Mills was a hero. And there were other heroes—squads of them at Silver Lakes—who helped preserve my pathetic existence by building back the wreck of a life that Otis Mills had salvaged. There were the doctors, nurses, social workers, psychiatric technicians, volunteers—and even other patients. Each and every one of them was instrumental in pulling me back from the brink. I had come so close, so fucking close, to going over the edge—but I was still alive, and after only a few days at Silver Lakes, I can honestly say that I was glad to be alive. The medication was working, and so was the program.

I was released after two weeks and back at work a week after that. Melissa was working as an aid at Yale New Haven Hospital for the summer and preparing for her first year of PA training at Northeastern University. Beginning in September, she'd be living in the Boston area for three years: two years working toward her master's degree, followed by a year of clinical rotations. At first, she was feeling hesitant about starting school—a little afraid to leave me alone. But I assured her that I was feeling fine, and as long as she loved me, I'd be fine from then on.

The sting of losing my beloved Christina had not faded (nor will it ever), but I knew by then what I had to do. Stronger, wiser, and with a new sense of purpose, I resolved to take life as it came, so I got busy living. That's what Christina and my dear mother would have wanted, and as I think back on it now, so did I.

Chapter 44

The White House by the Bay

Monday evening, November 25, 2013:

It had often occurred to me over the years, since receiving that cryptic response to my note when I was a ten-year-old kid, that November 26, 2013, might be the date I was to meet my maker. But in my note, I had asked for answers to some perplexing, if unspecified, questions. So, on that basis, I believed that if I returned to the big white house by the bay on that date, at least some of those questions would be answered . . . by someone. Thus, I had interpreted the terse, unembellished, and unsubscribed reply to my note as simply an invitation.

I took the note from my desk drawer, turned it over and over in my hands, stared at the date, and thought. So much had happened in the forty-five-plus years since the afternoon that timid little boy stood on the front porch of a house that no one else could see.

But Christina should have been here. Years before, we'd made a plan for the two of us to drive together to Far Rockaway, Queens, and for her to wait near a house she couldn't see while I, with no idea of what to expect, went inside. What love; what trust! My heart breaks to think of it, but evidently, the universe had more urgent need of her. As my grandfather Josef used to say, "Man makes plans; God has other ideas."

In her stead, William—my personal watchdog, as I liked to call him—agreed to come with me to Far Rockaway for my fateful visit. He and I planned to leave Branford by six o'clock the next morning.

I didn't sleep at all that night; how could I? So many thoughts were running through my head as to what might happen the next day. What would I find there at the house by the bay? Who might be waiting for me—would it be the old man I'd seen staring at me from the second-floor window? He'd have to be at least 130 years old; was that even possible? Was any of this possible?

All of it had begun to seem so bizarre! I had been anticipating this day for a very long time, yet on the cusp of its arrival, it felt anticlimactic, as though the most important events of my life—the only ones that really mattered—had already taken place. I was fifty-six years old, and despite my best efforts to enliven my existence, it nevertheless seemed so oppressively dull. I feared that Christina's death had taken the piquancy, joy, and adventure out of my life and that I'd become just another lonely old man.

Yet there was still Melissa, whom I loved with all my heart, and—equally important—who loved me too. It was for her, for myself, and for our life together that I summoned the courage to face the events of the following day—whatever they might be.

Tuesday morning, November 26, 2013:

It was the dawning of my 20,780th day on earth. I picked up William promptly at 6:00 a.m. in my 2010 Subaru Outback. We stopped at the Daily Grind for egg sandwiches, coffee, and *The New York Times*. We were on the highway minutes later, heading for Far Rockaway, Queens, New York.

"Augie," William said, coffee in one hand, a half-eaten egg-and-cheese on a hard roll in the other, "all of this is like something out of a Steven King novel. I love you, buddy, but I have to be honest with you—I've always had my doubts."

"So, my best friend in the world thinks I'm some sort of charlatan? Is that it, William, I'm a charlatan now—a fraud?" I said with a smile.

"I wouldn't put it that way, exactly, but it is an awful lot to swallow. Let's just say that you most certainly are one unique son of a bitch, and I'm ready to become a believer today, my friend. I'm totally looking forward to this."

"Glad to have you along, William. How's Jeremy doing?"

"He's fine—busy as hell. There's a lot going on at the hospital these days—I hardly see him. So, how are things with you, Augie? We haven't talked for a while."

"Okay. I've been so totally focused on today that I haven't thought much about anything else."

"You saw your therapist last week?"

"I did, yes. Ethan is great—he's been a big help, one of the best recommendations you've ever given me."

"Any suicidal thoughts?"

"No, none at all." William and I had agreed that this line of questioning would be completely permissible, considering my recent history. According to William, studies have shown that about 25 percent of those who attempt suicide will go on to make another attempt, while about 10 percent who attempt suicide one or more times will succeed.

"You probably get sick of hearing me say this, Augie, but you've been through a lot; you've come a long way, and I'm proud of you."

"Thank you, William."

It was 8:30 when we got to Far Rockaway; I parked the car on Almeda Avenue, and we got out. I ushered William across the street to show him the building where my family had lived so long ago. Nothing much had changed in the ten years since I'd been there last, but a lot had changed in my life—Chris, Mom, and Marco had all been with me on my last visit. William and I stood in silence looking at the building until my mind was fully able to grasp this essential truth and all its implications.

After a few moments in silent reverie, I took William by the arm and guided him back across Almeda Avenue. We headed toward the ball field and beyond until the white house by the bay stood before us, as peaceful and as patient as ever. Only I was able to see it, of course, and noticing my reverent gaze (seemingly directed toward empty space), William stood a little off to the side and waited quietly. I paused for just a moment until the rush of emotion passed, and then I turned and handed William the keys to my car and an envelope, inside of which was a note I had written for Melissa—just in case. After all, I knew I was going in, but recalling the last time I saw Anna Sokolova, I didn't know if I'd be coming out. I also reviewed with William the possibility that, at some point, it might seem to him that I'd disappeared. I'd no way of knowing for sure this would happen, but from all I'd learned, it seemed likely, so I thought it best to warn him.

The completion of these simple tasks was enough to instill in me a transient feeling of competence, and I strode purposefully up the seven transportive wooden steps, onto the broad front porch. I positioned myself squarely opposite the oversized front door, took a deep breath, seized the large brass ring that hung from the gaping maw of the lion's-head knocker—and knocked.

Chapter 45

Abraham

I immediately recognized the man who answered the door; it was my mother's uncle, Paul, the shoe store owner, who died in an automobile accident in 1962. "August, please come in; Abraham has been expecting you. My, you've grown to be a fine-looking man. I see your mother in you, August. Do you remember me?"

"Of course I do. You're Uncle Paul," I said.

"Very good, August," he said with a broad smile—the same generous grin he flashed when I was a kid and he'd just finished fitting me with a new pair of shoes.

"Please, follow me, Augie." Paul ushered me through the foyer and into a small sitting room furnished with two upholstered, high-back chairs. Set in front of the chairs was a round, dark mahogany coffee table, and on the table sat a large, leather-bound book—quite thick, like a ledger, with elaborately embossed gold detailing. It looked very old. "Have a seat, August—here, let me take your coat. Chilly out there, is it?"

"Not so bad," I said.

"Well then, you must have a head full of questions; I'll go and fetch the man who is best able to answer them. It's wonderful to see you, August; I'll be looking forward to seeing more of you in the future." He shook my hand; his grip was firm—and warm. He might have been a ghost, but he was very much alive.

As I sat in this lovely little room, waiting, I thought, *This is a dream—but it can't be—I'm awake, and this is really happening!* Then I recalled the story that Anna Sokolova told me many years before, about Petya, the monk, who, as a little boy in Russia, sought out and spoke with Irina Ivanovna, the woman whom the people of his village called "the witch." And I remembered well Anna's account of Petya's conversation with Irina:

"Some of the people say that you talk to the spirits out in the field in front of your house. Is that true?" Petya had asked.

"Yes, it is true. However, 'spirits' is not how I would describe them, Petya," Irina said. "They are deceased and thus no longer in our world, but they are quite alive in theirs."

"And what world is that?"

"The next world, Petya, the life beyond the death. You see, Petya, we continue onward after we leave our bodies—this world. We are called to a special place—a familiar place . . . It's a home, Petya, a house with loving family and dear friends. My family's home stands just outside, in the field in front of this little house."

"And why can you see it, while others cannot?"

"Because I have the gift, Petya, and if you have the gift, you see things, and you have to remember everything."

He walked quietly into the room and kissed me on the forehead—the bearded old man with the gray suit jacket, the same man who had stared out at me from a second-floor window of this very house so many years before, the man who had come to me in my dreams and comforted me. "August Nathaniel, shalom aleichem. It's a pleasure to see you again."

"Aleichem shalom," I said, the words barely escaping my mouth as I rose to greet him.

"My name is Abraham. I'm your great-grandfather; your grandfather Josef is my son." Abraham spoke softly, calmly. His demeanor immediately put me at ease.

"Sit, August, please," he said, indicating the chair I'd been sitting in, and sat himself in the other chair. "Please, call me Abraham. Tell me, how was your drive down from Connecticut this morning?"

"Fine," I said. "You know that I live in Connecticut?"

"Yes, I do. There are many things that we know when we get here; how that is, exactly, I can't say, yet we know. I knew who you were when you were a little *boytschick* looking up at me in the window. And you wrote that note—what a smart note that was for a boy your age. I knew then that you were a mensch, a gifted mensch at that—and do you know why, August?"

"I think so, yes."

"That's right—you see what others cannot see; you've seen what I could never see during my living years."

"But you're here talking to me," I said. "You're living."

"We call this the 'after-living.' Your brother, Michael, likes to abbreviate it; he calls it the A-L. What a fine man he is, and he is proud of you, August—Michael is very proud of you!"

"Michael is here?" I asked and began to choke up.

"Yes, he is, August. Your grandparents are here also, as are both your parents, Marco, and Christina. Christina is doing very well, and what a fine and beautiful woman she is. You are fortunate. I know that right now, you may not feel so fortunate. *Tsores zaynen far dem menschn vi zhaver far ayzn.*"

"I'm sorry?"

"An old Yiddish saying, August. It means 'Troubles are to man what rust is to iron.' It's the nature of our lives; no one is exempt—not a soul. The truth is, you will be reunited with Christina when it's your time to join us. But you're not ready just yet; you have more life to live. Here, let me show you." Abraham reached for the large book sitting on the round table before us. He opened its leather cover and began to leaf through the pages. "You see, this book is full of names and dates. For several centuries, the name of every individual who has passed through this house has been listed in these pages. These are our ancestors, August, yours and mine."

He continued leafing through the pages of the book. "See, August, more names, even names of those who have yet to be born. Birth dates, departure dates if you will, it's all here. But it's not the beginning and end dates of a life that matter; it's what one chooses to do between them that counts. Yet we spend so much time fretting unnecessarily about this and that." He sighed deeply and looked into my eyes—into my soul. "Yes?"

I understood and nodded. "Yes," I said.

"Some of the names are written in capital letters, see?" Abraham riffled back through dozens of what appeared to be thousands of pages of names and dates. When he reached the page he was looking for, he pointed out his own name:

YAKOV ABRAHAM FREEDMAN—May 15, 1956.

"Capital letters," I said. "What does that indicate?"

"It means that, during my time here, I am to be the 'house manager,' if you will. When our loved ones pass on, they come to this home; I greet them here, in this room, and have a conversation with them—acclimate them to their new surroundings, answer their questions, et cetera—not unlike the conversation I'm having with you right now. In this house, August, there is much that is similar to the world we have left behind, but there is as much, if not more, that is quite unlike your world. All of our needs are met here—that is, we do not have to work to sustain our lives. We are abundantly provided for; we want for nothing. Every one of us is at peace, even those who struggled mightily during their lives in your world.

"Here, August, suffering does not exist; here is where the trials of the living world come to an end. For those who have lived lifetimes of pain, either through physical trauma or emotional anguish—who were born on the wrong side of the tracks; who have known sickness, poverty, heartache, loneliness, addiction, depression, or oppression—for all of these trembling souls, their burdens are lifted, and they are free. Here, there is the promise of renewal. This home is like a bridge—the very bridge toward which all our many roads have led—the bridge that will, one day, take us to the other side."

"So, is this heaven?" I asked.

"Well, August, I don't know, only because no one has ever told me. We've often discussed it among ourselves, though; we discuss many things, many of which we do not understand. What we do know is this: When we leave the living world and enter the after-living world, we come into a home—a house—which is in a location familiar to us. Often, it's a location where, it seems to us, we've spent our childhood—as it will be in your case, August, and as it was in mine."

"Your childhood was in Far Rockaway?" I asked.

"No, no, August. My childhood was spent in Lodz, Poland. Here, we see what we want to see—what is familiar and pleasing to us. I see this home as being in a field that I used to play in as a boy, a large, beautiful green field in my home country. I am here with my family—my wife, Sarah, our children and grandchildren, siblings, friends, and parents—although my parents have since moved on."

"What do you mean by 'moved on'?" I asked. "We live, we die, we come to a house like this—then what?"

"To answer the first part of your question, August, we are only here for a predetermined period of time. Time for us differs greatly from time in your world. If a thousand days should pass in the living world—that is, in your world—it would be the equivalent of only one day here in the after-living world. I'll speak more about our concept of time shortly, but now, it will suffice to say that, at the dawning of each new day in our world, it is quite possible that one or more of us will be moving on (or moving forward, as we also say). Here, we know intuitively when it is time for us to move on.

"And as to the second part of your question, concerning our destination when we move on from here—the short answer is, I don't know. For the longer answer, allow me to begin by saying it's the same question we here often ask ourselves. You see, it's not very much different from the living years, when we all wondered and had our theories about where we would go after we died (that is, moved on from the living world to an unknown after-living world). Most said that good people went to heaven and bad people went to hell. Beyond that, some said we all went to a place called purgatory, where our souls were cleansed to prepare us for heaven. Still others strove to reach nirvana, which wasn't so much a place as a blissful state of mind, a process that might take several lifetimes, or incarnations, to complete. And others, more than would care to admit it, believed we went nowhere, that death was the last stop. How wrong they were, August!

"So, here in the after-living world, we ask ourselves what comes next—just as the living do in their world, with one exception: We know intuitively—that is, beyond what our reasoning minds can tell us—that whatever it is, it will be blissful. Personally, I believe that we will meet our Creator."

I was listening intently to everything Abraham said, but I couldn't hold back any longer and abruptly changed the subject. "Forgive me, Abraham, but would it be possible for me to see my family?"

"Ah, August, I knew you would be asking me that question sooner or later; I can imagine how much you must miss them. But no, I'm sorry—your place right now is with the living, not the after-living. However, your time will come, and when it does, you will be reunited with all of them—this time forever."

"You mentioned my father, Abraham—he is here?"

"Yes, and as I've said, August, there is no suffering here. Your father is a free man now, free to be his true self—free of the misery and pain that had clouded his living years and led to his early death."

"And the three of them—Dad, Mom, and Marco?"

"They all get along beautifully."

"Christina—Michael?"

"They are very well, August; they embraced warmly upon Christina's arrival. She's looking forward to having you with her soon."

I couldn't hold back my tears. Abraham handed me a white handkerchief; he, too, had tears in his eyes. He nodded and said, "*Ikh farshtay*, August Nathaniel, *Ikh farshtay*—I understand, August, believe me, I understand."

"Abraham, how can there be enough room here for so many people? The house doesn't seem big enough."

"That is only to your eyes, August. Space here for us, like time, is relative; there is ample space to accommodate everyone here because there needs to be—plus food to eat, books to read, beds to sleep in, and room to roam. We have everything that we ever needed or wanted during our living years—and more."

I had several more questions for Abraham, which he answered graciously. He then went on to expand on the difference in the perception of time between our two worlds. In summary, it seems that a thousand days in the living world is the equivalent of a single day in the after-living world. Those moving on from the after-living world do so at unspecified multiple intervals of one week of after-living time from the day of their arrival. Each multiple is the equivalent of seven thousand days in the living world—or approximately nineteen years and two months.

According to Abraham, most stay in this home anywhere from four to six weeks, after-living time, although there is no established limit. "Each of us knows, intuitively, when it is time to move forward. No one knows why that should be, and there is much animated speculation about it among the residents."

Finally, Abraham brought my attention back to the leather-bound book. "Here, August, I feel compelled to share this with you. See, the book is arranged by family lineage." Abraham turned the pages until he found the page he wanted. There it was, at the end of Abraham's index finger, with the date written to the right of it:

*AUGUST NATHANIEL GREENLEAF—January 25, 2033.

I stared at it, and it took a few moments before my brain grasped the meaning of it. "January 25, 2033—the day that I will die," I said quietly.

Abraham regarded me from beneath his heavy eyelids and nodded pensively.

"That's not quite twenty years," I said.

"That's right, August, seven thousand days for you, just a week for us here. Not at all a long time for your loved ones to wait to welcome you with open and loving arms. Here, time sometimes works in our favor.

"You will die on that January day in the midafternoon; it will be quick and painless, August. After you breathe your last, you will experience a sense of euphoria. Your first step into the after-living world will be right here, on the front porch of this house—as will be your last step out of it, when you move forward—toward whatever lies beyond.

"Look, your name is in capital letters; upon your arrival, you will become the manager of this house."

"And you, Abraham?"

"It will then be my time to move forward."

"Why me, Abraham? You're a man of great stature, I'm just a UPS—"

"August," he said, raising his voice ever so slightly, "you are a mensch, an honorable man. You have provided many mitzvahs, many good deeds, to the people in your life. It's time you were aware of this, my great-grandson. Hold your head high and revel in the time you have left among the living. Moreover, you are a special mensch at that; we here have been talking about you. Here, look!"

Abraham pointed at the page again. "See here—this asterisk? In leafing through the book, I found only two other entries with asterisks before their names. As I said, you are a very special mensch indeed." Having made his point, Abraham breathed deeply, patted my knee, stood up, and said, "Please remain seated, August. Paul will be back in a minute or two with your jacket and will show you to the door." He took a few steps and turned back toward me. "Seven thousand days, August—I'll see you next week. Mazel tov." This last one he said with a grin and a wink of his eye.

I remained sitting in the small anteroom, waiting for a man who'd died when I was a small child to show me out of the house—a house I'd first seen from my living room window more than fifty years before. I'd wondered then who lived here, and now that I knew, I felt a profound change moving within me.

I stepped down off the porch, and William was there to greet me—he was stunned. He stood rigid and speechless for several seconds, and then the words came tumbling out: "Holy shit, Augie, you were walking away from me;

you turned to the left, and suddenly you disappeared. Now"—he glanced at his watch—"an hour later, poof! Here you are again. What the fuck?"

I couldn't utter a word.

"Augie, are you all right? You look like you've seen a ghost."

"I have, William—two of them."

On our way home, he asked many more questions, and I did my best to answer them honestly. But I have to admit, my mind was occupied with all I'd just learned and what it might mean.

When we got to Connecticut, we stopped for coffee at a highway rest stop. Standing at the register in McDonald's, I reached into my back pocket for my wallet, and with it, I pulled out a fine white cotton handkerchief. I unfolded it, and there, embroidered in one corner of the fabric, were the initials YAF.

Chapter 46

My Last 7,000 Days

Thus began my last seven thousand days. That afternoon, after dropping William off and returning home, I lay on the couch awhile, trying to grasp fully what had taken place only hours before. It was so surreal that, in retrospect, it seemed like a dream. But it had happened, and that long-awaited date, November 26, 2013—inscribed by my great-grandfather on the back of a piece of notepaper decades earlier as an invitation to the enigmatic white house by the bay—was soon to be history.

After a brief nap, I sat at my desk and did the math. From that remarkable day in 2013 to January 25, 2033, I was to have nineteen years and two months to live. At fifty-six, soon to be fifty-seven years of age, I'd lived only 75 percent of my life. I would die twenty days after my seventy-seventh birthday—Melissa would be forty-one. I wished I'd have more time to be with her, but she'd be fully mature and established by then, and we'd have had over nineteen more years together. The thing for us to do was to make the most of those nineteen years. I decided not to break the news to her until the following weekend; in the meantime, I'd try to figure out the best way to do that.

I should have asked Abraham how, exactly, I would die. He had said it would happen in midafternoon and that it would be quick and painless. That appeared to rule out a long illness—perhaps it would be a major heart attack or severe stroke, either of which would imply that I'd be more or less functional all the way to the end. If that should be the way it actually went down, what the hell difference did the rest of it make?

What really mattered was that, until that fateful day, I would have a full, productive, and relatively healthy life among my loved ones here in the world of the living. It also mattered (as I'd just learned) that immediately after my earthly death, I would be reunited with my loved ones in the after-living world, that death is not the "final stop," and that there would be more, much more, to look forward to—of this I'd been assured.

I never remarried, nor did I ever date again. Friends occasionally offered to fix me up, but I'd politely decline; I suspected that my remaining years would be full enough without marriage. I was a lucky man, with many dear friends, and a loving daughter to look after me. I knew (because I'd seen it written) that Melissa would have a son; I also knew that, someday, they'd both be needing me—especially that little boy, yet to be conceived.

My final day of work at UPS was Tuesday, December 24, 2013—Christmas Eve. I officially retired thirteen days later, on January 6, 2014 (my fifty-seventh birthday), after thirty-five years of service to Brown. But I did not report for work during those last two weeks; I called in sick. My manager threatened to fire me, but I just laughed at him. I turned in my many brown uniforms and accessories on that day, but I kept one shirt and one pair of pants for old times' sake. They have hung in my closet through the intervening years as testament to the work I'd done. I was grateful, yes, yet keenly aware of the irretrievable time I'd given them over those three and a half decades of my life.

In late January of 2014, at Adriana's Ristorante (our favorite Italian restaurant in New Haven), over a meal of antipasto and zuppa di pesce, along with a "clean and vivid" Friuli pinot grigio, I told Melissa about my recent visit to Far Rockaway with Dr. William. I told her the whole story, from beginning to end, about meeting Abraham (her great-great-grandfather) in the beautiful white house by Jamaica Bay, what I'd learned from him, and what it all might mean. Even so, I withheld from her the exact date of my demise for fear that, when the time came, things might otherwise become awkward between Mel and me. I wanted no theatrics.

Over the years, Christina and I had barely mentioned the white house by the bay, or my uncanny memory—or any other phenomena associated with my gift. We had decided not to tell Melissa until she was old enough to cope with that knowledge and to integrate it into her own life. At that time, she was twenty-two years old and mature beyond her years. She deserved to know everything—to know about the two kindred spirits in Gettysburg who had seen a house at Little Round Top that no one else (except me) ever saw and about Anna Sokolova and the blue Victorian house at the end of her street in Guilford, which was invisible to everyone but the two of us. Thanks to Abraham, I was able to tell Melissa why those houses were there, who "lived" in them, and something about what went on inside. I shared it all with her.

"Honey, you're looking at me as if I had two heads," I said.

"This is an awful lot to digest, Daddy—I mean, houses that nobody sees but you, conversations with dead people, a big book with thousands of names in it, including your name in capital letters—plus an asterisk! Dr. William is right. It's like something out of *The Twilight Zone* or a Stephen King novel. Mom told me that you were special, Dad, that you had powers that others did not have, that most people couldn't even fathom. But wow! And I thought this zuppa di pesce was incredible!"

"You're a funny woman, honey," I said, smiling. "A very funny woman."

Whether she believed me or not was unimportant; I'd told her the last of my secrets, trusting that, given time, she'd be able to process it. What was important (to me) was that my daughter and I might share an open and honest relationship, unclouded by deception, guile, or suspicion, and that—for the nineteen years or so I had left—I could love her without reservation.

In April of the same year, I flew out to California to visit Jessica. I spent a week with her at her lovely home in Capistrano Beach. It would become an annual spring destination for me, and she'd come to Connecticut every fall. I liked California, and I especially liked being with Jess. I had not seen her since 2012, when she came to visit me in my darkest hours, while I was suffering through my nervous breakdown and had just begun my second rehabilitation.

One day Jess took me to one of her favorite haunts, an oceanfront restaurant in Laguna Beach, a town further down the coast. We ordered lobster quesadillas and fish tacos and shared a bottle of crisp California wine. We ate and talked as the waves of the Pacific rolled onto the beach below.

"Augie," Jessica said, "you know, you were my all-time favorite fuck."

I'd taken my wineglass from my lips just in time. "Oh, really?" I said.

Jess was capable of making outrageous statements like that without batting an eye.

"No, it's true, Augie. I don't really know why, but it is. You were incredibly good looking—Christ, you still are—and you had this vulnerability thing going on that I always found so damned attractive; all my friends did. Besides, you really knew how to make love—you knew what a woman wants, and in my experience, not many men did."

"Thank you," I said and took another sip of the wine.

"How was Christina?" she asked—as cool as a cucumber, she'd pushed the envelope again.

"Christina . . . ?"

"In bed, Augie. How was she in bed?"

"Oh—well, as in everything, Chris was a generous lover, and our lovemaking was wonderful. How she put up with me, though . . . there were times, early on, when I thought I might chase her away, that she'd walk out. But I was projecting; she always stood by me without wavering—*always*."

"That's because she was so deeply in love with you, Augie—in love with her little family. She and I talked, you know. During your rough times, she'd cry—not for herself, but for you. You had one of the best, Augie, and no matter what you may think, so did she."

"And you, Jess?" I asked. "What is it you've been searching for all these years?"

"Well, Augie, you kind of ruined it for me," she said, smiling. "After you, no one else could quite measure up."

"No, really," I said. "You've had so many good men in your life. How many times have you been proposed to since your divorce from Clint? It's a baker's dozen by now, isn't it?"

"More like a half dozen, but they were all so fucking immature, Augie. Evidently, all the real men have been taken; besides, I like my freedom. I've been like this forever—you know that. I have a great job and plenty of money. I can go anywhere I wish to go and fuck anyone I wish to fuck. I do my volunteer work with the girls, I go on my spiritual retreats for months at a time, and I have no one to answer to. Besides, Augie, you marry someone, and he wants children, but after what I'd been through, bringing another life into this world—well, that scared the shit out of me. That's all over with now, though, and I'm happy, Augie, truly happy—at peace with myself and with the world. And your being here this week, well—it's a special joy."

I smiled and raised my glass. "Back at you, Jess," I said—and finished my wine.

Melissa received her graduate degree from Northeastern University in the spring of 2015 and stayed in Boston for another year to finish her clinical rotations. In June of the following year, she moved back to Connecticut to live with me and to begin her career as a physician's assistant at the Yale New Haven Hospital Maternity Center. I was thrilled to have her at home again; her mere presence resuscitated what had become a rather lonely and melancholy place.

Actually, when she moved in, Melissa became the third occupant in our Branford home. Some months earlier, I had adopted a seven-year-old mutt named Scruffy. The dog's owner had died suddenly, leaving the poor little guy without a home or a friend. With my most recent battle against drugs behind me, Melissa had urged me to check out our local animal shelter. She thought a dog would be a good companion, one who, in needing me, might add meaning to my sedentary, solipsistic, small-town life.

Scruffy, while not the handsomest of dogs, really was a cool little guy—but he came with a giant attitude. He was not very keen on his canine brothers and sisters; cats were out of the question, and squirrels, rabbits, and other critters were on notice to run for their lives whenever the Scruffster was in the vicinity and free of constraint.

Humans were a mixed bag—either Scruffy liked you or he didn't, and it didn't take him long to decide. If you were in the latter category, there was nothing you could do to win him over. There was no kissing up to that dog: no bringing him toys, no proffering treats, no talking baby talk, and no petting him—you might wish you hadn't tried. He wasn't vicious, just opinionated; once you were on his shit list, you stayed there. He was a pending lawsuit on four legs.

But alas, my friendship with Scruffy was short lived; he died four years after I adopted him—cancer. God, I hate that word! It all happened so quickly; the limp, the lump on his left shoulder, the X-rays and tests, the diagnosis, the prognosis, and a very difficult decision. I sat with him for an hour talking about old times; I petted him while the vet injected the poison into a port that had been inserted into his right foreleg; I held his head and scratched behind his ear (his favorite spot) as he went to sleep. I sat with him for another hour, talking as though he could hear me and silently weeping—and as I wept, I wondered if pets were allowed in the beautiful white house by the bay.

Occasionally, Melissa and I would ride the train down to Yankee Stadium and take in a ball game. It was one of our favorite things to do; it took some mutual planning, and we'd be together, out of the house, for an afternoon and evening. Each year after my retirement, I purchased a partial season ticket plan that included twenty games. I had two seats about twenty rows behind the visitors' dugout, along the third-base line. Due to her work schedule, Mel couldn't make it to all twenty games, but she was able to get to about half of them. We'd take the Metro-North out of New Haven, down to the 125th Street Station, catch the subway to the Bronx, and arrive at the stadium ready to have a blast. At one late-April night game against the Boston Red Sox, in about the fifth inning (during a pitching change), the kiss cam was on the large Yankee Stadium screen. After focusing on several young couples, the camera was suddenly fixed on Melissa and me: there we were, on the 103-by-58-foot Jumbotron screen, and forty-five thousand paying patrons were waiting for a kiss. I sat there, frozen like a deer in the headlights, but Mel—who was two or three beers into the game by that time—did not disappoint them. To the delight of the crowd, she opened her arms wide, wrapped them around me, and gave me a big, long kiss on the cheek.

Well, on this particular night, there's this well-turned-out elderly couple sitting directly behind us. The woman, seemingly indifferent or oblivious to the age difference between Mel and me—or perhaps just assuming the obvious—taps Melissa on the shoulder and says with a smile, "What a nice couple you two make."

In a playful mood, Melissa says, "Yeah, he's my sugar daddy," and musses my hair.

The woman's smile quickly disappears, and looking down her nose from her superior perch, she says, "Oh—I see."

Now, as I'm turning around to set the record straight about my relationship to Mel, the old man turns and asks the woman (who I assume to be his wife), "What did she say?"

"She said he's her sugar daddy."

The old man, evidently hard of hearing, cups his left ear with his left hand and says, "Eh? What did she say?"

Betraying her irritation, the woman repeats, a little louder this time, "He's her sugar daddy!"

Undaunted by his wife's tone, the old man perseveres: "Ethel, I can't hear you; please, what did you say she said?"

Now at the end of her rope, the old woman shouts at the top of her lungs, for the entire section to hear, *"For Christ's sake, Marvin—he's her sugar daddy!"*

The well-oiled crowd around us laughs and hoots, and while I point to Melissa and mime "She's my daughter, she's my daughter," Melissa—who's totally into the scene by now—jumps up and down and pumps her fists; Ethel rolls her eyes with embarrassment and disdain, and poor old Marvin looks completely confused, thinking that everyone is laughing at him. But in truth, it's just another night at the ballpark.

I visit Christina's grave whenever she calls for me, but at least three times a year—on June 13 (her birthday), on January 15 (the anniversary of her death), and on October 6 (our wedding anniversary). I bring flowers—pink carnations, her favorite. As I lay them down in front of her headstone, my heart throbs, and my eyes moisten. On my knees, I talk to her at length about what Melissa and I are up to, and I fill her in on various odds and ends I may have picked up about family and friends—knowing full well exactly where she is and when I'll be seeing her again. After an hour or so, I leave the cemetery, feeling as though I've drunk deeply from the fountain of living waters.

When Alex Sokolova returned home and saw me sitting with his lifeless mother, he ran straight to his room, locked the door, and refused to come out. After two or three hours of wheedling, I was able to coax him into opening the door. I listened long while, through his tears, he complained bitterly about his lifetime of frustration. I had no idea that he'd harbored these feelings. Then I handed him his mother's note, and as he read, I watched his face soften and his body relax. When he finished reading, he looked up at me and smiled wistfully.

With information that Anna had provided me, I contacted Alex's cousin, Boris Sokolova (Alex's father's brother's son), in Killingworth, the one to whom Anna had given power of attorney over Alex's estate. Boris and I agreed that Alex should continue living in his home on Sharon Street. I visited him regularly, as did several members of his chess club, and (less frequently) Boris. With our collective oversight, plus the rental income from the first-floor apartment, his ample endowment from Anna's estate, and the help of local senior services, Alex thrived until July of 2021, when, at the age of eighty-eight, he contracted COVID-19 and rapidly succumbed. A brief memorial service, held at a local funeral home, was attended by a small gathering of his friends, whose identities remained concealed behind their masks, and all of whom left as soon as the service ended. Boris, Melissa, and I saw to the burial of Alexei Nikolaievich Sokolova's ashes next to those of his mother, in a cemetery near the center of the town of Guilford. But the only tears shed that day were mine.

In January of 2018, Melissa met John House. John worked with his father, Paul, in the family's arboriculture business, House Arborist & Tree Removal, LLC. John's mother, Kathleen, a CPA, kept the company's books and handled the payroll. I took an immediate liking to John, who had fallen in love with my daughter. In the summer of 2019, John proposed to Melissa, and she accepted.

They were married in September of 2021. Prior to walking Melissa down the aisle at Saint Theresa Church in North Haven, and having talked to Chris earlier that morning at the cemetery, I told Mel that her mother was very proud of her and would be sitting right next to me in the front pew as she and John exchanged their vows. Melissa wore Christina's wedding gown—and, I must say, she was radiant.

In 2022, John and Melissa built a house in the Branford village of Stony Creek, and they moved in a week before Thanksgiving of that year. What I knew broke my heart, but I never shared it with anyone, and my grandson,

Samuel, was born on October 22, 2023. With two working parents, little Sammy spent a lot of time with me, and before long, he became my sidekick.

I'll say this for Sam—the kid had spunk. He was smart and fearless; his mind was a sponge for information, and he got into everything. As children sometimes do with their grandparents, Sam and I developed a special friendship, and while he certainly loved his other grandparents, he and I became virtually inseparable. One day, when he was old enough to talk in sentences, and understanding that Paul and Kathleen were his grandparents, too, he asked me, "Grandpa, where's *your* grandma?"

"In a big, beautiful house," I told him, "far, far away."

A year after Scruffy died, I adopted a three-year-old Jack Russell terrier mix from Alabama. I named her Bowie, after the late performer David Bowie. She's really a good dog: excellent temperament, smart, fairly obedient, and super sweet—we bonded immediately. The day I got her, I took her to our local dog park. Bowie relished being there; she ingratiated herself with the dog owners and played well with all the dogs. She's the polar opposite of Scruffy, who had growled at all the dogs and half the people—God rest his tortured soul.

Every night, while I read, write, listen to music, or watch television, Bowie stretches herself across my lap and naps. Even now, as I type these words on my laptop, she's pressed against my belly, exhausted from three hours spent at the dog park earlier today.

On occasion I have visitors (most of them strangers) who come to me because they've heard I might be able to comfort them, that I know something they don't know—that there's good news, and they want to hear it. I'd never thought of myself as the type of person to convey such a message, yet I do it often. It began a few months after my visit with Abraham, when a friend from work called me. He had lost his seventeen-year-old son to a drug overdose and was bereft—inconsolable. He came to my house, and I openly shared with him what I knew: that we will be together again with our lost loved ones, that for each of us there will be a wonderful reunion. As he left, with tears in his eyes, he told me that he didn't know why, but he believed every word I'd said.

I had one or two other visitors during that first year. Within a very few years, though, with people talking as they do, it became known in our community that a visit to my home might help alleviate the grief that comes with the loss of a loved one, and the number of visitors increased significantly. They are not a burden to me. I meet with them in my den—a modest, friendly room, sparsely furnished with my desk, a comfortable sofa where my visitors sit, and a coffee table. There's a fireplace at the center of the far wall, opposite the door. A picture hangs above the mantel; it was painted for me, as a gift, by a well-known artist and dear friend. It depicts a large white house with a broad front porch, nestled among reeds and shrubs. Six empty rocking chairs are arrayed on the porch. Behind the house is a large body of water.

Windows on either side of the fireplace provide natural light during the day; after dark, lighting in the room is soft and diffuse, except for an accent light that illuminates the painting, and in winter, there is the glow of a low flame in the fireplace. At one end of the coffee table, opposite the fireplace, I've placed two spindle-back Hitchcock armchairs; I sit in one of these chairs when meeting with my visitors.

I set out a light refreshment—a pitcher of lemonade, some pretzels, maybe sliced vegetables, and a dip. I keep it simple. They open their hearts to me and tell me of their heartache. I listen quietly, attentively; I care, and they sense it. When it's my turn to speak, I am as brief as I can be—mostly, I'm here to listen. When I speak, I tell them of my visit to the beautiful white house by the bay and of my conversation with my great-grandfather Abraham. I answer their questions as best I can. I speak the truth; it's what they've come for. Some of them doubt what I tell them—I am not surprised. "This is all very hard to believe," they say. I lean forward and quietly tell them, "I understand, but it's the truth; it happened to me."

Occasionally, I'll hear from them afterward; more often not. Still, they come.

On a May morning in 2025, I woke up in the middle of the night with a burning pain in my chest. Half of me thought acid reflux (from which I'd suffered for several years), while the other half was not so sure—it felt different. The pain persisted in various degrees throughout the day, and by nightfall I was concerned enough that I drove myself to a local urgent care center, where they did some bloodwork, treated me for heartburn, and sent me home.

The next morning, I called my gastroenterologist; he was able to see me later that same morning. He put me on Prilosec, and no sooner had I returned home and walked in the door than my cell phone rang. "Mr. Greenleaf, my name is Joan. I'm a nurse at Connecticut Urgent Care. We have reviewed your bloodwork—you need to see your doctor as soon as possible. That's Dr. William Salinger, correct?"

"Yes," I said, "is there anything wrong?"

"There are some irregularities—I will fax those results to Dr. Salinger's office immediately."

I called Dr. William, and within an hour I was in his Branford office. After his nurse assistant performed an EKG, William gave me the news. "Augie, your EKG shows you've had a heart attack involving the inferior wall. We're calling an ambulance right now to take you to Yale New Haven."

"Is it really that serious that I need to go to the hospital immediately, William?"

"You know, Augie, I'm not usually dramatic, but this is the real deal."

"Can't I drive myself?"

"Absolutely not, and let me add, Augie, why the hell didn't you call me first!"

I was admitted directly to the CCU (cardiac care unit) at Yale New Haven Hospital. Soon after my arrival, a technician performed an echocardiogram, which produced video of my beating heart. Later that day a cardiologist reviewed the video and told me I was a lucky man; the heart attack was a mild one, limited to a small area in the lower part of my heart. They treated me with medications, and after three days, they released me with instructions to keep an eye on my weight, blood pressure, blood sugar, and cholesterol—and above all, to avoid stress.

My heart attack never unnerved me; I was actually quite calm throughout the entire episode. After all, I already knew the date of my death, and I was sure there'd be no changing that. So, I asked myself: Would it actually have mattered if I'd gone to the doctor or not—or if I ever went to the doctor again? After some thought, I decided that yes, it did matter. First, it occurred to me that I should go on living my life in as nearly normal a way as possible, as though I didn't have the special knowledge I had. To do otherwise would be to abuse a unique privilege and a poor way to show my gratitude for the gift I'd been given. Second, although I completely believed I would not die before my appointed time, there was still the question of quality of life. I had been given no guarantee that I would not be bedridden—or blind, or insane—for the remaining seven and a half years of my life, and so it behooved me to maintain my health as best I could. I owed Melissa and Sammy that much.

Today is Wednesday, January 6, 2027—my seventieth birthday. Tonight, I will be having dinner with Melissa, John, and Sammy. We will be driving into New Haven, home of America's best pizza—called, in the Elm City, "apizza" (pronounced ah-*beetz*). We'll probably wind up at Modern Apizza, my personal favorite.

I did the math again this morning: There are 2,211 days remaining before I join my loved ones in the world of the after-living. I believe that I've been using my days wisely, not squandering them as I might have done when I was younger. I still miss Christina very much, but time, and the knowledge that we will be together soon, have softened the pain I felt on losing her in that horrible accident so many years ago.

I'm blessed with a wonderful daughter and son-in-law in Melissa and John—and I get to spend plenty of quality time with my grandson and best buddy, Sammy. He is now in pre-K, and according to his teacher, he is a very bright boy and a joy to teach. On most days I take him to school at 8:30 a.m. and pick him up at noon. On occasion, one of John's parents, usually Kathleen, will pick him up and take him to their house for an afternoon visit and an early supper.

The other day, on our ride home after school, Sammy said to me, "Grandpa, you're special."

"We're all special, Sam,"

"Not like you, Grandpa."

"What makes me so special?"

"You remember everything, Grandpa."

"Who told you that, Sammy?"

"No one, Grandpa."

"Then how do you know?'

"I just do, Grandpa—I knew it when I was a tiny baby."

I was silently musing over what Sammy had just said when he added, "I love you, Grandpa."

"And I love you, Sam."

It was a cold February evening in 2030 when I received a call from Melissa; she was beside herself. John had gone to Vermont for a weekend of skiing with friends, but there had been an accident. All Melissa could tell me was that he had been skiing a double black diamond trail, and on his last run of the day, he lost control and hit a tree. She said that John's parents would be picking her up shortly, and they'd be driving up to Vermont together. I drove over to Mel's house to pick up Sammy, who'd be spending the night with me. When I got there, the three of them—Mel, Paul, and Kathy—were doing their best to stay composed for Sammy's sake. Melissa put her arm around me, and in a choked-up whisper, she said, "It doesn't sound good, Daddy. They say he's in critical condition. It's a head injury; he's in surgery right now." Although I'd known this day was coming, I was shattered when it came. Yet I was grateful that I'd be able to help Melissa and Sammy get through it.

All Melissa had told Sam was that Daddy had a skiing accident and that she, Grandma, and Grandpa were going to Vermont to see him. Sammy was quiet that night; he knew something was wrong—worse than he'd been told. "Grandpa," he said, "is my daddy going to be okay?"

"I hope so, Sam."

"Don't you know for sure?"

"No, I don't, Sammy. I'm sorry, but I don't."

"I wish you could tell me for sure."

"I do, too. Sammy, I do, too." Of course, I knew more than I was telling Sam, but I just couldn't deprive my grandson of this one night of hopeful sleep. I expected that tomorrow, Sammy's world would be profoundly changed.

Sammy was asleep by eight o'clock that evening. He was exhausted; he had spent the better part of his day outside in the snow, sledding with his friends. I laid him down on my bed, covered him up, and waited for the call—knowing all the while what the outcome would be.

The call came shortly after midnight. It was Melissa. Her husband, Sammy's father, Jonathan William House, was dead due to a traumatic brain injury. He was forty-one years old.

Melissa came home from Vermont drained of energy and emotion; we hugged, and with tearing eyes, I told her how devastated I was. She broke our embrace and, holding me at arm's length, looked me in the eye and said, "I've had a long three days, Daddy. I have a lot to do now, beginning with raising your grandson, and I'm going to need your help."

After John's funeral in Stony Creek, I suggested to Melissa that, if she wished to sell her house (which would eventually become a financial burden) and move back home, I'd be delighted to have her and Sammy live with me. In the summer of 2031, that's what she did. Later that summer, a year and a half after John's death, Melissa went out on her first date. At thirty-nine, she was an attractive woman—bright, kind, and with a contagious enthusiasm for life that was finally returning after her period of mourning John. I was elated to have my daughter back again, and Sammy, his mom.

Sammy grieved the loss of his father for several months, but the boy bounced back—his resilience is astounding. One Saturday morning, as we sat eating our Cheerios, he said, "Grandpa, am I really going to see my dad again?"

"Yes, Sammy, I told you that you will."

"Grandpa—"

"Yes, Sam?"

"Can you tell me how you know?"

"Yes, Sam, I can—but it will have to be our special secret. Okay?"

"Okay, Grandpa, I promise."

"Good, let's shake on it." I held out my hand; he took it, and we shook hands. "That's a gentleman's agreement, Sam."

"What's a gentleman's agreement, Grandpa?"

"When two good men—gentlemen, like you and me—make an agreement based on a handshake, as we've just done, that means they trust each other to do what they've promised to do."

"Am I a gentleman, Grandpa?"

"Can I trust you to keep our secret?"

"Yes, Grandpa, I promised—I will never tell."

"Then yes, you most certainly are a gentleman, Samuel Jonathan House, so pay close attention; I'm going to tell you this just one time.

"Many years ago, before you were born, I met a man named Abraham. He was my great-grandfather—your great-great-great-grandfather. He lived in a beautiful house; it was a special house, full of all my loved ones who had passed away. They all lived together in that house."

"Does my dad live in that house?"

"Yes, he does, Sammy. You see, Abraham showed me a big book full of names and dates—the names of people who had passed away already and the dates of their passing. And in that book were also names and dates of people who would pass away in the future. He showed me my name, and so when it's my turn to die, I will be together with everyone I ever loved who died before me—and it'll be the same for you, Sammy; you will be with your father and all your loved ones when it's your time. Do you understand?"

"Yes, I think I do. And when will it be your time to die, Grandpa?"

"Not for a while yet, Sammy. You needn't worry about that, okay?"

"Okay, but when will it be my time to see my daddy again, Grandpa?"

"Well, here's the other part of the secret, Sammy. When the time came for me to leave the house, after my visit with Abraham, he excused himself and left me sitting alone in the room with that great big book wide open to the page that my name was on. While I was waiting for another man—my mother's uncle, Paul—to show me out of the house, I turned to the next page in that book, and I saw many more names—and one of the names I saw was yours, Sammy."

"What did it say, Grandpa?"

"It said, 'Samuel Jonathan House is going to live a good, long life.'"

"Really, Grandpa?"

"Yes, really, Sam."

My friendship with Dr. William has spanned over five decades, and as is true of most friendships of long duration, ours has spawned many stories that, years later, we'd still recount with relish—including this one.

In 1990, Christina and I were invited to a Halloween party being thrown by a UPS coworker and his wife. Although my friend's personal income was commensurate with mine—which is to say, modest—his wife was a successful investment trader, and they lived in a large, well-appointed house in New Haven, whose size was ample for the party they were hosting.

William and Jeremy, who were dating at the time, came along with us, and the four of us arrived at the party together. Jeremy (who turned out to be one of the funniest people I'd ever met) had suggested that William and he go as UPS guys, and that Chris and I should dress as a nurse and doctor. I was able to finagle a couple of Brown uniforms in the appropriate sizes for the two of them, and William supplied two sets of surgical scrubs for Chris and me.

An hour into the party, we were all having a thoroughly good time; finger food was plentiful, and most of the guests were imbibing a sweet but potent alcoholic punch that our hostess had prepared in diluvial quantities. An oversized bong was making the rounds, and a sizable minority was becoming very, very happy. President George H. W. Bush (Yale '48) was among the guests; he was wearing an expensive black suit and a Bush 41 rubber mask; he might easily have been mistaken for a character out of some horror movie (*The West Wing* meets *Friday the 13th*). He'd been partaking liberally of the punch and weed, and their combined effect on him was becoming quite evident.

The president was accompanied by two Secret Service agents, who were also wearing black suits, each with a security earpiece in his right ear. These two played their roles well—as the president worked his way through the partying crowd, his agents followed close behind. Whoever he stopped and talked to was given a thorough pat-down by the agents; it was hardly a surprise that the president seemed to prefer the company of young, attractive females and got a vicarious thrill as he watched his agents perform their duties.

For most of the evening, our foursome was able to evade Bush 41 and his hands-on henchmen. Although a fun-loving person herself, Christina wanted nothing to do with the kind of fun being administered by the president and his cadre. Many of the other ladies, however, seemed to enjoy it—the punch and pot appeared to be eroding inhibitions.

While lying low in the den amid my UPS buddy's boy toys, our luck ran out. The four of us were engaged in an intense conversation—with *Miami*

Vice detectives James "Sonny" Crockett and Ricardo "Rico" Tubbs—concerning world hunger. How we got started on *that* subject is anyone's guess. Detective Crockett was dressed in a white suit with a white T-shirt and wore white Italian loafers without socks. Tubbs was attired in a pastel blue suit, a black shirt buttoned to the neck with no tie, and a pair of black patent leather shoes. The Crockett character, who actually looked a lot like Don Johnson, had been drawing quite a lot of attention from the ladies present (Christina included), and it didn't stop with them. Both William and Jeremy had big eyes for the Miami detective—the guy was so good looking that even I gave him the once-over.

Then, suddenly, here they were—the Three Black Suits, as Chris had taken to calling them. On entering the room, President Bush immediately approached Nurse Christina and stood directly in front of her; they were less than a foot apart when the president spoke. "Do you know who I am?" he asked, his voice muffled behind his rubber mask.

"Yes, I do," Chris said nervously. "You're the president."

"That's right, my dear, and you're a pretty one—I'm awfully glad that Barbara isn't here, because she'd be quite jealous. But before we talk, my security detail must ensure that you're not hiding anything dangerous under those fetching scrubs you're wearing."

The intoxicants were having their effect on me, too, and seeing this freakish version of Bush 41 up close, I found myself to be frozen in place; I couldn't utter a word as I watched this bizarre scene play out. I could see that Chris was off balance too—and a bit horrified. As 41 stepped aside, his security detail swooped in.

"Ma'am," one of the agents said, "we're going to have to pat you down now."

"Why both of you?" She was serious!

"Just doing our job is all," said the other.

"But he's not even the president. He's just some guy wearing a stupid mask."

"Either way, we're being paid to do our job," the first agent said.

Then my intoxicated and completely bewildered wife said, "What job? Who's paying you? This is just a fucking Halloween party!"

Seeing Christina's distress, Detectives Crockett and Tubbs moved in and stood face to face with the Secret Service agents. Thus relieved, Chris came straight to me. She stood behind me and peeked around my right shoulder at the evolving contretemps. Jeremy commented later that just at that moment, the tableau of the four men—dressed in black, white, and pastel blue—was "absolutely stunning."

Detective Crockett was doing the talking, but it was Detective Tubbs (I think) who pulled out his plastic pistol first and pointed it at the agent nearest to him. Or maybe it was the Secret Service guys who were first to pull out *their* fake pistols. In either case, Crockett—in his all-white getup, he remained as cool as ice—never broke a sweat or pulled out his own fake weapon. Instead, he said calmly, "Let's hold it right there, boys—no need for anyone to get hurt. The good nurse here is an ardent supporter of the fight against world hunger."

Never at a loss for words, Jeremy chimed in, "And she takes injured and stray animals into her home; she's currently tending to a raccoon named Whiskers, two squirrels with a total of six legs between them, and a smallish rodent-like thing that neither of us can quite figure out what the hell it is."

Then, just like that, it happened. Maybe it was too much of the punch and bong, or perhaps his brain had become overheated behind that hideous rubber mask, but whatever it was—down went our forty-first president without a shot being fired. And you know, it was a beautiful thing—the two sides immediately joined forces, and Crockett took charge. "Quick, get him outside into the fresh air," he said. And as Tubbs and the Secret Service agents carried the unconscious president to the patio, he added, "And get that stupid mask off his head!"

After the party, as the four of us were on our way home, I complimented Christina on her standing up to the president and his Secret Service agents, and asked her how she was feeling. But before she could gather her thoughts, Jeremy broke in, "Well—I don't know about the rest of you, but in my considered opinion, that Detective Crockett has one hell of an ass! Don't you think so, William?"

For years afterward, we recounted that story many times—four friends at an elaborately wacky Halloween party, a shared memory to last a lifetime—and Christina, every bit as buzzed as the rest of us, saying, "Who's paying you? This is just a fucking Halloween party!"

It's funny, that puzzled look on her face—I never saw that look again, not for the rest of her time with us. It wasn't like Christina to be puzzled, but we all have so many faces, at least one for every occasion, and on that Halloween night, the look was there on Christina's face, as if to say, "What's going on, exactly?" It's haunted me for a very long time—you know, since that terrible night in Rocky Mount, North Carolina, Chris pinned behind the wheel of my mother's silver Volvo. I picture her having that same look on her face, speaking the words of her puzzlement: "What the hell is going on here?"

Over the following months, even years, I made many calls to William for help. Some in the middle of the night, after the most dreadful nightmares, and some after the most tender dreams, when Chris had been right there with me, and I'd been looking into her beautiful, loving eyes, hearing her voice, feeling her touch.

William, my dearest of friends, was always ready to comfort me. He knew when to talk and what to say—to offer words that might assuage the pain of a heart completely broken. And he knew when to be silent—when words were best left for another time or another place. He was Michael reincarnate.

One winter's evening, not long after my visit with Abraham, I saw Chris for the last time in my life. We were lying together in our bed at home, her right leg crossed over mine, her head and hand resting on my chest. She said, "I love you, Augie." She said, "I'm so terribly sorry that I had to leave you." I told her, "You will never leave me, Christina." We kissed, and I fell asleep. When I awoke, it was 2:00 a.m., and Chris was gone. I couldn't get myself together; I couldn't stop crying. Still in my pajamas and slippers, I got into my car and drove to William's house. I rang the doorbell and a minute later collapsed into my dear friend's arms. I don't know how long we stood there in his doorway, but for however long it was, he was there, holding me, supporting me, loving me, his friend . . . while I wept.

Today is January 26, 2032. It's been over eighteen years since I met Abraham. I turned seventy-five three weeks ago. One more year to go—the days fly by.

Melissa has been dating a doctor she met at the hospital; his name is Kyle Okamoto. Kyle is an obstetrician-gynecologist, and a good man. Melissa and he make a handsome couple—I believe they have a promising future ahead of them.

Sammy's in the fourth grade now. His school principal says he's an intellectually gifted child; they have spoken to Melissa about moving him ahead a grade.

In October, Melissa, Sammy, and I flew out to Phoenix and spent ten days exploring Sedona, Arizona, and Zion National Park in Utah. My idea was for the three of us to spend some undistracted, uninterrupted time in an unfamiliar setting, where we would be encouraged to plan, think, discover, and react together—to share, as deeply as possible, our common experience. Melissa loved Sedona; Sammy's favorite was Zion. I liked them both, but mostly, I liked just being together with my daughter and grandson. I'd bought a zoom lens for my digital camera, and we took at least two hundred pictures. I don't want them ever to forget this time we spent together.

These past few months since returning home from Utah have been a period of reflection for me. I no longer carry regrets; I've learned that, during each phase of our lives, we work with what we have at our disposal. A young boy lacks the experience and wisdom of an old man; an old man no longer has the curiosity, energy, and stamina he had as a boy. We do our best—it's all we can ever do, and I believe—especially since my visit with Abraham, almost twenty years ago—that's what I've done.

I've thought about him often—the man who saved my life that night on the interstate. His sudden appearance at my lowest possible moment was truly miraculous. His name was Otis Mills; he was from Kentucky. He'd saved me from certain death and set me down safely on a patch of green grass. He'd known my name.

So, on a cold night in early January of 2033, a fresh coating of snow lay on the ground, and I was sitting comfortably in my living room, listening to a Gregory Alan Isakov album, when the doorbell rang. I became aware of a sudden chill, and under my L. L. Bean sweater, goose bumps dotted my arms. I opened the door halfway, and before me, illuminated by the light over the doorframe, stood Otis Mills. I was not surprised; I'd always known I'd see him again. I opened the door wide, and he stepped in, out of the cold air; I wrapped my arms around him and embraced him as I would a long-lost friend—which, in essence, he was.

Inside, we sat on the couch. Again, he wore jeans, but in place of the blue T-shirt he'd worn the last time I saw him, he was now wearing a white one. I knew not to ask him where his coat was, whether he was cold, or how he got here—such questions were of little importance beside the immense fact of his presence here in my house.

We sat quietly for a minute or so. Then he said, "August, second chances are a privilege, and you did well with yours. I'm very pleased."

I thanked him again for what he had done for me that night at the highway rest stop and told him that, during these last years of my life, I had finally found peace.

"We are all free, August," he said. "It's too bad so many don't know it."

"May I ask, Otis—who are you?"

He said nothing; he simply looked into my eyes, and in his eyes, I saw the same inner light I'd seen twenty years before—and I knew. I smiled, as did he, and I was warm.

We chatted for a while, and then he got up from the couch and said, "I have to go now, August, but before I do, I want you to know that your great-grandfather Abraham is very proud of you." His words caught me by surprise, and as I mulled them in my mind (Otis knew Abraham?), he started out of the room. I got up and followed him to the foyer, just in time to see the door close behind him. I hurriedly opened it again and looked left and right—but Otis Mills was nowhere to be seen. The snow lay a little deeper on the ground—fresh, white, and free of footprints.

This is my final night; I have no fear. The manuscript is complete, except for these last few lines, and for the prologue, which I'll write tomorrow morning. I'll say my goodbyes to them then, as though it were just another day; no fanfare, no tears—but not before we have breakfast together one last time, and I give Melissa one last hug and kiss. "Have a nice day, honey," I'll say. "I love you." Then I'll drop Sammy off at school, I'll shake his hand like a gentleman, and I'll hug him like a grandfather.

It's been a long journey, more than three-quarters of a century. I'll be going to bed shortly, knowing that I'll be with them tomorrow—Christina, Mom, Michael, and all the others. I'll sleep well, and dream of them tonight.

Chapter 47

Al Di La

Somehow I see them—they are all together here in the house by the bay—the whole family; there are at least two dozen of them. They're gathered in a large, beautifully decorated room with paintings on the walls and a crystal chandelier. There is an aura of joy and anticipation about them as they begin to take one another's hands.

Michael is calling out to me—"Come on, Augie, we're leaving now!"

I can hear him from my room, where I sit at my desk, working on another story: an account of the comings and goings of the after-living—my family and friends, and my own experiences—our lives together in this beautiful house.

"But I'm not finished yet," I call out to him. "There's more of the story to tell."

"That doesn't matter anymore, Augie," he says. "It's our time, now!"

"Come on, Augie!" It's my mother. "We don't want to be late, dear."

I get up, leaving my story behind—laptop, notes, reference material, printouts, and all—spread out on my desk. I walk out of my room, down a long, narrow, dimly lit corridor, and into the large, bright, comfortable room where they've assembled. I see Christina holding Michael's hand, waiting for me; she looks radiant. "Come on, honey," she says. "Take my hand."

We all walk out of the house—through the stair hall and foyer and out the great door. Hand in hand we cross the broad porch to the front steps, with me at the end of the line; on either side of us, the rocking chairs are perfectly aligned, facing outward, and still. One by one, as we reach the top step and step off, we become invisible to the others following—each vanishes in the clear air until my turn comes. I step forward, and we're all together again, floating in a luminous mist; I see the front of the line circling back toward me, and with my free right hand, I take Grandma Rachel's left. I feel no push or pull from either Christina or Rachel, and for all I know (lacking any other frame of reference), our little circle may be standing still—or moving at the speed of light.

Suddenly, I feel a flood of warmth and grace wash over me, and I'm immersed in an ocean of peace . . .

[We] who believe in physics know that the distinction between past, present, and future is only a stubbornly persistent illusion.

—Albert Einstein

"Hope" is the thing with feathers—
That perches in the soul—
And sings the tune without the words—
And never stops—at all—

—Emily Dickinson

Epilogue

Two men—one old, the other young—sit together, rocking on the broad porch of a beautiful white house near Jamaica Bay, in the borough of Queens, New York. The difference in their ages is due, almost entirely, to the fact that the younger of the two predeceased his brother by sixty-three years, which, for the younger man, had been just three weeks. In the world they now share, they've been reunited for two days and have a lot of catching up to do. They rock and talk about old times—before the younger man's death had separated them—and about their individual experiences during the time they've been apart.

As they talk, they casually watch a group of teenage boys playing baseball on a field at some distance from the house by the bay (the same field the younger man had himself played on many times during his brief sojourn among the living), and their attention is drawn to a tall, slim boy who's coming to bat. The boy exudes confidence as he walks from the on-deck circle to home plate, steps into the batter's box, digs in, assumes his stance, and takes a few practice swings. Once ready, he wastes no time—on the very first pitch, he hits a scorching line drive over the left fielder's head, and it seems to the two men watching that by the time the sound of the bat hitting the ball reaches their ears, the batter is already halfway to first base. As they watch him tear around first base and then second, the younger man leans over and says to his brother, "Look at that, Augie. He's rounding those bases like a young Jackie Robinson!"

His eyes still on the runner, the old man smiles . . . a wide and wistful smile.

שלום

Acknowledgments

We wish to thank those of our friends and associates who have contributed their time, sensibilities, and knowledge to reading our book at various stages of its development and offering their comments and suggestions for its improvement.

First (and foremost), we'd like to give special thanks to our compadre, Vincent DeJoy, who has spent countless hours working with us, helping to make this book a reality. Without Vinny's commonsense approach to American English and his eagle eye for poor word choice and stilted phrasing, our story would have been less readable and true to life—even the supernatural parts. His candor and goodwill have helped us avoid the pitfalls of pretense and pride of authorship, to focus on the job at hand, and his thick skin has allowed him to say whatever was on his mind without fear of contradiction (and contradiction there was). Thank you, Vinny—mere words can't express how much your friendship has meant to us—how about a big hug instead?

Though she lives in Florida, Kristin White has had occasion to spend weeks at a time in Connecticut—traveling with her two dogs, two rabbits, and a cat—to visit her mother. She has been of inestimable help in keeping us novices on track, both technically and artistically. We met Kristin at a writer's seminar sponsored by our local library, when she asked to join us at our table. Fortunately, we said yes, and since that day she has been a willing source of information, advice, and encouragement. She shares Stuart's deep interest in the paranormal and has been a valuable resource in our exploration of that realm. Kristin has read our manuscript thoroughly and critically—always giving us her frank opinion and occasionally adding some much-appreciated praise.

Among the many who have contributed to the actualization of our book, the professionals assigned to us by the Amplify Publishing Group (our connection to the reading public) were of critical importance in the process. Thank you, CW Patrick, for your guidance and direction; you're the best. Additionally, Gillian Barth, Ben Simpson, and Shannon Sullivan, all knew their business well; they were responsive, prompt, and equitable in considering those of our ideas that may have been at variance with their own. For all of that, we offer our sincere thanks. We'd like to thank our copy editor, Elizabeth, for introducing us to the joys of the *Chicago Manual of Style* (*CMoS*); from that day on, commas began to fall away from our manuscript like dandruff from an itchy scalp. We'd also like to thank Marco Primo, our illustrator, for your exceptional talent and patience as we refined our vision for the front and back cover.

As the first draft of our manuscript neared completion, and we began to think about publication, we worked briefly with David Cashion of Kevin Anderson & Associates. Mr. Cashion critiqued the manuscript and had several useful suggestions for improving the story, which informed subsequent phases of the book's development. Although we did not move forward with KA&A, we wish to thank David for his valuable contribution to our project.

Julie Davitz read an early version of the book, and with the practiced eye of a person familiar with the process, offered both broad and detailed comments on the organization and text of the manuscript, which we found very helpful as the book progressed. We hope she'll be pleased with the result.

We'd also like to thank Natalia V. Smirnova, PhD. A native of Saint Petersburg, Natasha enhanced the book's authenticity with her firsthand knowledge of Russian life, language, culture, and nomenclature. She also serves as the mother of our coauthor's three granddaughters—Valentina, Anna, and Tessie Connell. That said, perhaps we should also credit their father, Thomas.

Thanks to our many friends from various walks of life, who have given their time to reading our manuscript and commenting on it. To Alex, Anthony, Betty, Bill, Bob and Linnae, Bobby C., Cheryl, Cousin David, Dennis S., Denny and Val, Diane, Dotty, Ellen and Bob, Gary, Helene, Karen and Bob, Kathleen, Kia, Laureen, Leo, Linda, Lisa, Marcie, Maria, Melanie, Mike, Miles, Missy, Nancy, Pat, Patricia, Paul and Lisa, Rob, Tommy, and Tracey—thank you all for your help and encouragement. Although only your first names appear here, you know who you are.

Stuart wishes to thank his longtime friend, Chuck, for his sage advice on a range of issues not necessarily related to the book and, in general, for his constancy, loyalty and love. In addition, Stuart also wishes to thank Ethan for his support and guidance.

Finally, Stuart sincerely thanks his dear wife, Deborah, for her patience and support throughout the process of writing this book and for putting up with a weekly group of hungry, sometimes noisy (into the wee hours) rookie novelists. Stu also thanks his daughter, Sarah Goldstein, for her knowledge and guidance in the field of mental health, and apologizes to her and her husband, Eric, for his many ill-timed phone calls seeking their assistance in unlocking the mysteries of his balky laptop. All of them have read the book and liked it.

About the Authors

Stuart Greenblatt was born in Brooklyn and raised in Queens, the two New York boroughs he writes about in his first novel, *August Greenleaf's Last 7,000 Days*. At the age of fifteen, he moved to Connecticut with his mother, Ella, and older brother, Larry. His father remained in Queens, and not long afterward, he and Ella were divorced.

Stuart graduated from West Haven (Connecticut) High School, and after a series of dead-end jobs, he began his thirty-five-year career as a driver for UPS. The concept for this novel came to him early in his career—following a particularly memorable delivery—and he began filling notebooks with ideas for his story.

Shortly before retiring from UPS, Stuart began to suffer with recurring episodes of a debilitating depression, which led to him being hospitalized for several weeks. He credits his daughter, Sarah (a clinical social worker at the time), and the staff at Silver Hill Hospital in New Canaan, Connecticut, for helping him through that difficult period in his life.

In March 2020, Stuart finally sat down to write his novel. Later that year, he teamed up with coauthor David Connell, a dog park buddy, and the two began a collaboration, with Stuart providing the narrative arc and most of the content, and David working to bring Stuart's vision to life.

Stuart now enjoys retirement with his wife, Debbie, their eight-year-old Jack Russell terrier mix, Bowie, and their many friends in the shoreline town of Branford, Connecticut.

David Connell was born in Massachusetts three years before the Japanese attack on Pearl Harbor, and celebrated V-J Day three weeks before entering the second grade. He attended public schools, graduating from Natick High School in 1956. He enrolled at Colgate University, where he majored in philosophy and football, and graduated in 1960 with a BA but without distinction. As a hedge against a career in sales, he joined the US Marine Corps' officer training program, and upon graduation, he was commissioned as a second lieutenant.

In 1963, following his release from active duty, he entered the Pratt Institute School of Architecture in Brooklyn, where he earned his BArch in 1968. Married by then with two children, he moved to Connecticut to work with Warren Platner, a well-known interior architect and furniture designer. After over fifty years in the practice, he retired from architecture in 2020 to pursue other interests. These have included teaching himself the elements of poetry, writing doggerel that purports to be poetry (unpublished), and analyzing the work of other poets, mostly modernists (also unpublished).

Mr. Connell has three grown children and four grandchildren; he enjoys choral music and sings tenor with a local Soprano, Alto, Tenor, and Bass (SATB) group. A widower, he lives alone with his current dog, Alfred, on the Connecticut shoreline, east of New Haven, from where he can see Long Island.

August Greenleaf's Last 7,000 Days, coauthored with Stuart Greenblatt, is his first novel.